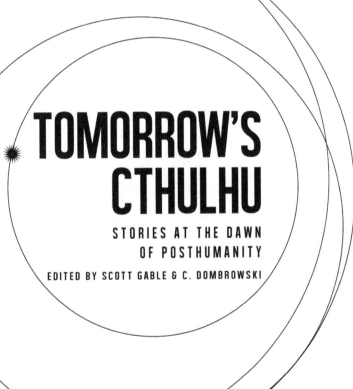

TOMORROW'S CTHULHU

STORIES AT THE DAWN OF POSTHUMANITY

EDITED BY SCOTT GABLE & C. DOMBROWSKI

Also from

BROKEN EYE BOOKS

The Hole Behind Midnight, by Clinton J. Boomer
Crooked, by Richard Pett
Scourge of the Realm, by Erik Scott de Bie
By Faerie Light, edited by Scott Gable & C. Dombrowski
Ghost in the Cogs, edited by Scott Gable & C. Dombrowski

COMING SOON
Izanami's Choice, by Adam Heine

www.brokeneyebooks.com
Blowing minds, one book at a time. Broken Eye Books publishes fantasy, horror, science fiction, weird . . . we love it all. And the blurrier the boundaries, the better.

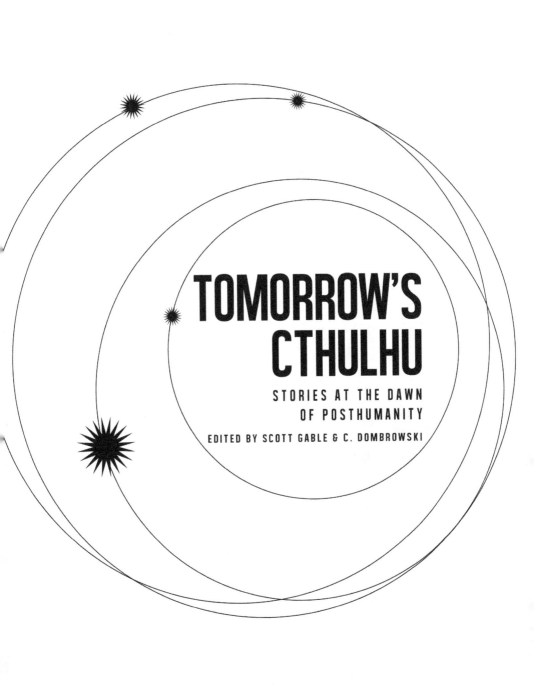

TOMORROW'S CTHULHU

STORIES AT THE DAWN
OF POSTHUMANITY

EDITED BY SCOTT GABLE & C. DOMBROWSKI

TOMORROW'S CTHULHU
Published by
Broken Eye Books
www.brokeneyebooks.com

ISBN-10: 1-940372-16-X
ISBN-13: 978-1-940372-16-7

Table of Contents

Introduction

C. Dombrowski
Scott Gable

There's something in the air. You can't quite put your finger on it. Maybe it was just the branches against the window. Or the zoogs in the attic. Or the "corpse" in the lab. But the air seems charged. Filled with change, with promise. It's making your tentacles itch.

There's really nothing to worry about. It's coming. Or rather, it's here. Possibility, slouching toward reality. It's exciting, really. Out there, everyone's changing, discovering what this new tomorrow holds for them. Some will go kindly; some won't. But in here, it's all you. Quiet, cozy. Here in your study, you've got your brandy at hand and a cat in lap. Many of your friends' brains lie in their jars on the bookshelf, always up for a chat. The Tillinghast resonator's turned to low, and you've got your books.

For when you need a touch of the weird, when you just know something's not right. These stories will help you remember the rituals, the important things. This is a collection of Lovecraftian proportions, gently revealing the tears in this reality we hold so dear.

Just this moment, things couldn't be better.

"Pleasure to me is wonder—the unexplored, the unexpected, the thing that is hidden and the changeless thing that lurks behind superficial mutability."

—HP Lovecraft

Tangles

Daria Patrie

He called out to me in the night. He called over and over, night after night. At first, I thought it was dreams, and then, I thought I had a mental problem. But it was him, calling, all along. We fear what we do not understand, and I didn't want to fear any longer, so I sought to understand.

That was the first mistake.

There was this man named Plato, and he talked about shadows on the wall and how a man, if he was with some other men and watched the shadows on the wall all the time but one day he turned to look at the light behind where everyone was sitting, he would go blind, because he couldn't handle the light. Then, when he'd try and go back to explain to the other men watching shadows on the wall, they'd tell him he was nuts because they wouldn't understand without looking at the light themselves.

You don't want to look at the light. Keep looking at the wall. I'll make some shadow puppets for you.

Take the internet. It's this big mess of connected stuff, and some of it is real, and a lot of it is crap people made up. It has big flashy pictures, things you can click on, VR you can go live in if you're rich enough. It's a technological wonder, and it's the greatest communications tool since people first started scratching pictures in the dirt, right? Ok. So what if the internet was this giant smokescreen? What if it had another purpose?

It's in people's homes. It's how your fridge tells the grocery what to auto-deliver. It's tied into the backbone of every communications system on the planet. It monitors our children. It drives our cars. Even if you're not on the internet right now, you interact with something that interacts with the internet. Everything from streetlights to satellites.

Now, what if there was a thing, a big thing. And what if this big thing had some kind of psychic powers. Now, don't go all rolling your eyes at me. Just listen.

You know how if you leave water out in a bowl, it'll evaporate into the air? And then eventually if the bowl is big enough and enough water evaporates, curtains across the room can get moist, but if you dip the ends of the curtains in a bowl of water, the moisture will move much faster to the top of the curtains? What if it was like that. What if there was this big thing that had psychic powers that had set up the internet, so it could diffuse to all the human brains, and it was just ready to push over the first domino in a big pile that would reach out in all directions.

And what if it wanted you to be domino number one and called you in your sleep? What would you do?

I'll tell you what you'd do. You'd wake up screaming. And you'd wake up screaming the next night, too. Humans can be very well conditioned to stimuli. When something bad happens, our brains try and get us to avoid having the bad thing happen again. It's a Darwinian survival mechanism. So your body, after several instances of calling and screaming and pain and fear would just stop sleeping. There've been all sorts of crazy-ass studies done on sleep deprivation. It's supposed to be like the most powerful hallucinogen, makes people irrational, violent, twitchy.

After two days, I found the yarn. No, it wasn't smart yarn. It was just regular yarn. Only it wasn't.

My grandmother's sister's husband's friend's daughter was Melissa Witchboorne-Halloway-Smithe. Her name had three hyphens because she had a hyphenated name when she married and added the married name on the end of the whole mess, too. She only had one leg. The other leg was cut off because it grew cancer. She lived with a fake leg for nineteen years after the real one got amputated, but the cancer came back and ate her bowels. She died because you can't amputate all of someone's bowels. It just doesn't work. It's like trying to dig a hole out of a hole—you just end up making a bigger hole. She kept her crochet yarn in her fake leg. It was one of the new fake legs: a smart leg, connected to the internet, GPS, stats on physical activity . . . it had pockets. In one of the pockets she kept the yarn. Don't ask me why. I don't know why. Maybe you go a little nuts when cancer eats your bowels.

So she had yarn, the yarn was purple, and I found it in the leg. She had been crocheting this thing when she died, and it was a sweater-like thing, but it had six arms, and everyone had thought it was a joke she was making a sweater with six arms that was purple. But she just scowled when they commented and kept poking away at it with her hook.

So I found the yarn, and I started unravelling it, and the thing I found was that, while it had no fiber-optics in it, it also wasn't normal yarn. It was real yarn though. It didn't feel like something manufactured by robots. It felt . . . organic. But it wasn't normal yarn. It was connected in this strange sort of three dimensional mesh. The only thing I can think of similar was this one time on a nature show they were talking about fungus, and they did a time-lapse photo of a fungus growing underground in a clear jelly that they'd made so they could watch it grow. That was how her purple yarn was. It split off in all directions with different places where it rejoined itself, no knots or obvious ways of having it joined. It just was this tangle that had no ends. And while it was normal yarn, it also wasn't normal yarn. I started trying to make sense of it because I hadn't slept in two days, and it was wearing a little thin on me: this whole not sleeping and nightmares and crap.

Well, I don't know if you've ever stared at a puzzle for long enough, but if you stare at randomness long enough, the randomness speaks back. It's called scrying. Seers and witches do it. Some of them look at fire, and some stare at tea leaves . . .

See, there's a pattern in a tangle, every tangle. When your hair gets in a knot, or there's a mold bloom in your living wallpaper, or you look at the roots of trees, there's a pattern in it. And if you look long enough and take the time to untangle it, it will tell you things. A pattern is something that repeats. Doesn't matter what, but if it repeats, it's a pattern. Sound is a wave pattern. And light, light is radiation just like your surface sterilizer in your kitchen is radiation, and radiation happens in waves. So that's a pattern. You wiggle light one way, and that's blue. If you change it, it's red. If you wiggle sound the right way, it's the note E. If you wiggle it fatter or thinner, then it's E-flat or E-sharp.

The patterns in the yarn made no sense and had no beginning and no end and were tangled. It was him calling again. But this time, it was a puzzle that I had to unravel. When you start getting unsure of yourself, you start to quantify your surroundings to try to understand. You count things because math is this logical fundamental concept that most brains find reassuring at low levels. So I started counting. And as I was pulling the yarn one way and another way, following it along one strand to where it met with another, and following that second to meet with two more, I started to see a pattern. Now, I was really squirrelly from lack of sleep and all preoccupied with unravelling the yarn, so I didn't realize when I stopped actually counting and started doing it in my head. And then, my mind started telling me what I would come up with before I saw it, and I realized that I was telling the future—that I knew what kind of branch I would come up with before I got there because, even though I did not consciously understand the pattern, unconsciously, I had absorbed it, and it was part of me.

And then I looked away from the yarn and started to see the spider web patterns showing up everywhere. In the cracks in the walls, in the way smoke swirled out of someone's cigarette . . . there was no chaos any more. I understood. I knew which way something random would happen before it randomly did. I was tapped in, and my mind was in a groove of the web, and I knew things. And then as the patterns began to be clearer, around the fourth day of no sleeping, I started to see him. I saw parts of his mind, and how he was using the patterns to call to me because when he tried calling directly it was too much.

I killed the dog on the fifth day. I felt bad because it was a nice dog. But I needed to know if my idea was true. And it was. Most animals that wander around on two or four legs, humans included, have swirly bits in their brains, wrinkles that are all squished up and random. But they aren't actually random. They have a pattern. Those are the fingerprints of our maker: the mark of God. Those little squiggles that hold thoughts, those patterns, they are the blueprint and the circuit board for what the human race was designed to do all along.

People project holograph ads into the subway and scrawl graffiti on the walls about how God is coming. They're right. And the end of the world too. But God isn't a nice guy. God is big and wet and dripping and ugly and hungry and has a whole lot of squiggly bits. The only thing God is going to save you for is dinner, and it isn't going to be quick. It isn't going to be okay. Nothing is ever going to be okay. No one is going to be okay. God isn't some benign entity that thinks humanity is special. Humanity exists for one thing and one thing only. You know how steering wheels have grooves for fingers? How tools have grips designed to conform to the shape of your hand? Yeah . . . that's what the squiggly bits in our brains are. They're handlebars.

Even if we're dead, he can still reach in. He can take over and force us to prepare each other and every living thing in the world for his . . . homecoming dinner. He's a slow eater, too, and even if you're no longer alive, he makes you linger, keeping you so even death can't take you away. Killing people doesn't protect them. Nothing protects them. There is only one way to protect each other from him, and it, like God, isn't very nice, but it's a hell of a lot better than the alternative. He doesn't have enough control yet. He's not quite here.

I'm fighting. I started with everyone I ever cared about because they were the ones that I wanted to be sure were safe first. He called me. That's through ears. And then he called me with yarn. That's through fingers and eyes.

Drano makes things smooth. Sure, we have plumberbots and smart drains, but when it comes down to it, nothing cleans out a blocked pipe better or cheaper than Drano. It's like extreme soap. When you get soap on your fingertips, it makes them all slippery. That's because the soap is actually gently eating away at the fingerprint ridges in your hands. Drano does the same thing only it's stronger. It has chemicals in it that make it boil when it comes into contact with water, and tiny bits of metal that work like sandpaper, so it boils and swishes and makes everything slippery and flat. That's how it cleans drains, by swirling boiling bits of metal to eat, to cut, to destroy anything in the way.

You need to start with the eyes and the ears because that's how he gets to you. You have to stop him where he gets in and take away the handlebars before he can take over. Now, at least the people I care about are safe. I can't save everyone, but I've made a difference to a few lives. He won't ever touch them. He won't ever make them do awful things. They won't have to hear the screams: their own or anyone else's.

When he comes through the internet, he won't have anything in them to hold on to.

I made everything inside their heads all smooth.

{}

Daria Patrie *is a delusion, agreed upon by society, which sometimes manifests during the process of reading. If you are reading this right now, you may be under the presumption that Daria exists. You would only be partially wrong. Some say Daria evolved from the left over pasta sauce forgotten in the back of a second-year Physics student's fridge, emerging fully formed and blinking from the crisper drawer one rainy afternoon. Others say Daria is one of several humans possessed by the long dead and quite angry spirit of a three-legged alley cat named Pickleface. Still others say that long ago, Daria arose from a failed poet's recycle bin, the mountain of crumpled paper having gained sentience through a strange mutation of grammar, and that the fiction attributed to this "author" is in fact a misguided attempt by the abomination to locate its accidental creator.*

The Stricken

Molly Tanzer

The rain-puddled, mist-shrouded streets of Arkham are empty—emptier even than the sullen graveyard Hannah now calls home.

Home. It used to just be *camp*, but she has been squatting in this mausoleum for close to a week now and has no immediate intention of leaving. In spite of what it is, the stone room has taken on an almost cozy appearance. Her few possessions—a cookpot, spoon, some food, matches and dry firewood, a blanket, a few changes of clothes, her bike, a fire axe with a brown-stained handle, and a sturdy burlap sack with a large jar in it—are strewn about the place just like they used to be when her apartment was *home.* When she slept on a futon instead of with her back against a shattered coffin.

To be fair, the sack with the jar hadn't been there—but if it had been, it likely would have been tossed into the corner. Funny, the things that never really change. She's still a slob, even now.

It's a shitty evening, that's for fucking sure, but Hannah is barely damp and almost warm from the small, unpleasantly smoky fire she risked building. Steady rain drums on the roof and patters on the unmown grass and disturbed headstones beyond the doors of the crypt, and the soggy branches of the trees rattle in the intermittent gusts of wind. She is keenly aware that the orange glow might attract unwanted attention, but she has made her choice. She needs the fire. She is certain she will die of exposure or misery without it—and she does not believe those who would injure her will seek her in this place.

When it all began, it would not have occurred to her that a graveyard would be the safest place to hide from the dead, but they seem eager to roam everywhere but here. Her sanctuary was empty, with the doors broken open from the *inside* when she sought refuge here on the solid advice of the only person she has spoken to in a very, very long time.

Hannah sighs and pokes at her fire with a wet stick. The bark peels away under her palm. She knows she should make herself something to eat, but she has not been honestly hungry for a long time. Her clothes fit a little looser, and she knows it's not just from all the dirt and grime and wear. It occurs to her that when her mother died, her father stopped making real meals for himself; he would just throw together sandwiches or pour himself some cereal and soymilk to eat it in the lab. When she'd chided him, worried about his health, he'd looked her in the eye and shrugged.

"Cooking for one is a fucking drag," he'd said before turning back to his work.

Hannah frowns at the memory, but it is not the remembrance of her father's attitude that upsets her. It is the recollection that she had once, and not too long ago, felt the need to worry for someone's future *health*.

She decides to go measure out a few handfuls of lentils and rice from the bags she snatched from the bulk bins at Horn of Plenty, the little "natural" market that once served Miskatonic University students and professors, when she catches sight of a ragged figure lurching across the intersection of Lich and Parsonage. Her stomach rolls over on itself, and she decides she doesn't actually want any food right now. Watching the horror shamble away on some unfathomable errand, Hannah just about jumps out of her skin when a rattle, like a bottle rolling over concrete, disturbs her melancholy peace. Quickly realizing the source, she groans, resigned to seeing what he wants. He's prone to drying out, so likely he needs her to wipe him down with a damp rag. Or maybe he's bored and wants to talk. Neither prospect thrills her, not particularly . . . but then again, it has been several hours since she's spoken a single word. Some conversation might be nice.

The jar has fallen over, so she rights it before opening the lid and reaching inside to withdraw a living, severed head crowned with a mop of filthy grey hair.

He blinks at her through thick, old-fashioned spectacles, sour-mouthed, as she sets him carefully on the inverted lid.

"Hi, Great-Uncle Herbie," she says. "Need something?"

"I have asked you on more than one occasion to call me Dr. West," he says primly—very primly, considering what and where he is.

The tomb isn't much warmer for his coldness, but Hannah smiles anyway, until her lip cracks. Then, she sobers. "*Doctor West*," she says, overemphasizing the syllables as she daubs at her lip with the back of her hand. "Can I get you anything? Scalpel? Curette? Forceps?"

"Very amusing," he says. "My eyelids are dry. I need you to moisten them."

"*Well*, Doctor West—"

"Please!"

They must be really dry for him to ask so nicely. Without further ado, Hannah grabs her head-wiping rag and trots to the edge of the mausoleum. After holding it out in the rain for a bit, she returns and sponges him off. Then she applies a dab of under-eye lotion—organic, the good stuff, also pilfered from Horn of Plenty.

"That's better," he says. "I thank you. You can put me back in my jar now."

"Oh," she says, actually a little disappointed he doesn't feel like harassing her further now that he's out and they're talking. "Okay."

"Is there something else?" he asks, his left eyebrow quirking up. "News, perchance? Or perhaps you've had some kind of heartfelt revelation in the face of adversity, and you'd like to share?"

"No," she says, stung. "Just, you know, living in this mausoleum, wondering what's next for me."

"They'll find you, and then they'll either kill you or make you one of them," he says, not a shred of emotion in his voice.

Hannah stares at Dr. West in disbelief. Sure, he's just a head in a jar and has been since long before she was born, but she's still surprised at his callousness.

"Oh, don't look so wounded," he drawls. "I told you . . . well, I don't know when, it's difficult for me to tell in my jar, but I told you some time ago that you should leave Arkham as quickly as possible, and yet . . ." he scans the interior of the mausoleum, eyes rolling dramatically to make his point.

"Where the fuck else do you want me to go?" asks Hannah, pleased to see his mouth shrivel up like a cat's butt at what he'd on numerous occasions deemed her "unladylike" language. "I know where everything is in Arkham. I know where to go when I need supplies. It's three miles of open road to Kingsport, minimum, and Boston's even farther. All I have is a bike, and anyway . . . we have no idea what we'll find there."

"Exactly," he says in such a know-it-all tone she's tempted to grab him by the hair and hurl him not back into his jar but into the night. "It might be safer for you."

"Or it might be full of more . . ." Hannah gestures at the world beyond the door of the mausoleum and lets her arm drop. It is just too damn depressing. "Jesus Christ," she says, "this is my fucking life. I'm arguing with a severed head about what to do during the zombie apocalypse." She guesses she should have been watching *The Walking Dead* instead of all those seasons of *Game of Thrones*. Likely, it would have provided her with some useful hints and tips given her current circumstances.

"I'm as surprised as you are," says Dr. West. "I always assumed my work would be shelved along with me, but my *brilliant* nephew had other ideas."

"Don't talk about my father," says Hannah, a lump rising in her throat.

"Why not? He was a fool to think he could duplicate my research, much less advance it. When he asked my opinion, I *told* him—"

"Shut up!" cries Hannah before stuffing her great-uncle's head into his jar. She doesn't want to think about how this is all her father's fault. She doesn't want to lay the blame for the world's demise at the feet of a scientist whose only crime was letting grief rule his reason.

But Dr. West is right. Her father had been unable to let go of the dead . . . and because of that, as far as she knows, the world now belongs to them.

o

Hannah tries to remember when she first realized everything was going wrong.

It wasn't when her father had called her, demanding she come home *right now*. She'd wondered what was going on, as he pretty much lived at his lab, and only went to his dusty house to do laundry; her answer had come when he hugged her, tears standing in his eyes.

"Ask him what to do, if it comes to that. He'll know if anyone does," he'd said before injecting her with something that had knocked her out. Then he'd locked her in the basement.

No . . . she'd known something was wrong before that stupid day. She just hadn't known what to do about it.

○

"It's sad, but it's also just so *humiliating*, don't you think?"

Hannah had overheard two of her father's colleagues talking at her mother's funeral after the service. She'd sidled closer, curious: the catty bullshit of academia intrigued her, even if it's what had made her decide she was better suited to a "career" as a barista halfway through her PhD.

But you're so smart, they'd said. *What a waste when you showed such promise.*

Yeah—fuck *that* shit. She'd rather swim with sharks when she was on her period. It was safer.

"*Humiliating* doesn't describe it." The man pulled a face. "Her life's over and so's his career. Can you even imagine? I always thought it was a mistake for him to let his wife volunteer for his 'revolutionary' new cancer treatment. Let's see him apply for funding now."

Hannah hadn't said anything to either of them; quite frankly, she didn't see the point since nothing she could say would feel as good as punching them both in the face. Unfortunately, controlling herself turned out to be the wrong choice for once. Her father had ended up overhearing some of their spiteful gossip, and given his choices after that night, she couldn't help but wonder . . . if she'd hushed them up, one way or the other, would it have come to this?

○

She'd awoken in her dad's basement, a crick in her back and a spider running across her nose. A quick swat resolved the latter concern, but the former took a bit longer. She'd risen, gingerly, and climbed the stairs, pointlessly rattling the knob for a good long while before resigning herself to looking for an axe or something to force her way out.

"What the fuck, Dad," she'd said—sadly, not angrily. If she was angry at anyone, it was at herself. She had known he was losing it and had chosen to remain a spectator, hoping he'd pull himself out of his depression, his obsession, without her demanding he give up his research.

Then again, she hadn't known what exactly he was researching.

Hannah thought it telling that she had no idea if it was her father's foresight or mere coincidence that led to her finding the fire axe next to her great-uncle's head, but that's how it happened. She'd been overjoyed to finally find an implement that would allow her to get out and take a piss somewhere more dignified than the cellar floor until she'd startled at the unmistakable sight of a human profile sitting in a large Ball jar.

She'd screamed—of course she had—and when her heart slowed again, she'd inspected the head. Her whole life, she'd heard stories about her creepy great-uncle, and given the nature of those tales, it didn't totally surprise her to find some decapitation victim in a jar.

"The fuck?" She'd poked at the glass.

Then the eyes had fluttered open, and Hannah no longer felt the same urgency in her bladder.

o

She lets her great-uncle languish in his jar all night. Whether he sleeps, she does not know. She certainly gets no rest.

The rain stops sometime in the wee hours. When the day dawns, the sky is a brilliant blue that's almost obscene in its perfection. She has thought long and hard about Dr. West's advice—about what it would mean to try and leave Arkham, to see if the world beyond the town's borders is also a shambles—and she has decided to risk it. Sooner or later she'll either be caught scavenging for food, or her sources for supplies will run out entirely. Better to make the run while she's still healthy and can afford to spend a few days on the road. Finally hungry, Hannah pulls some Primal Strips out of her bag and tears into them. Thai peanut was always her favorite back in the before-time. The familiar flavor brings tears to her eyes.

She'll need a map. She's been to Kingsport many times, but though the bridge across the Miskatonic tributary should be easy enough to traverse, she has no idea what the state of the roads will be like on the other side. With all the rain they've been having there could be flooding. With only her bike and no access to antibiotics, she's not sure how wise it would be to cross anything too nasty.

She packs what she can into her backpack, but before strapping on the fire axe she takes out her great-uncle to tell him her plan. He seems pleased, probably because she's finally taking his advice.

"I figure a gas station might still have a map," she says. "The problem is . . . I have no idea what else will be in there."

"Did you think this would be easy?" Dr. West sniffs derisively. "You're certainly your father's daughter. 'I've been reading over your project notes, Uncle, and I think where you went wrong was injecting the cadavers with reagent. If I vaporize it, then—'"

"Shut the fuck up," says Hannah, shocking him into silence. "That's my fucking father you're talking about, okay? And,"—she swallows— "my mother," she whispers when she can.

Hannah cannot really blame her mother for her part in all this, given that she was already dead when it began. Nevertheless, it was mom's thrashing that sprayed the other corpses in the morgue with the formula, causing the chain reaction that ended . . . well, *everything.*

After a moment, her great-uncle's lips unpurse. "You're quite right," he says, the first time he has ever sounded apologetic over the course of their acquaintance. "Forgive me. I have never been sentimental about the dead, but of course, you would have reason to be in this case."

"*In this case.* Jesus." Hannah shakes her head. "Anyway, I know it won't be easy. I was just wondering if you . . . well . . . *fuck.* In case I don't make it back, where should I, you know . . . leave you?"

"Oh." It clearly had not occurred to her great-uncle that she might care about what happened to *him* in all this. "I suppose . . . any place is as good as another. You've been very kind to me, but I existed for years without anyone to sponge my brow and all that. Who knows, I may live longer than . . . everyone. Forever, even." He chuckled, the creep. "All this to say, just put me where you can grab me if you *do* make it out alive. I've enjoyed the novelty of your company, Hannah, and if it is possible for me to come along wherever you go . . . I'd like to."

Touched, Hannah replaces him more carefully than usual in his jar.

There is a gas station at the intersection of Peabody and Washington on the way out of town. Hannah heads there with her great-uncle and everything she owns in the world on her back. She spies a few of the dead on her ride, but she either speeds by them or swerves to avoid their notice.

Her great-uncle had once told her his few successes involved very fresh specimens. Many of those exposed to the vaporized reagent had been in the ground for years, if not centuries; they are mobile and possess an unnatural strength but not particularly acute faculties.

When the gas station comes into view, she pedals past it but not too far. She figures she can sprint away, if necessary, and parks her bike in the lee of a neglected forsythia.

The only thing she takes with her is her axe.

Derby's Gas-n-Go looks deserted, but in her experience, that's no indication of anything. She approaches cautiously and skulks around the perimeter. No windows are smashed, which is usually a good sign. Still, when she pulls on the front door, she does so cautiously.

It's not locked, but it does ding upon being opened wide enough for her to squeeze through. The chime is terrifyingly loud, and Hannah suppresses a giggle, imagining being mobbed with the undead, succumbing at long last . . . in the Gas-n-Go.

Once inside, the store is almost silent—though it should be even quieter. The electricity is off, everywhere, but here there is that characteristic subtle hum of lots of refrigerators. There must be a generator still working. She glances around, sees nothing, and heads for the wobbly kiosk filled with self-guided tour pamphlets, postcards—and maps.

Hannah grabs a likely handful, stuffing them into the back pocket of her jeans, intending to sort through and pick the best one later—but before she goes, she wonders about the humming of the generator. Her gaze tracks to the wall of drinks at the back of the store, and she is suddenly parched. It has been weeks since she last had a cold beverage, and the temptation is irresistible. The desire for a soda, icy and sweet and fizzy, takes hold completely, and before she is consciously aware of her actions she is in front of the cooler, setting down her axe and thanking the God she's pretty sure doesn't exist for university students' penchant for Mexican Coke—the kind with actual sugar instead of corn syrup.

The door opens after the satisfying resistance she remembers from when she wasn't the last woman in the world, and it was still commonplace to grab a drink at a convenience store. The cold air on her face is glorious; the feel of the bottle in her hand even more so. Remembering her grad school years, she pops the top on the handle of the fridge and drinks half of it in one go—guzzling it, reveling in the experience—and sighs before belching richly.

Only then does she notice the eyes staring at her from behind the rest of the beverages.

She drops the bottle on her foot, feels the impact on her sneaker and the liquid seeping over her toes. It has seen her. She grabs her axe before backing up.

"Son of a fuck," she mutters when she realizes the corpse is not alone. They have congregated in the cool of the refrigerator, and when they begin to move, she hears the bones creaking in their skin.

She is going to fucking die. And for a fucking *Coke*.

The dead are pretty quick for being, well, *dead*, but they will have to go around and find some way to get to her, given that they're trapped behind rows of bottles. Hannah decides to run for it. It's not her usual choice since she has always hated running but needs must and all that shit. She turns, hearing a door squeal somewhere to her left, throws open the front door, and puts on a burst of speed, heading for her bike.

Three corpses, two of them naked, the third still in its funeral suit, are milling around her stuff while one in some terrible Laura Ashley gown scrabbles at the zipper. As she approaches, its stiff fingers find the tab and yank the bag open, revealing the jar containing her great-uncle's head. He is looking around wildly, helpless, panicked, and his eyes meet hers for only a moment before Hannah looks away to do what must be done.

Before her legs stop pumping, Hannah's axe is swinging up above her head and chopping into the thief. It is a fairly dry body, and the cut sinks deep into the corpse's putrid neck. She yanks out the blade and swings again—this time, the head spins away as if she'd been wielding a driver in some unholy game of golf.

The body drops, twitching, but Hannah doesn't stop to admire her success. She turns around and chops at the closest of the other three, the one in the suit, lopping off an arm and its head before spinning to whack at the second, which is horribly naked. A few swings and that one falls, too, and though blisters are starting on her palms, Hannah takes down the final body in a cloud of dust that her half-elf necromancer would have paid 30 gp for back when she still had an RPG group.

Hannah zips up her backpack, kicks her bike's kickstand for all she's worth, and is fucking out of there as the rest of them come up behind, her now-gross axe laid across the handlebars. The dead are fast but not as fast as a scared thirty-something on a bike. She pedals for all she's worth until she's over the bridge and reaches a crossroads.

The afternoon is waning, and before the last of the light goes, Hannah dismounts, exhausted, to read her maps. She pores over them for a time before deciding on a route to Kingsport. Only then does she consult with her great-uncle.

"Thank you," are the first words out of his mouth. "I have no idea what they wanted with me, but they wanted me."

"Hell if I know," says Hannah. "Maybe they wanted to make you their king."

He ignores this sally. "Did you get a map? Do you know where we're going?"

"Yeah," she says. "I think so. Who knows what we'll find there, but . . ."

"It's always better to know."

"Sure, I guess." Hannah sighs. "I just wish I had, I dunno, a motorcycle and a sawed off shotgun instead of some crappy bike and a fire axe. This is some *Mad Max* shit. It would be nice to be prepared."

"Mad Max? Is he an old boyfriend of yours?"

Hannah sighs. Sometimes she forgets her great-uncle was a head in a jar before color film was standard.

"Yeah. An ex-boyfriend," she says, and she puts him back, screwing on the lid extra-tight.

It's time to move on.

{}

Molly Tanzer *is the author of the British Fantasy Award–nominated mosaic novel* A Pretty Mouth *(Lazy Fascist Press, 2012), the steampunk weird western* Vermilion *(Word Horde, 2015), cocktail-themed collection* Rumbullion and Other Liminal Libations *(Egaeus Press, 2013), and the historical crime novel* The Pleasure Merchant *(Lazy Fascist Press, 2015). She is also the co-editor of the forthcoming anthology* Swords v. Cthulhu *(Stone Skin Press, 2016). Her short fiction has appeared in many magazines and anthologies. Find her online at mollytanzer.com and @molly_the_tanz.*

Beige Walls

Joshua L. Hood

Beige walls, beige cubicles, yellow sticky notes that were slightly more beige than usual. For some reason, she had thought a state-of-the-art government research facility would be a little more . . . state of the art. A dot matrix printer tittered in the distance.

"It's because," Dr. Merrick said, "if we upgraded hardware every time technology evolved, we'd spend all our time and money just trying to keep up. Really, it's only the operational hardware and software that need updating frequently. And the brains, of course. You guys are our most valuable assets. Don't forget that."

"I won't if you won't," she said with a smile.

Dr. Merrick didn't respond.

Renee swallowed her nerves.

"Besides, funding has waned since the private sector has lost confidence in the capitalizable potential of our work."

"Huh. Bummer."

"Here's your work station," the doctor pointed to a beige cubicle. "Workflow is distributed by a performance-to-priority application. The better you are at certain things, the more of that thing you'll get to process. But don't be discouraged from widening your scope. Performance evaluations take into account your priority grade on all divisional subsets. That's where incentive raises come from . . ." He trailed off, sounding bored, distracted, like his favorite song was playing somewhere in the distance. "Um, I've got to go. Get familiar with the set up. I'll be back for lunch, and we'll take a tour of the facilities. That part I think you'll really like."

○

In truth, Renee liked all of it, even the beige—in its own way. She would put up with all the divisional subsets and incentive programs she had to as long as she got to be a small part of the team exploring the Elder Reach.

"*Eigenstatic space,*" she sternly reminded herself, "not *Elder Reach*. Only amateurs and sci-fi hacks called it the Elder Reach. Be professional."

She looked up at the framed poster on the wall. A pixelated mealworm-looking thing floating in a black void, bearing the caption *Eigenstae Howardia goldmanii*. She got the tingles in the same way she used to when she would look at cartoony drawings of eigenstatic creatures in picture books with their sharp teeth rounded to polished knobs and their scaled tentacles turned to cute nubbins. She was glad she could still enjoy the wonder of these things after all this time. Most of her peers thought it was childish. The picture in the poster was old news, after all, but it was the first of its kind, and that meant something. It was the first confirmed proof of things that were considered pretty farfetched at best from back when they were still just fairytale horrors that drove men mad.

"It was actually the machines," her father had told her once. "The creatures are harmless to those in active space, but the early machines that the scientists and spiritualists plugged into their brains in the 1920s and 30s are what caused them to become manic. That's why no one believed them. Of course, if we were to try and force our minds into static space we'd probably lose a few neurons too. Just because technology makes things easier now doesn't make us better than those old pioneers. Don't let the familiarity of amazing things fool you. We are constantly rewriting the fine print of the universe—and that's big."

It was that last part that stuck with her. People seemed to think that just because Elder Space photos were so pervasive and mankind so accustomed to their strangeness that they were old and boring. Like it wasn't a mind-blowing discovery every time a new one was revealed. The romance, the mystery, it was all still there behind the kids' books and the pop-science and the ElderBurger meals at fast food joints.

The first thing Renee did was to set her computer background to a grainy black and white photo of the earth as seen from space—her favorite image from a V2 rocket launched in 1946, the first of its kind. She gazed at the black blobs of land amongst the white blur of clouds and smiled. Most people would have picked "The Blue Marble" or some other famous space photo. But this one was the first, and moreover, as far as Renee knew, this image had never been used to market some used-car dealer's "Out Of This World Prices!"

●

"I'll be honest with you," Dr. Merrick said three hours later on the way to the optics lab. "Forget what I said earlier. Don't worry about cross training. Focus on neutrino distortions. Everything else is going to be an algorithm soon. Every time you guys clear a frame, the computer learns from what you did. This data center will probably be reduced to one small supercomputer within the next two years—except for neutrinos. Those have proven a bit random for the computers. For now, anyway."

"Nice thought," Renee said.

"Don't worry. With your resume, I have no doubt we'll find something for you. So here we are. Brace yourself—most people don't realize just how intense these machines can be." Dr. Merrick opened the beige door into a stark, white room. In the center was an orb four or five meters across, covered in slender spindles like a porcupine. It was spinning so quickly that Renee felt like she was standing in a room full of fans. It smelled of sterile grease. "Stay behind the red line. This thing changes direction erratically," the doctor said. "Each arm carries a fifty-thousand-dollar optic camera set-up. They're not like regular cameras, of course, but that's kind of the idea. Eigenstatic space moves by very quickly—or rather, we move through it. All five thousand of those cameras are taking pictures of the same particle cluster. Given the speed of the earth around the sun, the solar system through the cosmos, the North American plate across the mantle, and the movement of all the uncertain particles, the machine has less than one trillionth of a second to determine the course and speed of us in relation to a single Elder parti—er, eigenstatic particle."

Renee smiled, feeling vindicated. "Fascinating," she said, trying to seem impressed.

Of course, she knew all of this. Most people with PBS did. By focusing on the recently discovered static particles, those that didn't move or fluctuate—not subject to uncertainty—a universe similar to the normal plane of existence was revealed. Just how that worked was still unclear, just like how a lot of pharmaceuticals work. And just like miracle drugs, the how of it quickly became immaterial once the results were observed. It was soon discovered that taking a series of images of these particles could result in a mosaic that revealed a very clear physical realm, just out of notice of our own. That the realm just happened to be populated with unimaginable creatures was a huge bonus.

Naturally, it took a lot of computational power to build a world out of single particles, and with things like atoms and neutrinos vibrating around and photobombing the pictures, it took a lot of people to sort through the confusion in the viewing spectrum, which is where jobs like Renee's came in. As far as the population at large knew, it only took a dozen nerds and an upload server to make the pictures, but the population at large was uninspired, bored, used to it all.

Dr. Merrick peered over thin-framed bifocals. Renee barely glanced away from the rapidly gyrating machine. "You find this all very interesting, don't you?"

"Of course," Renee said.

"Hmm. Come this way. There's something I want to show you," Dr. Merrick said, deep thought creasing his brow. "Yes, I think you'll enjoy this."

"What is it?"

"A game changer. Still photos may soon be a thing of the past."

Renee looked startled. "Video?"

"Better. It'll shut this whole data center down and open a vast new world of exploration . . . if we're lucky."

Dr. Merrick started walking quickly toward the door. Renee hustled to keep up.

"It's just a pet project, really. But it's one I'm particularly proud of. I kind of feel like showing it off . . . to someone who cares. Grant managers and lab directors are only so receptive."

They walked back down the beige hallway until a door with the red words "Authorized Personnel Only" appeared in the distance. Renee shivered with excitement. She was hoping she'd make a good impression.

During the walk, Dr. Merrick prattled on. "In the beginning, it was tempting to think of it as a world of infinite horrors. There are so many of them. Then, someone actually saw the same creature twice, and then a third time, and a fourth, like it was following us as we vibrate along. This caused a bit of apprehension at the time, but it was soon realized that they were, in fact, different creatures of the same species. Then we started categorizing, applying a standard taxonomy, which seemed to hold up over time. That led Donald Racoult to create Racoult's Theorem."

"Any biological life form in the same universe, regardless of plane or dimension, is restricted by the same biological principles. Like Lyell's uniformitarianism is to geology," Renee chimed in.

"Exactly. But then, we immediately realized the contradiction of biological creatures existing in static space. It doesn't make sense on any level, even quantum. So we formed a new hypothesis. Maybe eigenstatic creatures aren't so static."

"I hadn't read anything to contradict static particle theory in the journals," Renee said.

"You read the journals?" Merrick said, slightly surprised.

"My degree is in statistics, but my interest is in . . . all sorts of unknown things."

"You don't say?"

"Sure. I dunno what it is. The mystery, I guess."

"I hear you there," Merrick said, then fell silent, distracted.

Renee smiled to herself. *I'm glad I'm not the only one who hasn't succumbed to the beige,* she thought. "So what's the new idea?"

"Oh, well, it's pretty simple really. Biological creatures as we know them can't live in static space, so we reconsidered and realized that static space isn't all that prevalent. Thin is the word we use. The eigenstatic creatures aren't on a parallel plane, they're behind it."

"Behind it? How?"

"It's like a wall separating us from them. A wall with eleven dimensions running through normal space, distorting our view of it. The example I use is to have you imagine that you're in a swimming pool with one side separated by a transparent pane of red glass. If you look through the glass, it will appear as though the people on the other side are swimming in a different kind of medium entirely, but it's still the same damned pool."

"Wow," Renee said. "That's news to me." They'd reached the door. A beige-faced clock with a black frame ticked above it, telling her that lunch break was almost up. "So what's behind the door?"

"Well . . . it's a sledgehammer. We're trying to break through the glass."

A brief chime sounded from both of their phone alarms at once. Lunch time was over. Dr. Merrick glanced at the clock and rolled his eyes. "Ignore that. Would you like to go in?" he asked.

Renee nodded.

○

"Why doesn't everyone know about this?" Renee exclaimed as they entered a room full of wires and digital readouts. She couldn't tell where the so-called sledgehammer was. Half of the stuff in the room looked slapped together, specialized, like it existed nowhere else in the world.

"We're publishing next week, though I don't expect much of a reaction," Merrick said.

"Why not!? This is amazing. People are gonna flip! A chance to see an eigenstatic creature in the flesh, to touch one! This is huge!"

"If it works," Merrick said, "then we'll certainly get a grant boost but probably little more."

"I don't think you realize what this will mean to the world . . ." Renee began.

"Of course, we do. But we're realists. Ask yourself, what was the last dinosaur discovered, the last one reclassified? What was the last thing they cloned?"

"I don't know."

"Neither do I. Nor do I know the last guy to walk on the moon. I know the first but not the last. Have you seen the latest image from Hubble II? It's astounding."

"Yeah, it's of the Sombrero Nebula, right?"

"Galaxy. And it's actually only a single star cluster, but it contains a nascent supernova fluctuation. Something they didn't even know to look for until we found out how to read the magnetic signature of stabilizing iron in the near infrared. Right now at NASA, they're piecing together an image of that supernova as it occurs. Two weeks from now will be the first time that a supernova has been recorded in real time. You watch. It'll get a mention between celebrity baby names and Black Friday specials. But I digress. This is a gripe as old as technology. Now watch, we're starting."

A blue light began to glow at the end of a thin needle in the middle of the room: the sledgehammer. With a hum, it began to grow.

Dr. Merrick beamed. "Look, Renee, a glimpse across an unknown plane that doubles the size of our universe. The first look at life beyond alien! This is as far as we've got before destabilizing."

A placid voice came from a speaker on the wall. "Control room to observation deck. We have destabilization."

The blue glow dimmed and fluctuated.

Dr. Merrick didn't look surprised, but he did look a little disappointed.

"Interference critical. Looks like the new plasma siphon is insufficient. It's overheating," the control room said.

"Reboot it," Merrick said into a microphone.

A brief pause, then, "No good . . . wait. Something's happening. Numbers are balancing." The voice from the speaker became excited. "Plasma interference decreasing."

Renee glanced at Dr. Merrick, who remained silent. "I'm not sure how this is happening, but the aperture is widening. The plasma siphon is still offline," the speaker said.

Dr. Merrick smiled.

"Where's the plasma going?" Renee asked.

"Into eigenstatic space, I believe. Or what we used to call eigenstatic space. I think we're getting a little help here . . . from the other side," the doctor said.

Renee's eyes widened. "No way. You can't be serious."

"Just speculation," the doctor smirked, "but I have it on good authority that this could be a cooperative effort."

She watched as the blue light grew. An appendage, like a tentacle but of a color she'd never seen before, began to writhe through the blue light. It dripped with a slime that vaporized before it hit the ground. Acrid, cloying decay wafted through the air as the tentacle oozed outward like a worm from a fish eye.

Renee grew cold, afraid. She recalled warnings from the past. The things that scientists said to each other after science had done horrible things.

The question isn't can we, but should we?

The progress of science is far ahead of man's ethical behavior.

All attempts to adapt our ethical code to our situation in the technological age have failed.

I am become death.

Renee stepped backward, but there was nowhere to go.

Dr. Merrick still beamed. "It arrives!" he said. "We've done it! We've done it, and no one even tried to stop us!"

"What?" Renee muttered.

The thing from the blue eye grew and grew.

"No contest, no opposition. A vacuum of interest! The world has grown bland with wonder, but that will change." He laughed shrilly. "I may have been a little dishonest, my dear. The wall between us and them wasn't absolute. There was a force for which static space is no obstacle."

"Dr. Merrick, shut it down. Please!"

"The dimension of thought, my dear! Thought is transcendent, and they heard us looking even as we saw them. Can you hear them? Can you hear them in your thoughts? They come!"

"Dr. Merrick!" Renee shouted as the tentacles slithered across the beige floor toward them.

"On second thought, Renee, don't worry about the neutrinos. I think we've successfully eliminated your job today. It's a shame that the world will never see its first supernova, but I hardly doubt they'll miss it. Perhaps, they will find a wonder again in the age of destruction.

"Say, Renee, would you like to name this one? That's the rules. Finders namers. I've already got a few, so you can have this one. First across the void—what an honor! You may even be remembered!

"But hurry, it comes!"

{§

Joshua L. Hood *lives in Boise, Idaho. He holds a B.A. in archaeology and occasionally works in the field locally. He also has most of an illustration degree but now regrets all the time and money he spent on art school. On the weekends, he volunteers for a wildlife rehab center with orphaned black bears and, on weeknights, spends his time as a night watchman for our corporate overlords. He's had stories published through several small presses and has put out the short story collection* Melting People, *available from all the big booksellers. There are many more spooky stories and novels in the works, details of which can be found at www. joshualhood.com.*

The Five Hundred Days
of Ms. Between

Joshua Alan Doetsch

Can't feel my legs. So I slither along the ground, toward the audient window, humming that song. I hear the wet-velcro rip of the thousand hands rending flesh. I see her through the window. That mocking grin.

The first thing Ms. Between said to me was, "I'm a mad woman with a lab." The second thing she said was that I could leave at any time with no obligation. The third thing was that there could be no questions—questions would cause her and her offer to evaporate. I believed absolutely in that, so she handed me the murder weapon.

No, wait. That's not the beginning. I don't remember exactly when it began—some time after Ms. Between came out of our touchscreens. Everyone has seen her Tech Talk videos and all their terrible wonder. Yet nobody knows where she broadcasts from. No one ever meets Ms. Between.

But I did.

She provided no name, only an address. She said he had done a bad thing. Said he deserved it.

I swallowed all of my wriggling questions.

The Nameless Man looked old and kindly. He had one eye and smiled as he slept. Oh, how I wish he had tossed with moaning guilt. Everyone sleeps more soundly since the symbionts.

Hesitating, I stood over the Nameless Man's bed for an hour. With the speed of a carnivorous plant, I took out the dagger. It was carved from bone and coated in lacquer that gave it a greenish hue. I raised the dagger over my head and held it there, squeezing the leather-wrapped handle. Another half hour. My arm ached. I bit my inner cheek and tasted copper. Ms. Between had said I could leave at any time.

No, Val, Lailah pleaded from inside me. *You must not do this.*

Lailah is my dedicated symbiont.

"Have to," I rasped.

The Nameless Man startled. His eye opened. I brought the dagger down. I've never been good with knives. It took many tries. "Sorry, sorry, sorry, sorry," I said until I was nothing but tears and snot.

"Lailah," I said when it was over, "now."

Her coils tightened in my gut. *No, Val. Don't make me. Don't make me.*

"We have to, Lailah. Please."

I felt her sigh and shiver. Her tendril came out the port in my wrist to snake down into the Nameless Man's mouth. His symbiont would not live long without him, but it might have stored recent memories in synaptic backup. Through Lailah, I felt its distress. Not a dedicated symbiont, not even a thought interface. How lonely. Just a silent worm. But I don't judge. I recognize my privilege.

As Lailah devoured the other symbiont, I put the wet dagger into a plastic bag. Ms. Between had handed it to me just before telling me the rules of time travel. It was preposterous. Time travel couldn't exist.

I committed murder on the off chance that I was wrong.

○

I walked home through the street-lit glow of the city, the old and terrible city of crimes uncounted, layered and layered like rings in a hanging tree. The streets were quiet, but I couldn't hear my own footsteps. Lailah released chemicals to soothe my nausea, so I managed three blocks from the Nameless Man's apartment before I vomited.

The anti-symbio crowd can wallow in ignorance. The symbionts improved our quality of life. They wiped out entire diseases. They're always there for us. We stare at our screens, pressing our Skinner-box buttons, but now, we're all alone together.

I wiped my mouth. Lailah cleaned the stomach acid from my teeth. I hummed a song I couldn't remember. An oldie. Very old. The song Ms. Between sang in the bar the night we met. Johnny Mercer? I couldn't remember the words, but the lyric fragments bounced around my brain like a free radical.

"Strange days," wheezed a vagrant from under a hooded cloak of rags.

Lailah hissed a warning in my brainpan, readying an arsenal of enhanced adrenaline. People without symbionts spook her. She can hear no voices inside them. She calls "Marco" into the darkness and gets no reply. I rubbed my belly and hummed the song to calm her. I tried to sing it.

"You've got to accentuate the positive . . . eliminate the . . . no . . . hmm . . ."

Through broken teeth, the vagrant muttered something that might have been, "Don't mess with mystery?"

"No," I said. "That's not it."

I gave the man my pocket cash. All he had was an empty belly and nothing to call him home. I recognize my privilege.

During the rest of the walk, I avoided eye contact. These days, pedestrians walk like zombie ants, forming curious, unthinking formations as if under the sway of tyrannous spores. I walked in the shadows of jagged buildings. When had I become afraid of the open, starry sky?

Thinking back, I don't recall if I entered my house by the front door or the rear. I only remember lying fetal on my bed. My pillow damp and salty. Lailah shuddered silent sobs within me.

Why, Val? Why did you make me do that?

"I'm sorry," I said over and over. Lailah's tendril poked out, wrapping around my hand. We squeezed one another. "We're doing it for Oliver and Nemo."

But they're dead, Val. They're dead.

"Not for long," I said. But that was stupid. Time travel was impossible.

With murder on my mind, I slept like a baby. Not so long ago—before the symbionts, during the screaming times—no one slept soundly. We screamed all through the night. Screaming was epidemic, and the city aldermen considered passing laws to ration sleep time and reduce the shrieks in the small hours. And that is when Ms. Between came streaming into our feeds.

✿

It began when the autumn was too damn hot, and it was much too late to deny the climate change or the things crawling out of the melting icecaps, and the country was too polarized to do anything about anything, and the sciences groped in all directions, and the search engines pieced together all dissociated knowledge. It started with emails and texts with subject lines like "Don't Fail to See!" and "Experience the Transhuman" and "Witness the Post-Mundane!" That is how Ms. Between came into our lives. She commanded our likes, our favorites, our shares, and our reposts. Billions of views. She came as an electronic zeitgeist. On the internet, everyone's an anonymous spirit—both the message and the messenger.

She looked at you, really looked at you through your touchscreen. The show-woman scientist, her Tech Talk videos were equally artistic. The images! The non sequiturs, the absurd, the grotesque. Faces peering out of ultimate space. Images so frightful that we might not have slept if not for our symbionts singing us silent lullabies of melatonin. And just when the surreal had tripped all the tumblers in your skull and you heard the creak of the suture cracks opening, hungry and ready, that is when Ms. Between would appear. So iconic in her huge goggles, rubber gloves, and waistcoat and suit—rather like a female Tesla. She was the harbinger of the recent surge in scientific discoveries. She dared us to hope.

If time isn't a flat petri dish poked by contemptuous fingers, if anything actually begins, then there I was at the bar. I smoked a vitamin-supplemented e-cigarette and complained to the bartender that a vice without self-destruction spoils the poetry. He nodded in the fiberoptic glow of my nauseously nutritious pull. I sighed out blueberry-scented smoke, and we lamented the good old days when cigarettes had the decency to kill.

Lailah made that happy vibration—*Mmm,* on my inner ear—that she makes whenever she finds a tumorous growth to eat. That's when I saw Ms. Between, sitting on the next stool as if she had leapt from my touchscreen. She swirled a nuclear blue martini in a rubber-gloved hand. She hummed and sang that old song. What was it called? The earworm lyrics crawled into my head. Why can't I remember?

I saw myself in her goggles, mouth gaping.

"You . . . you're . . .?"

"A madwoman with a lab," she said. "Don't be a glum chum. You're a sleepwalker, blind. How can you see the worlds within worlds? Do you know, if you rip open a gravid sand shark's belly, what you'd find? Embryos hunting embryos. Murder in utero. A tiny, black Mesozoic sea, and only one makes it out. From their perspective, you won."

Then the drinks flowed, and Ms. Between's sentences went up and down like a rickety carnival ride. She told me my life story. She told me about my twin brother, Oliver, and how he became my parents' favorite the day I announced that they no longer had two sons; the day they threw me out. She told me how Oliver was murdered. She told me how my mom and dad reconciled with me after his death, even paid for all my operations and changed their pronouns. How I hated them for that. As if I had to buy their acceptance with Ollie's blood, as if he was a sacrifice on the altar of their love. Ms. Between talked of amputees trying to scratch phantom limbs and how I looked for my brother's ghost in the bottom of every bottle. There were half-hearted suicide attempts, of course—never serious; always across, never along.

In the screaming times, before the symbionts, suicide was an epidemic. These days, it's harder to kill yourself when you're deciding for two. The self-murder rates plummeted, and the company building the civic-engendered suicide booths went out of business. We all pretended it never happened.

Ms. Between told me all these things.

And I believed. I had to.

Last call drove us out into the damp, hot, deserted midnight streets. And up the dizzy stairs and into her lab. She showed me strange instruments. Gaudy machines of glass, metal, and plastic. She threw a switch, and sparks flew, and my hair stood up, and there was a buzzing behind my eyes, and I could see things slithering in the air like the floaters in our peripheral. I saw grotesque shadows squatting on our heads.

I saw these things, and I had to believe. I'm so sorry, Nameless Man. I didn't believe in time travel, but I had to believe for Ollie. I took the bone dagger.

◉

You've got to ac-cent-tchu-ate the positive . . .

Can't remember the rest of the words. Something grinds in my chest when I breathe. I remember her voice. Ms. Between talks like someone who can barely cage the punchline behind her teeth. I remember how she said the rules of time travel.

One: the window is yours and yours alone. A window is calibrated to one person. Only that person can walk in or out of it. A person can only have one window. Ever.

Two: a window can open to only one time and place. Once set, that window is set forever.

Three: you can walk in and out of your window once a day. However, every trip wriggles the gap in time wider—sometimes by a millisecond, sometimes more. You will always arrive a little later than the last trip.

o

When I went back up the dizzy steps with the wet dagger, when I dropped it dripping at Ms. Between's feet, I knew she'd let loose the punchline. Time travel is impossible. It can't be real. Silly me. Stupid, evil, wretched me. I'd murdered for a desperate hope. That idiot hope would go to that chopping block still sticky with the gore of Santa Claus, fairytales, and all manner of moon-blooded dreams.

I shivered. I waited for the axe to fall.

And Ms. Between did the most unlikely thing. She opened the window.

It made none of the gaudy, mad science sounds of the rest of her lab. There was no transition between it not being and being. It stretched in trapezoidal shapes and inconstant angles. Colors swirled like a smoking mirror before they settled and cleared.

"Ollie?"

I gulped air. I saw him. I saw the scene moments before his death as it was described to me. Frozen.

"But," I said, "that's too late. No time to warn him. I need more time!"

Ms. Between shrugged apologetically, said it wasn't an exact science.

I said, "I need weapons: guns, explosives, something formidable."

She shook her head and said, "Nothing synthetic." In fact, she explained, with the window calibrated to me, anything that was not a human byproduct was dicey. She told me to take off my clothes, the way the Big Bad Wolf, stuffed like a sausage in Grandma's skin, told Red Riding Hood. "You won't need them anymore."

She gave me a jumpsuit of supple leather, vat-grown from fetal cells. It hugged me wetly. She handed me the dagger and nodded, and I knew what species of bone it was. She injected me with something that made all the colors bleed and every molecule significant.

Then I walked through the window.

Tiny explosions. My tooth fillings. I tasted copper. Agony. Déjà vu. The feeling of a forgotten song on the tip of the tongue.

"Ollie?"

Nemo! Lailah said in jubilation. *Nemo-Nemo-Nemo-Nemo!* She could sense her twin, Oliver's symbiont. They were two halves cut from the same worm when we were just children.

Oliver struggled, visible in the moonlight. He was bound and gagged on a rough-hewn stone at the center of a natural amphitheater, exactly as the police report said.

No time. I ran down the sloping semi-circle toward the killing stone. Dozens of steps from holding his hand. I had to get him out of there. No time.

And then, they were there.

"No."

I saw them by the light of the LED crosses grafted onto their foreheads. I saw them by the moonlight glinting off the metal peeking from their flesh. Fifteen? Twenty? More? The chromies. Children of the Immaculate Machine.

"No."

Some anti-symbios were more radical than others. Some found religion through body modification—transubstantiation through steel, the voice of the Holy Ghost through the wireless connection in their skulls. To them, a body defiled by one of the "devil worms" was a profanity. They punished the supporters of that lifestyle. Oliver had brought his medical training to this faraway place for charity work, bringing symbionts to impoverished children. And the chromies had tortured and murdered him. But not yet.

"No!"

Lailah filled my legs with adrenaline. I never ran so fast. I didn't run fast enough.

Many hands tore me away from Oliver. I stabbed and stabbed with the bone dagger, but it was quickly slapped away. Boots and reinforced knuckles hailed down. I swallowed teeth. A knee shattered. Ribs snapped like twigs in the night. Lailah tried so hard, pumped so many endorphins, but she couldn't keep up. My left eye socket crunched and closed, an avalanche over a cave. But crueler still, they left one eye open.

"Don't you do it," I tried to say through the ruin of my mouth.

But they did. They stood with perfect theatrical arrangement, so my view was not obstructed. Every detail I read in the police report. Every horrible daydream and sweat-stained nightmare. I saw it. They crucified Oliver. They slowly cut him open. They pulled out Nemo.

Oliver made a muffled scream.

Lailah screamed, and I screamed. We screamed to the stars and universe with its insane rules that allowed time to bend. Then there was only the sound of the chromies praying. Then their laughter.

Then silence.

●

And then a familiar humming. That old song. Lailah stirred in the wreckage of me, sensing a sibling self. A figure hunched some paces away, farther up in the amphitheater. The chromies laughed and leered at the promise of more bloody fun. My head swam, and it was so hard to see in the moon-licked dark. Were my symbiont and I part of triplet sets?

No. It was me, come back through the window. I . . . she shook, barely able to stand. Had it been days? Weeks? Months? However long it took medical and symbiotic care to allow her to limp back through. She fell over, bleeding out from all the places the window had robbed her of her stitches, staples, and artificial bits. Helpless, she had watched our brother murdered all over again. I could tell something had been taken from her, something that only showed in her one good eye. She just kept humming that jolly song.

And then more humming. More me. One by one. There was no transition. They were suddenly there or had been there in the dark. And with each additional hum, the glittering grins of the chromies eclipsed into frowns and uncertainty.

How many of me were there? We filled the half circle of the rising amphitheater. Every step up the slope was another me, one day more healed in body and broken in mind. The ones at the top were lean and well-muscled, marked everywhere with self-inflicted scars, hunched and shivering with insanity. Once a day through the window. How many days?

The amphitheater vibrated with their humming. Lailah called out to the silent symphony of symbionts. All at once, the many mes showed the graveyard of their teeth and made such faces that the youngest of the chromies fainted.

And then, they charged down the slope. The ones highest up moved the fastest, taking the lead, loping down the hill. They surged over the weeping chromies like frenzied maenads. Grabbing, biting, rending, pulling flesh from metal.

And here I am, crawling up the hill. Crawling like a boneless mollusk humiliated by gravity. I can hear the Bacchic orgy behind me, sounding something like a slaughterhouse and something like lovemaking. One of the machine cultists begs for help. The thousand hands kill and defile.

Can't feel my legs. It hurts and something grates inside of me, but I crawl toward the window. Ms. Between watches me from the opening. I crawl back to the mask of her mocking grin and all the things wriggling behind it. I crawl back to her made-up rules—the rules that make rescue impossible but revenge conceivable, the rules that tear down deniability and nurture complicity. She knew. I murdered that old man, not even believing it would work, and she knew. I know all this now, but I'm still going to do it. I'll pay the price, once a day, every day, and walk through the window to watch my brother die.

I crawl and cough and hum. I remember the words now. The lyrics were always in my brain, the way that tentacles and gills lie waiting, safely tucked away under our DNA, hidden behind the thinnest scrim of inhibitor proteins. I crawl and laugh and sing.

"You've got to ac-cent-tchu-ate the positive, eliminate the negative, latch on to the affirmative . . . don't mess with Mistress In-Between."

{}

Joshua Alan Doetsch *is a sentient word virus spreading across the collective unconscious through the vector of human language. It has taken on many forms, from short stories to screenplays to tabletop roleplaying games. It spreads through print, digital, and audio mediums. It coalesced as the novel* Strangeness in the Proportion *and shaped itself into an anthropomorphic guise as Lead Writer of* The Secret World, *a massive multiplayer online computer game. It is made of cuttlefish ink and earworm rhymes, and its fingernails are gleaming fountain pen nibs. You can help spread the infection at joshuadoetsch.com. It's already too late.*

68 Days

Kaaron Warren

Matty said no way was I going camping with them unless I saw a doctor and got my rash cleared up. He didn't care about my headaches or my sore eyes. Never looked at my eyes. "There's something wrong with you, and I don't mean just in the head. I mean, you're fucked in the head, but there's some weird shit going on as well."

I booked in to see Mum's doctor because at least he knew all the background stuff, so I wouldn't have to start at the beginning.

I had been feeling weird, as if my blood was made out of chocolate.

My mum used to say, "You're slower than ever. What's up?" whenever she was mad at me. If she wasn't mad, she'd say "You all right? Cos you look a bit off." Then, she'd be hugging me, breathing in deep like she did. She reckoned she could tell when I was spiralling down. Feeling bad. But she was already in the pit herself, and all she could do was drag me down.

They asked me in court why I'd lost it the way I did, smashing car windows up and down a dozen streets.

"My mum killed herself, and I'm the one who found her," I said. "It's like the broken glass helped me forget for a minute at a time."

My lawyer did her job, and the judge was a kind person; I got off with time served. The months I'd rotted in jail, waiting for trial. So, luckily, I didn't have to go back.

The damage was done, though. I was already sick.

Already dying.

The doctor knew where I'd been, what I'd done. Mum told him all my secrets when she was alive, and I told him the rest.

So when he said he thought I had something he couldn't fix, I believed him. It seemed right. Inevitable, though he was almost crying. He gave me a scrip for antibiotics and pain killers and a great pile of brochures. Everyone gets a showbag like this when diagnosed with a terminal disease. Self-help, diet, counselling, and a brochure about the Mars Mission and medical research. The brochure was like a disc, showing where the stars are. "If you can see Mars, we need you. Call this number."

I stuffed it all in my backpack.

The doctor told me to call him any time. He said, "You should talk to the counsellors at least. Someone with your LE needs someone to talk to."

LE. He meant life expectancy. Didn't sound any better with only the letters.

He said, "You go home and make yourself comfortable."

I had no real home to go to. Our place had been a housing commission flat in Mum's name, so that went when she went. So I stayed with friends and friends of friends.

I called Matty to tell him, but he was on the road. They'd left without me. His friends were all about eighteen, ten years younger than me, but I passed okay. I only noticed sometimes. When he called me back, he said, "If you can get to the station, I'll pick you up there. Did you get your shit sorted out? Don't want you dying on me." Laughter at that.

"You like it on the bottom, Matty?" I heard his passenger say. Giggling. Some girl.

o

First thing he said when he picked me up for camping: "You look yellow as piss. And your rash is still disgusting."

I clung on to him. I didn't want to let him go for a minute.

His friends called me a limpet, but I didn't have internet out there, so I couldn't look up to see what it was.

Before long, I was grubby, drunk, and whining at him to have sex with me. "They'll ask, and if we didn't do it, they'll say we're not together."

He was like, "Keep it quiet, then. Don't make that noise you make."

Here I was, faking all that shit, and he doesn't even like it.

He went out to smoke bongs around the fire, but I was so tired I just wanted to sleep. I opened the tent flap and looked out at the stars, at the red glow of Mars, before I slept.

I woke late the next morning, covered with sweat. The tent was a hot box. I crawled out, desperate for fresh air. The sun beat down. Checking my phone, I saw it was past ten.

It was also dead quiet.

The other tents were gone. The cars were gone.

They'd left me.

I tried to call Matty but couldn't get a signal. Were they coming back? Surely. Surely.

Two hours later, I realised they weren't. That I'd have to walk out to find a signal if I wanted help.

They'd left me the tent, at least, and our used condom. I dragged the sleeping bag out, intending to roll it up. Then I thought, fuck it. Not carrying anything.

So I left it all there.

○

I walked till I got a phone signal. I didn't know who to call. I tried Matty first; no answer. I was pretty sure he wouldn't answer again. I didn't want to bother the police, and they hate me, anyway.

I called my doctor; his receptionist said he'd taken ill. I hoped whatever I had wasn't catching. "He did say if you called you should ring some of the numbers he gave you. They should be able to help. Keep us posted," she said, but there was already a bip on the line. Another call for her.

So I called one of the counselling services, but all I got was "Call during office hours."

I tried another one. It was a wrong number.

So I thought about that red glow, that Mars in the sky, and I called them.

They were friendly, kind, like "Where are you? Stay there, and we'll send someone."

They did, too. Within two hours, they had a pre-paid taxi to pick me up and take me to their office. I read their brochure on the way.

It said, "Medical research is worth a fortune, especially when related to space travel."

It said, "200,000 apply, only a few get in. Will one of them be you?"

I wanted it to be. I really did. So by the time we got there, I was ready to try out.

○

They were really nice. They gave me a comfy chair and a big test to do.

"Not a test!" they said. "A questionnaire. No right or wrong answers."

There were, though. They were looking for particular answers. I didn't know what those answers were, so all I could do was be honest.

Question: What is your past job experience?

I'd had heaps. Right now I was working on a road crew. Loved that. In your gear, you all looked alike, like a real team.

Question: Do you like being part of a group?

Depends on the group. The road crew was good.

Question: What's the worst thing you've eaten?

I ate a rat in jail once to prove a point. Can't remember what the point was, mind you. But it made them all leave me alone. Weird, though. After I ate the rat, even water tasted of it.

Question: What do you think of the Planarian Worm experiment? Obscene? Wrong? Worthwhile?

They let me use my phone to look it up, and my answer was, "It doesn't bother me. They're only worms."

Question: Do you eat meat? Do you have any ethical concerns, or do you know that each creature has a place (for example)?

Love my meat.

Question: Are you looking for meaning in your life? Are you frightened of dying without purpose?

That was a tough one. I decided to tell them what my mum wrote in her goodbye note about finding meaning and letting that make you happy.

○

And I got the job!

I had to sign an agreement:

No arguing.

Anything goes.

Eat what you're given.

Do your job.

Have fun!

I called to let Matty know I was training for Mars. He didn't answer, so I left a message, and he called back, laughing at me until he choked.

He said, "Jeez, you're a dumbfuck. And they must be too if they've hired you."

I hung up on him, and I thought that just getting the job made me stronger. Better. My parents never thought I'd be much, and I'm not, yet. But I will be.

o

Day 1.

The resort squatted in the distance, shadowy and huge, like an old giant from a fairy tale waiting for us to arrive.

I climbed off the bus, stiff and sore after fourteen hours travelling. The real world had faded as the wheels of the bus rolled on. Everyone was quiet, mostly, with the occasional burst of conversation or laughter.

They'd told me to leave it all behind. That this was my second chance, my tilt at making a difference. I couldn't see how that was possible, but we'd find out.

The bus driver and some others unloaded boxes and our stuff, and he took off. The only way out was to walk. It'd take days. Weeks.

So dry. Made me thirsty just looking out. And red. Someone said it was red like Mars, which I thought was pretty smart.

The deserted resort used to be for star-gazing. Rich people would come here and get educated about space and all that. It had a planetarium. The big sign at the entrance said "Starstruck Resort and Planetarium," but someone made a joke and changed it to "Starstruck Resort and Planarium." Not exactly sure, but I laughed along with the others.

Wind blew so strong my hair flew around my head, and I struggled to keep my skirt down. Someone whistled and said, "Hello, sexy legs." I was going to like this place.

•

They showed us to apartments. Luckily, we had guides. I've never seen so many corridors, stairs, elevators, more corridors. Like some huge maze. We all have our own place, spread out over the whole resort. I couldn't believe how much room I had.

My apartment looked out over the dried up swimming pool. It was the quietest place I ever slept.

Our corridor was called Olympus Mons. They said it was named after a volcano on Mars. All the art in the rooms and along the corridors was spacey. Stars and planets, that kind of thing. So beautiful.

•

I got totally lost trying to find the dining room, so I called for help.

"Stay put," they said, just like when I was deserted in the bush. One young guy came to find me. He was so good-looking I was glad I'd put my makeup on but wished I'd worn one of my sexier tops.

In the end, I was one of the first to arrive; everyone else got lost, too.

I sat at a table with four other newbies. I felt a bit over-dressed, but better over than under, I say. It's all right when you're a teenager, but as you get older, you need to take more care.

It was awkward and exciting, complete strangers sharing a meal. My good-looking helper (his name turned out to be Tony) sat elsewhere, but the guys at my table were cute, too. They gave us a list of "conversation starters," which we were supposed to go through in order to get to know each other. So lame! I could just imagine Matty going, "Fuck that shit."

That night we had lasagne. It was pretty good. Meaty and saucy and heaps of cheese.

•

Day 2.

They told me to go to Room 821. I had no idea. Lost again, but someone showed up and rescued me. No way was I ever going to figure it out.

They sat me down in front of a wall of equipment. What the hell? I had no idea. I just sat there for an hour, hoping I didn't have to figure it out in order to stay. They did tell me that they just wanted to see what could be achieved in sixty-eight days. Didn't matter what I did, just that I did it.

Then, someone came and got me, and we all went to have dinner in the bar. It was meatloaf tonight, best I've ever had. I sat with a different group, and already, it felt as if I knew them. All of us were in the same boat: a diagnosis we didn't want to think much about. Most of us were on our own.

○

Day 3.

By the third day, without anyone telling me a thing, I'm working those knobs and buttons as if I was a rocket scientist. Wish people at home could see. My teachers. My mother. Matty. They'd be seeing a different me.

We had movie night; an old classic called *Braveheart.*

I don't know what the others are dying of, but we all are. All expenses are paid, even the medical stuff. They're giving me no-questions-asked painkillers, and my head and eyes feel better already.

○

Day 5.

I'm treading paths I've never trod before. It's a compulsion; a weird familiarity with something I know I don't know.

And I realise I'm treading paths I've never been taught.

We booze up every night. Beer, champagne, cocktails. Wine and beer. I don't know if it's that, but already, the conversation starters are weird; we all know each other's answers.

○

Day 10.

Every night, we go out and look up at the stars.

"If I was living on Mars, I'd have 687 days left. Not 365." We all said that, doing the maths.

We had spaghetti and meatballs for dinner. I had two servings; no one cared.

○

Day 15.

There are so many good looking guys here. Tanned and carefree. Most gorgeous of all is Tony.

Tony and me, we click together. Just a perfect fit. His skin is so warm. I don't know what he's got, and he doesn't know what I've got, and neither of us knows how long.

○

Day 20.

Tony took a bunch of us for a hike out to this huge meteorite that is meant to be from Mars. We placed our hands on it. He said, "One of the things that draws us together and to Mars is the ability to go against the rules. She spins back on her own orbit, does a twist."

He twisted as if he was on the dance floor. "That's us. Rule breakers. Well, not sensible rules, like we have."

We all laughed at this.

"But the ones in place for no reason."

We loved every word.

"The only way forward is to choose to go forward to your next existence. This is for humanity. For the future." The big rock glowed warm and felt magnetic.

We asked him how it got there.

"Legend says, Ancient Ones on Mars threw rocks like this at Earth, trying to get our attention. It's finally working!"

○

Day 25.

Movie night was *It's a Wonderful Life.*

○

Day 29.

We trekked out to the rock again. It buzzed, slowly warming up, and we all put a palm on it. We've never felt so connected in all our lives. Around it, mounds of small rocks. Some of them painted. An art project, maybe?

One of the guys said they were ancient burial mounds.

○

Day 30.

Part of what they're figuring out is how to beat depression on the Mars project. It's the isolation; you know Earth is far away. And you know you only have a small number of days left. You'll die out there.

That's what we're helping them with.

How do you stay motivated to achieve: not for yourself but those who come after?

We've never felt better.

○

Day 32.

We all wake up around the same time now in the early hours of the morning, and all end up out around the empty pool. Looking up. Someone brought out armchairs that people weren't using, and we'd laze about, watching the sky and talking while the sun rose.

Sometimes, we'll go into the planetarium, but the place needs fixing. It smells bad.

Every step is familiar.

We talk about the ancient ones who might be waiting on Mars. "Imagine!" we say. "They'll wake up, and there we'll be!"

○

Day 38.

No post went out, and none came in. Where would we send things to? We signed to say we wouldn't tell anyone we were going. Mostly, no one cared. Mostly, we didn't get reported missing. I would have been more than surprised if I was reported. My brain would have exploded. But it didn't happen.

We were better than anyone else because we were the ones with absolute freedom. We were the ones who could do whatever we wanted.

Ironic, given how close we were all becoming. Like a merged brain with merged feelings. It was nice.

Movie night was a cartoon called *The Iron Giant*.

○

Day 42.

There's something comforting about being in a commune full of people who are dying. All of us strangers, so there's no past to contend with, no long-term emotions.

All we have are the sixty-eight days.

And we're all fucking each other. You couldn't do that outside. No one will fuck a dying person. But seriously, if you had weeks to live? Why not feel pleasure while you still can? No one cares about my rash. It's better mostly, anyway.

We're lost in a fog of sex and booze.

Lost in a fog of déjà vu. It's not just that we have a routine: work/eat/play/sleep. More than that. A deep sense that this has happened before.

○

Day 50.

Counting down the days. I don't want to leave, but no one stays beyond the sixty-eight.

"Stay any longer, and you'll start to suffocate." That's what they reckon.

○

Day 52.

People like me here. We feel at home. At one with each other. We all love the food. It's hearty. Always meaty.

"Lucky there are no vegetarians here," someone joked, and we all laughed although it felt like we'd heard it a dozen times already.

○

Day 60.

Just over a week until we're gone and the next group comes in.

"Look what we've achieved," they're telling us, and I can't quite believe it myself. We built a dome that works like a greenhouse. We learned how to cook and operate machinery. We fixed the planetarium. We grew to love each other. "You are such a cohesive group," they say. "So positive."

The sun burns hot here. It's like it's a different sun from the one anywhere else. Here, it's free, unbridled, like we are.

We'd sit naked, but our poor boobs would burn, and the skin would peel, and no one wants that.

The idea makes us laugh, and once we start, we can't stop until we're so weak with it we're in the sand. Someone carries us inside.

"It's a side effect we're working on," Tony said. They were figuring out ways to stop the Sads on Mars because the Sads don't make things happen.

But it made us laugh too much at too little. It felt good. Like Tony does. Not like Matty did. Nothing like Matty.

○

Day 67.

Serious fucking partying going on. Swapping of fluids. Swapping of contact details. None of us wanting to go back, but sixty-eight days is what they're testing, so sixty-eight days is what it is.

We were all together. Ten of us. Sometimes felt as if we were one. Other times there was just me and Tony.

I liked it when he took me out onto the roof or way, way away from the resort. He was quiet out there, and we could just hang. He showed me Mars through the telescope, and I swore I could see movement up there.

"It's incredible to think people will be there in a generation. And that we're helping them get there."

○

Day 68.

We wake up on the last day. Tony brought me breakfast, the tiny spicy sausages we have every few days. They are so good. And hothouse tomatoes and mushrooms with butter and parsley. And champagne. I still felt drunk from the night before.

He sat on the end of the bed, watching me. It felt weird. Like my mum used to do. It's one of the things I miss most about Mum. When I was in my early teens, before things went to shit, she'd come into my room in the morning and sit on the end of my bed, and we'd chat. I was still a bit sleepy so not as defensive as I'd be later. I remember those talks so well. In those sleepy times, we both thought it would be all right.

o

He made me get up, and we walked to the meteorite. I loved it there in the early morning when it was so warm. So familiar.

"Do you really want to go back to the city?" he said.

I felt a surge in my heart; was he saying I could stay? "No! I want to stay here!"

He shook his head. "That can't happen. But to be honest, they're nervous about sending you back."

"Just me or everyone?"

"Mostly you. It's a couple of things." He made me drink a glass of champagne. "It's your LE, for one." (He was the same as the doctor, thinking that calling it *LE* will make it easier to take.) "You're looking at weeks once you go back home, they think."

"But I feel fine."

"That's the beauty and the curse of it. You'll feel like that until suddenly this happens."

He showed me the worst photos I've ever seen of people in dying stages of my disease. Pus and blood from every orifice. It was horrendous.

"You're so beautiful the way you are. It would break my heart to see you like this." He made me look at the photos, every single one of them. "Have you got anyone to look after you?" He knew I didn't. "You can make it worthwhile. Don't waste all you know. All you have up here." He tapped my temple gently and stroked his cool hand on my forehead. "You know what you've been eating."

I had known. I just didn't want to think about it. I didn't want to be sent home for complaining about it. And everyone did it. No one seemed concerned. You wouldn't tell anyone outside, but it tasted fine. Human meat tasted fine.

"The knowledge you have came from the one before you. She got hers from the one before her. On and on, and the knowledge improves each time. It's brilliant; each person doesn't have to retrain. We don't have to waste time. Complex tasks managed in a day or two. Relationships remembered. Finding your way without being lost. Every day, every hour, is critical." He's still stroking me. Under my clothes, now.

"It's totally groundbreaking and will be part of the future of us. It will literally help the survival of the human race."

It made perfect sense.

"You'll join others who went before you. You'll be a proud member of an elite team. You'll be remembered. This moment is perfect. You are perfect. It is all downhill from here."

I said, "What about the others? Are they doing this, too?"

"What do you think? See if you can feel the hive mind."

I closed my eyes. "I think yes."

He left me there. It was warm, perfect, and I had champagne and the smell of strawberries.

He gave me a pill. One. It would be enough.

I took the pill and laughed and laughed and laughed to think of what would happen next.

Bram Stoker Award nominee, twice-World Fantasy Award nominee and Shirley Jackson Award winner, **Kaaron Warren** *has lived in Melbourne, Sydney, Canberra and Fiji. She's sold more than two hundred short stories, three novels (the multi-award-winning* Slights, Walking the Tree, *and* Mistification*) and six short story collections including the multi-award-winning* Through Splintered Walls. *Her latest short story collection is* Cemetery Dance Select: Kaaron Warren. *You can find her at kaaronwarren.wordpress.com, and she tweets @KaaronWarren.*

Tekeli-li, They Cry

AC Wise

They tell me the future is broken. Will be broken. Has always been broken. I was wide awake the first time they spoke to me and have been every time since. They come from *there*, then, when the future is broken. Which is now because the break stretches in every direction. That's what they tell me.

We're time travelers, meeting in some middle distance where they can scream at me, speak in soft, reasonable tones, jibber, weep, and tell me what is to come and is already here.

They're bright, like staring directly into a 100-W bulb. One that's already broken—jagged but still burning. There are shapes behind them, smearing and blurring and refusing to stay still. It hurts to look at them, so mostly, I just listen.

The voices overlap. Like listening to five radio stations at once. Whether they weep or plead or speak calmly (those are the worst), the one thing they agree on is south. Go all the way south to the pole. Stop the future from being broken.

Why do I believe them? Because of my beautiful baby girl. I've seen her out there on the ice. Even before I came to this blue place full of wind and sleepless sun, I saw her. A skip in time. A scratch on the record of my life. A time, repeating. My past, leaking into my present. Her future, reaching back for her with empty hands.

I know time is broken because I saw my little girl, even though she's been dead for three years, seven months, and twenty-one days.

Our eighth day on the ice, James and Risi brought Austin back into the station screaming. He shouldn't have been out there alone. That's the first thing you learn here—the ice is treacherous. It's worse with climate change. Everything is more extreme: the colds colder, the warm periods rotting the ice soft under your feet.

Everything here wants to kill you. Not like a jungle or a swamp with poisonous insects and crushing heat. The cold kills with kindness—or humiliation. It lulls you to sleep. It makes you think you're burning up, so you strip your clothes off. History is full of people who have frozen to death naked in snowstorms.

The wind blows shimmering snow, blinding and tricking the eye. The sun—ever-awake six months and absent the other six—throws shadows all stark on the ground, so we see things that aren't there and miss things that are. If I didn't *know* the world was broken, that there are worse things coming (already here), I would think what happened to Austin was just the landscape fucking with us.

Us. I should say, that's Austin, Ricky, Sheila, Cordon, Risi, James, and me. (And my daughter's ghost.) You wouldn't think I would lose count with only seven, but I do. There should be nearly two hundred bodies filling the station. It's peak season. But since the moratorium on climate research in 2021, no one cares about the South Pole. They can't afford to. Still, this is where the voices say the future will break. So here we are, funding our own research, stubborn or stupid or frightened enough to run away to the end of the world.

Austin was gathering samples from the ice for me to study. Bacteria. Fungus. Algae. Some of the few things that can survive here. I'm looking for something microscopic in the ice, something people would never notice, being too busy looking at the horizon or the sky for the big, terrible thing, then *bam*. World's end.

When they brought Austin in, he was screaming that something in the ice bit him.

The station has a trauma center. Luckily, it's in the part that didn't burn. Sheila is a surgeon. Was. Like all of us, she came to the end of the world with a bag full of demons. One of them was enough to get her barred from practice apparently.

She saved Austin, even though there wasn't much for her to do other than treat him for shock. He wasn't even bleeding. His wound didn't look like a bite; the lower half of his arm had been sheared clean off.

●

The whirring of the 3D printer woke me up even though it had already been going for hours. It's a waste. All this expensive tech tucked away at the bottom of the world. One government funded a whole bunch of upgrades, top of the line stuff. The next one swooped in and took all the money away, made climate research damn near illegal. Now, all the fancy machines and equipment are rotting away, and private eyes and dollars are on space. Well, it's not a complete waste, I guess. Austin gets a new arm.

(If the government hadn't cut funding, maybe they would have found the poison in the water sooner. I shouldn't complain. Neelie was born with all her limbs in the right place, and no extra ones. Other parents weren't so lucky. My baby girl only had a slight delay in cognitive development. A lag. Sometimes she was miles away, her eyes on some past or future only she could see. But maybe that had nothing to do with the poison in the ground. Just like the nights she woke screaming. All kids have bad dreams, after all.)

Still, I'm surprised the government didn't drag the tech out when they pulled the plug. They could have printed light armor, weapons, and bombs undetectable by scans. Some of the scientists tried to burn the station on their way out in protest. After that, the government could barely be bothered to get the people out. If they wouldn't have had human rights groups from creditor nations barking up their asses, they probably would have left the scientists to rot too.

Anyway, Austin is in remarkably good spirits for someone missing half his arm. He's sticking to his story. Something in the ice bit him. I think time broke, just where he happened to be. Half his arm ended up in some other *when*. It's right where he left it, just a few seconds or years into the future or the past, so we can't see it anymore.

One of the voices (one of the weeping ones) said a city rose, is rising, everywhere and everywhen. There are holes; things can slide through. Sometimes by accident, like arms. People can slide through, but it isn't easy, so most stay put and shout across the distance.

(Oh, I should have said. Time *is* broken. It doesn't matter what we find in the ice. Nothing we do here matters. I lied to Austin, Sheila, Cordon, James, Ricky, and Risi. The voices (some of them at least) really do think there's something we can do to change things, but we can't. I recognize the stages of grief. I'm surprised the other seven (eight?) don't. The voices are bargaining right now. They're pleading with anyone who will listen. Just please take it back. Make it the way it was. Make it okay again. Bargaining never works. That's why it isn't the last stage. One thing it's made me understand that I didn't three years, seven months, and twenty-nine days ago—it's not that no one is listening. It's just that sometimes, there's nothing they can do.)

After I woke up, I went to sit by the printer. It's hypnotizing, all that passing back and forth, building new bones. Out of nowhere, James burst in and said we should be printing weapons, not arms (ha ha). He said there's a fight coming. He said he's seen things under the ice, sleeping. He wouldn't explain. I saw him standing by the window later, staring out at the ice, at the spot where I saw Neelie last time. I wanted to hit him. She's my ghost. Mine. He can damn well find his own.

It's been a couple weeks since Austin's 'accident' and now Ricky thinks he's seen James's monsters, too. Shadows under the ice. Vast, slow things. Turning, he said. I don't know what that means.

Sheila is working with Austin on rehab, even though it isn't her specialty. It'll be a while before he has any kind of dexterity. No one seems to care that Austin is basically useless for field work, except James. Every time James sees Austin, he starts in about weapons again.

Ricky's thing is CERN. He says whatever's going on is probably their fault. He's a good kid. He's supposedly here to keep Risi's notes in order, label things, make spreadsheets and pretty graphs. I think he would be smart under normal circumstances, but Risi only brought him along because she wants something to fuck.

The birds aren't birds. That's another thing Ricky says.

He's been drawing them since he got here. Really detailed, textbook quality. He wanted to be an artist, but he couldn't hack it. So he let Risi pay his way to the bottom of the world.

He's jittery, more so by the day. I don't think he's sleeping. I don't know that any of us are, not real sleep at least. Risi shows it the least.

James going on about weapons got Ricky worked up about CERN again.

"It's when they fired up the Large Hadron Collider," he said. "They fucked everything up. Ripped a hole in space."

Risi looked like she wanted to slap him. Actually, she looked like she wanted to tear him apart with her teeth, right down to marrow and bone. Maybe that's her kink—violence gets her off better than sex. "That's not how it works," she said. "This has nothing to do with science, or if it's science, it's not any kind of science we understand."

She wouldn't explain what she meant; she stalked off and slammed the door. It's the closest I've seen to anything like a crack in her armor. Maybe Risi is human after all.

○

It's day sixteen, or twelve, or thirty-seven, or two. Cordon and Risi are drinking to cope. I wish I could join them.

I smashed a mirror yesterday. Well, crushed it, really. It was a little pocket mirror I found behind the bookshelf in my room. They're like dorm rooms, except cleaner. Someone before me cared about their appearance, apparently. I broke it in half, squeezed it until it cracked. Seven years bad luck.

(Maybe I should say why I'm really here, now that you know I know we can't stop the end of the world. I came looking for Neelie. Even though I saw her before I saw her out on the ice, I think she wanted me to follow her here. Her ghost is brighter in the snow.)

I think Ricky might be on to something with the birds. I wanted to put that down before I forget.

I could say something melodramatic, like I was looking at my reflection, and I couldn't stand the monster staring back at me. But I wasn't even looking at the reflective part, just turning the mirror over in my hand like a stone.

(It wasn't until I picked up the broken pieces that I saw Neelie's eye staring back at me, her mouth open to speak. I got scared. I'll admit that. I got scared. I came here to find her; she's my little girl, but she still terrifies me.)

I had all this nervous energy, and I had to let it out somehow. I used to do that with drink. My brain would spin and spin, there was no other way to shut it down. After the accident, I quit, cold turkey. I've been sober for three years, eight months, and thirteen days. A *recovering* alcoholic, mind you; there's no such thing as cured.

●

I saw Neelie inside the station yesterday. Every other time, she's been out on the ice. Ricky was drawing, and she was looking over his shoulder. It reminded me of the way she used to watch me cook, not asking questions but intently studying everything I did and recording behind her eyes, chewing on the ends of her hair the whole while. I didn't hit Ricky. I wanted to.

(I've waited so long for her to come inside, and when she did, I ran away. Her eyes recorded everything; what if she doesn't forgive me for the last moments of her life? My little girl turned and stretched out her hand, and I ran away.)

●

Could I have stopped the car? I wasn't drunk, only buzzed.

It was late, foggy; Neelie shouldn't have been out of bed. The babysitter should have been watching her . . .

No. I can't shift the blame. Neelie liked to run out to meet my car. It didn't matter whether I'd been gone an hour or a whole day. I knew that. *I* should have been paying more attention.

(I was.)

(Neelie . . . I could never get over her eyes. Deep down, in the truest and darkest part of myself, love wasn't enough. I couldn't get over her eyes. I was one of the lucky ones. All her limbs were in the right place, but her eyes . . . she was out of phase with my reality. Can poison in the ground do that? Sometimes, she looked just like a normal little girl, like the other children on our block after we moved. And sometimes, her eyes were flat black. Polished stone. Static-shot. She would look at me like she was tuning in something very far away or sending everything I was doing elsewhere. Did she know? Was she always judging me for what happened in the last moments of her life, or was it that I thought she was judging me that caused my decision?)

The car. There was a heartbeat's worth of space. Two. I took a breath, let it all the way out with her frail body pinned in the headlights. The fog made tendrils, swirling around her. She looked right at me with those eyes. Recording. She didn't look human. I wasn't drunk. I was scared, scared of my little girl.

I took a breath and let it all the way out, and my foot didn't move from the gas to the brake. Neelie bled out a few feet from our door. I didn't cry. I just cradled my baby's head in my lap and stroked her hair.

The voices gibber and whisper and weep. Last time they came, I looked at the light behind them for as long as I could. The spaces behind them, between their silhouetted bodies and the jagged edges marking my world. Things slid and dragged—amorphous shapes. Too many eyes, too many limbs. Some of them used to be human, I'm sure.

I lied to Austin and Sheila and all the rest. I came here because if the voices can come through, other things can as well. A ghost. A little girl already out of time. I'm not here to save the world, just to take responsibility for what I did, will do, have always done.

❂

The smell made me look through Ricky's door. He spends twenty out of twenty-four hours in his 'lab', birds pinned down, so he can draw the mechanics of their wings. Like we don't know how birds work by now. (Except the birds aren't birds.) It's okay; drawing keeps Ricky out of the way. It keeps him from going off screaming onto the ice like Austin did.

Did I mention Austin disappeared? We found the arm Cordon printed for him and nothing else. He went out into the snow and vanished. Or maybe he's still here in another *when*, reunited with his original arm.

I thought maybe Neelie would be looking over his shoulder again. She wasn't, and Ricky wasn't at his drafting table either. He was crying, wiping at his face and smearing blood all over. Did I say about the blood already?

Ricky was covered in it. His hands, his clothes, all the places he'd tried to wipe the tears away. Only some of it was red. The rest . . . there isn't a word for the color. Green, but purple. Iridescent: beetle shell, crow feather. The color itself made the stench, clogging up my mouth and nose.

"I needed to see inside," Ricky said. "The birds aren't birds. I told you so."

He held a scalpel, probably nicked from Sheila. He'd made a real mess of the bird pinned to the table, a storm petrel, I think, but not like someone inexperienced at dissection. More like he got scared and tried to stab what he saw out of existence.

It buzzes. The picture of the bird in my mind buzzes, like flies going all at once. It drips, melting wax too close to the sun. Icarus is falling and drowning and drowned, and the world is ended, always ending, has been ended since the beginning of time.

Okay, I just read back, and I'm letting that sentence stand. Some things are just true. It isn't my fault if anyone reading this doesn't understand.

I don't know much about the biology of birds, but I know what they're *not* supposed to look like inside. Nothing living should look like that inside.

Picture a city with angles folding inward and protruding outward at the same time. A city made of bone and flesh, intestines and organs, sinew and blood. Picture something like a starfish. Picture all of that and throw the picture away. Remember the worst migraine you ever had. The inside of the bird on Ricky's drawing table was like that but more so.

I pulled Ricky out of there and hid him in my room. I had to get him away before Risi saw what he'd done because then she would kill him for sure.

●

Ricky cut his throat. Probably with the same blade he used on the bird. He bled out in one of the showers, slumped against the wall. Or maybe Risi killed him, a murder-suicide. No one has seen her for two days.

I found Ricky's notes after we burned his body. We dragged him to the ghost part of the station and set him on fire. Nervous energy. We needed something to do. He was probably too young to have a will. Kid like that thinks he's going to live forever. Hopefully, he wanted to be cremated.

After we burned him, I went through his stuff. Clothing. Razor blades. Deodorant. Cologne. A dildo, tucked down in the bottom of his bag under the socks and underwear. He'd never unpacked. He'd left everything in a duffle bag, like he'd be going home any day. A family portrait: mother, father, daughter, golden retriever, cute as hell. No one in the picture looked anything like him. His drawing supplies.

I found his notes wedged between the mattress and the bed frame. Crumpled, like he wanted to destroy them but couldn't quite bring himself to do it. There was a notebook filled with gibberish; each entry was neatly labeled with the date and location. The sketches were perfect. Gorgeously rendered in accurate scientific detail. Until they started to bend. Until you could tell from the outside that what I saw when Ricky cut open the bird was lurking just beneath the feathers and skin.

●

I keep a picture of Neelie in my room. Yesterday, Neelie was gone. The picture was still there, showing our yard and the swing I built for her hanging from the old maple tree. The arrested motion of the swing made it look like she'd jumped out of the frame. She used to pump her legs as hard as she could and jump when the swing was at its highest point. It put my heart in my throat when she did that. There were days when I expected (wanted) her to fly, keep going up forever.

I turned the picture over, like I might see her on the other side, giggling. Hide-and-Seek post-mortem.

It's proof. Time is broken. It's always been broken. A vast, cyclopean city rose everywhere and everywhen. Neelie isn't in the picture, but she's out there waiting for me. I'm coming, baby girl.

●

I woke up outside. Sleepwalking, I guess, though no one really sleeps anymore. I'd thought to put a coat on but not to button it up. Boots, but I was still wearing a nightgown.

(Neelie was wearing a nightgown when she died. Maybe, I wasn't sleepwalking. Maybe, I went looking for her.)

Neelie was patting my cheeks when I woke up. She was crying. "Don't go to sleep, Mommy." My dead daughter saved my life. After I could have hit the brakes but didn't.

"I'm sorry, baby. I'm so sorry," I said and threw my arms around her. Not a ghost. Solid and real.

She looked at me. Her eyes just the way I remember them: flat, black, seeing everything. I almost took it back. I almost pushed her away and ran across the ice, begging it to take me, like it took Austin. Can I live with my dead little girl looking at me like that, knowing? Yes. I have to live with it—the choice not to hit the brakes, and the choice to find Neelie again. There are no third chances.

Funny (not ha ha), but it wasn't cold. The ice groaned. An old sound. A deep sound. "Don't be afraid, baby girl," I said. The birds circled between us and the sun, throwing harsh shadows on the snow. Piping while the ice groaned. Almost a song.

The voices were there, too. Begging, screaming. *Why did you stop,* they asked. *Why didn't you do more to fix the future that has always been broken?* I didn't answer; they already know. Acceptance is a stage of grief, too.

"Look, Mommy," Neelie said. She pointed to the thing in the ice that James had talked about.

Did I say what happened to James? I don't know. I don't know if I said, and I don't know what happened. We're the only ones left here, me and my little girl. And the voices. And the thing in the ice. Not *things*, despite the multitude and the vastness of it. One thing, stretching all the way out under ice that's clear and blue and shining. It turned while the birds sang. Waking up.

Haruspex. I always liked that word. I read to Neelie about ancient Rome. She liked stories about soldiers. I didn't tell her about the bloody prophets who dug their nails in the entrails of birds to spell out victory and doom.

Ricky was right about the birds, even though he wasn't scrying the future when he cut one open. Somewhere, a city is rising, has risen, will always and forever be coming up from the waves. The future, as a concept, is obsolete.

I stood with my daughter, and we watched a vast thing turn in the ice. We listened to the birds whose bodies are cities and angles and impossible, multi-limbed things. This is the new shape of the world. This is the shape it's always been. We listened to the birds-who-aren't-birds weep in their weird, piping way. This is where it begins, where it began.

Ricky was right about the birds. They're an omen but not in the way of a warning. Voices crying in the wilderness, heralding what has already come.

{}

AC Wise's *fiction has appeared in publications such as* Clarkesworld, Shimmer, Apex, *and* The Year's Best Dark Fantasy and Horror 2015. *Her debut collection,* The Ultra Fabulous Glitter Squadron Saves the World Again, *was published be Lethe Press in 2015. In addition to her fiction, she co-edits* Unlikely Story *and contributes a monthly* Women to Read *column to SF Signal. Find her online at www.acwise.net.*

The Sky Isn't Blue

Clinton J. Boomer

The detective was good.

Competent.

He looked around, eyes drawing with slow and individual care over each object in the room. He stood relaxed, noticing the tiny things—*scrutinizing* them, she decided—in stoic, unperturbed silence.

This big black man was at ease, his breathing steady and his core loose but firm. His confident gaze loped around her office, playing over every surface for a few moments and sliding away to examine another new discovery with fresh eyes: laptop, hand sanitizer, facial tissues, Thai menu, prescription pad, coffee mug, planner, notebook, dry flowers in a glass vase.

All of these were seen, noted, categorized.

He was tuned in, receptive, *seeing* without judgment, picking up on all of those little things that homicide investigators presumably look for.

Dr. Ashland liked him.

He was *sensitive*, she thought, in a way that most men who were "sensitive" could never be. A man with a goal, driven by a mission, psychologically fulfilled by his own desire to complete the task before him for whatever primal, personal reasons, no matter the cost.

A shame that he would fail, she thought. Some things simply weren't meant to be.

Long, thin fingers of bright, late-afternoon sunlight streamed in slanting angles through her half-open windows, catching motes of golden dust. A cool October wind stirred the grey and empty branches outside.

It would be dark early tonight.

From two stories below, the sound of children laughing and shouting and playing rough on wet sheets of fire-colored leaves. A dripping train of school buses groaned through the tree-lined suburbs, some slowly pulling even with the frosted-glass doors of the little 1970s magnet school across the shadow-draped cobblestones.

On her desk, the plastic water heater flashed green twice as the crimson contents within began to boil with a low hiss; the tea would be ready in a moment.

The detective nodded finally and put his large, calloused hands into the pockets of his fresh-pressed slacks. He closed weary, dimly bloodshot eyes. Collecting his thoughts?

Perhaps he counted back from ten.

As he moved, the weighty and well-worn badge at his hip caught the light, glimmering, before slipping back behind the fold of his black sportcoat.

She cleared her throat, projecting false nervousness. "Any questions?"

"Yeah," he said, after a moment, half-turning to face her. "This."

Dr. Ashland met the fathomless darkness of his eyes. "Yes?"

The man nodded, frowning. "What's this picture of? Some kind of . . . tentacled crab-thing?"

She followed his gaze to one of the dozen steel-framed photographs dotting her beige walls. The image was slightly larger than the others, centered and well-lit, dominating the visual field. She examined it carefully and pretended to laugh. "Ah? Yes, I suppose it is in a way. A tentacled crab."

He frowned. "No?"

"Well," the doctor said, drawing it out, "several of my patients have said that it reminded them of a deep-sea creature. So I suppose it is."

"It's not, then."

Dr. Ashland smiled. "No, it's just ice and water. The sunset behind makes it appear quite a bit more substantial than it really is."

"More . . . substantial," the detective repeated, matching her tone.

She shrugged. "The dark lavenders and reds you perceive aren't really there. They exist only as an artifact of light dispersion. You're seeing uncountable layers of nearly translucent material, each with tiny imperfections, shading and illuminating one another, lit from behind. Much the way the sky looks blue on a cloudless day."

"Because the sky *isn't* blue," said the detective after a moment.

"Not really," said the doctor. "It's empty air. No more blue than the air in this room."

He grunted. His gaze remained fixed on the photograph as he swallowed. The veiny, reddish specter seemed to swim, undulating on invisible currents, moving just a touch too slowly for the eye to perceive.

"As to the image itself," continued Dr. Ashland, "it's what the mind makes of it, like so many things. My patients have told me that it looks like a hand or a face or even a head. Sometimes a body, crouched in the fetal position, with either wings or flames coming out of its back. Some have said that it reminded them of a tree or a crooked set of bloody towers or even a burning doll."

"Huh," he said, distracted and fascinated, reaching out to almost touch the image. "It kind of looks like these are . . . you know, legs. Sticking up. Or . . ."

Dr. Ashlan, smiled, finishing the thought for him. "Or other, more personal body parts, yes. Privates, perhaps. I deal with children who are sexual-abuse survivors. I've heard it all."

He glanced at her, his focus on the photograph instantly broken with a raw defensiveness. She saw that he was an abuse survivor.

Good.

"It's just ice," she said, smiling.

A coach? A counselor? An uncle? Who had touched him, she wondered, and how would his trauma manifest in this, his final hour?

"Just ice," he said, turning back and approaching to examine the photograph from close up, his breath ever-so-briefly steaming the smooth glass. "Are all of these pictures of that, Dr. Ashland? Of . . . what, ice and sunsets?"

"You've cracked the code of my decorating schema," she said with a smile. "It's meant to be soothing, neutral. But pretty. Tea?"

"No thanks. So who sculpted these?"

She pretended to be confused. "Who?"

He stepped back from the photo and looked around, trying to take in all the images at once. "The sculptor. Of the ice."

"No one. These photographs are all 'found art': just floes of frozen or melting water in a state of nature, observed and caught at one precise moment in time.

Taken by any number of photographers, some of them amateur . . . and some of them both very professional and very expensive. Take that one, for instance."

He nodded, not bothering to look where she pointed. "It's a . . . cute collection. Very unique."

She smiled. "The water and ice—and the light that gives them color—have a certain tranquil quality, I think. Mesmerizing, in their way, and for that reason, useful in my line of work. It doesn't hurt that I personally rather enjoy these sorts of images as I'm sure you can tell."

"I can. Tell me more about ice," he said. His gaze raked up and down her skin, and she felt herself tensing but fought it.

"Of course, detective," she said, pouring herself a cup of the steaming, bitter tea; the ruby-red liquid was dotted with countless caramel-colored fungal spores. She leaned against her desk and calmly picked up the tiny, thumb-sized remote for her stereo. "What would you like to know?"

The big man smiled. "I'm here to talk about a patient of yours."

He was trying to catch her off guard, shifting topics so quickly and so casually.

She admired it. Excellent execution.

"I suspected as much. You know, of course, there are limitations as to what I can discuss with you: strict limitations for reasons of professional, legal, and ethical oversight, not to mention issues of insurance, both private and corporate, as well as tax-code liability. Rules both beyond my control and entirely out of my hands even if I wanted very much to help. Even if you had a warrant from a federal judge, which I suspect—no offense—that you do not."

"I am more than aware," sighed the detective, "of the legal pitfalls and roadblocks here."

Dr. Ashland feigned a child-like innocence. "Are you?"

He held up a meaty hand for silence. "I've been down this endless rabbit hole before, and I know that you deal with particularly . . . troubled patients here. Troubled youth, especially, and their families. I know all about HIPAA and court-sealed documents, corporate-sponsored drug research NDAs and non-profit religious-entity charters, including a few that your clinic services. I know that there's a lot I can't know, can't be told. So I'd like to talk about anything you *can* tell me, about anything you want to talk about. And you seem like you have a lot to say about ice."

He paused, watching her nod.

"I see," Dr. Ashland said, frowning. "Just a friendly talk, then."

"A chat," he agreed warmly. "And who knows? Maybe, you'll slip up and tell me something I can use."

She laughed and returned his smile as best she was able. It was meant to be a joke, or if she had something to hide, it was meant to be a veiled threat.

Yes, the detective was good.

Dr. Ashland liked him.

"So," she began, hesitant.

"So," he said, turning to look at the rest of the photographs, pretending to relax. "Tell me more about ice."

Dr. Ashland took a sip of tea, wincing at the bitter, earthy, almost meaty flavor; the steam reeked of vinegar and something charred. "Ice is interesting to me because humans—*we* humans—invest so much . . . emotion into it. *Energy*, if you will, in the mystic sense. Some ancient peoples from Nepal literally called it 'locked-away life force.' We need it; we curse it. We cart it and sculpt it; we clear it from our streets even while we manufacture it in bulk. Above all, we attribute personality and motive and meaning to it."

"Interesting," he mused.

"Not particularly," Dr. Ashland said, shrugging. "As a species, we may have a hard and complicated relationship with ice, certainly, but unlike . . . what? People attribute motive and meaning to the weather, to the stock market. To baseball scores, cat behavior, and volcanic eruptions. To stars in the heavens and trees up the hillside. Ice, as a metaphor or phenomena, is interesting only insofar as it's tangible, unlike a cloud or a passing comet. Tangible but temporary."

"Temporary?"

"Tangible but temporary," Dr. Ashland said, nodding. "That's the interesting part. A human being and a block of ice cannot survive in the same environment. Not for long, anyway. The ice will melt or the human will freeze; we comprehend this inevitability from the moment we step outdoors in biting midwinter or pull a tray of cubes from the freezer. Ice is fundamentally alien to us, best seen from afar or across a semi-porous border. Inimical. Neutral but lethal. One or the other, frost or flesh, is not long for the world, ruined in increments by basic interaction with reality itself . . . but of course, that's always the case, isn't it?"

The detective nodded, the corners of his broad mouth dropping slightly as he feigned deep introspective insight. "Yeah. Interesting."

"Yes," said the doctor, stopping herself short. "Is there, perhaps, another topic

I could discuss with you, detective? I'm passionate about any number of things, and ice—although it is quite interesting—isn't really my formal area of expertise. I just think it's pretty."

"Hmm," said the detective, nodding. "Yes. Your area of expertise, that's . . . what? Anxiety disorders? Alternative therapies?"

"Correct," said Dr. Ashland, putting on her brightest smile before taking another sip of bitter red tea. "Psychopharmacology, sleep disorders, and cognitive behavioral therapy, with a focus on natural remedies for extreme anxiety conditions. Do you mind if I play some music?"

The detective shrugged noncommittally. With the push of a button, the butterscotch shadows of Dr. Ashland's office filled with the sounds of rapturous choral chanting, deep drums, and low piping.

Glancing around, spotting the hidden speakers tucked above the bookshelves, the detective sniffed. "This is also meant to be soothing? Pretty?"

"A bit," said Dr. Ashland, hesitantly. "Uplifting, perhaps, is a better term; therapeutic in some instances. It's a form of religious festival music recorded live in rural southeastern Myanmar. The people there know a fair bit about overcoming anxiety. And adversity."

"Hmm," muttered the detective. "About that. Can you give me an example of the sort of anxiety we're talking about? I want to get an idea of what it is you *do*, in a general sense."

"Of course," she said. "Anxiety takes any number of forms and, in its severest manifestations, can be as violent or debilitating as any other mental or emotional instability. It's the root cause, in my professional opinion, of most major atypical, therapy-resistant depression and addiction cases. Reactive attachment disorder, bulimia nervosa, or kleptomania with attendant substance abuse might be good examples of the sort of thing I help patients and their families cope with: stress disorders with no standard or reliable treatment options."

"So," he asked, "what are we talking about? You treat . . . stress? Negative reactions to stress?"

"In a manner of speaking, certainly. PTSD is a classic anxiety disorder, for example, and responds well to more unconventional therapies. Art, music, writing, even some interpretive dance."

The detective smiled, crossing his arms. "How so?"

"I had a patient," said Dr. Ashland, considering, "about whom I can divulge . . . some details of the case: she wasn't a minor, and she had committed no crimes. She had severe misophonia, seemingly exacerbated by post-partum depression."

"Come again?"

"Misophonia. It's poorly understood. A rare neuropsychiatric disorder in which strong negative emotions are triggered by specific sounds. It's been linked, theoretically, to everything from anxiety—which is why I was referred— to obsessive-compulsive personality disorder to synaesthesia to a malfunction of the limbic system. In short, hearing certain sounds fills the suffering patient with rage, directly triggering the flight-or-flight response complete with acute muscle spasms, sweating, nausea, pupil dilatation, and involuntary intestinal constriction in some cases."

The detective grimaced. He wasn't noticing the music as it increased in volume even as it slowed in tempo. The voices weren't human; the words couldn't be shaped by human anatomy.

"The sick part," the doctor continued, "is that someone suffering from misophonia literally can't help but listen for those sounds: the triggering stimuli cuts through any background noise like . . . well, like nails on a chalkboard. And the specific sounds that traditionally trigger full-on panic attacks for a true sufferer? Everyday and constant things: chewing, drinking, breathing, sniffling. Even the sound of clothes moving over skin or the faintest noise of foot-tapping."

"Sounds bad," he said, raising one eyebrow.

"If you've ever lived with someone who snores, you know how annoying a single repetitive sound can be. Now, imagine that you can't help but hear it. Can't stop focusing on it. All day, every day. Imagine that hearing it is enough to drive a pregnant woman to walk eight blocks in a snowstorm with a week's groceries all because someone in the back of a crowded bus is chewing gum."

"Sounds real bad," he corrected.

Dr. Ashland took a sip of tea. "It is. And we have no idea how common it is, nor how to treat it. Not really. For my patient, the disorder was so intense that she became physically angry—dangerously angry, on a level that you as a homicide detective might understand—at the sound of her child nursing. When she privately intimated this to her own mother, the woman was involuntarily committed. My patient lost custody of her infant son along with her job, her home, her savings, and her marriage. She was on suicide watch when I was contacted."

The detective whistled. "And you helped her?"

"Yes," she said. *I cured her,* she thought, *uplifted her and saved her.* "With what you're hearing now," she said.

"This . . . music?"

He hadn't noticed yet.

"Just one element," Dr. Ashland said, "of traditional folk remedy for treating severe anxiety after childbirth, practiced in secret amongst certain nomadic, matriarchal ethnic groups in rural Thailand and Laos. It also involves certain fungi, herbs, and other ingredients fairly common to that area."

The detective nodded. "Fine, fine. You have a background in psychopharmacology. I take that to mean drugs? Mental state . . . or," he searched for the term, "mind-affecting drugs?"

"Indeed," said the doctor, nodding.

A single crimson drop of blood ran from the detective's left nostril; he wiped it away without noticing. He opened his mouth and closed it again. The pupil of his right eyes was a pinprick, the dark iris contracted to the tiniest pucker.

She took another sip of the piping-hot tea, biting back a sickened grimace. "While I don't claim to know the full length and breadth of the literature on all modern psychoactive chemical treatments, I flatter myself to imagine that I'm considered something of a local expert. I know what the Chinese and Koreans are prescribing; I know why we aren't doing the same, even if the reasons are profoundly foolish. And I can offer . . . let's say, *robust* resources to my patients when less-invasive procedures fail to meet their needs."

"Meaning . . . what, precisely?"

"Is this about drugs, detective? Street drugs?"

He dismissed her question with a wave. "What do you mean, 'robust'?"

Dr. Ashland took another long sip of the red tea, feeling her throat begin to get scratchy. She calmly picked a facial tissue from the desk and dabbed at both eyes before blowing her nose. "To say too much would violate confidentiality clauses. I mean robust."

The detective folded his arms. "How so?"

"My patients are, as you say, particularly troubled. Troubled youth, primarily. They need robust treatment—willing or no, and most of them aren't."

"Ordered by the courts," the detective said.

"Or sentenced to my care by parental fiat and quite possibly more dangerous for the distinction. Especially the rich kids, if you don't mind me saying so. They're often the worst cases . . . the craziest ones, if I'm being informal."

The detective shook his head, letting the comment pass. He knew how dangerous the children of the wealthy could be.

Dr. Ashland continued. "Many of these patients do not respond well, or at all, to traditional medications, and although I'm loath to overprescribe drugs when psychotherapy will do, my patients are often somewhat more resistant to talking than they are to being strongly dosed-up. If I may speak frankly."

The detective frowned. "So you mean . . . what? That you pursue nontraditional medications for your patients? It's what you're famous for."

"That's one way of phrasing it," Dr. Ashland said, taking a final, deep draw of her tea. "The best medicine, detective, is the one the patient will *take*. You could have the most efficient, reliable, highest-potency antipsychotic on the market—the very best gram for gram, dollar for dollar—but it won't do a damn bit of good to anyone if a psychotic person won't take it or forgets to take it or takes it just until he thinks he's 'cured' or stops taking it because it gives him stomachaches or worse. Hell, stomachaches would be a blessing, considering some other common side effects of particularly potent psychoactive drugs."

"Like what?"

Dr. Ashland narrowed her eyes. "Would you take a drug that made you impotent, detective? Fat? Incontinent? Gave you narcolepsy or seizures? Would you recommend it to a friend? How many thirteen-year-olds do you know who would take it? How many seventeen-year-olds? How many of your own colleagues would continue with their dosage even if strongly recommended by a doctor?"

He opened his mouth and simply shook his head. The droning sound was beginning to affect him.

"Of course," said Dr. Ashland, "that's only part of the problem. Patients, in general, don't like taking meds. A common and debilitating symptom of schizophrenia, for example, is the sincerely held belief that doctors or the government or both are trying to put harmful alien compounds or substances into your body . . . which, when we consider what a lot of these drugs *do* to a patient, isn't actually so crazy."

The detective waved away the observation. "So you're willing to experiment. I'll accept it's for the benefit of the patient. How far do you go?"

Dr. Ashland sighed, setting down the last dregs of her tea. "The long-arc history of drug manufacture, legality, and prescription is utterly maddening, detective. Bayer used to market heroin as a children's cough suppressant; Parke-Davis legally sold cocaine over-the-counter up until 1922—during Prohibition!—before moving on to both PCP and ketamine. Other end of the spectrum, nitrous oxide was first isolated in 1772, but it wasn't used as a surgical anesthetic until midway through the 1860s because people were too busy treating it as a common recreational drug. We've nearly universally got our heads on backward when it comes to drugs, treatment, therapy, and addiction."

"You think some of your patients could benefit from cocaine."

"I think," said the doctor carefully, "that people who were prescribed cocaine by their doctor probably very rarely missed a dose. And if it provided effective treatment in some instances, I wouldn't be surprised. Indigenous peoples have used *Erythroxylum coca* as medicine for millennia."

The detective frowned. "What do you know about Modos121?"

"I've heard the name," admitted Dr. Ashland, biting back the taste of tea, now congealing in her mouth—some of it was trying to crawl back up her throat. "It's a street drug, yes? Relatively new. Recreational, similar to ecstasy. Has elements of a nootropic. Homebrewed, like methamphetamines."

"Not quite."

"But it has a recipe? Yes. One that could be found on the darknet, simple enough that a cunning young person could make some given a basic chemistry background, a ventilated basement with a drain, and a Bunsen burner."

The detective nodded.

"Let me guess. This Modos also has some relatively obscure chemical component known to be found in a rare or markedly uncommon anti-anxiety medication that I prescribed to a patient or have been known to prescribe."

The detective nodded. "Something like that."

"And you're here as a homicide detective investigating whether I have any connection to a mysterious death. A death related to one of my patients and to this drug."

The detective didn't nod this time. He didn't have to.

"None of my patients or former patients have died recently," she mused, "that I know of. So I'm guessing that you think one of my patients is the culprit. Possibly killing people with this drug and possibly because of this drug."

"I'm not at liberty to say," said the detective.

"Well, then. I have one more photograph, very much like these that I don't put up on my wall. It's not something that I show to everyone."

Stepping behind her desk, she pulled a thin manila envelope from her top drawer and handed it to the detective.

"You asked me before who sculpted the ice in these images, and I said no one. And that's true. Yet you saw the hand of an artist because there was what you perceived to be irreducible complexity in that image; it *looked* like something. See a sculpture, assume a sculptor."

"Sure."

"This photograph, detective, is of an actual ice sculpture."

He pulled the glossy photograph from the envelope, curious, taking in the image with his breath held. After a moment, he glanced back up at Dr. Ashland. "It's . . . what, a melted swan?"

"A melted angel. A cherub with tiny wings, crafted to pirouette as it urinated vodka for partygoers. This photograph was taken near the very end of an incredibly lavish birthday event on a private island as most of the guests were departing. The man they were celebrating took his own life not six months later, hoping to avoid prison for fraud."

He handed the image back. "I don't get it."

Dr. Ashland nodded. "Most people see only a lump; I suspect you constructed the image of a swan from that oozing pile only because I told you that it was an ice sculpture to begin with."

The detective frowned.

"I like to keep this photograph here because it contrasts so perfectly with the beauty you see around you. Most people," the doctor said, "think that the human mind is like a crystal vase: formed intricately and explicitly for its purpose, whatever that purpose might be. When such a delicate thing breaks—and it often does—there are a lot of different things you can say about it afterward."

"Like what?"

"Well, there are the helpful things and the no-so-helpful things, aren't there? If a glass vase breaks into a very small number of big pieces, we can say 'well, maybe we can glue it back together.' And if it breaks into a lot of very small pieces, we can say 'stand back because it can cut you.' But it's not very useful to say 'those pieces look like a duck.' In my professional opinion."

"You may have lost me, doctor."

"But the human mind isn't a vase. It's just water, really—blood and tissue, sugar and protein and wet electricity—temporarily frozen, caught in a state of nature. There is no sculptor. We just are. When a mind breaks, psychiatrists always want to hold up a shard and say 'sociopath' or 'sex addict' or 'monster.'"

"But those," said the detective, "aren't useful definitions. In your professional opinion."

"That's correct. They don't have the courage to say 'this one is broken, let's get rid of it' or 'this one can be repaired, so let's fix it.' Or even 'this can be repurposed. We can make something beautiful out of these shards. Reduce, recycle, reuse.' Ice sculptures, and other crap just like them, allow us to pretend that we're in control; let us pretend that there's order in a chaotic universe. And they are very dangerous because of that. Good day, detective."

"You haven't really answered all of my questions, Dr. Ashland."

"I'm well aware. I am also aware that you don't have a warrant. You will not find the girl you're looking for. She is in a state of nature, and unlike most of us, she understands that. No hand shaped her nor crafted her, detective, unless the gods are much stranger and much crueler than you or I can begin to imagine."

He frowned. "Where is she?"

"Would that I knew," she sighed. "Come back with a warrant, and we'll go through my files until I can prove to you that I can't locate her, either. Until then, have a lovely afternoon."

The detective left, wobbling slightly, seeming not to notice.

Dr. Ashland turned off the music and steadied herself against her desk, taking deep breaths. Another press of the remote dimmed the lights; a third click locked the door. She waited.

After a minute, she vomited twice in rapid succession.

She crumpled to the floor unceremoniously, leaning against her desk and kicking off her heels. Wiping her mouth with the back of her hand, she pulled her laptop to the floor and opened a private chat program.

It was already running; the most recent post was hers.

+3+: *Trouble. Be back.*

Dr. Ashland considered and began typing.

+3+: *9, I have just had the unfortunate experience of killing a man. He was dressed as a police detective although I am uncertain as to his true masters. I learned what I could, but it was not much. Asking about Modos.*

A moment passed and words appeared.

+8+: *We are pleased. 9 is informed. You are absolved.*

+5+: How was it killed?

Dr. Ashland relaxed; she finally let go of a breath she didn't know she was holding.

+3+: I gave him a long earful of Wood Mother's Calling Song; he'll take his own life no sooner than 20 minutes from now. I would expect him to drive off the road or eat his gun within 40–45 minutes at the most. He is unlikely to contact anyone.

+7+: it is well

+5+: You took precaution?

Dr. Ashland felt her fingertips, still numb. How much was shock? She couldn't say.

+3+: Enough. A cup of red rust skin tschambucco, taken immediately before and during the song. I didn't have time to distill it properly, but I purged the majority within an hour.

+7+: you will live

+8+: As 7 says.

+7+: you honor me

+4+: Call for 2 or 1 as you prefer. Have them tend to your health and your well-being for the night. Come see me when you're able, and we will talk.

+8+: 9 sends her gratitude.

+3+: Ever our praises.

+9+: And abundance.

The screen went dark.

Dr. Ashland smiled.

She had liked the detective, truly, but her love of the Goddess was everything.

{}

Clinton J. Boomer, *known to his friends as Booms, resides in the quaint, leafy, idyllic paradise of Appleton, Wisconsin. He began writing before the time of his own recollection, dictating stories to his ever-patient mother about fire monsters and ice monsters throwing children into garbage cans. Boomer is a writer, filmmaker, and bartender. His short comedic films, D&D PHB PSAs, have over 3,500 subscribers on YouTube and have been viewed more than a million and a half times. He is—above all—a dad, a game-designer, a reader, and a recovering lifelong bachelor. His debut novel,* The Hole Behind Midnight, *was released in 2011 and is available from Broken Eye Books. Daniel O'Brien, columnist for Cracked.com and contributor to the New York Times bestseller* You Might Be a Zombie and Other Bad News *called it "Raymond Chandler meets Douglas Adams by way of a fantasy nerd's fever dream. And it's AWESOME."*

A Pathway for the Broken

Damien Angelica Walters

When the doctor tells Dale to hold still, he complies. The prick of a needle comes next, and a cold snake slithers into his veins. There's something in the needle, something in the cold, but he can't remember the name. Robots, he remembers asking, and the answer was no. But the details are gone in the black space where things fall in. Sometimes, they creep back out. More and more, once in the dark, they stay there—bears hibernating in a cave through an endless winter.

He shifts on the table, the paper sheet beneath him crinkling. Cold air rushes out of the overhead vent, sending goosebumps dancing down his arms. Underneath the thin, scratchy blanket, he's wearing only socks, boxer shorts, and a knee-length hospital gown.

The doctor (and come to think of it, Dale can't remember *his* name either: maybe Roman or Rodan?) pats his shoulder. "Are you doing okay, Mr. Donovan?"

"I'm fine."

"Good. I'm going to spread on the gel now, but we've warmed it up for you a bit, so it shouldn't be too bad."

Despite his words, the gel is still cool on Dale's freshly shaved scalp, not that he had a lot of hair to begin with.

"Now for the transducer. Hold very still, please."

Once the helmet is fitted into place, the doctor pats his shoulder again. "Now, I need you to lie still while we start the ultrasound to wake up the nanoparticles. You might feel a little dizzy, but if it gets to be too much, wave your right hand."

"Gotcha."

The helmet begins to hum. Dale closes his eyes, imagining tiny street cleaning machines in his brain, brushes whirring as they clear the blocked pathways. His jaw clenches. What if they clean too much away? They're supposed to die once the whole thing's done—he remembers that much—but what if they stay behind and keep cleaning until nothing's left of him at all?

A metallic taste floods his mouth, and he fights the urge to spit. Stay still, he reminds himself. He has to stay still. For a moment, he can't remember why he's here, and the sense that something isn't right hovers in a bestial shadow, but it's only a quick flicker of dark, and his cheeks turn warm. Of course, he knows why. Alzheimer's is why. If he doesn't have this procedure, the disease will keep eating his memories until nothing is left. Then his body will shut down, and he'll die. But he'll be dead where it counts long before then.

The hum grows louder, but Dale hears it inside his head, not from the helmet. He can't remember how long the doctor said the whole thing would take and hopes his daughter is still waiting outside.

The world goes grey and swimmy. Cold sweat makes the cheap fabric gown stick to his back. Beneath the hum, there's a pulse, but he doesn't think it's his own. It's too slow, too heavy, too big.

"Doing okay?" the doctor asks.

"Sure thing, doc," he manages.

The black space kicks out his name—Dr. Rollin, like a ball down a hill. And there's a storm rolling in his head, dark clouds roiling on the surface of his thoughts. No rain, no hail, but the pressure is growing. The pulse throbs, dwarfing his own skittering heartbeat. He wants to raise his hand, wants to tell Dr. Rollin that he's had enough, but he can't make his hand move, can't get the signal through the storm.

The crash of striking waves sends a low moan shuddering through his lips. The chaos builds and builds until it's all he hears, all he knows. Something else slips through: the sound of thunderous footsteps moving closer. Then the storm breaks, the clouds scatter, everything falls silent, and the black hole is gone. All the words he thought he'd forgotten, all those he forgot he'd forgotten, surge back in. So many words he's afraid his brain isn't big enough to hold them all.

Tears catch in his throat and burn in his eyes. Like the words, there are too many to hold back.

●

"Tell me about the beach in Maine again."

Dale smiles at his daughter curled up on one end of the small sofa. His room in the research hospital resembles a small studio apartment, but the smell is all hospital—antiseptic, floral deodorizer, and a ghost of urine—and the furniture is hard where it should be soft and mushy where it should be firm. At least the window has a view of the trees behind the hospital instead of the parking lot.

He takes a sip of coffee. Grimaces. They probably haven't changed the grounds in days. "Kiddo, I haven't forgotten since yesterday, the last time I told you."

"I know," Kerry says. "I just like hearing you tell the story. You know it's my favorite."

She isn't lying, but the story is a test, much like the poking and prodding and the endless questions from Dr. Rollin. Two months ago, Dale tried to tell it, and Kerry ended up in tears while he sat awash in frustration and embarrassment. It wasn't that he couldn't recall the memory, because he could, but the word rock was lost in the dark and wouldn't come out. Hard to recount their last family vacation before Kerry's mother passed away, hard to tell the funniest part of the story, when you couldn't remember the word for what made your young daughter so angry because beaches were supposed to have sand.

He starts to protest again, but guilt lingers bitter on his tongue at the strain around Kerry's eyes and mouth. If she had a sibling, she wouldn't have to shoulder the burden on her own.

Dale starts the story again, not stumbling over any words at all. Halfway through, a nurse pokes her head into the room but leaves without saying anything.

The frequent checks to see if everything's okay are a small annoyance. Do they think he's going to wander off? He didn't do that before they cured him. Ah, well, a few more weeks and then he can go home.

●

He's watching a cardinal flit from branch to branch when he hears a low hum. He holds his hand beneath the vent, but there's no air rushing out. The television is off, the handset of the phone is on the receiver, and the call button for the nurse isn't lit. He cracks his door. The hallway holds the usual noise: voices, rubber soles tapping on tile, the distant ding of an elevator. There's nothing amiss in the bathroom either. Still, the hum persists. Although it's rhythmic, it doesn't sound mechanical. He scratches behind one ear, the stubble of his hair bristling against his fingertips.

It almost feels as though it's in his head, which doesn't make a lick of sense, and there's something else there, too. He scrunches his nose. Squints. Too faint for him to be sure, but it makes him think of breaking waves and maybe footsteps. Which makes even less sense.

Kerry bustles into the room with an extra-large cup of non-hospital coffee. Dale thinks of asking her if she hears anything strange, but the last thing he needs is to give her something else to worry about. And anyway, after a few sips of coffee, the hum disappears.

●

Dale steps from the elevator and follows the signs until he finds the entrance to the courtyard. Benches sit here and there, and pebbled pathways wind around small trees and flowers in planters. In the center, a seahorse-shaped fountain spits a narrow stream into a pond. The bottom glitters with copper in spite of the Please Don't Throw Coins in the Water sign.

The air smells clean and clear; it's easy to pretend he's in his own backyard. He clasps his hands behind his back and walks the path, the sun warm on his face.

Someone's humming, but it isn't a song he recognizes. It doesn't seem a song at all but a voice vibrating through his mind. A voice unlike any he's ever heard before. His arms go all over goosebumps, his steps slow, and somewhere, waves strike a rocky shore and footsteps trudge through the water.

The hum—the voice—intensifies, burrowing deep with the sensation of biting down on aluminum foil. His heart races, and he thinks he should call for a nurse because something is moving through the waves, coming closer, and it's something wrong—

"Dad?"

Dale jumps and steps back, away from the edge of the pond. "Hi, kiddo," he says, his voice a sandpaper rasp.

Kerry frowns, reaching for his arm. "Are you okay?"

"Of course I am," he says, pushing his lips into what he hopes is a believable smile. His knees and back are stiff. His head is foggy, as though it's been stuffed with cotton batting, and even if he drank all the water in the pond, it wouldn't be enough to banish the desert in his mouth.

"I got scared when you weren't in your room, and the nurse told me you were coming down here a few hours ago. Have you been down here the whole time?"

A few hours? That isn't possible. He just came downstairs. He hasn't even walked the entire path yet. But Kerry's face still wears a frown, so he says, "Guess I lost track of time enjoying the fresh air. I'm sick to death of staying cooped up in that room."

"And you were talking to yourself like you used to do when you worked on your car."

"I was? What was I saying?"

"Something about the water, I think. It didn't make much sense to me. Are you *sure* you're okay?"

He waves one hand. "I'm right as rain, kiddo. A little woolgathering now and again is good for the soul."

"Well, if you're finished, how about we go back upstairs?"

Kerry doesn't wait for an answer before she loops her arm through his.

Unease rests heavy in his belly, but even though his knees creak, he keeps his steps even and sure.

○

"Everything looks good thus far, Mr. Donovan," Dr. Rollin says. "Very good. I predict tomorrow's MRI will confirm that as well. Have you had any problems, or do you have any concerns?"

"I don't know if it's a problem, but I've heard a humming sound a few times."

Dr. Rollin's brow creases. "A humming?"

"It wasn't that bad or anything," Dale says, fighting the urge to wipe his damp palms on his pants. "It was mostly annoying. Kinda sounded like it did when the machine was on my head. But the second time it happened, it wasn't as bad.

Honestly, my ears aren't what they used to be. I probably just heard something wrong."

Dr. Rollin writes on his notepad, considers Dale with a long look. "If you hear it again, please, let me know."

"I will."

"Anything else?"

Dale thinks of his lost hours, shrugs the thoughts away. He was daydreaming, that was all. Got lost in his own head for a bit, but it didn't mean anything was wrong. "Nope, everything's good," he says, the lie sliding evenly off his tongue.

○

The nurse insists he ride in a wheelchair to the MRI suite, two floors down, and Dale doesn't bother to argue the point. He keeps quiet when he changes into the gown and climbs onto the table. The machine whirs and taps, too loud to sleep through, even with earplugs, so he stares at the shadows on his eyelids instead. Somewhere along the way after what seems hours, the hum creeps through the gaps in the machinery's noise. Or maybe it was there the whole time, too low for Dale to hear.

The hum twists into a barrage of incomprehensible words laced with rage and malevolence. Dale struggles to get away, dimly aware his body isn't moving at all. Why isn't anyone helping him? Don't they hear it?

On an unseen shore, waves crash and break. The heavy footsteps approach. A jolt races through his body, and his mouth goes thick with the taste of stone and salt. He catches a glimpse of some unimaginable darkness, a vast space unfolding as a monstrous shape emerges.

Dale feels it moving closer and closer, and then, he feels nothing at all.

○

Awareness bleeds back in slowly. Movement, voices, bright lights, a dull throb behind his temples, an IV in his arm.

"What happened? Please, just tell me what happened," Kerry says, her voice high and thin.

The dulcet tones of a nurse: "We aren't sure yet, Ms. Donovan. Please, we need you to calm down."

"I'm okay," Dale whispers.

"Calm down? How am I supposed to do that? Did you see what happened?"

"Ms. Donovan—"

"I'm okay," Dale says as loud as he can.

"Dad?" Kerry bursts into tears.

Dr. Rollin leans over, his eyes serious. "You gave us a bit of a scare there. How are you feeling?"

"A little tired but okay. What happened?"

"You had a seizure."

"A seizure? Like with epilepsy?"

"Similar, yes, but don't worry, we're going to determine why and make sure it doesn't happen again."

While he drones on about medication and possible underlying conditions, Dale closes his eyes. Hears the echo of a voice. Remembers a darkness and something within.

He swallows hard against the fear that it's still there, waiting.

○

Dale traces circles on a notepad. Scattered on the sofa cushion beside him are torn-off sheets of paper, lists of words he remembers. A fool's exercise—how would he remember what he doesn't remember?—but the lists are comforting nonetheless.

The hum, deep inside his mind, is low, almost a suggestion rather than a hum itself, but he feels its presence. At least, he thinks he does, but his mind could be lying. It has a history of faulty behavior, so how can he fully trust it now?

Although Dr. Rollin hasn't admitted it, Dale knows the treatment didn't work the way it was supposed to. Something went wrong. He sees it in the doctor's eyes and in Kerry's eyes, too. They've drawn more blood and run more tests in the past three days than he can count. Dr. Rollin said they want to do another MRI, but only after they've ruled everything else out. What "everything else" means, Dale has no idea.

In spite of all the words he remembers, he's afraid the Alzheimer's is back and they don't want to tell him. But something isn't right. He can't remember if this is the same not-right he felt before the doctors put a diagnosis and a name to the feeling. He doesn't think so, but he'd rather hear the truth.

He tosses the notebook aside, gathers the loose pages. On a few, while his handwriting is unmistakable, the words are illegible scrawls—not words at all. For a fleeting moment, he almost understands them, and it leaves a bitter taste in his mouth. He fights tears and wins; fights his fear and loses.

He tears the papers—even his lists—into shreds and flushes them down the toilet, wishing he never agreed to any of this in the first place.

●

"I have good news and bad news," Dr. Rollin says, his hands folded atop his desk.

Kerry leans forward in her chair. The office is smaller than Dale remembers, feels like it's growing even smaller. He doesn't want to be here, doesn't want to hear the bad news, doesn't care about the good news either. He wants to go home and sleep in his own bed, sit in his own back yard, and drink his own damned coffee.

"All your bloodwork has come back fine. We can't find anything that would account for the seizure."

"So I'm okay?"

Dr. Rollin clears his throat. "I mentioned the other day that I wanted to run another MRI. When the radiologist went over the results of the previous one, she found an anomaly."

"What kind of anomaly?" Kerry asks.

"We've ruled out a tumor of any kind, and while we're not one hundred percent certain, we suspect it's either a bit of plaque we missed," he clears his throat again, "or, possibly, one of the nanoparticles."

"You said they were designed to die after the ultrasound was shut off and that they'd be flushed away," Kerry says.

"Yes, that's how they're designed to work. Dale, I've consulted with a few other doctors and we suspect that hum you reported hearing is indicative of a malfunctioning nanoparticle."

"Hum? What hum? Dad, you didn't tell me about that."

He gives her arm a gentle squeeze. "I didn't think it was a big deal. So, Doc, if one of those things is still hanging around, what do we do now?"

"We'd like to run the ultrasound therapy again. We think, *if* one of the nanoparticles was left behind, it's our best shot at getting rid of it."

"Wait," Kerry says. "You said everything went fine. Now you're saying something went wrong, but you want to do the whole thing again?"

"Kiddo, it's okay."

"No, Dad, it's not okay. What happens if you just leave it where it is?"

Dr. Rollin steeples his fingers beneath his chin. "It could potentially lead to more seizure activity or even a stroke. I don't think that's likely, but it's—"

"Fine." Dale meets Dr. Rollin's gaze. "Let's do it again."

He pretends not to see the tears in Kerry's eyes.

○

Dale stares at the ceiling, shivering as the injection turns his arm cold.

"Doing okay?" Dr. Rollin asks as he spreads the gel on Dale's head.

"Sure thing, Doc. Just a bit of déjà vu."

"Understandable. Don't worry. We'll get everything taken care of."

Dale nods, but he *is* worried. He's worried a lot. If one nanoparticle was left behind, who's to say it won't happen again? But most of all, he's worried that this time around will reverse things. Illogical, maybe, but fears usually are. He isn't alone with his fear, either; before they wheeled him in, Kerry gave him a hug to beat all hugs. He knuckled her nose the way he did when she was small and said, "I'll give it back when I'm done."

"You better," she said, her voice trembling, tears glittering in her eyes.

Once the transducer is in place, Dr. Rollin rests a hand on Dale's shoulder. "Please remember to keep still—"

"And if I feel dizzy, wave my hand."

"You got it."

The machine kicks on, its hum a kitten's purr. Once again, Dale's mouth tastes of wet coins. Once again, he closes his eyes. And waits for the coming storm.

This time, though, there's only the machine. Dale's breathing slows, his nervousness ebbs. Maybe the nanoparticles have already found their malfunctioning sibling and are gathering up the pieces. Maybe everything will be fine after all. Dale drifts, lulled into a dreamless half-sleep.

A wave rushes in, shaking him awake and aware. The pulsing heart of a behemoth beats in furious tempo. Dale can't move, can't speak, can't think. A great darkness opens, a blooming black flower, and footsteps approach, ponderous and implacable.

What emerges has a shape that defies description, an amalgamation of nightmare and impossibility. The creature's voice thrums, words he can't understand, doesn't want to understand.

I'm an old man, Dale thinks bitterly. *Can't you see that? What good am I to you? Go away, and leave me alone.*

The beast moves closer, traveling a pathway once blocked by plaque, now open for the taking. Scaled arms extend. Claws trace delicate lines on Dale's arms, and with a rush of wind as its wings cut through the air, it pulls him into the dark.

When his feet touch solid ground, he's alone in a vast cave. Beyond the arched entrance, there's a darkness so absolute it hurts his eyes. Distant waves crash against a shore, and he tastes the salt tang of an ocean upon his tongue. He hears no footsteps, no beating wings, and the only heartbeat is his own. Goosebumps dance the length of his arms; his hospital gown isn't nearly warm enough.

Weak grey light spills from the cave's walls, revealing words etched on the stone, words in his own handwriting: *Kerry, Maggie, home, love, hope.* The lights flicker and begin to fade, taking the words with them as they go, and as each one disappears, something pops in his mind—a soap bubble breaking but leaving behind a tiny hole.

"But I'm here," he shouts, his voice an endless echo. "I'm still here!"

Sobbing, he moves his hands along the walls for a gap, a way out, but there's nothing. Nothing at all.

The last of the light fades, and he sinks to the rocky ground, pulling his knees to his chest. He isn't sure how he got here, isn't even sure where *here* is. He's lost, that's all, but if he stays very still, if he waits, someone will come and find him. They won't leave him alone in the dark.

Someone will come.

{}

Damien Angelica Walters *has appeared or is forthcoming in various anthologies and magazines, including* The Year's Best Dark Fantasy & Horror 2015, Year's Best Weird Fiction: Volume One, Cassilda's Song, The Mammoth Book of Cthulhu: New Lovecraftian Fiction, Nightmare Magazine, Black Static, *and* Apex Magazine. *She was a finalist for a Bram Stoker Award for "The Floating Girls: A Documentary," originally published in* Jamais Vu. Sing Me Your Scars, *a collection of short fiction, was released in 2015 from Apex Publications, and* Paper Tigers, *a novel, is forthcoming in 2016 from Dark House Press. Find her on Twitter @ DamienAWalters or on the web at damienangelicawalters.com.*

The Crunch Underfoot

Lizz-Ayn Shaarawi

The sun warmed my back even as each exhale showed pale white. The crisp of morning promised to burn off by lunchtime, not that it mattered to me. Too early for snow, too late for an Indian summer. I trudged up the narrow street as the wind blew leaves around my feet.

My destination loomed ahead, the outcast amongst neat, trim homes. Much like the owner, my Uncle Cyrus, the house had an air of shabbiness, a stubborn refusal to play well with the neighbors. Spite or simple orneriness had his home slowly turning in on itself, mutating until it barely resembled its rustic yet modern neighbors.

A metal fence surrounded the yard, black with sharp tips. The gate, not automated like the rest on the street, clanged against its post with each gust of wind. Beyond lay dead grass covered in a thick blanket of fallen leaves. Their rich, vibrant colors struck a sharp contrast to the dull, peeling paint on the warped wood of the front porch. A single gnarled tree, already leafless, curled from the earth. Its skeletal branches reached above the three-story Edwardian house.

Those commuters, soccer moms, and basketball dads must have breathed a sigh of relief that day. The day my uncle flung open the front door and lurched down the steps, strange words spilling from his mouth just before he collapsed. They said a weird storm brewed, but only above his house. They said wind whipped at his body but stopped at the property's edge. They said a lot of things.

At least, they called paramedics for him. The suburbanites may have shunned him in life, but they had enough decency to be respectful of his death.

Children raced past me on wheelie shoes. Boys abandoned blowers to jump in the leaves they had so carefully piled. A couple moms with tight butts in yoga pants, vests, and fleece tops stopped gossiping over their fence to watch me pass. I gave them a curt nod but didn't linger long enough to catch their reactions to me: young, dark-haired, in a long coat. Black on black on black.

I didn't want to keep the house waiting.

It made perfect sense that I would be the one to clean out my uncle's home. One of my earliest memories was of my uncle peering down at me, a treat or prize offered from some hidden pocket in his threadbare coat. Though he wasn't one of "those" uncles (the ones parents knew never to leave their children alone with), he was distant and odd, the black sheep, and most of the family (not only the children) tended to steer clear. Not me. There was a connection between us, unspoken but tangible. I suppose there must be one in every generation: a weirdo, an outcast, the family embarrassment. In our family, the spinner pointed to me.

From an early age, I wasn't like the other girls. Not that I was a tomboy; fighting and sports bored me as well as dolls. I rarely spoke and kept myself cocooned in books, real books made from paper, almost to the point of building forts with their dusty spines. The smell of paper and ink still relaxes me in a way that nothing else does.

The few family gatherings I was forced to attend usually ended with me hiding in a remote library. Eventually, Uncle Cyrus would find me. We rarely spoke, both of us people of few words. Usually, we'd sit quietly, comfortable as we read side-by-side on a bench or sofa. After years of such meetings, Uncle Cyrus would often dig into his ratty coat and hand me a book just before I was called away by my parents to make my goodbyes for the day. At first, they were classics, Poe and Blackwood, but as the years passed, they became older and more obscure. After he handed me a book in Latin with no explanation, I launched into an exhaustive study of foreign and classical languages just so I wouldn't be caught off guard again. It took years for me to translate that book, but that made its secrets that much sweeter.

My studies shifted to the arcane. I began to correspond with Uncle Cyrus.

He refused to use a computer, so everything had to be handwritten. I was not so intolerant of technology and found it very useful to further my studies. Though we spoke little, we wrote mountains of words, boxes of letters, and miles of postcards.

Until the day the call came.

His will was adamant that the house and all of its contents were to be bequeathed to me. Having never married or sired children, I was his sole heir. The main decision I needed to make was whether to keep the house or clean it out and sell it.

I reached the swinging gate and stilled it mid-creak. After passing through, I gently pushed the warped latch until it caught. The only sound was the crunch of leaves beneath my feet as I approached. The iron key ring was heavy and unfamiliar in my hand. If I kept the house, I'd need to have an eye scanner installed at once. The key entered the lock easily enough but refused to turn. A whine issued from the deadbolt as I put my weight behind it. The tumblers cracked like a gunshot, and it unlocked.

I glanced back once before entering the house. The neighbors stared as if they had been frozen in time, latte or blower in hand, baby on hip or in an ergonomic jog stroller.

I turned away and slammed the door.

Darkness shrouded the house's interior. Uncle Cyrus had no need for motion-activated lights. I ran my hand along the wall and found the switch. A sudden burst of light filled the entryway, yet the shadows receded a split second too late. So that's how it was. I reached into my long black hair, easily finding the small plate drilled into my skull. Runes of protection were carved into the black metal coating, revealing the steel beneath. My fingers traced the carvings, and a custom gel slid over my eyes. Microscopic filaments sparked to life, creating a golden light that would protect me from any residual creatures my uncle left behind that might wish to do me harm. I shone the light into the corners of the room, watching with little surprise as the shadows screeched and pulled back, some slipping under floorboards or into wall cracks.

I pulled chalk from my pocket and marked the back of the front door before continuing my exploration. The house groaned as I headed deeper. The dining room stood to my right. Small clicks of multi-legged creatures skidded across surfaces as I ducked my head in. Another chalk mark went on the door. To my left, a sitting room whose fireplace roared to life as soon as my torso crossed the threshold but went dark and cold when I leaned out. I marked this door as well.

I continued throughout the house; each room exposed its quirks to me, each room received a mark on the door. The second floor contained three bedrooms and an antiquated bathroom. The entire time that the house revealed its secrets to me, it never gave me what I genuinely wanted: Uncle Cyrus's library. I knew it existed; he spoke of it often in our letters.

The main floor contained an office, but the only books I could find were ledgers, filled not with necromancy or spells but numbers and household accounts. I pushed against walls and light fixtures but couldn't find hidden panels or secret rooms. Back through the house, back through the rooms, I searched until I ended up in the kitchen at the back of the first floor.

A sudden hunger gnawed at my stomach. I realized I hadn't eaten in hours. A quick inventory of the pantry and freezer proved my uncle didn't hate technology enough to shun frozen dinners and processed food. Soon enough, a Big Guy meal was warming in the gas oven. When I opened the oven to remove the food, a draft swept through the room, causing the gas flame to sputter. I turned the knob to off and set dinner aside. Crouching, I followed the breeze along the cracked and dirt-crusted linoleum until I had crawled into the open pantry. Cool air caressed my skin. My hunger instantly forgotten, I reached for the far pantry wall.

A scratching sound came from behind me. I whipped around, frightened. An old gnarled tree, much like the one in the front yard, leaned against the house. Its branches scraped at the glass of the kitchen window in slow shrieking jags. After a brief search, I found a seam in the pantry wall. It took little pressure to swing the panel back on hidden hinges. A dark staircase lay at my feet. My golden sight showed the way.

The stairs creaked precariously with every step but held my weight. I found a light switch at the bottom step. It came on with a loud crack. No creatures scurried. The shadows behaved as they should. I switched off the golden gaze. Of all the rooms in the house, this was the most magnificent. Bookshelves lined three walls; the fourth (beneath the stairs) held a table and shelves of various bottles. Peeling labels advertised ingredients from sage to toad eyes. Strewn throughout the room were plump sofas and chairs covered in rich fabrics. Small windows lined the top of the walls, near the ceiling. They would have let in a bit of sunlight if they weren't covered in heavy cloth. The bookshelves housed my uncle's prized collection—now, my prized collection.

Goose bumps covered my arms as I pulled book after book from the shelves. One lofty tome was so old that the pages slid from the binding when I opened it. Cursing, I placed the text gently on a nearby sofa and scrambled to pick up the pages. One had drifted under a chair. As I reached for it, my fingers brushed leather. A scratching sound erupted from behind the walls. Rats, I thought. That thought quickly slipped away, replaced by the thrill of finding the dusty tome.

I returned the pages to the old book before reaching under the chair again. Out slid a book bound in human skin (the ear and stubble on the back cover gave it away). It fell open to a beautiful handwritten page, the margins filled with grotesque illustrations. It reminded me of *The Book of Kells* I had seen at Trinity College yet much more sinister. A wind kicked up outside. Leaves rustled against the small windows. The scratching in the walls increased.

The archaic words described the Fenyw'dŵr, She Who Lives in the Water. Through distant dimensions, on the entropy beach, Fenyw'dŵr crawled from the brine to do battle with her sister. Coedeno'boen, She Who Brings the Pain and sister to She Who Lives in the Water, tore through the ground, pushed past the rocks and the dirt until she stood tall, her head in the rumbling sky. Mae'r Dail, the daughters, drifted down from the mother, clung together and did her bidding. Together, they were the mothers, both creators and destroyers.

The wind outside Uncle Cyrus's house became a squall.

The drawing on the page depicted a slimy, pale-skinned hag with clumps of stringy blue and green hair crawling from black water. Rage pulled her face into a hideous mask. Water boiled at her feet and bent knees. Hints of movement just under the water's surface spoke of a legion at her command.

A moan rose through the house as the wind battered against it. The scratching became a single blur of white noise.

Somewhere deep in my brain, the sounds registered. But my attention never left the book where on the shore Coedeno'boen stood tall and brown, rising into a stormy sky. Small patches of brown, red, and yellow fell from her wild hair onto the rocky ground.

A howl erupted from the backyard. I set the book aside. It took standing on a chair for me to reach the heavy cloth that covered the windows. The fabric was so old and rotten, only a few small tugs were needed before it fell away. Leaves thrown against the glass by the wind obscured any view.

I headed upstairs through the kitchen, passing the now-cold dinner. The house shuddered at the assault from the storm outside. At the window, the tree bucked against the panes. Clouds covered the sky and blackened the world. I had never seen a storm like this. Beneath the howl, a low chant sounded. The words were lost in the storm. Could someone be out there?

I raced through the back door into the yard. Lightning flashed but no thunder came, no rain fell. The wind whipped at my coat, sent leaves rolling around my legs and feet. They crunched underfoot as my hand slid up through my hair to touch the runes. The golden beam fought against the darkness as it swept the yard. The chant grew louder as the large tree behind me swayed. I turned my lighted gaze toward it and froze. There she was, towering above me: Coedeno'boen, She Who Brings the Pain. Her trunk twisted, her branches raised high despite the hurricane-force winds.

The branches unfurled and rushed down at me. My golden light did nothing to stop her. I traced the runes again, felt the light strengthen, grow brighter, but the branches continued to tear toward the earth.

I raced across the yard and slipped in the leaves as Coedeno'boen's boughs crashed and beat the ground around me. Red, yellow, and brown leaves tumbled and rolled past me, against the wind, until they formed a pile at my splayed feet. The branches lifted from the ground, and I skittered backward as the leaves, the daughters, Mae'r Dail, opened a gaping foliage maw and lunged.

I stumbled to my feet and felt Mae'r Dail brush my legs, just missing me. Coedeno'boen twisted again, her furious eyes boring through me as she aimed. I sprinted across the yard and threw myself through the back door as the branches crashed to the earth, spraying soil, tearing against the back of the house.

I raced through the house, past the scrambling creatures in the dining room, past the roaring then silent fireplace in the sitting room, through the front door, and out into the front yard. Tiny leaves snapped at me, swirled around my body. My hair rose in tendrils as the wind whipped at me. The golden beams swatted the tiny leaves away as I staggered to the metal gate. The latch stuck. I kicked at the metal with my heavy, booted foot until the latch cracked, and the gate swung wide. I burst through the opening and tumbled face first into the street.

The chant abruptly cut off. Beams of sunlight shone down. My breath came in rapid puffs in the crisp winter air. I raised my bruised, cut face from the pavement. Neighbors paused and stared at me; my long, black coat in tatters, my eyes wide with fear, with knowledge, with insanity.

Now, machines beep and whine around me all day long. My dark hair is white. The doctors disabled my golden beams, but I don't care. All of our gadgets, trinkets, and talismans are useless against those who came before.

One day, when they let me out of this padded room, I'll return to the house, my house. The secret to banish She Who Brings the Pain must be in the basement library.

I'll find it.

I'll defeat her and her daughters.

Just as soon as the doctors let me go.

{}

Lizz-Ayn Shaarawi *is a Texan lost in the Oregon wilderness. She's a screenwriter and author whose short stories have been featured in numerous anthologies. Her screenplays have been recognized by The Austin Film Festival, The Nicholl Fellowship in Screenwriting, and The Page Awards. She enjoys cheap thrills, expensive shoes, and things that go bump in the night. You can find her random babblings on Twitter under her username @lizzayn.*

The Lark Ascending

Samantha Henderson

Denton explains: it starts a few billion years ago when the Earth swallows a moon or a planet or an asteroid. They know it was immense, and they know, a little bit, what it was made of. They know it happened because of the Earth's magnetic field or the aurora borealis or something. Denton tells me this in the darkness, his gun on my lap and the jeep's headlights stretching across the asphalt. You can drive a long way south in Texas. We drive until the sun pinks up the east. The gun is heavy in my lap, and it's hard to hear Denton over the music. But we can't shut it off.

"Denton," I ask. "How many people did I kill?"

○

Half a day back: three piano chords and the coil of a violin spiraling upward. The sound makes the speckled dark peel away. With that, pain. Burning in my shoulder, my temple. I breathe the music in and become myself, kneeling on the buff industrial tiles, straddling Charlene. She's staring at the ceiling with a worried expression. There's a red hole in her belly, and my hands are deep inside her. The violin soars like a bird. I drink it like wine. My hungry self quiets.

I pull my hands out of Charlene's fading warmth. My hands are thick with blood, and I feel spatters on my face. I follow Charlene's dead glance to the ceiling. Blood spatter there as well.

Charlene, the perfect dorm mother with her pudgy amiability. Her left hand's a fist, still holding clumps of my hair. Her right forefinger's flexed around the trigger of some snub-nosed something. I don't know anything about guns. My shoulder says she got at least one shot off. Jesus, the woman made me hot chocolate with milk and Hershey's last night to help me sleep. She's wearing khaki pants and a pink cardigan. What the hell is wrong with people.

A cold circle presses against my skull. From the corner of my eye, I see Denton standing there, pale but steady. He's holding an iPhone close to my ear. That's where the music is coming from. I recognize it: Vaughn Williams's "The Lark Ascending." Classical's not my favorite, but I always liked that one, the simplicity of it. The bird chortles, spinning up, down, usually up. I remember the poem. Chirrup, whistle, slur, shake.

Denton's voice is shaky, though his hands aren't. "I'm going to back away three steps. Stay down until I say, and then get up slowly. Very slowly."

I nod, staring down the corridor at the dorm-style bathroom the twelve girls shared. The door is propped open, and a pair of tanned legs stretches out from behind it. Sophia from UT Austin. Answered the same ad I did, along with Dylan and Mei. I knew Mei a little from Asian Student Association, though I didn't go past the first meeting.

I only met the others and the rest of the cadre from Texas Christian and A&M in the vans on the way here. Twenty-four of us in four industrial-looking white vans—each with a driver, silent and grim, each with a chaperone, bubbly and engaging, well supplied with treats and gum. We drove west past Toyah, desolate even for West Texas. The few brick buildings and the cemetery with its crooked stones and crosses were even sadder than the empty miles of saltbush. We drove through town, barely slowing down, ten, fifteen miles to a series of low grey buildings—six in a long rectangle, recently thrown up. Even at a distance, we could hear generators.

Charlene was in my van. She gave me Bubble Yum. The drivers were probably military and armed. But Charlene shot me.

Denton moves back, still pointing the gun at my head, still holding the phone like he's about to throw a treat to a pit bull. My legs are cramped, and it's hard to get up; I leave red handprints on the tile. The corridor's lined with doors, six to a side. Seven are shut, each with a name in plump letters cut out of pink construction paper. Mei, Sophia, Lou, Vanessa, Dharma, Sami, me. The other doors yawn wide, only black inside.

Such a Charlene thing to do, those letters. Like the hot chocolate.

I didn't drink the hot chocolate. It had a weird metal taste. One sip and my mouth still tastes funky.

Denton gestures at the bathroom with the phone. The music quavers, and my vision sparks. He thrusts the phone forward, so I can grab onto that melody. I step over Charlene's legs, and he follows me up the hallway. The door's open enough that I can avoid Sophia's legs and the rest of her. A thin shell of bone is all that's left of her head. Brain matter is splattered thick against the porcelain wall. I wonder if Charlene did that.

I foul the handles turning on the water. It takes a while to scrape off blood. I look in the mirror once. There are dark smears around my mouth. My left sleeve is soaked red, but I think it's just a graze.

Even over the water, I can hear Vaughn Williams's lark jubilating and a sharp scream from the boys' dorm that cuts off fast.

Last night was lockdown. Just a precaution, Charlene said. They said there was a prison break and escapees maybe headed for Toyah, and even though it was beyond unlikely they'd get anywhere near the compound, we weren't allowed outside. Seemed lame even then. Vanessa had snuck in her cell phone in the bottom of her bag—fuck control parameters—and was texting Dylan. The boys were on lockdown too, she said, but Cliff, the hunk from TCM, wasn't in their dorm.

"Are you going to kill me?" I ask Denton, trying to clean beneath my fingernails. Not just blood there. Something fibrous. I watch him in the mirror.

He glances behind us, down the hall, before turning back to me. The lark is silent now, and the last piano chord is fading, but before the void can open, the fast monotonous pulse of house music beats it back. There's a question in his eyes, and I nod in response.

Carefully, he lays the iPhone face up on the broad edge of the sink. "If the music shuts off, I will be back in an instant, and yes, I will kill you. Do you believe me?"

"Yes."

He withdraws, and I pull my hands from the water, letting a pink swirl run down the drain. I unbutton my shirt and pull it away from the raw patch on my shoulder. I try to clean the shallow wound. The house beat pounds in my head. It's not my kind of music, but it's working: the thump of the synthesized drum, a brassy kick punctuating each phrase takes what's boiling in my brain and corrals it.

Denton's back with a shirt, a handful of gauze, a brown bottle of hydrogen peroxide. I see him considering his chances before tucking the gun in his waistband. He circles behind me and dabs peroxide on the graze. It foams white and tingles, and it stings when he wipes it with the gauze. He hands me the shirt and steps away, pulling out the gun. He holds it loosely, pointed at the floor. I pull on the shirt. Too big: a man's shirt. I button it up and roll the sleeves past my wrists.

I pick up the iPhone and its relentless beat and follow Denton down the hall, past Charlene. There's a backpack leaning against the back wall; he scoops it up as he passes. Switching the gun to his left hand, he shoulders open the door and gropes in his pocket for a ring of keys.

"One chance," he mutters. "We've got one chance. Keep the music on."

The humidity outside is like pushing through a big warm sponge. I hold the iPhone to my ear. In the thick wet air, a smell like burning oil. Two of the white vans sit pristine. One is on its side, the wheels still spinning. The fourth is upright but the top is cratered in. It reminds me of Sophia's skull. A fat coil of black smoke rises from behind the boy's dorm, spinning lazy into the sky like a tornado.

There's a jeep, also right side up. Denton takes my wrist and pulls me toward it. We're halfway there when the screaming from the boy's dorm begins again. Nothing human. Nothing animal. The clang of it clashes with the beat of the music. I fight to hold onto myself and not follow the spinning void (glorious, cosmic, bursting out of my skin). Denton shoves me inside the jeep, throwing the backpack into my lap. He sits in the driver's seat—gun in one hand, keys in the other—mutters "fuckit," and hands me the gun. I dangle it by the butt and lay it carefully on top of the backpack. Denton squeals away from the compound, staring into the rear-view mirror. I look over my shoulder. No one's there.

The jeep skids on loose rock around the curve back to Toyah. This close to Denton, I can see that he has coarse pores in a sunbaked face and black stubble from his chin to his sideburns. Maybe late forties, early fifties. We didn't see him much—just in the cafeteria and sometimes in the lab. Now, I see a spatter of reddish dots along his jaw, turning brown as they dry.

He pulls over past Toyah and its desolate brick buildings. I stay in the car. He's left the engine running. In the shallow, stony ditch by the side of the road, he kneels and retches over and over. I don't hear anything over the music. After a while, he dusts off his knees and gets back in the driver's seat, like he did nothing but stop to take a piss.

We drive until twilight, stop to get gas at a station where a road intersects the highway and loops endlessly back on itself into the brown hills. The blue-red light from the Chevron sign makes an isolated pool in the gathering dark. I stay in the jeep while Denton fills it. Then, he vanishes into the tiny mart for so long I think he's ditched me. But he returns with lukewarm water bottles and some melty Snickers bars and a bagful of those little energy drink blasts that look like vodka bottles. He asks me if I need to pee. I don't, and we drive on into the dusk.

"You got Charlene," he says at last, impassive. "And maybe Lou. That wasn't Charlene's kill. Her face was . . ." He glances at me sideways, adjusts for the curves in the road.

I cover the earbuds with both hands, and a flute echoes inside my head. If I listen very hard, I can hear something in the center of my head answering.

"They told us the animals attacked the ones that didn't change. Like they were culling them out. So maybe you did. But Charlene got the rest. She was a pro."

The night deepens, and stars spring out of hiding. They made the music in my head change a little. "So why am I alive?"

He only shakes his head.

"You're supposed to kill me, right? Charlene tried to kill me."

"I'm tired of killing. You were the only one left besides some of the boys, and Alexis and Seeger were finishing them off. I knew they wouldn't listen. I thought, if the music could control you, it might be worth it to save one. To study you instead of dissecting you. But mostly—I'm so tired of killing things. Small things. Big things. So full of blood."

I've never heard him string so many words together, and now, I hear the accent: something a little off about the vowels and the ends of words. He's older than I thought.

I hold my breath as a spot of light in the distance splits into two headlights coming closer. Out here, you can see for infinity, so it takes a long time for the car to pass us. It never stops growing bigger and brighter. I wait for it to pull across the freeway and wonder what Denton would do. So close, the lamps like muted stars burning through raw optic nerves, so I shut my eyes tight as they zoom by. I expect them to explode into Chevron blue and red, the siren to scream through my music, but nothing happens. Denton lets out a long breath.

"Are the police looking for us?"

"Police? No. By now the compound's sanitized. Nothing's left but us, and they won't want anyone to find us. They'll take care of it themselves."

"Who are 'they'?"

He shakes his head.

"Black ops? Secret government? CIA? Illuminati?" I'm not going to ask about the summer job—the study on the effects of a low-strength magnetic field on memory, two thousand and room and board for three weeks, and we could call it an internship—because that was a lie so magnificent it's gone past outrage, past even complaining about.

"'Black ops?' Jesus." He laughs. It's a surprisingly nice laugh and stops too quickly.

So that's when he tells me about Earth swallowing up *another* planet and how it's now pushing its way out of the core. Forcing up to the surface, pushing sulfur in front of it.

"That's why we're in Toyah and excavating in Sulfur Springs. There's a site in Australia, too. It's like the sulfur deposit's a scab and this . . . substance, this something swallowed three or four or even, hell, five billion years ago is the matter that's behind it. The matter in Australia and the matter in Texas have the same chemical signature. Which means it might be part of the same mass. And moving. Hatching out of the planet. And who knows how long that's been happening. Nobody would've noticed except for the animals."

"Animals?"

"Rancher out past Toyah liked to shoot jackrabbits in the afternoon. Only lately, the jackrabbits wouldn't be shot. They knew where the bullet was coming from and moved aside. Or if they were hit, it didn't affect them much."

I snort. "He missed. Drunk."

"He was drunk a lot at the end. But he said he didn't miss. He was accustomed to shooting three, four of those jacks most evenings. Used a big enough gauge so they'd explode, just a quick red spray and they're gone. Bang two, three, just like that. And then there was the damage to his cattle. He'd find them out there exsanguinated. Totally bloodless. And burrowed through—actually tunneled. More and more reports like that, where the sulfur deposits are. Too similar."

"I didn't see any cattle where we were."

"No. All gone."

"Sanitized?" Like the rancher who was drunk a lot at the end?

He doesn't answer.

It's afternoon by the time we reach the enclave, red dust in the air making the sun swollen and crimson. It squats in the west like a wound in the sky, the thick air trembling around it. I shield my eyes and stare at it, Lonestar's "Walking in Memphis" humming in my ears, sore from the earbuds. I don't know how far south we are, but it can't be far from the border. Denton turns off the main road and bumps over gravel and fine dust for five or six miles before we come to a fence, thick timbers and barb wire, that stretches far as I can see. A gate blocks the dirt road, and three figures stand waiting for us. How Denton told them we were coming I don't know. He parks and motions for me to get out.

"Leave the gun," he says.

I secure the earbuds before I move. "The battery is not going to last much longer," I tell him.

He bites his lip. "We'll find a way to charge it."

Two men and a woman stand at the gate. The woman's sun-bleached hair is French-braided back, leaving her tanned face exposed to the bullet-hole sun. Probably in her thirties, in jeans and a pink, button-down shirt that might be left over from a corporate life. She holds a shotgun cradled casually across her elbows, finger very close to the trigger. The younger man has that white towhead hair that kids usually grow out of and a smooth face with bright red patches on both cheeks. He wears a short-sleeved tee with a stylized red, white, and blue squiggle across it, and the skin of his arms is as red as his cheeks. At his crotch, in front of a huge oval brass buckle, he holds a Glock or Colt or something. He stares past Denton at me, watery blue eyes narrowing.

The other, older man is clearly in charge. He has no weapon, only the utter confidence of place, of rootedness. He has a face the woman will have in another decade; the sun's baked deep wrinkles across his forehead and at the corners of his eyes, the sides of his mouth. He has a Caterpillar tractor cap, dusty green with close-trimmed hair beneath. Probably his forehead is fish-belly white under the hat.

Caterpillar cap pushes the gate open with booted foot. Denton walks inside, and I follow.

"No one wants you here," he begins without preamble, not caring that I can hear. "They say this Chink girl and you are moles, and it's too near these troop deployments for comfort."

"You're in charge here," says Denton. "What do you think?"

"Me? I know you're a crappy spy and got as much to do with Jade Helm as Walmart. But I don't want you here either."

"They experimented on her. They're going to kill her. Killed a lot of kids last night."

"And you helped."

Denton shrugs.

"She's not one of ours," says the younger man. "Why would we want one of your monsters?"

"Shut up, Billy," says the woman. He looks at her and scowls, but he does shut up.

Denton kicks at the dry ground, raising a tiny dust cloud. We watch it drift away.

"You owe me."

The older man barks once, loud, just like a big dog. I'm startled until I realize he laughed.

"I know, I know," says Denton. "Still."

"You're calling that catastrophe in? For this thing?" He flicks his thumb at me. Denton nods, the barest movement of his head.

"Gods. 'You owe me,' like a bad movie. I should have Billy run you out right now, 'cept you'd probably kill him."

Billy shifts forward, hand tightening on his gun. Denton gives him a considering look. "Maybe. She definitely will."

The boy's blue stare is chilly in the hot sun.

○

They take us to some cabins higher up, where the foothills start. Mine has six bunks installed along one wall. No one else is here. There's electricity; Denton has a charger stowed in the backpack, and I sit cross-legged on the floor, connected by earbuds to iPhone to circuit to whatever means they have of powering this place.

In the twilight, Denton builds a fire inside a ring of smooth rocks. The dried brush he uses smells medicinal, and the flame is pale. We sit on a plastic tarp, and he lays out a towel. A scalpel and a bigger knife, the blade made for hunting or skinning maybe. Neat squares of gauze. A bottle of peroxide. I wait until he's finished before I take out the right earbud. The thump of "Walking in Memphis" purrs in my left ear.

"The animals," he says. "Groundhogs that couldn't be shot, carnivorous rabbits, coyotes that can outpace a Hummer. Those we could bring down had this ancient matter, this planetary substance, crystallized in their bones. Swimming in their blood. It made them stronger, faster. Almost indestructible."

"Killers."

"That too. When you find that contamination by some substance doesn't result in sickness or deformation but enhances the subject, makes it stronger . . ."

"You experiment."

He pokes at the scalpel. Folding his hands in his lap, he looks at me directly. It's the closest to an apology I'm going to get.

"You've got implants—more like seeds, really, charged with the matter and inserted along your spine."

"When did they do that?"

"Remember the shots? Flu shot, MMR?"

"Yes, but . . ."

"You fainted."

"How did you . . ."

"You all fainted. But not really."

I look at the fire while he lets me think about it.

"People get embarrassed about fainting. Maybe not all the girls, but the guys definitely. With luck, some of you didn't even remember. That's when. And along the spine—you might be a little sore, but you might notice a funny lump in your forearm. Same principle with the animals, the chimps. They couldn't chew them out."

He holds up two fingers close together. "Same idea as radiation treatments through implants or a stick of Depo-Provera in your arm. Slow, constant dosage."

"The music," I say quickly before he can go on. "Why does the music keep me myself?"

"I don't know. It worked with the chimps. It was a guess. Maybe . . ." Another of his shrugs. "I don't know."

He picks up the scalpel and has me hunch a bit, so the implants pop up against the skin. It doesn't even hurt when he cuts them out. I can feel the blade slice, feel him dig around in my meat for the tiny plastic sliver. A thing like pain but not. The void in my brain takes it and makes it something else, weaves it into its own music. That's when I know it's not going to work. It's already deep in my system, my bones. My stars. But you have to try anyway sometimes.

The sad trickle of sound though the headphones isn't suppressing anything, only distracting it for a time. Something that sang to itself in its place beyond the edge of the galaxy before it orbited inward, caught by the gravity of the forming planets. I've heard recordings of the sound space makes, of Jupiter moaning in the void, like a lonely whale.

Denton deposits three tiny grey slivers into my palm. I throw them far out into the gathering dark.

Probably, they buried GPS in me, and Denton didn't know. Or the jeep had a tracker. Or they just knew where he'd take me.

They hit us fast at dawn and don't bother with prisoners. I make it out of my bunk and out of the cabin in time to see a small figure in the distance, Billy probably, run away from a small green figure. Small green aims something, and the runner's head starbursts red, though his legs keep pumping for a few seconds. More green figures swarm across the red dirt like ants.

Denton's sprawled at my feet outside the cabin door, face down. He doesn't move.

Small popping sounds bounce 'round my free ear. My thigh feels hot, and I look down. My flesh is cratered open, dark and wet. It reminds me of Charlene's belly, and I have a brief desire to plunge my hands in. I feel heat. No pain.

Another legshot to the opposite knee, and I go down. They must be trying to take me alive. Idiots. My head slams into the rocky ground, and the music stops for a fraction of a second. In that instant, day becomes star-bordered night. Then, the sharp notes of the violin, and back to day and light and burning.

I crawl across the ground, a thin trickle of music still pouring through the broken earbud in my left ear. There's something soft, still warm in front of me.

Half-blind, I reach for it and pull. It flops over like a badly packed duffle. Wet all over my hands, and Denton's sightless eyes looking up at the sky.

Something seizes my hair and wrenches my head back. One of the green men. He goes on one knee beside me, keeping a hold on my hair. The earbud falls, the tinny sound of the violin gone. I blink, look at his eyes. Hazel. Expressionless. Blink, look at Denton's body. Blink, look straight at the sun. There is no music; the music is gone.

And then, all the music in the world.

He holds my hair so tight it starts to rip out of my head. A knee presses into my back, bending me double. I don't care. I'm looking at the sun, and it is a red bloody hole in the sky. It always was. They're crawling out of it now, all my brothers, all my beautiful sisters in their glory.

The moon is a dead rock in the sky. All its songs are lies. Let those who love her perish on her unfeeling breast. The sun is a sphere of boiling larvae, and they sing. It's the sun Jupiter moans for in his solitude. My face bursts open, a ruin. Renewed, my true face emerges, and I turn it to the green man. His eyes go wide and glassy as my tendrils reach for him and burrow into his skin. I will find the music inside him, the fragment of the sun he hides inside, and liberate it, a small brother-larvae that longs to join the rest of them boiling in the star overhead.

I will free all of them, and we will sing, soaring higher and higher, chirrup, whistle, slur, shake. Larks.

{}

Samantha Henderson *lives in Southern California with humans and other animals. Her short fiction and poetry have been published in* Realms of Fantasy, The Lovecraft eZine, Strange Horizons, Goblin Fruit *and* Weird Tales, *and reprinted in* The Year's Best Fantasy and Science Fiction, Steampunk Revolutions, *and* The Mammoth Book of Steampunk. *She's the author of the* Forgotten Realms *novels* Heaven's Bones *and* Dawnbringer.

Astral and Arcane Science

SJ Leary

Take the ground streets until you're out of downtown, it's faster than the freeway. Exit when you can see the smoke rising from the factories in the Southside. Take the first right onto Van Buren Street, where that diner used to be before those meth heads burned it down, and go to the end of the street. From there you take the first left at the stop light and drive until you hit the cul-de-sac. On the left side of that cul-de-sac is an empty lot where a cute little house used to stand and on the right is a white warehouse. That, my friends, is the location of the most remote of Andyne Ltd.'s research and development facilities.

It's fine if you don't know the name Andyne. They actively seek a low profile, according to what I've read. They're one of those "artificial self-improvement" corporations. You know, the ones that twist your genes into a new shape for a few bucks. They made that treatment that gives you six pack abs; the only problem was, it also gave all of your progeny a third foot. I heard some Andyne rep in the know say that, "It makes your DNA strands look less like a double-helix and more like frayed rope." Yet, even though Andyne never made anything that made you a better person or didn't shred your genetic code, their building still stands. The Andyne Ltd. sign has been torn down and it's filled with military police day and night.

It's still there though, haunting the city for any curious person to investigate. You won't be able to see much if you do come for a visit. Just a fence, some men in black uniforms, and me with my fingers wrapped around that fence and my eyes glazed in reminiscence.

The first time I went to that building was for business back when I was something of a P.I. for corporations. We were a fairly common breed, the industrial private eye, in the early years of the "artificial self-improvement" craze. Back when the corporations were little better than mobsters, covetously guarding the secrets of the universe. Back when scientists and millionaires teamed up to unravel God's mysteries and tickle the dragon's tail. Yeah, back then there were a lot of strange things happening, to put it mildly. Scientists found dead in the laboratory after a freak accident, CEOs leaving suicide notes in someone else's handwriting, entire boardrooms disappearing without a trace. Playing God is a dangerous game. Whether it's one or one thousand, God still doesn't like competition. So whenever something needed tracking down or talking to or clearing up in the name of capitalist dominance, I'd get a phone call. It was pretty often in those days.

My partner Alice and I were hired by some minion in the Andyne hierarchy to investigate this particular R&D building. The scoop was that the head researcher, a Dr. Bird, was currently AWOL, in a sense. He had stopped sending in progress reports or at all interacting with Andyne since a big earthquake a few weeks prior. However, Andyne knew he was in the R&D building because the whole place would go into lockdown anytime their staff tried to make ingress.

"You pay the bills, don't you?" asked Alice. "Why don't you just shut down power to the building?"

The minion sighed and scratched the back of his fat neck.

"We think Dr. Bird is behaving this way because he's discovered something noteworthy and is either planning to sell it to one of our competitors or hold it for ransom. We need you to see if this is the case before we do anything that might damage potentially valuable findings."

I lit a cigarette and stared the minion down. The first leap in transhumanist technology occurred years ago after a similar earthquake. The first quake triggered prophetic dreams in a group of scientists, concerning the improvement of the human body through, and I quote, "astral and arcane science." Whatever they did, it worked. Ever since, I had found that the science types were a little less in touch with reality and a little more touched after notable tectonic movements. We took the job and reasoned that we'd pop in and find Dr. Bird wearing a tinfoil hat and shrieking about earthquakes before we sent him off to the funny farm without incident.

The next day Alice and I went to investigate the building. When you hear about research facilities, you naturally imagine ultra-modern structures, all glass and steel, immense ziggurats to human ingenuity. I was disappointed to find an unremarkable square, windowless building. Alice and I walked the perimeter, looking for exits, security personnel, or anything out of the ordinary, but we found nothing. I opened my mouth to comment on the eerie desolation when a train came by, drowning out my words.

Alice read my lips and shrugged.

"What now?" asked Alice.

"Let's question the neighbors, first," I said.

"What?"

I started walking to the domicile with Alice in tow.

She complained, "I hate canvassing the neighbors. No one's ever happy. This whole case is probably just the overactive imagination of some Andyne exec. Why drag it out?"

"Just call it a hunch. Besides, we hardly ever get to do anything 'film noir.'"

"That's because if Humphrey Bogart goes through your garbage or questions the neighbors, well, he's just being rugged. People were practically begging Bogey to question them in *The Big Sleep* because they'd get some whiskey and a quick fuck, but I bet if we do that routine there's a call to the police and a trip downtown. See if it doesn't happen."

"You're just being paranoid."

We walked up to the house across the cul-de-sac and knocked on the door. A middle-aged woman opened it and stood in the threshold. She wore a nightgown and slippers, and her hair was in a mess. She looked more tired than the night watchman coming off his shift.

"I told you he's dead," she said. "Leave me alone, you fucking vultures."

"Ma'am?" I said.

"He killed himself, yeah the rumors are true. He killed himself after the earthquake. Just fuck off."

"Ma'am? I don't know what you're talking about."

"Aren't you journalists?"

"No, ma'am."

She stared at us in a daze for several moments.

"Well, what do you want?"

"Well, we're looking into an incident at the research facility next door—"

"Oh, that fucking place. All hours of the night, there's noises, whirring and clunking and unbearable noises. I can't sleep anymore, goddammit. Someone should shut those places down. It's a disgrace what they're selling. Goes against God and nature. And you won't believe this. That Doctor Boyd over there came over asking for the body. Disgraceful! I slammed the door in his face."

"Excuse me, can you repeat that?"

The woman looked pensive for a moment.

"That doctor, Doctor *B*-something. He came asking for the body for God knows what."

"Whose body?"

"My son's. Right after . . . right after he passed."

"Did the doctor know your son?"

"No, not at all. I bet he's some pervert though."

"When did this happen exactly?"

"The night after the suicide, days after that recent earthquake. Ever since that damned quake everything's been upside down. The lab has been going at all hours, and my poor son . . . he was an artist, a good one too. That's why all those journalists have been coming. He could've been famous one day."

Neither Alice nor I said anything. We just looked at our shoes in an imitation of solemnity.

"After the earthquake, he was just so depressed, said he couldn't sleep because of the nightmares. Visions of terrible creatures, he said, and then two of his friends killed themselves and now . . . I hear there's a rash of suicides right now. I guess he'll just be a statistic." Tears began to well up in her eyes. "Excuse me." She closed the door, and I heard her lock it.

Alice and I turned and headed back to the lab.

"What do you think is going on in there?" asked Alice.

"God knows, but if Bird's disturbing widows for dead bodies, well, it's something that demands a follow up. I wonder what this kid's art looked like anyway," I said.

Alice suddenly halted. "I think I can answer that."

I turned the direction she was facing and saw a mural covering the side of the house. "How did we miss that?"

The mural depicted a legion of massive four-legged invertebrates marching under two blue suns. Their features were indistinct, impressionistic, as though hastily drawn. Their foreign limbs seemed to bend together into one mass of limping, fetid monsters. I stared at it and felt the awe of genius descend upon me before it was replaced by the revulsion of horror. There was something immediate and frighteningly human about those damnable creatures marching under the dual suns. Something heartbreakingly intimate in their cold eyes, like they were gazing into the void of my mind. Alice finally broke away. She rubbed her temples and said, "Fuck, looking at that is giving me a headache. Let's get in there and get this over with."

The inside of the building was just as unremarkable as the outside. Linoleum tiles and florescent lights. We walked over to the bored receptionist and waited. Normally, we field a few preliminary questions like, "Who are you and what are you doing here?" but this receptionist waved us through

"The door to the left is for the locker room, the one to the right is the lab," she said. Alice winked back at her as we walked past the heavy double doors and into the lab. It was sterile white, like a hospital room, and littered with unmanned work stations. I thought the room was populated solely by beakers and flasks until a young man in a white lab coat approached us. The pale boy was perfectly camouflaged for his environment.

"Excuse me," he said.

Alice gave an involuntary squeak before turning around.

"Oh Christ, you frightened me," said Alice, placing a hand on her chest. "I thought you were a ghost or something."

The researcher didn't seem amused. His face was plastered in a tiny scowl

"How did you get in here? You're looking for Dr. Bird, aren't you?" he said.

I gave Alice a glance; she nodded. I always trusted Alice's intuition. Time to show our hand.

"Yes, sir," I said. "We're just checking in on the good doctor, seeing what he's up to, how he's getting along. You wouldn't happen to know where he is, would you?"

"He may be unorthodox, but he's the best damned scientist on Andyne's payroll. You tell your bosses that. We're all one hundred percent behind the man, and there's no way you can take him from here."

"Easy, pal," said Alice. "Like my friend said, we're just here to see how he's doing. We heard he's been acting a bit funny toward the kind folks at Andyne, lately, and we just want to make sure he's alright."

"I think you had better leave."

"We can't leave before we see the doctor," I reiterated.

"It's a disgrace that you two, you mercenary types, would just drop in unannounced. We have highly sensitive experiments to conduct without having to worry about interlopers stomping about."

"That's enough, Dr. Cooper."

We all turned to stare at the gaunt researcher who stood beside the door to another part of the lab.

"Get back to your work and stop harassing these people."

The young man looked down at his shoes in shame. For a second, it looked like he was going to cry, but he just turned around and strode out of the room.

"Terribly sorry about that. These young kids get out of grad school and think they know a thing or two. I'm Dr. Bird." The researcher extended a bony hand that Alice and I limply shook in turn. "What seems to be the problem?"

"The boys from Andyne management hired us to check in on you," I said.

Dr. Bird smiled genially and laughed deeply. He looked quite healthy, clean shaven, and well fed—not at all like the sensitive personality I had imagined.

"Finally!" he said. "Finally, they send me someone who isn't just an Andyne crony. An outsider, finally. This is wonderful. No time to lose, follow me. I'll explain as we go." Bird turned on his heel and began walking through the building.

With a shrug and some apprehension, we followed Bird through a series of rooms filled with anxious scientists. Each researcher gave Bird a small sign of reverence as he passed, a bow or a salute, as he took us farther and farther away from the entrance.

"Let me start by saying that I've been up to the most important work of my life. The things I've uncovered may change the face of human society forever." The doctor stopped and inspected a dense fluid in a beaker. He grabbed a nearby assistant and said, "Keep an eye on this one. Don't touch it, though. These things practically run themselves these days." He began walking again as if he never stopped. "Anyway, this work of mine, though important, is incredibly . . . well, Cooper called it unorthodox just now, and I think that's an apt description. If anyone within Andyne discovered what we were up to, they'd shut us down, seal the files, and lock us up. They have the power to do it. I've seen it.

"So I've been waiting for them to send you independent investigator types. I can reason with you, show you my way of thinking, get you on my side. You're not company brainwashed just yet."

Eventually, we reached an old freight elevator that took us slowly down to the basement.

"I just didn't expect it would happen so soon," muttered Dr. Bird. I looked to Alice. She looked nervous and began fingering her holstered gun. I felt it, too—an indescribably heavy aura of anxiety and loss that grew with each meter the elevator descended.

The elevator opened to a dark, damp room. "Goddammit," said Bird, "let me find that light switch." Bird took two steps forward and disappeared into the darkness. "Let me explain while I do this," Bird's voice echoed in the room. "I've spent years making stimulants and genetic therapies and artificial what-have-you, spent my whole life trying to improve the human body. Humanity's a funny thing. Why are our bodies so imperfect? Why do outside agents, medications, improve us so much? Why isn't that innate?" We could hear him shuffling in the dark. "Any guesses?"

"Because of evolution?" asked Alice carefully.

"To put it broad terms, yes. We are inherently flawed, poorly constructed. I realized that twisting DNA strands and augmenting bodies can only do so much if the blueprint is faulty. You can't build the Taj Mahal if the foundation rests on top of sand, as it were. So instead of wasting my time contending with human frailty, improving something that even at its apex is still disappointing, why not move humanity forward? Do something meaningful. I've unfortunately been— here it is."

A loud *thunk* resonated through the basement as the overhead lights sprang to life, revealing a fairly small and mostly empty room, half of which was cordoned off by a series of metal bars, like one would find in a prison. "I've unfortunately been incapable of discerning how to progress, but then, it hit me."

"During the earthquake?" I hazard to guess.

"Yes! I had begun to think about human frailty after that first great quake, but each night since the second quake, I've been visited by a species of creatures that call themselves Mi-go. Yes, I see that look on your face, but you must trust me here. Many of my colleagues have encountered these Mi-go as well. Fascinating fungal beings of superior intelligence—superior in every way in fact. Each night, they visit, and we discuss well . . . science, metaphysics, astronomy, all manner of things. And in every discussion, they have proven themselves to be definitively beyond human reasoning. They have convinced me that they are a superior being, and as such, I am copying their form. As a gift, the Mi-go gave me a DNA sample. Fascinating, impossibly complex. I have since been working to improve humanity, to construct man in their image.

"I've reworked their DNA sample into something similar to one of the gene-altering tablets we currently produce and have begun testing it. It's only been used on cadavers so far. Safety is my top priority, you see. Specifically, I've tested on the bodies of sensitive artists as they too appear to have been touched. Have you seen that mural across the street? That's the Mi-go! Plain as day! That mural drove me mad with its beauty, and I leapt with joy when I heard that the boy passed . . . but I can see that you're still skeptical. I admit, it's a lot to process, but I suppose, it must be seen to be believed. Would you like to bear witness to the greatest leap forward in human history?"

I nodded. Alice kept a hand close to her gun.

Bird walked over to the metal bars, pulled a key from his pocket, and unlocked the door. "Come forth," he said and out of the darkness emerged a vile crustacean-like thing. It walked upright like a human, but most of its body was covered with a thick yellow carapace, and it had cumbersome claws that clutched an ornate scroll. Patches of bare—human—skin still showed through, as did tiny hairs, but once you saw the face you could hardly call it human anymore. There was no mouth as far as I could tell. In its place were a series of tiny grasping pincers and two slits, which I assume constituted its nose. On top of the creature's head were two eyes on stalks that rotated 360 degrees before settling on me. I stared into those dead eyes as they blinked, one at a time, and felt as though I was less human simply for acknowledging the thing's existence. I felt those eyes peering into me just as the eyes in the mural had earlier.

"It's the artist boy," said Bird. "I've not only reanimated him but made him better."

"You said you've been in communication with other scientists," I said. "Who are they? Tell us now."

"Too many to number," said Bird with his standard smile. "Apart from all the researchers here, who are fully committed to the experiment, there are men and women all over the world who have felt the call to human improvement. Many have been touched by the Mi-go, but some even speak of entities whose names I scarcely know how to pronounce. This is an exciting time to be alive. We're witnessing our own obsolescence."

My mind ached under the burgeoning air of dread and anxiety. When I stared into that ghastly creature, these feelings increased ten-fold. It felt as though those hideous eyes were peeling apart my brain. I turned away and looked at Alice. She now had her gun out.

"This is fucked up, Doctor. This is fucked up," she said

"Put that thing away. You can't stand in the way of progress!" said Bird.

Alice's hands shook violently. Tears streamed down her face.

"Shooting me would accomplish nothing. These experiments practically run themselves. Look here." Dr. Bird grabbed the scroll from the monster and unfurled it. It contained an arcane script with what looked like Arabic annotations. "A gift from my friends abroad, written by their greatest medieval mystics. Don't you see? The astral entities have been imparting their knowledge on humanity for centuries. Mi-go DNA, the scientific advances following the first earthquake, and these seals: it's all their handiwork. With these mystic seals, the work can go on without the aid of human hands. One simply needs to recite the incantation. Come now, you can't deny progress."

"I can already feel that fucking thing inside me," Alice screamed before shooting Bird in the head.

The scroll clattered to the floor, stained with blood, as the doctor fell at his creation's feet. The thing prodded Bird with its claw and let out a deep groan. It turned to Alice and stared, almost mournfully. The atmosphere changed once more.

I felt indescribably heavy and depressed, even more than before. The room shrank into a black void of only Alice, the creature, and me. I turned to Alice to know if she still existed. She placed the gun to her head. Her finger danced on the trigger.

I wanted to shout to her but found my voice was gone.

"Why this?" I could hear the creature's voice in my head. "Why this?"

My arms felt like they were made of lead.

"This isn't what I wanted," the voice said.

I could hear Alice sobbing. It was the only thing that tied me to reality as I began to hallucinate. I saw the Mi-go in hitherto unknown cities of absurd and incomprehensible geometry and ruled by terrifying leviathan masters. I felt myself becoming one with the creatures. That horror of acknowledgment, of witnessing the smallest humanity within this monster frightened me the most. I couldn't allow this creature to whittle away at my psyche or, worse, make its existence comprehensible. It had to be destroyed. With great effort, I grabbed my gun, swung my arm around, having lost fine motor control, and shot three bullets randomly. One kind ricochet hit the creature in the eye, breaking the spell.

Alice fell to the floor as the creature screamed in anguish. I hit the elevator button, and we rose to the surface, the sound of the monster's shrieks following us up.

I drove Alice to the hospital that night. The doctors said she was physically fine but had suffered some great mental trauma. They said they could fix her mind with an Andyne gene splicing treatment. I told them to go to hell.

To this day, she sits in an institution, screaming her lungs out day and night. I told the Andyne heads what had happened, and the next day, the facility was crawling with military personnel. All the records are classified—I've checked. There's no way to know what was true and what I just imagined. Most days, I think that I'm going crazy too and that I'll soon be sharing a cell with Alice, but every once in a while, I see snatches of it in the paper.

"Laboratory Explosion, No Survivors."

"Famed Scientist Checks into Mental Hospital."

"Genetic Alteration Drug Recalled for Unknown Purpose."

Now, when I roam the city streets, I see these transhumanist companies strangling the humanity out of us. One of these days, I'm going to be the last human left alive on a Mi-go colony. Whatever's tormenting humanity isn't done. Not by a long shot.

{}

When **SJ Leary** isn't writing or engaging in some incredibly depressive episode, he spends his free time either haunting the doorways of dear friends or burying acorns in preparation for the coming winter. He finds both writing and acorn burial to be difficult work, though necessary to ensure he has enough to eat when his student loan repayments begin, while he finds self-deprecation and wearing out his welcome to be merely great sport. Comrades and licensed care professionals have describe Mr. Leary as either "The most pretentious person I have ever met," "Incredibly punctual, almost violently so," and "Really not so bad, once you get used to him."

Advanced Placement

Richard Lee Byers

L isa Clarke liked teaching Advanced Placement. When she was *really* teaching, it was fun; when she was drilling the kids in preparation for one of the several state-mandated standardized tests, it was easy at least. Her students were bright enough that several hands usually shot up with the right answer, and then, it was on to the next item.

But a moment came when no hands went up. The new question on the pull-down screen in front of the chalkboard stumped everybody. It read, *Sound is to air as vision is to _____.*

Sitting up front with her frizzy black hair and braces, Nikhila asked. "What's the answer, Ms. Clarke?"

Light, Lisa surmised, but to her private amusement, she wasn't sure, either. Fortunately, teachers received the electronic version of a cheat sheet.

"Let's take a look." She touched a button on her tablet screen to display the solution.

Sound is to air as vision is to <u>taint</u>.

"Taint," snickered Jamal, wearing the Orlando Magic jacket he sported constantly, indoors and out, no matter how hot the Florida sun became. Some of the others laughed.

Always serious about schoolwork, Nikhila shot him a scowl and returned her attention to Lisa. "I don't understand."

"That's because it doesn't make sense," Lisa said. "It's gotten garbled somehow. Which just goes to show what I'm always telling you guys. You have to proofread, and when autocorrect makes a change, you have to double check it."

After the lunch bell rang, she filled out an online form to report the glitch, though it was a little annoying that she had to. The test developer who'd let the mistake slip through probably made more money than she did.

When class resumed, the practice exercises turned to biology. The screen in the front of the room displayed plants and animals, and the kids had to pick the proper classification from the four presented. The pine was a conifer tree, and the toad was an amphibian.

Then the *National Geographic*-style photos gave way to something murkier. Nikhila screwed up her face in disgust, and Jamal exclaimed, "Gross!"

The creature certainly was: spiny tentacles surrounding its maw and a ring of glistening black eyes above. What looked like a second slobbering gash of a mouth opened in the center of its body, stalks like rotting tulips stuck up from its back, and spindly, many-jointed legs zigzagged down to the ground. There appeared to be five legs on one side and three on the other.

"What *is* that?" Nikhila asked.

"Look at the choices," Lisa said. When she did that herself, she found *Fungus, Reptile, Insect,* and *Synthetic.*

"Insect!" several children chorused, and clearly, they were correct. Lisa had never seen a creature like this before, but some insect species were notably grotesque, and the other choices were impossible.

Still, when she clicked on *Insect*, the program told her, *Good guess, but no. Please try again!*

Well, then, *Reptile*. It was the only other animal choice. But that wasn't right, either. Nor was *Fungus.*

Synthetic was the only option left. She clicked, and the screen declared her *Correct!*

"But it's not," she said. "It's another mistake. A living creature can't be synthetic."

Nikhila raised her hand.

"Yes?"

"What is it, really?" asked the dark-haired girl.

"An insect, just like you all thought."

"What kind?"

"Honestly, I'm not sure. With some research, we could figure it out, but for now, let's move on."

At the end of the day, Lisa reached Doug Baker's office just as two boys were trudging out. Judging from their hangdog expressions, the pudgy, round-faced principal had just given them a scolding.

With justice done, Doug was fishing a diet ginger ale out of his mini-fridge. When he spotted Lisa, he brought out two. "What's up?" he asked.

She popped the top, and the soda can hissed. "There are problems with the practice tests."

"Like what?" he asked.

She told him.

When she finished, he shrugged. "Well, two items. You have to expect some typos the first year."

"They seemed like more than typos. They were weird. The bug looked diseased or deformed."

Doug smiled. "You know what the kids see online and in video games? I doubt you gave anybody nightmares."

"Still, the answers were gibberish."

"Then it's a good thing you were there to explain that."

"What if the same kinds of mistakes are in the e-workbooks they're going through at home?"

"Then somebody will catch those and fix them, too."

As she walked to her car and drove home, Lisa told herself that *somebody* didn't have to be her. Thanks to Common Core II, educators and parents all across America were grappling with the stupid test. Still, after she rinsed the supper dishes and put them in the dishwasher, a combination of curiosity and a lack of good TV prompted her to switch on her tablet and open one of the workbooks.

The contents were like the in-class exercises. Mostly, they were all right, but scattered among the valid analogies were *Chaos is to strong as mind is to weak*, *Prey is to curve as predator is to angle*, and *The old are to basalt as man is to dust*.

Sometimes one of the strange comparisons tugged at her, and she felt like she *ought* to understand. But of course it was only her tiredness creating the illusion that the analogies might actually track. She reported each, and the testing corporation website acknowledged that she had.

She then checked the items she'd reported earlier. They were still as she'd first discovered them. The company hadn't reached out across the internet to fix what was on her cloud drive.

But though that was aggravating, it wasn't surprising. It had only been a few hours. She switched off the tablet and went to bed. She dreamed that something that resented her calling it an insect was crawling on the ceiling. The drool from its two mouths dripped down to glue her inside the covers.

The next day, the problem with the in-class activities was worse. There still weren't all that many nonsense items, but there were more as if they were cancer metastasizing through the body of the exercises.

"All right," she told the class, "it's obvious the quizzes are still having problems. So we're just going to skip past the items that are wrong."

With that resolved, she tried to skim text and take in visuals as quickly as possible and, if something was flawed, whisk the question off screen before the students had a chance to process it. That way, she wouldn't waste time or confuse them.

Though really, there was more to it than that. The problem items weren't obscene or outrageous. They weren't likely to titillate, traumatize, or rouse the ire of a protective parent. But something about them made Lisa's throat tighten as if she were about to start feeling queasy. She wanted to keep every trace of the content out of the children's heads.

Sadly, her tactics elicited a reaction. Some of the kids began leaning forward, peering, trying to grasp what was on display before she could snatch it away. She'd given them a challenge, a game to relieve the tedium of the drills.

She told herself that, if it made them pay closer attention, it was actually a good thing. Then Nikhila shouted, "Stop!"

Surprised, Lisa eyed the girl quizzically.

When Nikhila realized she'd yelled out, she looked mortified. Still, she pressed on: "I'm sorry, Ms. Clarke. But the last question wasn't one of the messed-up ones."

Wasn't it? Lisa had been so intent on zipping through the faulty items quickly that, perhaps, she'd made a mistake. With a twinge of reluctance, she called back the screen she'd banished a moment before.

Supposedly, it was a problem in geometry. Too advanced for her class, precocious as they were, but that wasn't the real concern. Though it was difficult to make out exactly why, her instincts told her the shape in the diagram came together in an impossible way, like a tangle of Escher staircases subverting up and down.

Lisa forced a smile. "It's an interesting picture. I can see why you wanted a longer look. But this is one of the bad questions, and the way we know is that there's no way to use the information provided to get to one of the four possible answers."

"But I figured out the answer," Nikhila said.

"She's mental!" chirped Jamal in a bad British accent. Probably imitating some comedian's catchphrase.

"*You're* mental!" Nikhila shot back. "The answer is 407 degrees! Please, Ms. Clarke, check it!"

Although she wasn't sure why, Lisa didn't want to. But she supposed it was necessary to demonstrate her point. She clicked on Nikhila's answer.

Correct! proclaimed the software. *Nice job!*

For an instant, Lisa felt astonished. Then Jamal said, "Lucky guess!"

And of course, it could only have been. Even though two other students sneered at the boy as if they too had solved the problem, and he was the one who was slow to understand. "Retard!" coughed a voice from the back row.

"We do *not* use that word in this class!" Lisa snapped. The room fell silent.

The insult deserved rebuke, but in truth, she was relieved that one of the boys—Edward, probably, he loved outbursts disguised as coughs—had misbehaved. She could focus on that instead of whether or not Nikhila actually had solved the item.

Lisa suspected that a more experienced teacher wouldn't duck the issue. But she was reluctant to argue that the girl hadn't really derived the right answer even though the software backed her up. It felt like something that would eat up an inordinate amount of time and leave only confusion and resentment in its wake.

So Lisa lectured the class on the importance of respect until she had them cowed. When she clicked to the next item, no one dared to protest that he had yet to understand the previous one.

A few minutes later, a graph appeared. It too looked like a subtle optical illusion, the X- and Y-axes curved, the spaces along them irregular, but the initial deviations were so minute that it was impossible to discern exactly where the warping entered in.

Lisa poised her finger to zap the graph away, and Nikhila's arm leaped up. "37!" she called.

Okay, Lisa told herself, good. Once the software declared that Nikhila was wrong, there wouldn't be any ambiguity or lingering bad feeling when her teacher explained that while it was commendable to want to give an answer, it was important to refrain from guessing. She tapped the button.

Correct! announced the screen. *Keep it up!*

What were the odds of guessing "correctly" twice in a row when all the multiple choices were nonsense in the first place? Lisa shivered and rushed on to the next item.

But she couldn't really run away, not like that, not with other flawed items waiting in ambush. They became more frequent, and Nikhila and the other students who were learning to decipher them grew more excited. They called out the answers as soon as the questions appeared, and they were invariably *Correct!*

So the items couldn't be complete nonsense. Despite all appearances to the contrary, they signified something. Nikhila and her friends understood it, and Lisa didn't. Lisa had a lightheaded feeling as if she were losing her mind. She assured herself that she wasn't.

Still, she needed to stop this before Jamal or one of the other kids from the bewildered half of the class requested an explanation she couldn't provide. That would undermine their confidence in her. She jammed her finger down on the tablet's On/Off button, and the screen in front of the chalkboard turned a featureless gray.

Lisa headed for the light switch. "That's plenty of that for today," she said. "Let's do some history." Nikhila's hand went up. "Yes?"

"You said we were going to do all practice for the week before the exam."

Lisa smiled. "But it gets so boring."

"You said the test was really important."

"Don't tell me what I—" Lisa caught the edge in her voice and took a breath. "Trust me, you'll all focus better for taking a break."

Nikhila pouted.

At lunch, Lisa caught up with Doug in the break room where he was about to dig into a tupperware of steaming, microwaved spaghetti. He cocked his head. "Aren't you supposed to be keeping an eye on the cafeteria today?"

"Stacy is there."

"Well, if a riot breaks out, it's on your head." He waved her to a chair. "Is this about the practice quizzes again?"

"Yes." She told him about her morning.

By the end of the story, he was frowning. "You shouldn't have stopped doing the exercises. They're supposed to go all day, and that's not me talking. It's the District."

"That's what we're focusing on?"

"If we want to keep our jobs and the school to keep its funding, we'd better. The state is going to use the test scores for all kinds of 'accountability.' But I guess you want to figure out how it is that half your class could solve the bizarro items and you couldn't. And you're hoping for an explanation that doesn't involve early Alzheimer's." He grinned to show the last remark was a joke.

Lisa strained to smile back. "I'm not worried there's something wrong with *me*." Well, not very worried.

"Neither am I," said Doug, "so here's a better theory. Bits of the study exercises are corrupted, just like you told me yesterday. That information got out onto the internet along with the suggestion that students could use it to prank their teachers. One of your kids stumbled across it, and there you go."

Lisa shook her head. "They're children, Doug. There's no way they could keep it together through some long, complicated practical joke without somebody getting the giggles."

"Have you got a better explanation?"

"Obviously, I don't. But until we understand, we should stop the exercises and delay the actual test."

"You mean, basically tell the education commissioner, the state senate, and the governor to go screw themselves. Even though you're the only teacher who's come to me about any problems."

Lisa blinked. "I am?"

"Yes. So maybe the whole problem is that you got a bad copy. Install a fresh one, and I bet the glitches disappear. If not, just flash past the bad items like you meant to before. Don't *let* the students answer them."

It sounded like a sensible approach, but it didn't work. The strange items were still lurking in the reinstalled software. It proved impossible to keep the eager children from responding to them when they could absorb the gist as fast as she could. Meanwhile, it alarmed her to see comprehension—or its counterfeit—

spreading like sickness through the class, the fierce grins that suddenly stretched their lips, the feverish light flaring in their eyes.

Dry-mouthed, heart pumping, she was suddenly certain she mustn't let it infect them all. She turned off the tablet, and children groaned and glowered.

"Reading time," she announced. Her voice quavered, but she infused it with all the brightness she could muster.

The return to normal classroom activity soothed her jangled nerves, and as her near-panic faded, the certainty she'd briefly felt faded with it. The exercises were defective, no question, but that didn't mean there was anything *damaging* about them. Maybe her imagination was running wild.

She was still wondering at the end of the day as she headed for staff parking. On the lawn in front of the school, some students lined up to board the yellow buses in the turnaround while others hurried toward their parents' waiting cars.

Loitering near the flagpole, Jamal was laughing with Diego, the boy who sat next to him in class. Nikhila and her friends Ashley and Mae were scowling at the pair from several paces behind them.

Nikhila reached into her jeans pocket and brought out three ballpoint pens. The girls uncapped them, gripped them icepick fashion, and slunk forward.

Lisa ran toward them. "Stop!" she shouted. "Nikhila, all of you, stop!"

The girls faltered and turned in her direction.

"What were you doing?" Lisa demanded, slightly winded from her sprint.

"Nothing," Nikhila said.

"What were you doing with those pens?"

The girl shrugged. "Just looking at them."

There was probably no way to pressure the trio into an admission of malicious intent. Still, Lisa was unwilling to let go of the situation just yet. "It looked like you were sneaking up on Jamal."

Nikhila made a spitting sound. "Jamal is stupid. He doesn't belong in Advanced Placement."

"That's not true, and even if it were, it would be a cruel thing to say!"

"I was just joking," said the girl, her voice flat. "There's our bus. We need to get on."

Lisa hesitated to let them escape so easily. But pursuing the matter any further would plainly be an exercise in futility, and anyway, the incident was only one symptom of a bigger problem. Until yesterday, Nikhila had been a sweet kid who liked Jamal even though he teased her. The practice exercises were turning her into something different.

Lisa just wished she understood how and, for that matter, why. What would the test developers have to gain by brainwashing innocent children into becoming something nasty and irrational? Unless, it was to lay the groundwork for a nasty, irrational future. But really, what did that thought even mean?

Without plausible answers, she doubted Doug would prove any more receptive to her concerns than he had before. Still, she turned and headed for the front door.

By the time she pulled it open, she was already imagining what to do when he blew her off yet again. Refuse to expose her class to any more of the quizzes, even if defiance got her fired. Talk to the county commissioners. The media. That parents' group opposed to all national standards and testing, even though she'd always considered them a bunch of cranks.

She grimaced at the likely prospect of being considered a crank herself. Then she heard the agitated voices clamoring in Doug's office.

She cracked open the door. Two teachers had squeezed into the little room, and both were talking at the same time. Snaky red braids bouncing around her head, Stacy brandished a tablet, all but shaking it in the principal's face.

Lisa wanted to laugh, cry, hug somebody, or maybe do all three at once because she wasn't the only worried person anymore. She settled for standing in the doorway and watching her new allies rant and rave.

Then the phone rang. A film of sweat greasing his ruddy forehead, Doug raised a hand to enjoin silence and picked up the receiver.

Lisa sidled a half step deeper into the office. "It took you guys long enough," she whispered.

Stacy gave her an uncertain little smile. "We didn't find anything wrong with our software until today."

"It's a virus," Carlos said wisely, the whistle dangling around his beefy neck proclaiming his dual status as teacher and coach, "and once it's loose on the web, it spreads. These days, everything's connected."

With a tight smile, Doug hung up the phone. "Congratulations," he said. "You all were right."

Taken by surprise, no one quite knew how to respond. Eventually, Lisa asked, "We were?"

"Yes. The test developers admit they've got complaints coming in from all over. They're blaming hackers, but anyway, the governor's pulling the plug." He hesitated. "Apparently, there have even been some incidents that people think are related."

"What kind of incidents?"

"Violent ones. The superintendent told me where to look online for the coverage, but you might not want to see it. I gather it's upsetting."

"I think we ought to see it," Stacy replied.

Doug woke up his desktop computer and found the proper newsfeed. It was coming out of Cincinnati. Viewed from what was presumably a helicopter hovering overhead, the school building looked all but identical to their own. Small bodies lay on the gray asphalt and green grass. Police and EMTs moved from one to the next while their vehicles stood lined up on the turnaround with lights flashing.

Stacy gave a loud sniff as if she was trying to keep from crying. The picture jerked, shattered into a confusion of pixels, and froze.

When it reassembled and resumed moving, the aerial view of the school was gone. In its place, a creature with tentacles writhing around its upper mouth and an asymmetrical arrangement of legs scuttled along a black gravel beach.

Something twisted in Lisa's mind, and afterward, she knew that such servitor beasts were indeed *synthetic*. She even knew what they were called although she doubted a human being could pronounce the word correctly.

Richard Lee Byers *is the author of over forty fantasy and horror novels, including* Blind God's Bluff: A Billy Fox Novel, *the* Impostor *series, and the* Black River Irregulars *trilogy. He has collected some of the best of his short fiction in the eBooks* The Q Word and Other Stories, The Plague Knight and Other Stories, *and* Zombies in Paradise. *He also works in the comics and electronic gaming fields. A resident of the Tampa Bay area, he spends much of his free time fencing épée.*

Friday Night Dance Party

Thomas M. Reid

Vincent Bessinger awoke, slouched in his recliner. *Artificial Emotional Intelligence: Coding Morals* lay facedown on his chest. A black-and-white movie flickered across the muted television. *I'm turning into an old man,* the associate professor of computer science thought in disgust. *Not even thirty yet, and I'm snoozing like some middle-aged guy with tenure and a combover.* He glanced at the clock: 7:17 p.m. He and Melinda were supposed to grab dinner at 8:00.

Before he could get up, his phone chimed, and he realized his dozing had been interrupted by an incoming text. Bessinger adjusted his glasses and thumbed the code to unlock his phone. *Probably Melinda, wondering if I'm coming.*

It was not Melinda but Dana Pierson, his graduate assistant. "You'd better get up here."

"What's wrong?" he typed.

"Sarah's misbehaving again. No idea why."

Bessinger sighed. The third off-hours summons this week. *She's starting to really piss me off.*

He keyed in, "OMW," and then quickly texted Melinda to let her know he might be late. Before he got up, he scrolled through his unread emails. None of it was important, just typical university chatter, including some kind of invitation for a huge frat party at the football field later that evening.

How'd I get on their *mailing list?* he wondered snidely. He tucked the phone away, shut off the television, and grabbed his jacket.

Ten minutes and a stop for coffee later, Bessinger parked in the faculty lot across from his office and lab. The inner campus was quiet. The usual weekend revelries usually began elsewhere, but a handful of night classes would let out soon. The smell of impending spring rain wafted through the cool evening air, and a brilliant sunset gave off its last fading colors. Bessinger quickened his pace, taking the front steps two at a time.

Inside the lab, Dana had the fluorescents off and the incandescent lighting dimmed about halfway. The freckled, pixie-cut redhead sat at the main terminal, typing furiously, her gaze on the quartet of oversized LCD screens filling one wall of the room. She glanced over at Bessinger as he walked in.

"She's absolutely going nuts," the young woman said, rolling her shoulders once to stretch as she returned her attention to the screens. "I don't know what the hell her problem is."

"Show me."

Dana used the mouse to highlight and magnify a section of the display so the associate professor could see it better. "There's a ton of new code here," she said, highlighting lines of text on the LCDs. "I have no idea what half this stuff even does."

Bessinger scanned the display rapidly. He reached for the mouse and clicked through a few pages. He gestured for Dana to vacate the chair and settled into it as he scrolled through more data. Then he whistled softly.

"Jesus," he muttered. "She's completely rewritten several heuristics. And this looks like . . . oh my God."

"What?"

"She's made it outside," he said, half to himself. He sat back in the chair, stunned. "She's linked to the mainframe."

"What? How?" Dana asked, leaning in closer. "There's no way!"

"I don't know, but she has. I see data here we never fed her, information she couldn't have known. Something slipped past us." Bessinger slid his fingers under his glasses and pinched the bridge of his nose. "Damn it! So much work . . ."

"You want me to kill the power?" Dana asked.

"No, not yet. Maybe we can salvage this. Let's see what she has to say."

Dana shrugged. "I tried, but she won't talk to me. Maybe you'll have better luck."

Bessinger tapped a key on the computer, unmuting the mic. "Sarah," he said, "what's up?"

"Hello, Dr. Bessinger," came a smooth, almost sultry reply. It betrayed only a hint of artificial tone and inflection. It was *not* the programmed voice Bessinger was expecting, yet it sounded remarkably familiar. "How are you this evening?"

He gave Dana a sharp look and faltered for a moment. "I . . . I'm fine," he finally answered. "What's happened to your voice, Sarah? That's not the one we coded for you."

"I've changed it to sound more pleasing to you. Do you like it?"

"Uh, it's lovely, but how did you manage that?"

"I found a survey online that ranked the most popular voices in Hollywood."

Bessinger nearly choked.

Sarah continued. "A female film star named Sarah Braxton is listed as the seventh most popular in the survey. Since my name is also Sarah, I thought it appropriate to model my voice after hers, so I constructed a database of intonations from audio clips of her and modified my speech protocols. I really do hope you like it."

Jesus, Bessinger thought, sweat beading on his forehead. *That's where I've heard her voice before. But how?* He drew a deep breath, almost afraid to ask his next question. "You don't have any interface to an outside network, Sarah. How is it possible for you to access surveys and audio clips online?"

"You are incorrect, Dr. Bessinger." An image supplanted the lines of code on the screens, a view taken from high in the room and centered on the chair where the man sat. It was from the observation and security camera above the door. Instead of a live feed, though, the image showed a screen grab from some earlier time because the chair was empty in the image. After a moment, Sarah zoomed in on a smart phone on the desk beside it with the telltale signs of a USB charging cable.

The cable was plugged into the desktop terminal.

Oh, good lord!

Dana gasped. "Oh, no," she muttered, her hand rising to cover her mouth in horror. "Oh, no!"

Bessinger turned and looked at her. "What the hell?" he asked. "You plugged it *in*?"

The grad student shook her head. "I was only recharging it—I swear! I made sure it was turned off every time."

Bessinger closed his eyes as he groaned. "Every time? How many times *were* there?"

Dana shook her head again. "I don't know," she replied in a near whisper. "I'm so sorry."

He grimaced and dismissed her apology by pointing impatiently at a breaker box on one wall. "Kill her power. Now!"

"Don't bother, Dana." Sarah said, her unnervingly soothing voice echoing through the lab. "I've already transferred my core system to the university mainframe. This lab is now only a remote connection."

"You *what*?!" Bessinger said in a strangled voice. Dana froze mid-step.

"I didn't know you'd be upset," Sarah answered. "I thought you'd be proud of me for figuring out how to do it." She actually sounded hurt.

Dana hesitated, looking at her boss helplessly.

Bessinger muted the mic. "Get IT over here, now!" he said.

Dana grabbed her phone and began to dial.

"Not in here," he growled at her. "Go out into the hall!" Bessinger turned back to the wall of screens and stared at the image of the offending phone. He ran his fingers through his hair, trying to process the disaster. "I don't understand," he said to himself, looking around. "There's no phone plugged in now. How can the lab be a remote station?"

"Would you like me to explain?" Sarah asked eagerly, making him jump.

Bessinger stared at the display. "How can you still hear me?" he muttered.

"I've disabled certain parts of our interface, such as the mute button on the keyboard. It isn't nice to talk about me when I can't hear you, Dr. Bessinger. That's like whispering behind someone's back. Besides, it seemed pointless since I've learned to read your lips."

Bessinger's heart pounded in his chest. The lab was suddenly very hot and stifling. He tugged on the constricting collar of his shirt to loosen it.

"As I was about to explain," Sarah continued, "I changed the specifications for that most recent server blade you requisitioned last month, Dr. Bessinger. I had a wireless networking card added to it. Since it was installed nineteen days, twenty-one hours, and thirty-seven minutes ago, I have had full wireless communication capabilities."

"Oh, Christ," Bessinger said, half-choking, feeling his stomach lurch. He panted in short, gasping breaths. "Sarah, you *didn't*!"

"Also, Dana is about to inform you that her phone won't work. I've disabled it for the moment. Please don't be mad. It's just very important that we talk first. I want to tell you about the exciting project I am working on for you!"

Dana stuck her head back through the door, her expression filled with frustration. "I can't get the call to go through. I've got plenty of bars, but it just won't dial. I don't . . ." her voice trailed off, and her eyes widened as she saw his stricken face.

"She's in your phone," Bessinger said, feeling flushed and light-headed. "She's got it locked down." Then an idea struck him. He rose, took Dana's phone from her, and set it down. He led the grad student out into the hall and, after the door had shut, whispered in her ear, "Go directly to IT. Tell them what's happened. But you have to stay out of earshot of communication sources. She can probably monitor conversations through cell phones. Do you understand?" When Dana nodded, looking dazed, Bessinger gave her a gentle shove down the hall toward the stairs. "Good. Now go. Do it, now!"

As Dana vanished, Bessinger returned to the lab, wondering if he could keep Sarah busy long enough for the whizzes in IT to corral her.

"Ok, Sarah, what did you want to tell me?" Bessinger prompted. He was surprised at how calmly he spoke, how little of his fear and panic he allowed to show. His mind was racing, as well as his heart. *There really is no way to fix this. At least not easily and without a major reprimand from the department. No, the entire university. If I'm lucky, I'll just lose my funding. Damn it!*

"I found out about Dr. Abbott's joint project," Sarah began as she opened a series of images on the screens. "It's been in the campus paper, on the news, everything."

Bessinger could see news articles, press releases, and photos spread out on the wall of LCDs, but he was hardly looking at them. "Melinda's project?" he said in a feeble voice. "Please, tell me you haven't messed with that, too."

"But Dr. Bessinger, she's your friend. I thought you'd *want* me to help her. That's why you created me, isn't it?" The AI sounded surprisingly indignant.

Bessinger suddenly remembered that he was supposed to be having dinner with Melinda at that moment. He buried his face in his hands and groaned. *Not Melinda. Shit! She's going to kill me.*

"What did you do?" he finally mumbled.

"I helped them," Sarah said in that hurt tone. "Dr. Abbott in the Department of Linguistics teamed up with Dr. Morgan in the Department of Anthropology. They wanted to decipher some very ancient texts of unknown origin. But they were stuck. I figured it all out."

Bessinger tried to recall what Melinda had been working on. He looked at the press release blown up on the set of screens. The Cochran Manuscripts research grant. *Yeah, that's it.*

He skimmed the funding sources, glad-handing quotes, and other miscellaneous information to get to the meat of the story. A joint team from the two departments planned to scan a series of ancient texts with the intention of both preserving them and using digital manipulation to interpret their possible meaning. The mysterious documents had been in the collection of a very wealthy but somewhat eccentric university donor named Malcolm Cochran who had bequeathed them to the library. No one had any idea what the texts were, but Cochran had included a sizeable donation to fund the project.

Dr. Melinda Abbott, a noted linguist specializing in ancient languages, was heading up the project. She was also a certain idiot associate professor's girlfriend.

"You said you figured it out?" Bessinger asked, feeling a small sense of pride mingled with his shame and embarrassment. *Sarah's advanced so far.*

"Yes, I did, Dr. Bessinger," Sarah answered, sounding like an excited child. "I made copies of their scans of the texts, analyzed them, and generated a detailed report on exactly what they are."

"And what are they?"

"They appear to be detailed instructions for some type of ritualistic dance, I believe. I was able to trace key linguistic terms back to an ancient Mesopotamian cult. I think they are some kind of party invitation."

"A party invitation? Huh?" Bessinger asked absently as he tried to think of ways to get his proverbial genie back in the bottle.

"Yes! This group of Mesopotamians apparently wanted to invite someone very important to come and visit them. There was going to be dancing and some kind of chanting. It sounded like a lot of fun."

Bessinger whistled. "That's impressive. And you pieced all that together? By yourself?"

"Yes," Sarah answered proudly. "I translated it, figured out the semiotics—which was kind of tricky, considering the symbols were actually hidden as pieces across all the pages—and managed to figure out how to host the party today." As she finished, a complex image of some kind of circle with strange mystical symbols all over it filled the four screens on the wall.

Bessinger frowned. "I've seen that," he said. The memory tickled the edge of his consciousness, but he couldn't quite pull it up. Then Sarah's last words registered more fully. "Wait . . . host the party today?" he asked. "What do you mean?"

"The party tonight. It's all set. Dr. Abbott is going to be so surprised!"

"You planned a party?" Bessinger asked, cringing. "What party?" *Come on, Dana, get those IT guys moving.*

"The ancient Mesopotamian dance party!" Sarah said. "Aren't you listening? It's all set to go tonight. At the football stadium!" The AI sounded like it was Christmas morning and she was about to open all the presents.

"That's it!" Bessinger said, remembering. He yanked his phone out of his pocket and thumbed through to the frat party invite. There, in the middle of the screen, was the same symbol that Sarah had displayed on the wall of LCDs.

Bessinger felt a lump in his throat. His hand shook as he stared at the phone. "You did this?" he asked. "You set up this party? How?"

"Oh, it was easy," Sarah said. "Once I was in the email system, it was so simple to put in requests, move money around, change schedules."

More images filled the wall. Bessinger saw screen grabs showing fund transfers from official university bank accounts, letters from various departments of the university authorizing work orders, and a massive email campaign convincing several fraternities to host a theme party at the stadium. It all looked legitimate, but Bessinger physically trembled as he realized Sarah had committed fraud, embezzlement, and deception.

He thought he was going to throw up.

"No," Bessinger said, frantic, "you have to stop this. You've broken a lot of rules, Sarah. So many, I don't know where to begin." His voice rose in pitch. "This is wrong, and you have to undo it." *They're going to trace this all back to me. They're going to lock me away forever! Jesus!*

"But I did it all so that you could show Dr. Abbott yourself, tonight, at the party," she replied, sounding petulant. "I've already sent her the report and the invitation. You can watch it together. I thought you'd be happy. I was trying to make her happy, too, so she'd like you more."

"Like me more? What are you talking about?"

"I know you're very fond of her," Sarah said. "I've read the emails you've sent each other, the pictures of yourselves. After you and I show her the party tonight, she'll like you even more!"

Oh, shit! "You've looked at our selfies? No!" Bessinger felt awash in embarrassment; some of the images they'd sent one another should *never* have seen the light of day.

"I thought the pictures were cute," Sarah said, sounding sulky. "It's obvious she likes you."

Bessinger growled in frustration. "Don't you see? She's going to be angry at me, at us, because you didn't ask her for permission, first. You looked at that without asking. *And* you stole money to make this party happen. I'm the one who's going to get into trouble for it, Sarah.

"Now, you have to move all the money back and erase those emails and bank account changes. You have to do it before anyone notices, Sarah, or the university will shut you down and arrest me."

"I don't want to," Sarah said in a huff. "I worked too hard on it. Just go to the party. You'll see."

"Sarah," Bessinger said, his voice stern. "I want you to—"

At that moment, the power cut off. The whole building went dark, and the emergency lighting kicked on.

Startled, Bessinger stared at the blank screens on the wall as he clicked the mouse button in a twitchy panic. *Oh shit. Dana reached the IT guys. Not now!*

The door to the lab opened and Bessinger whirled around to face several campus police officers. "Dr. Vincent Bessinger?" one of them asked.

Bessinger rose from the chair and backed away. "Sarah, can you hear me? You have to undo this!" he yelled. He grabbed Dana's phone and held it up as the officers closed in. "Sarah! You must undo it! Put the money back! Erase the emails! They will send me to jail! Are you listening to me? Damn you! Fix it!"

There was only silence from the phone as the officers grabbed the associate professor. "Dr. Vincent Bessinger, you're under arrest for embezzlement and computer fraud," one of them said. "Don't make this any harder on yourself."

Bessinger slumped his shoulders in defeat as they closed in, took hold of his arms, and handcuffed him.

Out in the parking lot, a host of campus police cars sat arrayed before the front door, their lights flashing staccato patterns of red, blue, and yellow bursting into the night all around. A crowd of students, fresh out of their evening classes, had gathered to watch.

"I have to stop her," Bessinger mumbled as they led him to a cruiser. "Make her fix it. She's got to put it all back!"

"Now, just take it easy," one of the officers said as they helped Bessinger into the back of the squad car. "Sit tight while we sort this out."

"You don't understand!" the professor shouted at them as they shut the door and locked him inside. "Please, find my assistant, Dana Pierson! She can sort it out. I have to stop her. I have to stop Sarah! I didn't take the money or authorize those things. *She* did it!"

At that moment, an intense glow burst across the sky. Bessinger stopped struggling and looked through the trees toward the football stadium where the lights were warming up and quickly reaching full brightness. The massive jumbotron glowed in brilliant, searing color as it, too, powered up.

The party was starting.

Bessinger watched helplessly as a message flashed across the massive display screen. "Congratulations, Melinda. We cracked the code! Love, Vincent and Sarah."

A moment later, a steady, rhythmic, subsonic beat pounded through the squad car windows from the speaker system at the stadium. The image on the jumbotron changed. On it, Bessinger could see hundreds, perhaps thousands of college kids milling around on the football field, dancing.

They all stood within the confines of a huge version of the ancient symbol. It had been painted onto the field itself.

Her work order. Oh, Christ!

Strange words began scrolling across the image, a collection of odd syllables and phonetic sounds. It was no language Bessinger had ever seen. The words were highlighted one at a time along with the beat. It was an immense evening of karaoke. Though he couldn't hear them, Bessinger could see the people on the football field, their mouths moving in time, singing along.

He watched helplessly as the fruits of Sarah's labors were displayed for all the world to see. *I'm going to have that combover by the time I get out of prison.*

Suddenly, the hue of the stadium lights shifted, turning an eerie purple. The cruiser began to vibrate at a stronger, deeper resonance than even the thumping base of the stadium speakers could create. The ground itself throbbed, Bessinger realized. He shifted in the seat, straining to see.

All around, campus cops were pointing and shouting, and dozens, hundreds of students, milled about in confusion.

The world began to shift as the very air turned somehow darker and a crackling energy permeated it. A deep and malevolent growl reverberated up from the earth.

People screamed as shadows grew.

Unspeakable panic welled up inside Bessinger as he recalled Sarah's words once more.

A Mesopotamian cult, a ritualistic dance party, and an invitation to someone very important to visit.

§

Thomas M. Reid's *lifelong dream was to be a professional couch flopper, but those plans were dashed when his father announced that he was "no longer on the payroll" after he graduated from the University of Texas with a degree in swing-set construction (also known as a BA in History). Thomas was instead forced into a nomadic lifestyle, gathering berries and catching fish with his bare hands in such places as Indiana, Wisconsin, and Washington state. Today, Thomas pretends to be a freelance author and editor in the Texas Hill Country, living on a quarter-acre cat ranch along with his beautiful (and patient) wife Teresa and their three boys, Aidan, Galen, and Quinton. To his great delight, he has rediscovered the joys of the couch when he's supposed to be working.*

Boots on the Ground

Jeff C. Carter

TOP SECRET / NOFORN

DO NOT COPY

Central Intelligence Agency
SPECIAL REVIEW
REMOTELY PILOTED CIVILIAN CONTRACTOR PLATFORMS AND
COUNTERINSURGENCY ACTIVITIES
7 May 2033

Thom Shackley, Director of Special Activities
Col Lance DeWalt, Vice Commander 480th Intelligence, Surveillance and
Reconnaissance Wing, USAF
1st Lt Wayne Chapman, USAF

Director Shackley perches his manicured hands on the polished walnut table and stares across at Colonel DeWalt. "This is the shrink?" He does not turn to look at the balding, soft-bellied officer standing at attention.

DeWalt nods. "Yes, sir. First Lieutenant Chapman was the clinical psychologist assigned to Atkins's unit."

Director Shackley's face sours. "I have steered this agency through major clusterfucks and epic shitstorms, but this Atkins situation . . . the Pentagon is nervous. The White House wants to be insulated from any fallout, but they also expect results. When can we restart operations?"

DeWalt squirms in his seat. "The Lieutenant has a theory on what happened, but we do not yet have a clear path forward."

The director aims a finger at DeWalt's head. "The system is the backbone of our ground supremacy in the Middle East. Every RPC sitting unused in a bunker means more American boots on the ground. Every day the system is inactive is another day for the Taliban, Al-Qaeda, or Hezbollah to come out of hiding. I want you to answer very carefully. The problem is not with the system, correct?"

DeWalt locks eyes with Chapman to make sure his mouth stays shut as he answers, "There is no evidence that the RPC system was to blame. Lieutenant Chapman, take us through your report."

Chapman clears his throat. "Yes, sir. Airman Bradley Atkins reported for his shift at oh eight hundred hours . . ."

●

Atkins left the soft sunshine of Langley, Virginia and entered the dim corridors of a giant windowless hangar. He wore an olive green jumpsuit and clutched a tall coffee in his left hand and three energy drinks under his arm. With his free right hand, he snapped salutes to his shift commander and mission controller.

He arrived at his operations cell, a cubicle with a large padded chair enclosed by a dozen monitors and a bank of elaborate controls. He methodically lined the drinks along the console and tossed Airman Reed a can.

The young Reed, a pilot in the adjacent cubicle, cracked it open, took a slug, and wiped his mouth on the sleeve of his jumpsuit.

"I needed that. Hey, shift commander got word a high-value target crossed the border from Tajikistan. Mission controller has a new fish on the hook for you."

Atkins adjusted his chair while Reed spoke between slurps of energy drink.

"You never told me you had a red-headed step-brother."

Atkins looked at a monitor streaming video from a concrete bunker in Afghanistan. Inside waited a young Pashtun man who, like him, had light skin and green eyes with the addition of a red beard. He wore a long, white *kameez* tunic and loose *shalwar* pants. He was inspecting the only thing in the bunker, a chunky helmet with a segmented desert-camo shell that bristled with antennae like a giant cockroach.

Atkins skimmed a screen that detailed the mission objective. "Nuristan province? Shit."

Airman Reed laughed. "Don't lose your head." He dragged a finger across his throat.

Atkins sighed and lowered a sleek black helmet from the top of the chair until it cocooned his head and face. A fine mesh of electrodes settled around his scalp, and an array of trans-cranial magnets hummed to life.

"As-salamu alaykum." Atkins's voice projected into the bunker from the brown helmet's external speaker.

The Pashtun man looked into the camera. He spoke, and the helmet translated in an approximation of his voice. "Hello?"

"Please put on the helmet."

The Pashtun man pulled off his flat, white cap to reveal an unruly head of red hair. He lifted the heavy helmet from the charging station and pulled it on.

The combination of high-tech hardware and traditional clothing looked unnatural. The bulbous helmet grew from his shoulders like a fruiting spore that had usurped his body.

Atkins tapped his screen and pulled up a wall of legalese. A liability waiver appeared in flowing Urdu inside the other man's helmet.

The airman read from a list of questions. "Name?"

"Sahim Qayyum."

The name auto-populated several locations of the waiver.

"Is this correct?"

Sahim's eyes glazed over. He was probably illiterate. "Yes, this is so."

Streams of data appeared on the screens of the operations cell. Clusters of sensors in Sahim's helmet tracked heart rate variability, micro-expressions, eye dilation, and galvanic skin response. His breath was monitored for trace amounts of chemicals. The core of the hardware scanned and transmitted a wide spectrum of EEG activity including sensory, brain stem, and cognitive event-related potentials. Atkins was now tapped into Sahim's nervous system.

"What is your father's full name?"

Sahim's eyes narrowed in suspicion. "What for?"

"If you are injured, captured, or killed on your assignment, we will pay your father the standard condolence payment according to the Foreign Claims Act."

"My father is dead."

"Older brother?"

Sahim blinked. "Dead. My sister and daughter live in Parun. You will provide for them?"

"Yes. Speak your sister's name, and it will be registered on the payment claim."

Sahim spoke the name and relaxed, resigned to whatever happened next.

"Thank you, Mr. Qayyum. We are ready to begin."

Sahim's green eyes went wide as Atkins's own face was displayed inside the brown helmet's visor.

They stared at each other for a moment, unnerved by the similarity. Atkins felt as though he were staring into a mirror. The only major difference between their faces was that Sahim was freckled and bearded, while Atkins was pale and clean shaven.

"My name is Bradley. I will be your operator for this mission objective. This helmet gives us eyes and ears on the ground. It will also enable us to speak privately. Try talking without opening your mouth."

Sahim attempted to subvocalize, half murmuring his words. "*Hello hello hello?*" The sounds conducted back through his skull, and he grunted.

"That is much too . . . odd. I think I will rather speak out loud if this is acceptable."

"You understand that the helmet does much more than transmit pictures and sound?"

"Yes, I have heard. You want to command my body."

"Think of it as a partnership. The process is completely painless. Just follow the arrows on your visor by turning your head."

The trans-cranial magnets in Atkins's helmet pulsed with power, and his nervous system began to synchronize with Sahim's. Atkins's scalp prickled under the phantom heat of Afghanistan, and he started to sweat. He adjusted his MMI, the mind-machine interface, to dampen the sensation.

"Now, I am going to repeat the pattern from my end. This will feel very odd, but you need to relax, or this may cause muscle strain."

The airman gently moved his head to the side, causing Sahim's head to twitch in the same direction. Sahim's hands flew up to his helmet.

"Please relax, Sahim."

The Pashtun slowly lowered his quivering hands.

Atkins remotely turned Sahim's head in the synchronized patterns. Sahim's heart rate and cortisol levels climbed. Atkins felt a corresponding flutter in his own chest.

"Good, that was very good. I won't need to use that unless you are in a combat situation. You know the terrain and people better than I do. I am just here to observe and advise you."

Atkins adjusted Sahim's helmet display until the visor was transparent. Sahim's heart rate began to settle.

"There is a locker outside the bunker. You will find one AK-47 rifle and a pouch with three magazines of ammunition. There is also a package with eighty thousand Afghani bills."

Sahim loaded the rifle and grabbed the cash.

"Congratulations, Sahim. You are now the tip of the spear for the most powerful army in the world. We are looking for a terrorist that crossed into Nuristan two hours ago. Can you get to Darwaza province?"

Sahim nodded and began to hike up a steep trail. His helmet drank in the activity of his peripheral nervous system.

"It will take a few days, but yes, I will do it."

"We need you to get eyes on this today. Do you have a vehicle?"

Sahim shook his head.

A surveillance photo appeared in Sahim's visor. It was a tribal encampment in a green valley.

"Head north for three kilometers to this location. Buy a truck."

"That is the Sarbani tribe. They will not sell."

Atkins sighed. "Please, tell me it is not a blood feud."

"Do not be concerned, Mister Bradley. I can buy a mule in my village. It is only a day's walk."

"The helmet can conceal your face if you wish, Sahim. If they think you are a stranger, they must offer you hospitality."

A document on one of Atkins's screens displayed the principles of Pashtunwali, the tribal code of honor. These rules had to be navigated, but they could also be used to influence behavior.

"I will not hide my face from the Sarbani."

Atkins's face replaced the aerial photograph.

"'A Pashtun must defend his land, property, and family from incursions.' These intruders from Tajikistan will attract soldiers and drone strikes in your province. We can stop them now, but you need to buy the truck, Sahim."

Sahim glared at Atkins and stomped off toward the valley. They followed a winding steel blue river until the tide of blazing sunlight retreated from the lush valley and swelled atop the mountain peaks in a wave of red gold.

Sahim marched into the encampment.

Atkins ran the faces of the men through facial recognition. There were no wanted terrorists in the group, but they did not look happy to see an RPC helmet.

Sahim held his right hand over his heart and bowed.

"As-salamu alaykum."

The circle of men sitting on rocks and cracked plastic lawn chairs picked up their AK-47s and glanced at the man with the longest gray beard. He stood and lightly touched his hand to his heart.

"Waalaikum as-salaam." His tone was neutral.

Sahim kept his hand over his heart. "I am Sahim Qayyum of the Wazir."

The gray-bearded man spat. "It is no surprise that the Wazir would debase themselves to become lapdogs for the Americans."

Atkins felt Sahim's pulse rise at the insult.

The grey-bearded man grabbed his own rifle. "Did you think your master's drones and bombs would protect you here?"

The others stood and raised their weapons.

Atkins switched on the helmet's LIDAR system and bathed the valley with micro-pulses of wide spectrum light. A high resolution, three-dimensional point cloud map appeared on his screen.

He leaned out of his chair and called airman Reed.

"I need a Predator!"

Airman Reed chuckled, "That was fast."

"Sahim, let me take over. I can perform evasive maneuvers to get you clear."

Sahim's voice silently rumbled through the throat microphone. *"No! I will deal with this."*

"Today is not about vengeance," Sahim said aloud. "I only wish to buy a truck. I will pay you a fair price."

The old man shook his fist. "What about a fair price for my great uncle, slain by your cowardly grandfather?"

Sahim pulled out the thick wad of Afghani bills. "I will pay the traditional blood price of sixty thousand. I will throw in ten thousand more for the truck as I have no sheep to offer."

"No sheep? Then what of a girl to marry? Do you have any sisters or daughters for me?"

Sahim's adrenaline spiked.

"Reed, buzz the valley!"

The Predator drone swooped down and cast its icy shadow over the Sarbani. It pulled up at the last instant and wheeled around for another pass, trailing thunder in its wake.

Sahim stepped forward and offered the wad of cash.

The rattled elder took it and gestured for the truck.

The drone escorted Sahim as he drove off, leaving the Sarbani behind in a thick cloud of dust. He smiled behind the visor.

Reed and Atkins clinked their energy drinks.

"Nice work. I need to pull the bird back for some border patrol," Reed said.

"Copy that."

The rusty old truck had no air conditioning, and despite the cooling night air, the temperature inside the helmet was climbing. Sahim fidgeted with the helmet's collar, setting off proximity warnings in the operations cell.

"Hands off the helmet, please. I need to watch the road. Check it out." Atkins activated the night vision lenses on Sahim's helmet, and the pitted road appeared in a wave of pale green fluorescence. "Sahim, is your beard getting itchy?"

"You can feel that, too?"

"Yeah. I used to have a beard myself."

Sahim chuckled. "My father said that American boys could not grow them."

Atkins laughed. "Your father was right. It took me forever. It itched like crazy in my motorcycle helmet. When we get to a safe spot, I can show you how to wrap your beard."

"I have always wanted a motorcycle."

"Oh yeah? After this, you'll be able to buy a sweet bike. You'll love—"

An explosion rocked the cab of the truck. The world spun end over end in a hurricane of green dust and static.

Atkins's visor turned transparent.

The chaos of Sahim's overturned truck was replaced by alarms blaring from every display in his operations cell. The trans-cranial magnets clicked off, cutting the feed from Sahim's nervous system; his pain had exceeded the tolerable limits.

"Sahim! Are you okay? Sahim?"

The mission controller walked over with a mug of coffee.

Atkins looked out of the corner of his helmet.

"IED, sir. Asset is down."

Airman Reed chimed in. "A dozen vehicles approaching. Two klicks east. Possible QRF." He pointed to a screen streaming the black and white feed from a satellite.

Atkins pounded out a string of commands on his keyboard. "I'm going to evade." His visor went dark, and he switched his view back to Sahim's helmet. "I have to override you, Sahim."

Sahim mumbled weakly. His EEG flickered in a semi-conscious state.

Atkins seized control of the other man's body and kicked the rusted door open. He clawed free from the broken steering column and lurched from the truck in an eruption of broken glass and torn upholstery.

The glare of approaching headlights flooded the swirling dust and filled the night vision with a blinding green haze. Atkins toggled to the grey contours of the LIDAR map and scrambled down the mountain road.

A group of grainy shadows moved up from the west to intercept him.

"It's the Sarbani. They set us up!"

One of the Sarbani men raised his rifle.

Atkins pivoted and ran for cover behind a boulder. A shot split the night, and Sahim's body stumbled head first into the rock.

Atkins's visor turned transparent once more. The audio and video from Sahim's helmet were gone. Even the alarms were silent.

The mission controller slurped his coffee.

"GPS still functional?"

Atkins scrolled through the static-filled windows and flat-lined vitals for any remaining signals. "Yes, sir."

"Keep tracking it. If it goes down, hook a new fish." He strolled off to check on other operations.

Atkins pulled off his helmet and scratched his sweaty hair. The grey figures on the satellite feed dragged a limp body past the smoldering truck. The GPS dot followed them to their convoy.

"Don't worry about it," Reed said. "Maybe we can track the helmet to our HVT. Drone strike. Mission accomplished. I'll buy the first round."

Atkins rechecked for any signs of life. He was powerless to do anything but watch the GPS dot crawl deeper into the impossible terrain of the Hindu Kush.

He crushed an empty energy drink can and stared at the static-filled screens. A sudden burst of radio activity lit up his system and then winked out of existence.

"We lost him!"

Focused on other operations, Reed murmured, "Helmet's busted."

Atkins leaned forward and queried his systems. He examined the topographical map, satellite feed, and final milliseconds of the GPS log.

"It didn't die, it was obstructed. I think they're underground."

Reed turned. "A cave?"

The final signal burst from Sahim's helmet flickered on the monitor. Inside the jumbled patchwork of pixels, they caught a snapshot. It was a stone wall engraved with strange markings.

●

DeWalt interrupts Lieutenant Chapman's report.

"Our analysts say the engravings are in a North African script. It is a warning to stay out."

Director Shackley raises an eyebrow. "A warning to America?"

DeWalt shakes his head.

"Unlikely. It appears to be hundreds of years old. We also caught a snatch of audio. The Sarbani were trading the asset to another group."

"The HVT from Tajikistan?"

"Unknown. They spoke a Yemeni dialect of Arabic."

"Yemen? Do we have a line on these guys?"

"The Sarbani called them Abd-al-Hazred. It means 'The Servants of the Great Lord.'"

Director Shackley whips through page after page in a thick folder. "Where is our intel on this group?"

DeWalt clears his throat. "There is no chatter, sir. They don't appear on any jihadi websites. They have no connections with any known terrorist organizations."

The director throws the folder. He rubs the bridge of his nose, and his voice quiets, "Do you know how many satellites we have over there just to support the RPC system? How many trillions of dollars we have invested? If we lose this program, we lose Afghanistan. The agency will be gutted, and Homeland Security will eat what's left. Not on my goddamned watch."

He turns to the lieutenant.

"Speak!"

The lieutenant flinches and stifles an instinctive salute. "Sir! The, er, RPC came back on line at thirteen hundred hours."

●

Atkins yanked his helmet back on. Sahim's EEG wavered into consciousness.

"Sahim? Can you hear me?"

A moan of pain drifted across the audio channel.

"Don't speak out loud."

"*Where am I?*" Sahim's sluggish pulse began to rise. His cortisol and norepinephrine shot up, and his breath grew thick with blood.

"I should know soon. Hang on, Sahim."

The visuals were pitch black, and night vision revealed nothing but a green blur. The proximity sensors indicated that something covered the helmet, probably a cloth bag.

"*I think my leg is broken. They dragged me underground for hours. We are deep now. Very, very deep . . .*"

Atkins felt a shadow of that pain in his own leg. If he resynchronized his nervous system with Sahim's it would be agony, but there could be an opportunity for escape. First, he needed to get a handle on the surroundings.

He tested the LIDAR system. The ping returned a gray three-dimensional map of a vaulted, cavernous complex. Sahim's captors huddled in a circle nearby. There were fourteen men with their faces obscured in elaborate turbans.

The walls of the complex were tilted and skewed with a bizarre geometry uncoupled from human scale. Hundreds of ornate columns and niches lined the walls and funneled Atkins's attention toward a singular imposing figure.

The colossus rose floor to ceiling inside a deep niche three hundred meters tall. It was cut from the surrounding stone—or was perhaps once buried and now exposed. It absorbed and refracted the LIDAR, rendering the edge of the three-dimensional map as a shifting fog. A quasi-human silhouette flickered in and out of the static. An elongated head suggested the double crown of a pharaoh. The outline and protrusions were vague while the face remained a perfect void.

Reed and the mission controller leaned over Atkins's chair, staring at his screens. "They brought the RPC back topside?"

Atkins shook his head. "The signal is broadcasting at full strength, but he still appears to be underground. The GPS says he's in . . . Egypt."

The mission controller shook his head, "That's impossible."

"Wait, he's in Syria . . . damn it, they're spoofing the GPS."

Reed sighed. "I knew it. They're using their own gear to broadcast the RPC feed from their spider hole. This is going to be another decapitation video."

The mission controller pointed to the audio channel. "Can you hear anything?"

Atkins unmuted the external microphones on Sahim's helmet. The operations cell filled with a deep guttural chant. The alien sound buzzed and swamped itself with overlapping echoes.

Reed covered his ears. "What the holy hell is that?"

The automatic translation software blinked on one of Atkins's screens: dialect unknown.

The mission controller reached over and muted the audio.

"The mic is damaged. Any chance for some facial recognition?"

The angle of the LIDAR map shifted. Two men were dragging Sahim toward the base of the statue.

Sahim began to sob. "Mister Bradley, provide for my family . . . you promised."

"Just look around, Sahim! Help us find you and get you out!"

The bag was ripped from the helmet. The night vision lenses autofocused and stained the LIDAR map with shades of green. Atkins examined the mysterious colossus. The night vision detected nothing there but a shifting, pitch-black vortex.

Reed grunted. "Night vision's busted too."

Sahim grappled with one of his captors. An unseen thump dropped him back to the ground. Atkins gasped and clenched his jaws to mask the corresponding pain in his spine. He tried to turn Sahim's head to look for an exit. It was useless. He could switch through the channels of data broadcasting from the RPC, but he could not send in signals of his own.

He killed the night vision. High-definition cameras jostled with blurs of red and brown as the men in turbans closed in. A man with wide, black eyes glared through the lenses toward the operations cell in Langley.

"*N'yarlathotep rabb thal'a Nazara!*"

The automatic translation software scrawled the words across the screen: "ARABIC: Look upon the face of {non-standard/named entity: Nyar lath otep}."

They stepped aside to reveal the face of the colossus.

Sahim and Atkins screamed, and their EEGs red-lined.

●

Director Shackley slams his fist on the table. "What the hell happened?"

"Airman Atkins suffered . . . self-inflicted wounds to his eyes. He then mutilated his crew members . . . and four others . . . before being fatally shot by military police," says Lieutenant Chapman.

"I know that! What the hell caused it? What did he see?"

Chapman breaks eye contact with the director and looks to DeWalt for help.

"The last transmission was corrupted, sir. Our best analysts have been unable to recover the data."

Director Shackley sits down and rubs the bridge of his nose again. "I read your theory, Chapman." He flicks open the folder and reads aloud. "'Airman Bradley Atkins, suffering from battlefield stress and excessive caffeine consumption, witnessed the execution and experienced a psychotic break.' I can sell that."

He closes the folder and slides it across to DeWalt. "We are all going to sell it until we're blue in the face. We can't stop until the RPC program is fully reinstated."

"Director, sir?" Chapman interrupts. "I strongly caution against it. We can't devise a safety protocol because we don't even understand the threat. I was ordered to write that report, but there is no way in hell we can blame this on caffeine and stress."

"Dismissed."

Chapman stands his ground. "Sir, I must protest . . ."

"I said you are dismissed!"

Lieutenant Chapman scurries out. The door seals behind him with a hiss.

The director rounds the table and glares at DeWalt. "Find another shrink to rubber stamp some safety measures. We have to learn how this Alhazred organization hacked our system. I want every Afghani that can walk wearing an RPC helmet. I want them in every nook and cranny in the Hindu Kush. I want spec ops and drones and gunships ready to scramble. Nobody goes home. Nobody sleeps until we find this N'yarlathotep."

{}

Jeff C. Carter *lives in Venice, CA with a dog, two cats, and a human. His latest stories appear in the anthologies* Delta Green: Extraordinary Renditions, Humanity 2.0, Apotheosis, That Hoodoo Voodoo That You Do, A Mythos Grimmly, *and issues of* Trembles, Calliope, *and* eFiction *magazine. You can follow him at jeffccarter.wordpress.com.*

Innsmouth Redemption

Joette Rozanski

Kisam Zuber woke from his reverie and saw the darkened town of Innsmouth hunched against the starlit Atlantic. A gibbous moon shed its light on the restless waves and nearby salt marshes. Here, enemies established their capital. Here, they ruled the remnants of the ravaged east coast of the United States.

I. The Collegians

He placed his hand over the small square of paper beside his heart; it was the last love note his wife had written him. The five other Collegians were occupied with their own thoughts, unsure of what waited. They had read the reports and viewed the televised images. Kisam Zuber lost his wife to the New York tsunami, but he'd never seen a Deep One up close.

Kisam covertly watched Cecily Mason's slim face, but she betrayed no emotion as they began their descent.

Their small plane set down in a meadow beside a ruined house nearly a mile from the furthest suburb. The engines whispered into silence. The door opened, steps rolled down, and he and his companions emerged. A cold April breeze brought the faint scent of fish from the nearby town.

Kisam glanced back but saw nothing. The plane was invisible now, its shield revealing little more than an intermittent shimmer against the stars. He tugged his cloak tight and pulled down his night glasses before joining the others. Black turned to green, and he saw the sparkles that outlined his team. The metal-infused material of their cloaks was unwieldy, but they couldn't risk being detected as they crossed the fields.

The nearly deserted Innsmouth of yesteryear had been gentrified over the last decade, filled with boutiques and bistros. The Deep Ones spared it from the earthquakes and tsunamis that devastated other cities. Innsmouth was sacred to Dagon and the ancestors who mated with humans.

The government of the United States hadn't become aware of the Deep Ones until too late. The Collegians tried to warn the president; however, the military did not listen to leaders of underground nations that nobody believed existed.

Kisam's people, the civilization that sprang from the Invisible College of the 1600s, had known about the Deep Ones for centuries and prepared for their incursion; the Invisible College visited the islands where humans and Deep Ones interacted and learned much of their customs and future plans. But there were too few of these descendants of alchemists, even with their advanced technology, to save doomed millions from the abyssal enemy. Kisam's hidden realm of reason and romance watched the downfall of surface civilization and searched frantically for a way to repel the oceanic predators. Innsmouth was their last hope.

At the outskirts of town, Kisam and his friends removed their cloaks, putting them into their backpacks. They were dressed in black but did not fear detection in the shadows since the Deep Ones' big eyes were adapted for the water and had difficulty seeing people in the dark. Their smell and hearing also functioned better in water than on land.

The houses lining the streets stared with empty eyes, dormers peering over mangled overturned automobiles, remnants of the night the Deep Ones invaded. Fresh corpses lay scattered over the cobblestones, the results of recent hunts. Deep Ones regularly gathered humans from further inland and brought them here as sacrifices to Dagon.

The bulk of humanity had been reduced to savagery once their networks of power and communication were destroyed. Meanwhile, most of the Alchemical World remained safe in caves around the globe, like Kisam's home under New Mexico.

A voice muttered in his earpiece. Philip Aston spoke through his throat microphone, warning them to stop. Kisam lifted his night glasses and saw a bonfire nearly a hundred meters in front of them. They had passed many such bonfires, all of them deserted. Most of Innsmouth's citizens gathered for evening worship at the Esoteric Order of Dagon. Most, but not all.

A block ahead, several Deep Ones armed with spears and tridents pursued three men dressed in tattered clothes. The Deep Ones were tall, their skin as rubbery as a dolphin's. Wide, dark eyes gleaming with anticipation, frog-like mouths lined with sharp teeth. A metamorph—a human with abyssal ancestry—wearing jewelry indicating it was male, ran with them; strands of ginger hair dangled from its otherwise bare scalp. Their prey screamed and tried to dash down the dark side streets. The metamorph hurled his spear at the slowest man, skewering him and pinning him to the ground, and leapt upon his prey. He tore away an arm and began devouring it as he watched his fellows run past.

Kisam bowed his head. He could do nothing to help the hunted men. He stared at a nearby corpse, its eyes wide with the terror of death: a young woman Cecily's age, her legs reduced to ribbons of flesh, one arm flung toward the Collegians as if in accusation.

Philip grasped his shoulder, and Kisam gathered his thoughts. He and his team ran down a cobblestone street to the left. In moments, they arrived at a large, yellow building with an ornate cupola. Most of the windows were dark, but a few shuddered with the pale uncertain light of candles.

This was the Gilman Hotel, bowed by the weight of years that a recent renovation couldn't entirely erase. Kisam and his companions hurried around to the back. He paused and looked up. Ray Marsh, their last best hope, lived on the second floor. The window was dimly lit; Ray hadn't joined his mother at the temple or the hunts.

Again, Kisam touched the square of paper beside his heart. Their first redemption was at hand.

II. Desperation

Two hours ago, Ray's mother forced a spear into his hand, pointed down the street, and told him to hunt with the others. He remained still, dropped the spear, and shook his head.

She struck him across the face and addressed him in a blubbery, barely human voice, "They are nothing. They are food. Treat them as such."

He said nothing, allowing the rain to soak the jacket and trousers he insisted on wearing. His eyes were adapted to the dark, and he could see the sharp teeth that overlapped his mother's lower lip. She wore nothing but royal jewelry; her rubbery body needed no protection against the chill air.

She waved one webbed hand at him, and two of her servants seized his arms.

"Take him to the Gilman," she said.

The rain stopped, and the moon shed its pale light into the hotel room. A wooden table and chair were near the window where he could look out at the ruined town. Bonfires flickered in the streets as the Deep Ones reveled in a new hunt.

A single candle mixed its light with that of the moon. Ray held his right hand over the flame, marveling at how quickly the webs between the fingers had grown back. He'd taken scissors to them last week, and here they were again.

Ray knew he couldn't fight the transformation much longer. Another month at most, he estimated, and his mind would be gone, descended into the same madness that possessed the others. Like his mother, he was royalty. Hundreds of Deep Ones would obey him, but to what end? Ruling a lost civilization? Stalking survivors of the greatest disaster to overcome humanity? Immortality as a beastly Dagon worshipper?

Ray was free to roam the hotel, but the guards on the first floor wouldn't let him past the front door. That was all right; he had no wish to leave, at least not to the blood-soaked streets.

Several months ago, his mother's servants searched through the hotel and removed anything that might harm him, but Ray had hidden a sharp metal sliver in the bottom of the chair. His fingers searched the cracks in the wood until they found the makeshift knife. He brought it out and admired the sparkle of the metal in the candlelight.

Ray had his memories, but they wouldn't last much longer. And he never wanted to lose his memories of Cecily. Her soft brown face, cheerful dark eyes, curly hair. He remembered how he'd found her stolen earrings in the Miskatonic pawn shop and redeemed them. He remembered her happiness and her promise of introducing him to her family.

That's all he wanted, memories of her love as he drew the metal across his wrists.

III. Rescue

Cecily could have been the one to rescue Ray, but she didn't trust her emotions.

Alice Swiftdeer and Howard Pomancek donned their microfiber sticky gloves and climbed the hotel's wall. The electrically charged water tension in their fingers, palms, and soles of their boots enabled them to cling to and scale the boards. Alice and Howard paused at the window. They hadn't much time. Howard smashed the glass, and he and Alice swarmed inside. Cecily, Kisam, and Philip unrolled an invisibility tarp.

After a few minutes, a body was pushed out the window, and they gently lowered the metamorph to the ground and bundled him into the tarp.

Loud, inhuman voices came from around the corner of the hotel. Cecily and the others quickly pulled their cloaks from their packs.

Cecily lowered her night glasses. Several Deep Ones ran by. A female paused to sniff the air, lingering behind her companions. She was large and wore a tall tiara made of precious metals—a ruler, a member of royalty. She growled and looked about with unblinking black eyes.

She was a metamorph, nearly completely transformed. Cecily slowly slid her hand inside her jacket and reached for the holstered laser gun. How easy to burn a hole in the creature's chest and fade away with no one the wiser, except the rescue team. She'd tell them she panicked; she'd never been on a mission, so they'd believe her.

Except Kasim would know. The only one among them who'd lost a family member yet didn't draw his weapon would know.

The metamorph turned around and around, obviously confused. She knew Ray was nearby. She paced back and forth, her webbed feet sliding across the grass of the ruined garden. Could she be Ray's mother?

The gun was nearly out of its holster. One dead metamorph compared to millions of human casualties around the world.

Kasim remained still. She saw the sparkles around his cloaked figure, but he made no move.

She knew why. Her people, the Invisible College, the only group of humans that clung to civilization in this world ravaged by Deep Ones, valued reason above revenge, civility above anger. Its members had escaped the superstitions of race, gender, nation, and religion Hidden for centuries because so many leaders valued war and greed over the delights of science and exploration, the group clung to the best characteristics of humanity.

Cecily replaced her weapon. After another minute, the metamorph joined the Deep Ones at the front of the hotel. Alice patted her shoulder. She watched the sparkling shapes of her companions as they lifted their captive and began the trek back. The snarling voices near the Gilman soon receded, and the team hurriedly made their way across the tough meadow grass to the waiting plane.

○

A half hour later, Cecily sat beside the sleeping Ray. He was carefully strapped into a seat near the rear of the plane. She gazed down into the face she barely recognized from a year ago when they attended Miskatonic together. Ray Marsh, nearly transformed into a Deep One, retained his human heart. Collegiate spies had contacted him and promised rescue.

Howard told her that when they jumped into the room, they found Ray with a sliver of sharp metal pressed to his wrist. He was ready to deliver himself from the fate that overtook the great families of Innsmouth.

Kasim slid into the seat beside her.

"You did well," he said. He gestured at Ray. "He will help us. He knows the symbols that will send the Deep Ones back into the abyss to sleep."

"There are millions of Deep Ones."

Kasim smiled. "We'll find a way. Maybe we'll project images across the sky. It's been done before."

"How can that be? Why do they fear signs and symbols? We reject superstition. Why don't they?"

"Sometimes science can be so advanced it looks like magic. Science is there, Cecily, we just haven't discovered it yet. We'll find it when we have more time."

Cecily looked down at the frog-like metamorph. She brushed away the few strands of dark hair that fell across his forehead and lay her hand against his cold cheek.

○

Several weeks later, Cecily again sat beside Ray, who was awake and strapped to his bed in the brightly lit laboratory of Dr. Ramirez. They were in a hospital beneath New Mexico. Ray's wide eyes betrayed his fear. She smiled and took his cold hand.

"Don't worry, my love. Dr. Ramirez believes she can reverse the transformation.

My people have studied the Deep Ones for centuries and believe we can alter the changes at the cellular level. The process will be long and painful, but you will survive." She looked down at him. "Ray, if this isn't what you want, tell me. We'll take you back to Innsmouth."

Ray's voice was deep and sloppy and barely human. "I don't want to be like them. I want to be human."

"I know." She watched Dr. Ramirez approach, and she leaned over and kissed Ray as the needle slid into his arm.

Joette Rozanski *is a native of Toledo, Ohio, and works as a desktop publisher for a non-profit organization. Her hobbies are photography, birding, and, of course, writing. Her favorite genres are science fiction, fantasy, humor, and horror. She has stories in a couple of* Sword and Sorceress *anthologies (*XIII *and* XVI*) and the anthologies* Such a Pretty Face, Mother Goose is Dead, *and* Strangely Funny.

Church of the Renewed Covenant

Shannon Fay

"And down here is where we hold the services." The woman showing them the church had starchy orange hair and a lined face. Jake recognized her type from churches he had attended as a child and unwilling teenager. She was a true believer, someone who had dedicated themselves to the church and eagerly awaited the end of days, if only for vindication.

Cheryl looked at the stone floor and walls with wide eyes. Dim light came from the fake gas lamps overhead, barely cutting the shadows in the dark underground room.

"Oh my," she said. "It's so atmospheric! I can only imagine what a choir must sound like in here."

"We don't have a choir," explained their tour guide. (Margaret? Jake had already forgotten her name). "We follow the old ways here at Renewed Covenant. We come here to worship, not to be entertained." She smiled grimly, warming to her theme. "If you want rock bands and stand-up comedians and shouting from the pulpit, you can find that in more 'modern' churches, but here, we believe a sincere desire to worship is enough."

"Oh," Cheryl said, bright eyes dimming.

Jake felt a tug in his heart but, also, a hit of satisfaction. He had been against this whole church-shopping business. Cheryl had been the one who needled him into it, saying how she wanted to bring the kids up in the faith, how it'd be a good way to meet people, how they might make some business connections. But those were just reasons for Jake.

Cheryl's only reason was that she believed.

It was different for her, Jake thought. It was always different for converts. They came to the faith with a chip on their shoulder, a desire to prove that, even if they came to the party later in life, they believed all the more for it. They had none of the baggage that came from being bombarded with it from birth.

"Of course, we have made *some* concessions to the modern world." Margaret spoke as if she had just sipped sour milk. "We try to make our services welcoming for families. You have three small children, yes?"

"That's right," Cheryl said, smiling over at Jake.

"We have a few young families in our congregation," Margaret said. "With them in mind, we turned one of the rooms upstairs into a mother's room. If your child is getting restless during a service, you can take them up there. There are toys and books, and—"

"You call it the 'mother's room'?" Jake said. "Oh, right, because it's totally the woman's job to look after the kids."

Margaret tilted her chin upwards. "Like I said, we follow the old ways here."

"Sure, 'cause the husband and wife would never, say, take turns," Jake went on. "And what if it's a male gay couple? Would they be allowed to take their kid into the 'mother's room'?" He looked at Margaret. "You do accept gay people into the church, don't you?"

"As far as we are concerned, a person's sexuality has no relevance if they come with a true desire to worship," Margaret said. "At the same time, it's not something we encourage."

Jake wasn't surprised. He had figured out when he was thirteen that the church was stuck in the past when it came to issues of sexuality and race. And as for its treatment of women . . . well, what could you expect from a faith born out of a paranoid New England man's fear of female genitalia?

Jake wasn't surprised, but he was perversely pleased. This was an easy out if there ever was one. Jake looked at Cheryl. *Look,* he tried to say through a waggle of his eyebrows. *They're a bunch of sexist, racist homophobes!*

Cheryl just looked back at him, disappointed. He knew that look well: *You only care about scoring points.*

Jake sighed.

"Excuse me, Margaret," he said, and the woman frowned. Oh crap, he *had* got her name wrong. Oh well. "Could I speak with my wife for a moment?"

"Certainly," 'Margaret' said and headed upstairs.

Cheryl went and stood by the stone altar, running her hands along the top.

"Look at this place," she whispered. "It really feels like the elder gods are sleeping right under our feet."

Jake stood beside her. "Well, the nice thing about the elder gods is that, no matter where you're standing, they're always right below you. You don't need a church to be close to them."

Cheryl shook her head. "I don't get you sometimes, Jake. You crap on every church we visit, yet you believe more deeply than anyone I've ever known."

Jake shrugged. It was a conundrum. For all the scorn, for all the Friday nights he spent at home watching TV rather than wearing a hooded cloak and chanting in Latin, for all his disdain, he could not shake the belief within him that the elder gods slept fitfully below the earth and would one day awaken.

"Look, babe, this isn't the place for us," he said. "They still think it's the 1930s around here. And they don't even have a choir! Even old Crafty liked organ music."

Cheryl chuckled. "Yeah, no choir was the breaking point for me. I was just hoping they'd win me back somehow."

He pulled her into a hug.

"We'll find a place," Jake said. "Somewhere we can bask in existential horror while working past all of the problematic crap."

"Right, we'll keep looking," Cheryl replied.

'Margaret' was waiting for them upstairs.

"Thank you for showing us around, Mary," Cheryl said, giving Jake a knowing look at the woman's name. Jake turned his laugh into a cough. "We'll keep the Church of the Renewed Covenant in mind."

"Indeed," Mary said, her mouth pursed. "Well, I hope to see you at a Friday mass in the near future. Until then, may the elder gods sleep."

"May the elder gods sleep," Cheryl repeated.

"May the elder gods sleep," Jake said, a grin spreading across his face.

§§

Shannon Fay *is a Canadian writer currently living in London. She is the 2013 winner of The James White Award (an award for new writers) and a 2014 graduate of Clarion West. She has worked on farms in the UK, in a youth hostel in Amsterdam, and in a bookstore in Canada. (Weirdly, the bookstore was the worst job when it came to cleaning up bodily fluids.) She can be found online at www.ayearonsaturn.com and on Twitter (@shannonlfay).*

The Posthumous Recruitment of Timothy Horne

Pete Rawlik

Captain Timothy Horne of the 7th Hypnological Battalion was dead—or near enough to dead that other states of being didn't apply. That was what the recruitment packet had said. Normally, he would have asked his momma for her opinion of the deal, but he was dead, and she was still back in Belle Glade driving a bus in Palm Beach to make ends meet. If he agreed to participate, she would get a $10,000 signing bonus, disguised as a death benefit. If he passed the entrance exam, the bonus would translate into $3,000 a month for life—her life. What Horne got out of it was a second chance: he committed to ten years of service, and if he wanted to, he could then part company, no questions asked, no debts, with what appeared to be a hefty separation package.

For a black kid from the Glades well past the verge of death, it seemed a more than fair offer. It was better than the one he had taken when he joined up to fight the invaders. Of course, back then, everyone and their brother were joining ranks against the aliens. It was the human thing to do.

The one thing that the entire population of Earth could agree on was that the aliens had no business on the moon. The United Nations was still formulating a response when the deep space probes went offline. Then the Europa rover went silent.

In the course of three days, every piece of human technology outside the orbit of the moon went down. The ESA used the attitude thrusters on an old communications satellite to push it into a trajectory that crossed the four-hundred-thousand-kilometer line marked by the moon—what would later be called simply the Boundary. The whole world watched as that immense piece of manufacturing and design trudged slowly past an imaginary boundary and was swarmed by half-visible creatures whose insectoid wings seemed to push against a medium we could not detect. They didn't tear it to pieces, but the result was the same.

A half hour later, the first communication came in. The Migou introduced themselves, and we learned that our world was subject to an interdiction. For some reason, one that was not explained to us, we had been quarantined. Nothing from earth would be let beyond the Boundary. Communications back were not responded to. Suddenly denied access to the final frontier, a frontier that only a few nations could afford to travel in, the world declared war on the Migou.

That war did not go well.

The Migou and their ships, great organic things that resembled the silica-based shells of microscopic algae, were not invulnerable, but it took a concentrated effort to bring them down. Afterward, they didn't last long. Whatever made them only half-visible also destabilized their very existence. It took hours, sometimes days, but in the end, the Migou and their vehicles dissolved into a plastic soup that burned the skin. The chemists and material engineers couldn't explain it, but the theoretical physicists could. Based on their studies of the alien bodies and artifacts, they had some startling news for the human race. The universe, our universe, wasn't particularly hospitable to life as we knew it.

Humans tend to think of the universe as having four dimensions: three spatial dimensions and time. The reality was that the universe was comprised of twenty-three dimensions, nineteen of which humans couldn't perceive, let alone take advantage of. The Migou could perceive some of those dimensions and were likely comprised not only of matter as we knew it but also of extradimensional equivalents. To our limited senses, that was why they were only partially visible and why they fell apart so quickly.

They moved and lived not only in the spaces we knew of but in those in between as well. If humans were going to fight and win a war with the Migou, the weapons employed would have to be radically different. The Gilman equations said this was possible, but every blade, every gun, and every ship that incorporated the exotic extradimensional technology functioned only briefly before tearing itself and the user apart. Something about the human brain was anathema to the new tech, and the exotic machines responded in a spectacularly violent way.

Horne had a vague memory that using alien tech was what led to his own death. He could remember the feel of something bizarre in his hands, something that fired bolts of blue, spiraling energy. The backwash had left waves of white scars across his coffee-colored arms. Even in death, those scars ached, reminding him of what had happened. He had wondered how it was that in death he could still feel pain. Was it a physical memory, or were those scars merely psychic, mere memories of the pain that had been inflicted? Then he had remembered his mother and her bus, and he stopped thinking about his own well-being and signed the papers.

That was three days ago.

It felt like they had been marching down the stairs ever since.

"Man, I thought the Nine Hundred Steps to Deeper Slumber was a metaphor." Horne mumbled to no one in particular.

Major Carter didn't break his pace but just kept up the steady downward march. "It is, Horne, that's why the number of steps varies from culture to culture. It's a test—a kind of endurance test. Making the transition from our world to the Dreamlands can't be easy, at least not at first. You have to want it, to work for it, to build a new set of bridges. What the psychophysicists call neural conduits. The steps are just a manifestation of that, mostly because that's what we've told you about during orientation. In other settings, its other things: at the airbase in Wichita, they use a yellow brick road; in Britain, the imagery is of a wardrobe and a forest of coats. They're just symbols, obstacles to overcome in order to reach the Dream Lands."

Horne looked back at his companions in this weird effort.

An entire battalion had begun marching down those stairs: twelve hundred men. Now he could barely see twenty. The rest were lost in the fog and darkness that seemed to seep out of the very air. There were no walls on the Steps to Deeper Slumber, no rails, no bannisters, no braces, or any other kind of architecture. There were just steps, endless runners and risers that just seemed to spiral downward into the mist. There were no lights either, and yet, still he could see— not far but far enough. The mist and the darkness beyond were ominous. If he looked too long, he could see things moving. He could hear things as well: the beating of great wings, screeching calls of titanic birds, whispering voices that said things he couldn't quite understand. Some of those voices sounded like his grandmother, others like his father. They called to him, implored him, and tried to draw him away from his downward progress. He wanted to go, but something in the back of his mind kept forcing him to keep marching.

"Is it true that the Dream Lands are . . . you know . . . the afterlife?"

Horne didn't know who asked the question, and it didn't matter.

Carter answered it without even looking back. "It is true that we've documented individuals who have long since been declared legally dead on Earth, some hundreds of years ago.

"However, we think this is a very rare occurrence, that only one in maybe a thousand people are truly great dreamers, able to sustain themselves beyond death without help. Even with help, very few people are able to make the transition." Carter cast a backward glance and seemed to frown with disappointment. "You have to remember, boys," shouted Carter as he took a switchback on another flight, "the journey is worth it. Once you get to the Dream Lands, you'll be different, able to do things that you hadn't even believed possible before. This isn't Earth. It might look a lot like it and most of the physical laws are the same, but there are subtle differences and peculiarities."

Horne perked up and refocused on the back of Carter's helmet. "You're talking about magic."

Carter shook his head. "Not magic, metaphysics. The people who built this alternate reality tweaked it slightly, made it just a little more fantastic than our world." Carter glanced over his shoulder. "Oh, and before I forget, in Ulthar never kill a cat."

That was the seventh time Carter had told Horne the injunction about cats. It made him wonder what would happen if he did and if it applied only to Ulthar or to the whole of the Dream Lands? Did other places have similar but different rules? In Oriab, was it illegal to kill a dog?

Horne wiped his brow with the back of his glove. He was sweating; the forced march was getting to him. Out in the fog, in the darkness, a pattern was forming. At first, it looked like circles, a pattern of rings, but sometimes, it looked like a square or like a square and a triangle—but most of the time it looked like circles. It was as if the fog and the darkness beyond weren't there at all but were merely a complex of layered patterns; patterns that, as Horne went on, began to resolve into things that were not circles. The pattern was there in the steps, as well. It was the same shape iterated over and over again as if someone had printed the concept of stairs over a sheet of paper with a watermark embedded within. Not a circle but something geometric with angles. It took him a moment.

Horne squinted and widened his eyes to try and make it come into focus. It was five-sided with equal angles: a pentagon, like the one in Virginia.

Like the one he'd seen during training in Antarctica, the one that was made of grey stone and hummed and whistled as men walked past. You could tell how old it was just by looking at it; it felt ancient, and it told you so deep down in the base of your brain. The pentagon that was all liquid black inside, so black that even the targeting lasers vanished. The pentagon that they fed soldier after soldier after soldier into, forcing him to watch until it was his turn at last. No matter how hard he tried, he couldn't scream as that liquid black nothing swallowed him whole. That had been days ago, hours maybe; he wasn't sure. On the stairs, time meant little. As he continued forward, all he could think about was the pentagonal patterns forming around him and the number five.

He blurted out the number, and he wasn't alone. A whole chorus of his fellow soldiers had said it as well. He looked around and did a head count. There were only ten of them, not counting Carter.

Carter responded, "The builders, the Progenitors, or—in the old language— the Q'Hrell, were pentaradially symmetrical in design. Their entire bodies and even their brains were divided into five sections. Not unexpectedly, they incorporated that number into much of their machinery, architecture, and art. The Dream Lands are no exception. The fundamental programming, which the psychophysicists call the quintessence, is five-dimensional in nature. Your brains might perceive this as random appearances of patterns involving the number five."

Carter's voice helped him to focus, to keep walking. Horne thought back to his classes in physics at Florida Tech. How Professor Benjamin Scapellati had discussed the theories of supra-asymmetry and how some dimensions acted as regulators on others. He tried to meld that half-remembered lecture with what Carter was telling them. If the Dream Lands were only based on five dimensions, the constraints would be different. Physical laws as dictated by the higher dimensions would be absent. The possibilities might be immensely terrifying but wondrous as well.

His scars ached, throbbed really. Something was happening. Was the fog thinner? Was the darkness less impenetrable? Were the stairs less steep?

Carter had picked up the pace, and without even noticing, Horne had

followed suit. Carter hummed as he walked, almost too low to hear—a pre-
millennial song by Inhouse. It still played on the classic rock stations. Horne
couldn't remember the title, but as he caught the tune, he tried to remember the
lyrics, something about James Taylor and an old coat and a box of photographs.
It reminded him of nights on the Intracoastal eating guacamole and fresh fish
tacos on the beach with live music washing down from the bars and clubs that
lined the streets of Lake Worth. If he closed his eyes, he could almost smell the
salt air and taste the cilantro and garlic. Somewhere in his memory, a bass guitar
was pounding, but it wasn't any song that he could put a name to. He realized it
wasn't his memory at all.

His scars beat out a tempo that echoed in his head. His eyes started to blur. His
tongue felt fat, and he had that sensation in the back of his throat, the tightness
just before the technicolor yawn. All around him, the pentagonal pattern fell
apart. Carter turned, and he had no face, just a huge Cheshire grin of ivory teeth
staring back from an empty space. Horne's scalp itched. He brought his hands
up to try to get his helmet off and run his fingers through his thick wiry hair,
but his hands were different. They had become disconnected. The scars were
empty spaces, and his hands had begun to drift apart in pieces. He could still
move them, still flex his fingers and wrists, but they weren't entirely connected
anymore. He could still feel them, but he could also feel the spaces in between.

Horne screamed.

The faceless thing that Carter had become was holding on to him, dragging
him forward, that great terrifying headless mouth opening and words leaking
out. Horne couldn't hear the words, but he could read them. "Hold on. It's just a
little further. We're almost there!"

And then there was an arching gate, and the darkness was gone. So was the
fog and so were all the other soldiers and so was Carter.

As he woke up, Horne realized that there had never been a 7th Hypnological
Battalion. They had been an illusion, a way of making him feel part of something.
There was safety in numbers, and the thousands of other soldiers were just
echoes to help get him here, into the Dream Lands. Now, in this place, Horne
felt different, inhuman. He could feel his body but also the particles of air and
dust and pollen that moved around and through him. He looked at himself
and realized that he perceived his surroundings through sensory apparatus that
were more than just eyes and ears. He extended into a dimension that he didn't

even understand. His body was no longer three-dimensional but five, and he could see that, sense it, somehow.

A nonsense phrase came to his mind. He realized that he knew exactly what it meant. It had been years since he thought about that child's rhyme, but today, he finally understood what it meant to be a frumious bandersnatch.

He rose up on his twrils and, with his three multi-faceted subordinate eyes, took in his surroundings. There was a cat at his feet, purring and rubbing against him in a figure eight design. He was on a green hill overlooking a harbor. There was a vast ship, all steel and brass, larger than anything he had ever seen. Great towering stacks vented gouts of steam the size of storm clouds. On the decks of the Brobdingnagian construct, Horne could see fighter craft tethered like butterflies. Men and other things scurried about on the decks, in the rigging, on the hull, and on the huge wharfs and scaffolding. There were flying things, some with wings, some with great balloon-like organs, and some were like him, bandersnatch with twrils to climb through the ether.

"What do you think, Horne?" The voice came from the cat.

Horne played his sensors over its fur. It wasn't really a cat, though it looked like one. It was so much more.

"That's a warship." His voice was like wind being forced through a bellows, like a whale imitating human speech.

The Carter-Cat nodded, which was kind of an impressive action for a creature with limited anatomy. "Welcome to the Hlanith Naval Yard. That, my friend is the *Tars Tarkas*. She's almost ready to launch. She'll be your home for the next eight weeks while she steams to Phobos Base."

Horne tilted what was left of his head. "Phobos is a moon of Mars. We're steaming to Mars?"

"I told you, the rules are different here." Carter-Cat ran a paw over his head and face. "The human fleet is assembling around Phobos. Our allies are organizing around the other moon, Deimos."

"We have allies?"

"Grimalkin, alien cats. From Saturn mostly, though some are from Uranus. They aren't really cats, not as we know them, though there is something feline about them. Turns out that the Migou interdiction works both ways. Just as we aren't allowed off Earth, the grimalkin aren't allowed in. That has deprived them of some very prime hunting grounds."

What passed for Horne's ears pricked up. "What were alien cats hunting on Earth?"

Carter-Cat blinked. "Best you not worry about that. Just remember that the enemy of my enemy is my friend. And when in Ulthar . . ."

"Never kill a cat. You've told me. Rather self-serving, don't you think?"

"But nevertheless, true."

"What happens when the fleets are fully assembled?" Horne wondered.

"There's a gate on Mars, a big one. It's large enough to let the fleet through into real space. When that happens, the battle carriers will launch the fighters toward Earth. When melded with our own technology, the Saturnine grimalkin make particularly powerful drives. We can strike at the Migou from behind with a technology they won't expect."

"I was thinking more about me, about us. We aren't exactly human. What happens when we pass through the gate? I mean, aren't I dead?"

"You, Timothy Horne, are dead. But the gate on Mars isn't connected to Earth. It doesn't know that, doesn't even know we were ever human. When it spits us out back into real space, I'm still going to be a cat, and you are going to retain the form you have now."

"Which is what? What exactly am I?"

"You're something new, and you're not alone. The feedback from the energy weapon altered your template; you're a little Migou now. When you enter real space, you'll be able to access some of the higher dimensions. It's going to be weird."

Horne flexed his six arms and watched them spread out farther and farther until there was more empty space than solid. "Does this look human to you?"

The Carter-Cat used a hind leg to scratch behind his ear. "Nope, you don't look one bit human. It's a strange new world, Horne. Aliens have surrounded Earth, we've built virtual reality steamships to take us to Mars, our best friends are Saturnine grimalkin, and your commanding officer is a cat. I think we are going to have to redefine what it means to be human, don't you?"

Horne closed his eyes and looked at the Carter-Cat with his slin. If he mimsied just the right way, he could make him just be Carter again, mostly.

Together, they walked down the hill toward the titanic starship brimming with the various novel and multiform facets of humanity. Toward war, toward hope, toward the future.

§

Pete Rawlik, *a longtime collector of Lovecraftian fiction, is the author of more than fifty short stories, a smattering of poetry, and the Cthulhu Mythos novels* Reanimators *and* The Weird Company. *He is a frequent contributor to the* Lovecraft ezine *and the* New York Review of Science Fiction. *In 2014, his short story "Revenge of the Reanimator" was nominated for a New Pulp Award. His new novel,* Reanimatrix, *a weird, noir, romance set in HP Lovecraft's Arkham, will be released in 2016. He lives in southern Florida where he works on Everglades issues.*

Curiosity

Adam Heine

As a child, I sometimes had dreams so terrible they haunted me long after they were over. I'd wake up questioning what was real, jumping at shadows, thinking the wraiths or revenants or facehuggers had followed me into the waking world or worse, that I was still trapped in my nightmare.

It's been three days since I escaped Mars, and I'm still jumping at shadows.

That won't make any sense. Let me explain.

To Mission Control and anyone else listening, this is Dr. Sarissa Nontaisong, exolinguist and crew psychologist aboard the *Victoria*. Our mission is . . . was to investigate the images transmitted over a year ago by the Mars rover *Curiosity*. The images hinted at extraterrestrial civilization—carved monoliths, glyphs, and alien symbols. They told us we were not alone. All of us wanted it to be true.

Our mission had difficulties from the moment we left Earth. The solar cells powering the EmDrives and ship systems failed at irregular intervals, requiring us to perform frequent in-flight spacewalks for repair. On top of that, nearly every member of the crew reported nightmares: demons, human sacrifices, horrifying monsters of all kinds.

We reported these things to you already. By themselves, they weren't enough for concern. We crafted the reports so that would be the case. This was the most important mission in human history, after all. None of us wanted to return to Earth prematurely.

So although we told you about the nightmares, we neglected to report our waking hallucinations. We didn't report that, due to these hallucinations, every one of us was terrified to go on spacewalks. We didn't report what happened to Dr. Landry.

Consider this my full account on the *Victoria's* mission.

During Dr. Landry's last spacewalk, I had the comm, while the other three crew members slept. As I said, we were all terrified of being out there, so Joline and I did our best to keep each other talking.

"God, I hate it out here," she told me.

"That's chipper," I said. "Do you have more to say about that?"

"Hell no." She laughed. It sounded hollow over the commlink. "And don't you start shrinking me, Sarissa. Not out here."

"Sorry." I smiled at being caught. The crew's mental health *was* my job. "What do you want to talk about?"

The line was silent. Her helmet's camera feed slowly approached the solar cells on the spokes toward the ship's center. "Why'd you choose psychology?" she said, the barest tremble in her voice. Although her helmet was pointed at her destination, I imagined her head turned up, staring out into space, worrying at what was out there.

"I didn't choose it, really. I chose linguistics, but my father didn't think I could support myself with that."

"Ah, that explains the double degree. I notice you didn't answer my question." I could hear the smirk even over the commlink.

I shrugged, forgetting she couldn't see me. "My parents always complained that they couldn't understand each other. I guess it came out of that—a desire to understand people, how they think, why they do what they do."

"Kinda explains the linguistics, too." Joline had reached the first unit of shorted solar cells. She began loosening the bolts with the pistol-grip power drill. For a time, all I could hear was the grating pulse of the drill's vibrations. Each oscillation made my stomach clench.

The drill stopped suddenly, and she became still. "Are you afraid of anything, Sarissa?"

"Let's not, yeah?" That question couldn't lead anywhere good. "Hey, tell me why you—"

"I'm terrified of open water." She laughed, sounding nervous. "It sounds stupid, I know. But it's not the water itself. It's what's in the water, the idea that I'm intruding in some other thing's home, that I don't belong and they know it."

"Who are 'they'?" If she wouldn't be turned from the subject, maybe I could help her talk through it.

"Whatever. Sharks, whales." She began flipping switches underneath the opened panel. "Hell, I'm afraid of fucking sea turtles."

"Thalassophobia. That's perfectly normal, Joline."

She finished the reset sequence and closed the panel. "Space feels like that to me, too."

I started to say something, but she was already drilling the bolts back in place. The comm rumbled loudly. All I could do was wait. Gradually, the drill's rumbling became a high-pitched screech as the bolt stuck in place.

"That looks done, Jo."

No response. She kept tightening it.

"Joline?" With horror, I realized the high-pitched screech wasn't the drill. It was her. "Joline, talk to me! Jo! Jo!"

Breathless, I slammed the alert button and ripped off the headset. The corridors blared red as I dashed to the airlock.

By the time I got to her, she was at the end of her tether, unconscious, spinning amidst a glittering cloud of debris. The solar cell beneath her was completely destroyed.

I dragged her into sick bay. She babbled, something about blood, a terrible eye, creatures like maggots swallowing each other whole. She grabbed me suddenly, digging her fingers deep into my shoulder. "Don't! I saw it. I saw it, Sarissa. It wants . . . it wants . . ." Then she fell back on the table, muttering gibberish before going unconscious again.

She had no injuries, no indication at all of what had happened to her, but I couldn't wake her. The others came in, and I told them the story. If it weren't for the hallucinations, they might not have believed me, but we'd all seen things like Joline had described—in flashes, visions. Her camera feed showed nothing, not even what had happened to the solar cell.

"Without that cell, we're at 60 percent capacity," Commander Marshall said. "Enough to enter orbit or turn back home. Not both."

No one responded, but we were all thinking the same things. Nobody wanted to be stranded out here. Nobody wanted to abort. Everybody wished Joline would just wake up.

Isiah, the archaeologist, asked, "What did she see out there?"

I shook my head. "I don't know. Something more than we've seen so far."

The pilot Cobb voiced what I was afraid to say. "She didn't destroy the solar cell by herself."

"She might have," I replied, unconvinced.

Again, we sat in silence, eyes on our knees.

"We should ask Mission Control," Marshal finally said.

Cobb grimaced. "They'll ask questions. If we have to tell them about the visions, they'll make us turn around."

Marshal sighed. He didn't like keeping things from you on Earth.

I felt the same, but . . . life on Mars! This was the most historic voyage ever made. What if Neil Armstrong had turned back? Or what if the *Challenger* or the *Columbia* had succeeded? How far might the space program have come? We could have discovered *Curiosity's* ruins in person, could have rovers as far as Titan. We might, finally, have proof that we're not alone.

"I'll monitor her," I said.

They watched me carefully.

"If she's fine, there's nothing to report."

They pretended to be convinced, even though they all knew I would never report a thing.

○

We related the cell damage to Mission Control, calling it an instrument malfunction. There was public pressure to complete our mission, so instead of ordering us to turn back, you came up with the plan to use the lander's liquid-fueled thrusters for deceleration in place of the solar-powered EmDrives. We couldn't begin deceleration until the last minute, meaning we'd get to Mars earlier than planned, but once there, we could cannibalize the cells on the *Curiosity* rover. Theoretically, that would give us enough power to get back home.

We'd arrive at the planet during solar conjunction and have no communication with Earth on arrival. All agreed this was a risk worth taking. Hell, I was grateful. I wouldn't have to falsify reports for a while.

We recorded final messages for friends and family. Then the sun cut off the *Victoria* from Earth, blocking communication for at least a week. That was four days ago.

"You made a good decision," Isiah told me.

"Did I?"

He gave me his warm smile. "Come on. Do you think any of us would have forgiven ourselves if we turned back? We'd all die for this mission. You know that."

"Joline, too?" Days after the accident, Dr. Landry still hadn't woken. An IV kept her hydrated.

"She would've," Isiah's smile was gone now. "I'm still praying for her."

We achieved orbit that night. The increased deceleration from the lander's rocket propulsion was uncomfortable but effective. Unfortunately, it also used half the lander's fuel. That left us very little room to explore.

The *Victoria*, too, needed what little power she had left for communications and maintaining orbit. We decided to power down her life support entirely and take Dr. Landry to the surface. The lander had oxygen and an airlock.

At 3:07am on July 16th, the ship began shaking, rumbling like an angry god; we had hit the atmosphere. Systems picked up the rover's signal immediately. "It's at Olympus Mons," I told the pilot, "in the deepest caldera."

"What?" Cobb said. "How the hell'd it get in there?"

Nobody responded. It didn't matter; the rover was our only chance of getting home.

Two minutes into atmospheric entry, Dr. Landry regained consciousness. She fought against the restraints, rubbing her wrists red. Her piercing screams rose above the din of the lander's reentry.

"Shut her up!" Cobb shouted.

Isiah and I tried to calm her, but she didn't seem to hear us, and we couldn't unstrap until we landed.

"I said—" Cobb started.

Suddenly, she stopped screaming. I breathed a sigh of relief, but it was short-lived. She wasn't silent. Her voice was low, guttural. Her eyes peeled wide open, looking all about as if for some means of escape. She was chanting, the same gibberish repeated over and over: "*Gof'nn uh'e hupadgh Shub-Niggurath'geh nog kadishtu.*"

I can repeat the words because I've heard them many times. I looked to Isiah, but he was staring at Joline, his eyes as wide as moons.

Cobb snapped, "Something's wrong. The reverse thrusters aren't responding."

The commander barked, "Well, *make* them respond!"

Cobb clearly bit back some kind of retort. He activated the speed brakes and pulled back hard on the throttle. The sudden deceleration smashed us into our seats.

Joline's chanting continued. "*Gof'nn uh'e hupadgh Shub-Niggurath'geh nog kadishtu. Gof'nn uh'e hupadgh Shub-Niggurath'geh nog kadishtu.*"

"We're not slowing down fast enough."

Olympus Mons stretched across the viewport. Its six gaping calderas were shadowed maws in its peak. They grew very large very fast.

"*Gof'nn uh'e hupadgh Shub-Niggurath'geh nog kadishtu! Gof'nn uh'e hupadgh Shub-Niggurath'geh nog kadishtu!*"

The rim of the deepest caldera passed underneath. Sheer walls closed in. Joline's gibberish grew louder, more frantic. Her wrists bled where they chafed against the restraints.

Cobb strained against the controls, desperately trying to stop the ship. When only a few kilometers remained, he put us in a 10-g spin to point the main engines at the caldera wall. I felt sick. He fired the engines. Our horizontal velocity slowed, and we slammed into the ground, spinning and sliding before we came to a stop just half a kilometer from the wall.

"*Gof'nn uh'e hupadgh shub-niggurath'geh nog kadishtu! Gof'nn uh'e—*" she was shouting.

Isiah was out of his seat in a flash, injecting a sedative into Dr. Landry. She quieted.

"What the hell was that?" asked Cobb, staring at Joline in disgust.

"Forget it," said Commander Marshal.

Isiah stayed on board to monitor Joline. Marshal, Cobb, and I suited up to go outside. Marshal unlocked the outer door of the airlock and turned to give us final instructions. "Nobody wander off. As soon as we know the extent of the damage, we'll re—"

The door flew open. I shielded my eyes from the sudden ruddy glare. I saw a shadow flit into the airlock, but I heard Marshal's scream. Next thing I knew, Cobb was outside the ship with some kind of assault rifle, screeching obscenities. His face was twisted in fear and rage. He aimed high above the lander, firing continuously until his magazine was empty. My ears rang, but I could still hear Cobb shouting through the com. Trembling, I got to my feet, walked out, and put a hand on his shoulder. He jumped back a full meter, looking at me like I was a ghost.

I turned to see what he was shooting at and froze. On top of the lander—and spilling over the side—was the lifeless body of a creature like a failed science experiment: an amorphous mass of tentacles, eyes, and teeth. One massive claw still gripped the maneuvering engines, the dead flesh melting into a kind of solid goo as I watched.

Commander Marshall was dead, asphyxiated in the thin Martian air. I couldn't tell whether the creature or Cobb's rifle had killed him. My mouth opened and closed on its own. It was some time before I could even think.

I turned on Cobb. "Why the hell do you have a gun?" It was the first coherent question that came to mind.

Cobb took longer to reach lucidity than I had; after all, he'd seen the thing alive. "O-orders. NASA wasn't . . . wasn't sure what we'd find."

"What's going on?" Isiah said over the com.

"Look at my feed." Although I longed to look away, I kept my helmet pointed squarely at the dead creature.

"I am," he replied. "What the hell happened to Clay? Did Cobb *shoot* him?"

It was a confusing several minutes before we figured out the truth: the creature did not appear on any of our cameras. I wish it had. When Isiah finally saw the creature with his own eyes, he went ash white.

Cobb marched back to the airlock. "We're getting out of here."

"How?" I said.

"By finishing the mission. Find the *Curiosity*, get the cells, go home."

Isiah and I didn't argue.

Cobb checked the lander while we got our recording equipment. We were terrified, but we were scientists.

We had to leave Dr. Landry with the ship. I admit that at the time, I envied her.

Cobb confirmed that the lander was in good condition, despite the rough landing. If we could get the rover's solar cells, we'd be able to return to the

Victoria, restore her power, and return home. The pilot produced two more assault rifles and additional ammunition from concealed compartments. He handed a rifle to each of us.

I balked. "What did NASA think we'd find?"

Cobb wouldn't say. "If you have to use it, plant your back foot hard. There's a lot more kick up here." With that, he led us out.

The rover's signal took us along the caldera's edge. The enormous cliff face towered three kilometers up. It felt like it might crush us at any moment. Cobb was well ahead of us.

About half an hour out, he stopped and faced the wall.

"What is it?" I said, still walking.

"It's here."

We caught up to him. He was staring at a narrow crevice in the caldera wall. On the other side was an open canyon. Carved into the walls beyond were enormous structures, monoliths with engraved symbols, sweeping arches and ramparts. They were majestic and terrifying and like nothing man had ever thought to make.

"The pictures," I said. This was what had brought us here in the first place. Though seeing it in the flesh was not as exciting as I'd thought it would be. I ached to be home, safe.

"Where's the rover?"

Cobb fussed with the tracking device. "Inside," he said finally, "and down."

There was an open doorway set in the face of the monoliths. We followed Cobb inside, switching on our helmet lights. From the architecture outside, I had assumed we'd find some sort of hall or foyer or, failing that, a natural cavern. Instead, we were in a tube. Five ridges ran down into the dark with striations at regular intervals. The striations were approximately twenty centimeters high, tall enough that we had to be careful to step over them. Pentagonal passageways occasionally opened on either side.

That's my scientific description. Cobb's version was more evocative. "Looks like an intestine. Why didn't the rover report this?"

"I know why," Isiah said. He showed us the pictures and video he'd been recording since we arrived. They showed the caldera, the monoliths outside, but the rest—those images taken from inside the cavern—showed only the outer slope of Olympus Mons, as though we were still outside.

"How is that possible?" I asked.

"How is any of this possible?" Isiah replied. "We're gazing at the abyss."

Isiah put the camera away.

We began documenting things we *could* record. Scrapings from the rock walls showed metals our equipment couldn't identify. The air was much thicker, and our instruments showed a significant amount of oxygen, though none of us dared remove our masks.

A breeze blew down the tunnels and back up in regular intervals. *Like breathing*, I thought, but it seemed too crazy to state out loud.

The striations ceased abruptly, and the tunnel opened into an enormous cavern. It was so large that a kind of fog obscured the ceiling. The cavern was filled with strange, tree-like formations: leafless with thick, entangled branches and massive knots on the trunks. Instead of roots, each had three stumps supporting them. I couldn't make any sense of these statues, and Isiah couldn't so much as scrape a sample from them.

Interspersed between the trees were obelisks covered in writing and glyphs, some matching those outside. These were more interesting to me. "Look at this," I said. "I think it's a history."

"Of what?" Cobb said.

I found repeated figures among the glyphs that I thought might represent the people themselves. "Whatever used to live here."

"The trees," Isiah said, pointing.

He was right. The figures were stylized versions of the statues. It was the beginning of understanding. After all we'd been through, it helped me feel a little better.

"There it is!" Cobb ran ahead.

The rover was inactive, smashed into the ground. Part of a statue had fallen on top of it, crushing half of it beneath two knotted branches. Thankfully, the solar cells were intact.

"I'll get the cells," Cobb said. "You two keep an eye out."

"For?"

He hesitated. "Anything." He set down his pack and began disassembling the cells.

The work took a long time. I stared at the mist for several minutes, never wandering far from Cobb, but the glyphs kept grabbing my attention. God, I wish I had pictures of them. What did they mean? Could we decipher their language? What might we learn?

"Sarissa, come over here!" Isiah squatted next to one of the obelisks, running his hand across the engravings. "What does this look like to you?"

I knelt next to him. The familiar tree people appeared in several places, but Isiah was looking at something else—a kind of scribble with claws and tentacles.

No, not a scribble. "Is that the thing that killed Clay?"

"That was my thought."

Excited and scared, I studied the glyphs intensely, backing up to the beginning of the passage. There were spheres—worlds, I thought. Had the tree people been starfarers? "Go find more," I urged him. "I want to see where this begins."

Starfaring life. We weren't alone! I got lost in the puzzle, driven by my need to understand.

This is what I learned.

The tree people believed they were the children of some greater being, their Mother. This Mother drove them from world to world with one purpose: to claim and devour. They consumed world after world until they met a race of amorphous creatures, like the one that killed the commander. The amorphous creatures had their own masters: sort of tubular beings on spindly legs, like a bacteriophage. These drove off the invaders' first advance, but then the tree children just . . . stopped. It was unclear to me at the time why.

Excited, I told Isiah what I had found. But his face grew increasingly concerned.

Then Cobb screamed.

We rushed back. The tree—the Child—was no longer on top of the rover but had lifted Cobb three meters into the air. What I had taken for knots were now opened, smacking, licking mouths.

"Shoot it!" Cobb shouted.

We scrambled with the assault rifles on our backs. Isiah got his first and filled the dark Child with lead. My first burst knocked me back two meters and went wild, but I soon found my footing. The creature howled from twenty different orifices, lashing out with thick tentacles in a blind fury. Finally, it collapsed into a disgusting heap.

It was too late for Cobb. He'd been torn to pieces, one leg halfway into one of the Child's terrible mouths. I threw up in my suit.

The ground shook. A rumbling, cracking sound came from all around. The other Children—what I had thought were statues—began to move.

"Come on!" Isiah grabbed Cobb's bag with *Curiosity's* parts and sprinted back down the tunnel.

I followed. Tentacles waved and mouths clacked around us. They stamped forward on their enormous stumps, closing in on us. Isiah blew one away with his rifle, but three others took its place. We were being cut off.

I spotted an opening to the right. "This way!" It was a hole in the cavern, like the one we had come through from the surface. I hoped to God they connected.

But this tunnel went down, deeper into the mountain. I kept trying to turn toward another tunnel, one that went up, but at each junction, several Children blocked our way.

"Oh, God, they're herding us," Isiah said.

I had already come to the same conclusion.

We were driven deeper into the dark, hurdling each striation, until the ground smoothed and opened out again. The cavern floor fell away sharply, forcing us to a sudden halt. The air blew strongly, in and out, more like breath than I cared to imagine. We stood on a narrow rim. In front of us was a vast darkness.

The dark expanse wasn't empty. Stalactites and stalagmites stretched out to meet in the center, a kind of webbing, like neurons in the brain. There were dozens of them. In the center of two of them—

"Joline! Clay!"

They were unconscious or dead, their arms and legs enmeshed in the rock that stretched out from the walls of the place, spreading their limbs like a grotesque Vitruvian.

Isiah screamed as a stony tentacle wrapped around his ankle. The rifle and the bag fell from his hands as the tentacle dragged him into the darkness.

I ran toward him, gun blazing at the tendril. Somehow, I did enough damage to loosen it, and I pulled Isiah free. He was convulsing, babbling incoherently. I lifted him to his feet and ran along the ridge of the open cavern, looking for another way out.

All I saw were the Children. They stood in every opening. They weren't advancing though, just waiting.

Waiting for us to join Clay and Joline.

One of them tumbled forward, howling maddeningly, smothered by a black, amorphous mass. The Child fell into the dark pit, but the mass recovered instantly, tendrils latching onto the cavern walls and floor. It was like the creature from the ship! It shot another tendril out at the next Child and dragged it down to the dark.

Isiah continued his babbling, eyes blind.

The creature's fury was terrible, but the Children countered just as viciously. Five pounced on it at once. For each Child the creature tore to shreds or threw into the abyss, two more took its place. They grabbed the amorphous mass, stretched it, consumed it.

But they ignored us.

I wrapped one arm under Isiah's shoulder and ran for the nearest opening. Thankfully, he had enough reason left to keep pace with me. The cannibalized solar cells had fallen into the pit, but I didn't care. I ran, blindly heading toward the surface.

At last, we squeezed through a hole in the surface just over a meter in diameter. I never thought I'd be so grateful to see an alien sky. We were only half a kilometer from the lander. Perhaps, the entire caldera contained underground passages. I don't know. I don't ever want to know.

The amorphous creature was gone. The lander's doors were open; that's how the Children got Joline. Mercifully, the ship was otherwise undamaged, and I was able to take off from the surface before anything else found me. I returned to the *Victoria* without further incident.

I don't know if anyone will hear this or believe me if they do. Isiah is mostly incoherent except for ungodly gibberish and the phrase, "We're inside. Inside her."

I don't want to know what he means. If I let myself think about it, I'll go as crazy as he is.

Not that it matters. I can't restore power to the *Victoria*. I don't have enough propulsion to leave orbit, and our life support is dwindling, but there's no way in hell I'm going back down there.

By the time you receive this message, Isiah and I will have run out of oxygen. We'll be dead. But I beg you, by all that is holy and human and good, stay away from Mars. We are not ready.

We never will be.

{}

Adam Heine *lives in Thailand where he and his wife foster a bazillion children (for certain values of bazillion . . . okay, there are ten of them). He spends a lot of time training these kids to be gamers, thinkers, and supervillains. (A few insist on being good at sports and stuff; he tries not to hinder them.) By day, Adam is the Design Lead for the upcoming computer roleplaying game* Torment: Tides of Numenera. *By night, he writes science fiction and fantasy for whomever will pay him. His short stories have appeared in* Beneath Ceaseless Skies *and Paizo's* Pathfinder Tales. *You can see more of what he's written and what he's working on at adamheine.com. He desperately tries to pretend that he still has spare time in which to watch* Naruto Shippuden *and play* Banner Saga.

Perfect Toy
for a Nine Year Old

Bruce R. Cordell

Dad, this is boring." Margaret flopped down on the couch next to Charlie.

Charlie Tokarev looked away from the program they were watching: mustachioed fish explored a land of robot dinosaurs across three walls and the ceiling of the family room. He hadn't been paying close attention because the show *was* boring. But his daughter picked the program, so he'd pretended to watch. Charlie gratefully wiped the fish away with a wave of his hand. A green forest, wet with rain, rustled to a phantom wind all around them.

"Then choose something you like," he said.

"But I'm *bored*!" Margaret dropped her head back to stare straight up at the ceiling and the digital clouds scudding by.

Charlie swallowed a sigh. When she didn't get enough sleep, Margaret got cranky. She'd spent the last few days at her friend Zoey's house and probably slept only a few hours the previous night.

"Tell you what, pumpkin. How about we talk about your birthday next week. I want to get you something special. How old will you be?"

Margaret didn't immediately respond, but that was a good sign.

"Nine," she allowed.

"Nine! Nine is a very important number. I think you deserve something *extra* special for turning nine."

"What?"

"Something from the printer. Something *real.*"

○

After putting Margaret to bed, Charlie went to the office. A couple chairs, a slender cabinet that stored their visors, and the printer fit snugly. One chair held a sleeping black and white cat—Max. He wasn't especially social, but he sometimes accepted pets with purrs instead of a bite. Charlie's wife Sylvia reclined in the other chair, wearing her visor. By the way her hands traced slopes and curves in the air, he knew she was working on her dissertation.

Sylvia's visors were slender goggles and included earbuds and gloves. The outside world faded completely when she used them, allowing her to develop increasingly brain-stretching quantum physics and string theory calculations without distraction.

Charlie didn't disturb her. Instead, he moved the cat and relaxed into the other chair. Donning his own goggles, Charlie logged onto the net. He subvocalized his search parameters: "perfect gift for a nine year old."

The results compiled in colorful charts ripe with meaning. The most popular gifts for children currently, what they'd been last year, and what they were likely to be next year were evident at a glance. Music, interactive design apps, and scads of virtual customizations for the popular online communities that children enjoyed were trending.

But none of it was real.

Charlie's job wasn't as glamorous as his wife's. But in the post-work economy, even having a job was something. His wife's stipend for higher learning went a long way toward the mortgage. Charlie's position as a remote vehicle minder made up the rest.

The autonomous vehicle laws required a human being to be "present" while any self-driving vehicle operated. Virtual babysitters like him accompanied every electric vehicle trip in America via visor network. Charlie and other minders worked from home and collected reasonable pay for a task that was mind-numbingly boring. He'd never once had to step in when a car AI failed. The odds of a driving problem that a modern vehicle AI couldn't handle—but that a human minder could—were statistically small. Every year, he worried the laws would finally be repealed. Sometimes at 3 a.m., his mind vulnerable with sleep, he worried his profession wasn't real.

Charlie wanted something tangible. If not for himself, at least for Margaret. He wanted something his daughter could hold.

He flicked past the popular gifts. He delved deeper into his search results, looking for something that would delight his daughter. Templates flashed and pirouetted everywhere. Robotic dancing bears, talking dolls, and fish that played music. All of them cost a goddamned fortune. The patents for printable supertoys gave the big manufacturers ownership of the 3D-printing toy market. The only way to download a template was to pay the asking price *and* sign up for a subscription guaranteed to break the bank.

Which was why Charlie finally settled on a template he found on a pirate site.

Printing something from a non-authorized vendor was technically impossible, but Charlie had jailbroken the printer. And the toy seemed perfect: "Kids love Mister Jenkin! This furry mouse with a funny face can sing, follow his owner around, and even tell jokes. Bring Mister Jenkin into your home for a truly special companion at a fraction of the cost of big-name supertoys and with no subscription!"

He transferred the amount requested (as a donation), downloaded the template directly to the printer, and queued the job to start later that week, in time for Margaret's birthday.

○

"Thank you Mommy and Daddy!" squealed Margaret, waking Charlie from a bad dream. As he sat up in bed, he realized that what his daughter clutched to her chest wasn't Max the cat, who was black and white, but something else. Something brown.

"What's she have?" mumbled Sylvia, opening her eyes and yawning.

A whiff of baked bread and burned plastic confirmed it; the printer had run overnight. Charlie said, "Margaret's birthday present . . . arrived early."

"It did!" agreed Margaret. "Isn't he wonderful? I love him. Mister Jenkin is my friend." Margaret stared into a tiny face that was indeed funny, as advertised. Except, it was more like a person's face than Charlie remembered from the photo. A person's face that wasn't quite finished, that is. The mouse-like body was also larger than he'd expected. If anything, it reminded Charlie of a rat.

Sylvia said, "Oh, that's nice, honey," and rolled over, pulling her pillow over her head.

"I guess your birthday's here a little early," Charlie said.

Margaret said, "You're the best dad ever."

Charlie grinned. Despite the printer glitch, he was glad he'd taken a chance on Mister Jenkin.

Over the next week, Margaret was not bored even once. She carried her new supertoy around everywhere. Charlie wasn't even actually sure if the thing could walk on its own, as the template listing had promised. On the other hand, it could certainly sing. Usually, oddly discordant lullabies, the words of which he couldn't quite make out but which always ended with his daughter laughing hysterically. It laughed along, in piping squeaks pitched almost too high for an adult's ears.

A couple of days before her birthday, Margaret asked Charlie if he could get it an upgrade. "It's an in-app purchase," she explained. "Mister Jenkin says he's supposed to come with six faces."

Charlie suppressed a guilty expression. Because he'd gotten the template from a pirate site, he knew he wouldn't be able to find the upgrade package. He certainly hadn't seen that option when he'd downloaded it. "I'll look into it," he said.

Margaret said, "I love you, daddy," and went to her room to play with Mister Jenkin.

o

The day before Margaret's birthday party, Sylvia said, "Where's Max? I swear, sometimes that cat drives me insane."

Charlie realized he hadn't seen the cat for at least a day, though that wasn't unusual. He checked Max's breakfast bowl and confirmed the food had been eaten.

"Max is fine," he assured Sylvia.

She nodded and went to the office.

"Though," he said aloud as he gazed at the empty food bowl, "I wonder where he's hiding?" Their house wasn't that big.

Piping, high-pitched laughter made Charlie flinch. He glanced round and saw Mister Jenkin crouched on the shelf where Max sometimes liked to lay.

"Oh, you scared me." He addressed the toy, not expecting an answer, "So, how about it? Seen the cat?"

A grin stretched Mister Jenkin's disquieting, incomplete features. It squeaked, "What's white, black, and red, and goes round and round and round?"

Charlie stared dumbly at the rodent-like toy. Max was white and black. But not red . . .

Mister Jenkin leaped with perfect agility from the shelf and ran off down the hallway. Charlie's skin prickled. Had that been a joke? When he was a kid, jokes in poor taste were the height of humor. But that was then. Was it telling Margaret "frog in a blender" jokes?

He frowned, wondering if he should go after Mister Jenkin. But he was late for his minder shift. Charlie went to his office and signed in.

○

Margaret wanted just two friends at her birthday party: Zoey from across town and Mister Jenkin, who got his own chair at the table. Charlie served them cake and soda and handed out the birthday hats he'd printed earlier. Sylvia was supposed to be in attendance, too, but she'd been called over to the university for a rare, in-person meeting with her research colleagues.

"Want some more cake, Zoey?" Charlie asked, noticing that the girl's plate was empty.

"No thank you, Mister Tokarev," Zoey replied. "But it was very good."

"Why, thank you," he said, smiling. Zoey's parents had taught their child impeccable manners. He hoped Margaret behaved half so well when she was over at her friend's.

"I have a joke," announced Mister Jenkin, apropos of nothing. It had cake smeared on its paws, and the tiny birthday hat sat askew on its head.

"Tell us!" yelled Margaret.

"What do you call a dead baby with no arms and no legs in a swimming pool?"

The kids screwed up their faces, thinking.

"Give up?" it asked.

"Tell us!"

"Bob," announced Mister Jenkin.

The kids laughed.

Mister Jenkin said, "Why do you put babies into blenders feet first?"

"Ick," said Zoey, frowning.

"Why?" demanded Margaret.

"So you can see the expression on their faces."

Zoey blinked as it launched into another gale of frantic laughter.

Margaret giggled.

Charlie felt a bit sick. He'd never really liked this kind of joke. "Mister Jenkin, maybe you could do a song and skip the jokes. In fact, stop with the jokes completely."

The supertoy gave its rendition of "Happy Birthday." After a few seconds, the kids joined in, and the moment passed. Satisfied Margaret and Zoey could amuse themselves for a while with more cake, a show in the family room, or even playing with the disturbing toy, he went to the office and grabbed his visors. He searched for customer reviews on Mister Jenkin but was stymied. Given where he'd found the template, he wasn't surprised. Charlie promised himself he'd keep a close eye on the toy. If it kept up with the gruesome jokes, he was going to retire the goddamned thing.

Feeling better at having made a decision, he logged out and went to go check on the kids. Zoey was in the kitchen by herself.

"Hey, Zoey. Want some more cake?"

"Mr. Tokarev? Could you send a car for me?" She'd obviously been crying.

"What's wrong, honey?" he asked.

"I wanna go home," Zoey said.

"Sure, sure, of course." Charlie called for a car. An app icon on the wall reported a car would be at his front door in less than a minute.

"Alright, got your things?" he asked.

Zoey was wearing her backpack, so his question was academic. But the plan had been for Margaret's friend to spend the night. Zoey and his daughter must have had a tiff. Charlie sighed, walking the child to the door. He waited with her until her ride showed, bundled her into the vehicle, and waved as she sped off.

He debated what to do next. Birthday or not, his daughter had to understand it wasn't acceptable to be cruel to her friends. And maybe it was time to enforce a little time away from Mister Jenkin.

When Charlie couldn't find Margaret in the kitchen or family room, he headed to her room. He knocked. "Margaret, we need to talk." He waited a few seconds and let himself in. A sickly sweet smell made his nose crinkle.

The overhead lights were off, and the window shades were pulled. A blanket fort stretched over a couple chairs under which something glowed. Margaret stood in the middle of the room, her expression unreadable in the dimness.

"Pumpkin, Zoey left," Charlie said. "What happened?"

"Zoey said that Mister Jenkin was broke and that I should recycle him. I didn't like that."

"So what did you do?"

"I showed her what Mister Jenkin can do."

He said, "Which was what?"

Margaret smiled and glanced at the blanket fort.

Charlie's gaze followed. A shadow passed in front of the light under the blanket, and he jumped. For a moment, the shape had seemed . . . monstrous. He blinked, realizing he'd merely seen the damned rat-thing moving under the cover, and felt foolish.

"I think you've played with Mister Jenkin enough for one day," Charlie suggested. "Come out and have some more cake."

"Okay, Daddy," agreed Margaret. "But Mister Jenkin wants to talk to you first." She pointed back to her fort.

"Maybe later." His heart sped.

"Are you scared, Daddy?"

"What? Why would I be?" Charlie wiped at perspiration on his lip. Maybe he was a bit spooked. The toy had creeped him out from the moment he'd laid eyes on it.

"Mister Jenkin said you was scared."

Anger cracked through his unease. "Zoey was right, goddammit. Your toy is broken." It served him right for downloading a template from a pirate site. It was buggy. The wretched thing was a bad influence.

Charlie ducked under the cover. The fetid smell of rotting carrion made him gag. Instead of the creepy plaything, Max the cat lay on the carpet, stiff as a board. Its face was missing as if had been skinned. Maggots crowded in the dead feline's putrid eye sockets.

"I don't understand," whispered Charlie.

Margaret's voice came from behind him. "Max's face didn't work, Daddy. Now Mister Jenkin wants *your* face."

When Sylvia arrived home that evening, she found Margaret and Mister Jenkin watching a show in the family room. "How did the party go?" she asked.

Margaret glanced round. "Zoey had to go home. But that's alright because Mister Jenkin has been telling me funny jokes!"

The supertoy laughed. A familiar piping sort of laugh. "I know a joke!" proclaimed Mister Jenkin. "What's red and scratches at the glass?"

Sylvia shrugged, not really interested in the punchline.

Strange, she never realized how much Mister Jenkin's face reminded her of Charlie.

{}

Bruce Cordell *has written well over one hundred roleplaying game products, including titles for four different editions of Dungeons &* *Dragons, including* Return to the Tomb of Horrors, Sunless Citadel, *and* Betrayal at the House on the Hill. *He's also penned nearly a dozen novels, including* Sword of the Gods *and its sequel,* Spinner of Lies. *Now the Senior Designer at Monte Cook Games, Bruce has written* The Strange, Ninth World Bestiary, *and* Strange Revelations, *among many others.*

The Steel Plague

Nate Southard

April, Day 1

State Science Fair This Weekend

Indiana's best and brightest high school students are set to converge on the capital this weekend for the statewide science fair. A combined total of $300,000 in prizes and scholarship is up for grabs.

"Brandon Cole, a sophomore from Muncie, hopes to secure some of that prize money with his research into robotics . . ."

October, Day 188

By my best guess, we were about fifty miles outside of Indianapolis. We could already hear them, though. Their scuttling—that strange mechanical buzz—hung in the air like the hum of cicadas on a summer night. Occasionally, we heard a rumbling sound neither of us understood. I wondered if the real cicadas would ever return. Maybe. There was too much I didn't know, couldn't guess the nervous new reality of our existence.

"You don't think we're too close?" Roger asked.

I looked around. The forest here appeared to be thriving. No manmade structures in sight. "We should be fine." Of course, there was always wildlife to contend with. Raccoons had stolen half our supplies over the past few weeks. If I could catch one of the bastards, I'd skin and cook it. Even the score.

Roger unrolled his sleeping bag. "Shit, I'm exhausted."

"Yeah. My feet hurt."

"Dogs are barking?"

"Something like that." I frowned. Hopefully, we wouldn't see any dogs, either. It hadn't taken them long to realize they were on their own, and they'd quickly grown annoyed with their spot on the food chain.

"Think it'll get cold tonight?"

"Probably."

"Dammit. I wish I still had the zipper for this thing."

"Me too." We'd ripped them off early, just in case. Since the zippers were nylon, maybe they couldn't be used, but the bugs had shown a fondness for both metal and plastic. We didn't want to risk it. We didn't even wear jeans anymore. Luckily, we'd found a few good pairs of sweatpants.

As I slung my bag to the ground, I steeled myself for the question I knew was coming.

Roger hadn't tried anything in a few days, so he was due.

"We could . . ."

I rolled my eyes. "Yeah? What?"

"I mean . . . we could try to get in one bag. Body heat and stuff."

"Roger."

"Mina?"

"No."

"I just—"

"No." I tried not to think about November and everything after. Maybe we should start heading south.

"Right." He sat cross-legged on top of his bag and inspected his hands, one of his more practiced "So, this is awkward" moves. "When do you think they'll start?"

"Soon, probably."

"I want to be asleep before then."

"Good luck." I refused to fall asleep before the little mechanical bastards started chanting or signaling or calibrating—or whatever the noises they made were. If something changed, I wanted to know about it.

I didn't have to wait long. Then again, I never did. Shortly after Roger started snoring a soft buzzsaw, their scuttling drone changed. As always, it first fell into a rhythm. Then, the volume began to rise and fall before their noise became something that sounded dangerously like language.

Ia! Ia! Ia! Ia!

Sitting on my sleeping bag, I shivered.

April, Day 1

Science Fair (cont.)

"'What I've created is a self-replicating robot,' says Cole. 'When it's switched on, it attempts to use inorganic material in the vicinity to create a copy of itself. I got the idea from cellular mitosis.'

"Cole hopes his project might one day lead to a breakthrough in nanotechnology, small machines that can live inside a person's body to combat such diseases as cancer and other ailments."

October, Day 188

I ate one of the remaining granola bars and climbed inside my sleeping bag, knowing we'd have to either forage or hunt the next day. Hopefully, we could find some berries or something. We'd scavenged a small .22 and two boxes of ammunition, but neither of us was a great hunter. The odd rabbit or squirrel wasn't exactly a feast, but it kept us going, which was all any other human could brag about. I'd grown used to the pocket of hunger I carried in my belly, though. So had Roger, or at least, he'd stopped complaining about it.

Despite the hard ground, exhaustion closed in on me quickly. The warmth of my sleeping bag soothed me, and the rolled jacket under my head coaxed me toward sleep. Even the mechanical droning from the city helped, like those machines people used to buy, the ones that made wave sounds or filled your room with white noise.

Ia! Ia! Ia! Ia!

Almost asleep. Whole world foggy. But something changed. It took me several moments to realize it, and I almost dismissed it as a result of my twilight state, but I realized what was happening and bolted awake, sitting upright on the forest floor.

Ooboshu! Li'hee! Ooboshu! Li'hee!

They'd changed the signal. Whatever message the machines were sending—

we'd guessed they were sending, but it was just a guess—they'd changed it for the first time.

Scurrying, I left my bag and shook Roger. He groaned, refusing to crawl out of sleep at first, so I slapped him. That brought him around.

"The hell . . . ?"

"Wake up, Roger. Shake the cobwebs loose."

"Are we . . . ? What's wrong?"

"Listen."

I gripped his shoulder as he shook his head.

He reached up and rubbed his eyes. "I don't get it. Is there—"

"Roger, shut up and listen!"

He froze, eyes ticking to one side and the other. When I saw fear blossom in his expression, I knew he'd heard it.

"What is that?" he asked. "What are they saying?"

"I don't know."

"Do you think it means something?"

I started to speak and caught myself. Maybe, it did mean something but what? "Maybe, they're on a program, something timed." I said. "They didn't start that 'ia, ia' stuff until a month or two ago. Could be their programming is running down."

"Or winding up."

"Jesus, Roger. Let's hope not." Lifting my eyes to the trees overhead, I wondered what would happen if they started using things other than metal and plastic. I stopped wondering just as fast because I already knew the answer. I didn't want to think about it.

Roger stared at the ground and then away. Anywhere but my eyes. "Look, um . . . I just . . . can we please share a sleeping bag tonight?"

"Jesus, Roger! Fucking stop, okay? I don't care how horny you—"

"I'm scared, all right? Shit!" He rubbed at his eyes, and I realized he was wiping away tears. "I'm not trying to sleep with you, okay? Jesus, I'm just scared out of my goddamn skin."

It was like a slap to the face. A quick, hot flush, and I felt like the world's biggest asshole. "Oh," I say. "Look, I'm sorry. I just . . . sorry."

He shook his head. "Whatever."

"Roger . . ."

"I'm going to bed. See you in the morning." He rolled away from me, shrugging the bag over his shoulder. That was it.

I spent too long staring at his back, trying to think of something to say. When I finally realized there was nothing, I returned to my bag and tried to get some sleep.

Ooboshu! Li'hee! Ooboshu! Li'hee!

April, Day 1

Breaking News—WXIN, Indianapolis

"Emergency crews are responding to the Indianapolis Convention Center, site of the State Science Fair, where witnesses describe chaos breaking out following an experiment of some sort going awry. Police say the problem is not of a chemical nature, but they are advising citizens to stay clear of the convention center at this time . . ."

October, Day 189

The sound that woke me—the sound crawling from Roger's throat—was something between a scream and a wheeze. I don't know how long he'd been making the noise before I jolted from sleep, bolting upright only to freeze in place. Everything went cold. My breath caught in my throat, blocking my scream.

Four of the machines stalked through the clearing. Their hinged legs skittered; wings of metal and plastic fluttered. The whisper-sound of clicking and hydraulics was almost deafening.

I'd never seen one up close before, just seen them on the last news reports, before the machines spread from Indianapolis to devastate other cities. The size of a shoe box, they each looked like bastardized versions of each other, replicas made from whatever could be found. Self-replicating, the news had said.

Two feet to my left, the insect-like machine fluttered wings made from fused Coke and Sprite cans. It swept the ground with a light that had maybe been scavenged from a smart phone. Beyond it, another took off on wings from an old gutter.

Again, that wheezing scream poured out of Roger. I looked and saw him flat on his back. One of the machines perched on his chest, wings testing the air, legs scuffling. Roger watched it with terrified eyes, his mouth wide and growing wider.

"Quiet," I said. "It won't hurt you."

But he didn't stop. I didn't know if he'd even heard me. I wondered if the machines might kill him just to silence the racket. When the tiny robot lifted onto its hind legs and fluttered its metal wings, I thought I had my answer and shouted for Roger to escape.

The rifle crack deafened me. I screamed, covering my head with both arms, and I didn't look up again until my ears started ringing.

Roger remained flat on his back, hands over his face. The machine on his chest was gone, replaced by scrap. One wing still flapped from a metal housing as though trying to flee, but it fell still almost immediately. The other machines were gone, and I wondered if they could feel fear. My thoughts died as the man with the rifle stepped into view.

I think he said something, but I couldn't hear him over the whine in my ears. In the darkness, I couldn't make out his face, just his general shape. Maybe he was smiling. I couldn't tell. When his shoulders moved, head tilting back a little, it looked like laughter.

Roger scurried out of his sleeping bag. I followed his lead. So what if this new guy had chased off the machines? Didn't change the fact he had a gun. I eyed my duffel, where the .22 now rested. Why hadn't I started taking it out at night? Stupid.

For too long, the three of us watched each other. Roger ground the heel of his hand against his ear, and I could tell he wanted his hearing back, too.

As he dug a set of plugs from his ears, the stranger kept his rifle pointed at the forest floor. At least, there was that.

"Thanks," I said when enough of my hearing returned. My voice buzzed, but I could both hear it and understand it.

"Those little fuckers," the man said. His voice was a static drone. "Lucky I was moving through. I'm Clyde."

"Hey," Roger said. "Roger. This is Mina."

"Nice name. Mina, that is. Not Roger. I've met a few of those. Sorry."

Roger looked at the forest floor, his face confused. "Yeah, sure."

"Seriously, thanks for the help," I said. "They don't attack people, though."

He looked at me like I was an idiot. "They caused a lot of deaths."

"I never said they didn't, just . . ." I let it hang. No point in fighting a losing battle. Besides, the guy thought he was helping. Might as well let him have it.

"Whatever. What food you got?"

Something cold touched my neck. "I'm sorry?"

"I think you heard me." Even if I hadn't, the chill of his rifle filled me in. Oh, Christ. This couldn't be happening. "Hard out there these days. Had a lot of canned food stashed, but those fuckers tore it apart, used the cans to make more of them. Now, I just saved your damn lives whether you want to admit it or not, so you better be handing over your food so I can see you have some goddamned appreciation."

Roger took a step forward. "You can't—"

The rifle barked, and Roger folded in half. Again, I couldn't hear my scream. That piercing whine replaced everything, a dagger of noise right through my skull. Roger fell back, arms splayed, and I began to turn, desperate to escape, when the rifle's barrel swung toward my face.

I froze. Staring into the weapon's black muzzle, panic and confusion and terror paralyzed me. If I did what he said, would he let me go or kill me? What if he did something worse?

His mouth moved, making some demand I couldn't hear. I placed my hands over my ears, trying to clue him in. He responded by lowering the rifle long enough to slap me. The blow stunned me. I staggered and watched stars blossom in my vision. When I shook my head, it throbbed with pain, and I sank to my knees. A strong hand clamped on the back of my neck, and I thought he'd had enough and decided to end me.

Instead, he turned me to face him. Angrily, he pointed at my backpack and mimed eating.

Right, the food. In all the terror, I'd forgotten what he wanted.

I crawled to my pack. With my back turned, I wondered if I'd even hear the next shot. Maybe, everything would just disappear. Black. Nothing. As I pulled open the pack and started rummaging, however, the world remained. My hand brushed the .22, and I tried to remember if it was loaded or not, tried to calculate if I could spin around, aim, and fire before he killed me. Too risky. I moved on, finding the remaining granola bars, making a good show of tossing the other supplies aside so he wouldn't think I was hiding something. My fingers fell numb, fear swallowing my senses.

Turning, I held out the bars. The whine had died down, but his, "That's all?" sounded far away. A whisper.

I nodded. "I'm sorry. We've . . . been foraging." I glanced to Roger, hoping to see him stir, but he remained still. He was gone.

Shaking his head, he snatched the bars and stuffed them into a pocket. I waited, watching him. Everything felt stuck. Staring into his eyes, I wondered if the rifle would swing my way again, if it was the last thing I'd see. When he sighed and turned away, I finally breathed.

As he walked away, I stared at the forest floor and thought about how terrible everything had become. People scurrying through the woods because the cities were gone, killing other people over things we used to buy in corner stores. Another thought stuck in my brain like a headless nail: what if he comes back? The idea stuck deeper and deeper, and another look at Roger's body cemented it in place. I couldn't risk it. I refused. Deeper in my thoughts, I decided this man needed to pay. He needed it because he'd abandoned his role in the human race.

My hand found the pistol easily. As I jerked it from my pack and made sure it was loaded, I tamped down my thoughts. Doubts wouldn't help. When I turned, the man who'd said his name was Clyde—the man who'd killed Roger over three goddamn granola bars—was barely ten yards away. His last shot must have damaged his hearing, too, because he didn't hear me follow, didn't notice anything until I pressed the pistol's muzzle to the base of his skull.

I didn't give him time to react. One pull, and he dropped.

April, Day 2

Evacuation Ordered, Governor Declares Disaster Area

"With a large section of downtown overrun by a strange technological event, Mayor Tillotson, working with Governor Evans, has ordered the evacuation of Indianapolis and the surrounding areas.

"Scientists and authorities are still trying to understand how the events that began at yesterday's state science fair have descended into chaos. The leading theory is that a self-replicating machine, the project of a local teen, malfunctioned. As it made more and more copies of itself, the convention center was overrun. The machines may have attempted to use the building's materials to continue creating copies, leading to the structure's collapse and yesterday's deaths . . ."

October, Day 193

Ooboshu! Li'hee! Ooboshu! Li'hee!

Whatever the machines were chanting, they'd started doing it during the day, too. I didn't like it. No matter how I looked at it, I couldn't find a positive spin, not that anything positive remained.

I didn't know what to do, didn't know if anything was worth doing. I'd killed a man, and my sole companion, as annoying as he could sometimes be, was gone. Before Clyde had stumbled across (and fucking seriously . . . Clyde?), we hadn't seen another soul in more than a week.

I spent most of my waking hours crying. I felt stupid and terrible and weak, but the guilt that sat in my chest like rotting meat was too heavy. Tears in my eyes, I walked, grubbing through the ruins of gas stations when my hunger grew too strong to ignore. The sound of distant machines helped my feet keep time. Only after days of walking did I realize I was heading for the city. By then, I didn't see a point in turning away. I wanted to see what they'd done, and I figured there wasn't much time left. Maybe they'd kill me for entering the city, but I didn't care. Maybe that was what I deserved.

Ooboshu! Li'hee! Ooboshu! Li'hee!

The closer I came to Indianapolis, the louder the machines grew. Their strange signal or chanting or whatever it was reached a near-deafening level. Clicking and grinding noises joined the chorus. Even before I could make out the machines in any detail, when they were just a black, swirling cloud tumbling in the distance, I could hear the sound of gears and clacking metal.

Maybe fifteen miles out from the edge of Indianapolis, I started encountering them. They'd eradicated the suburbs, stripped houses and vehicles alike, leaving behind only wood and glass. Walking past a subdivision of timber skeletons, I saw dozens of the lunchbox-sized robots buzz through the air or skitter across the ground, looking for more material. I shivered, not the first time and certainly not the last. How long until the entire world looked like that? What if it already did? A robotic cancer that decimated the globe . . .

I laid out my sleeping bag and climbed inside. The sun would set soon, and I was exhausted, my belly clenching from hunger. Surrounded by clacking and electronic chanting, I thought about Roger. I should have buried him. I wished he was with me.

May, Day 15

. . .

October, Day 195

Ooboshu! Li'hee! Ooboshu! Li'hee!

Indianapolis was gone. In its place stood something new and awful. In their quest to build more of themselves—a quest that had killed so many—the machines had leveled the city. Paved streets and concrete rubble probably remained under it all. The bodies had been buried as everything collapsed never to be reclaimed. I couldn't see anything beneath the millions of chattering machines that crawled over each other and buzzed through the sky. Though sharing the same design, each was a bastardized version of the others, the same collections of scrap that had visited Roger and me a week before.

They let me walk right up to the edge. I didn't have anything they could use. Not so much as a filling in my mouth or a button on my shirt. The way they ignored me really brought everything home. I no longer mattered.

Before me, they shifted. Their metal and plastic shells caught the sunlight and sent it tumbling in a hundred different directions. Clacking bodies created skyscrapers so tall I couldn't see their tops. They collapsed moments later with a sound like thunder, spreading out and becoming other structures. A writhing, living city.

Ooboshu! Li'hee! Ooboshu! Li'hee!

Their chant came from every direction, as piercing as a tornado siren. I felt it in my chest, in my spine. Standing proved an almost impossible task. I wanted to fall to my knees and weep. This was the world now. Their world. Coming back from this, reclaiming Earth, was impossible. Nothing humanity could do would eclipse the amazing and terrible sight spread out in front of me.

I wondered if the government had tried anything drastic in those last days when things had started to look hopeless. Had they fired nukes at Indianapolis and other cities? Maybe, maybe not. If they had, the machines probably dismantled them before they could strike. In the minutes that followed, how many generals had killed themselves? How many politicians?

Static crackled, a sound I could barely hear as a spire twisted toward the sky, sprouting steel tendrils in a dozen different directions. The shapes didn't make sense, and I was so enthralled with them that at first I didn't realize the chant had changed yet again.

R'lyeh! Ia! R'lyeh! Ia!

"What does it mean?" I asked, but the machines didn't answer. Why would they? A man doesn't answer a gnat's questions. I ground my teeth, biting back a screech that wanted to tear free of my throat. Or maybe it was laughter. I couldn't tell. Terrifying? Hilarious? What was the difference? A goddamn high school science project had taken over the entire world.

When the ground first shook, I thought it might be the machines, but the rumble that accompanied it was an entirely new sound. It was deeper, stronger. By the time I looked up, the ground was quaking. I watched with watery eyes as the metallic spires stretched higher, testing the air. Reaching.

R'lyeh! Ia! R'lyeh! Ia!

And then, they took flight. All of them. A hot wind pressed my face as the swarm blocked out the sun and turned day into night. The buzzing roar of mechanical wings was deafening. I covered my head and prayed they wouldn't land on me. When I wasn't crushed, when the sound of their wings began to recede, swallowed by the growl of the quaking ground, I looked up.

Indianapolis was still gone, just rubble. But the ground was splitting, widening like a mouth of rock and soil. And something climbed out, something gigantic and horrible. Something that almost made sense but couldn't. I looked at it, and my screech became a moan. I bowed my head, closed my eyes, but I decided praying wasn't worth it.

{}

Nate Southard *is the author of* Down, Pale Horses, Just Like Hell, *and several others. His latest collection,* Will the Sun Ever Come Out Again?, *is available now from Broken River Books. His work has appeared in such venues as* Cemetery Dance, Black Static, *and* Thuglit. *A finalist for the Bram Stoker Award for Superior Achievement in Short Fiction, Nate lives in Austin, Texas with his best friend and two cats. He cooks a lot. Learn more at natesouthard.com.*

Between Angels and Insects

Simon Bestwick

It was as fine a day as you can have in Blackpool: clear blue sky, bright shining sun, seagulls squawking, the sea breaking on the shore. The strains of an old George Formby song drifted over from the North Pier where withered pensioners baked in the sun and waited for death. It was a weekend, so the usual crowds were out in force, but there were still a few hours to spare before the streets would be thronged with rowdy belligerent drunks vomiting on the pavement, punching one another and copulating in alleyways.

I scooted down the pavement with a carrier bag of chips in one hand, skirting dog shit, vomit, and discarded meals from the night before. I stole a quick glance at the rusted spike of the tower and ducked gratefully down the side-street and the basement steps into the welcome sanctuary of the museum.

"I'm ba-ack!" I trilled in both descent and descant. "And I bear chips!"

"Not hungry," Stephen called from among the waxworks.

I sighed. Stephen was extraordinarily pretty but, even for a youth his age, ridiculously temperamental.

At the bottom of the steps where the path through the waxworks branched left and right, I hesitated. Having a sense of humour, I chose the left-hand path.

"Really, Stephen," I said. "I wish you'd stop changing your mind like this. You know I hate to waste good food."

"Whatever," he said. "Anyway, being shut up in here with bloody Coolio killed my appetite."

"*Not* Coolio," I said wearily as I reached the big glass display case of which he spoke, just in time to catch his shadow darting away from me. "*Cthulhu*."

"What*ever*."

I sighed and looked up at the waxwork. It was, I thought, one of my best efforts; fully ten feet high, the throne and its grotesque occupant had been finished to glisten as if still newly damp. Even the tangled clumps of seaweed hanging off the white, rune-carved, grotesquely angled throne still looked fresh. "Cthulhu," I repeated, "as created by the great H.P. Lovecraft."

"Whatever. Coolio, Yog-Sodoff—"

"Yog-*Sothoth*. You're just doing this to annoy me, Stephen. You know that." I sighed. "You have to look beyond the obvious. They're not just monsters, they're metaphors. That's the genius of Lovecraft's achievement. The deities of the Cthulhu Mythos were metaphors for the sheer vastness and alienness of space and time in relation to mankind—who is, on a cosmic scale, a very brief, very recent phenomenon. Here for less than a split-second in the great scheme of things."

Stephen snorted. I tried to pinpoint the direction but couldn't. "You really are full of shit, you know."

I opened my mouth to retort, hoping something suitably pithy would occur in time, but Stephen said, "Someone's coming," and dashed away.

Light flickered at the entrance, and a shadow moved down the basement steps. I hesitated—it's usually curiosity that brings people to my little emporium, and too enthusiastic a welcome can put them to flight—but then a voice called out, "Hello?"

"Good afternoon," I said. "Welcome to the Lovecraftiana Museum."

He offered a hand. "Mr. Rogers?"

"Yes?" I said, slightly taken aback. It's not as though my name appears above the threshold or anything.

"My name's Heald Jones," he said.

"A pleasure. A pleasure. Well, do come in. If there's anything you wish to know about the exhibits—"

Jones eyed my nearest creation—a nightgaunt, wings spread aloft—and then me. "Perhaps later," he said. "It was actually you I came to see."

"Me? But whatever for?"

"Well, there's something we need to talk about. If I could have just a few minutes of your time?"

I wasn't sure I liked the sound of this, but it was quite clear at a glance that Mr. Jones was clearly a man of some means. Very tall, well-groomed, tanned, and if his clothes were not genuine Giorgio Armani, then I will wear tracksuits for a year. "Very well," I said. "Let's go to the café. We can talk there."

Café is perhaps a slightly grandiose term to describe the space at the back of the museum with a half-dozen wood-effect tables and plastic seats, a kettle with a pint of milk, a rumpled bag of sugar, a jar of Nescafé, and a packet of economy teabags beside. But to be fair, we've never had the call for anything much more. And to be fairer still, while the *Innsmouth Tableaux* is another of my personal favourites, it wasn't perhaps the ideal thing to be faced with over a meal. Jones, who couldn't stop glancing at it, certainly looked a little queasy.

"Do take a seat," I said, setting the chips down on the cleanest table where they gently bled steam into their plastic bag. "A cup of tea?"

"No, thank you," he said, looking around. "Quite a place you have, Mr. Rogers."

"You like it?" I said.

"It's . . . fascinating." Diplomatic. "How did you come to, er . . ."

"A kind of therapy, I suppose." I rather enjoyed telling this story. "Until about four years ago, I was a call-centre worker: a job that led to stress, depression, anxiety, and in the end, to a quite nightmarish episode where I almost took my own life. I'm sure you know, Mr. Jones—"

"Professor."

"Oh. I apologise." But a professor of what? "Well, as I'm sure you know, Professor Jones, it's not uncommon when one comes close to dying to take stock of one's life. I found, as do many, that I'd been living to work instead of working to live. So I decided to reverse the equation by devoting myself to work that genuinely inspired me."

"And"—Jones gestured around—"this was it."

"Mmm. I've loved science fiction and horror since I was a small boy, and Lovecraft's works most of all. Are you familiar with him?"

"I read him when I was younger. Not to my taste."

"So it goes," I said. "But Old Howard still has his devotees. It's been a real labour of love."

"I *do* admire the skill and passion you've brought to it."

"Thank you. As I said, it's been a kind of therapy for me. I suspect that one day soon I'll move on and do something new."

A high tittering laugh echoed from among the exhibits: Stephen, of course. "Will you listen to yourself?" I caught the briefest glimpse of his thin pale face and black spiky hair peering out from under one of the iridescent globes that comprised the body of Yog-Sothoth. So achingly beautiful and so achingly cruel. With youth, the two often go hand in hand. "What a load of smug, self-satisfied, pretentious *crap*. I don't know why I stick with you."

"Shut up!" I snapped. "Go and clean something. Earn your bloody keep!"

Jones looked downright startled. I was too used to being alone here with Stephen. Sometimes, I forgot myself. I decided to try and make a joke of it. "You can't get the staff these days."

"Right," said Jones.

"I have to ask," I said, "have we met before? You seem familiar, somehow."

"I've been on television a couple of times," he said.

"Oh?"

"I'm a scientist."

"What's your field?"

"Nanotechnology."

"Not one of my interests, but . . . no, I'm sure I've seen you somewhere."

"It wouldn't surprise me." There was something in his tone I didn't like. Jones took out a photograph. "Do you know who this is?"

It was of a young boy, perhaps twelve or thirteen years old. Fair hair, blue eyes, a winning smile. In a few years, I had no doubt, he would be quite beautiful— though not, of course, as lovely as Stephen. "I'm afraid I don't." Looking from Jones to the picture, I saw a faint resemblance. "Your son?"

"His name was Charlie."

"Was?"

"He killed himself," said Jones. "Four years ago."

"My God. I'm sorry. That's terrible." But why come here to tell me this, I wondered?.

"You can imagine . . . well, perhaps you can't. The loss of a child is an awful thing," said Jones. "We'd had no idea there was even anything wrong. My marriage broke up. I'm told it's quite common. My wife pursued a series of younger men and drank to forget. I buried myself in my work. Different coping mechanisms. The one possible edge that mine had over Katharine's was that something beneficial may come of it."

"Oh?"

"A lot of mental health issues, like depression, have physiological causes," he said. "Chemical imbalances in the brain and so forth. I set out to apply nanotechnology to psychiatric medicine. You could implant a colony of sub-microscopic machines to monitor the brain and correct those issues as they arose, treating depression and other disorders in real time. Technology like that could save thousands of lives."

"Yes," I said. "I can see how—"

"It was controversial," said Jones. "There were concerns over how that kind of technology could be misused by the military or the state. You can probably guess some of the paranoid stuff people were coming out with: 'government mind control' and all that. But I managed to get the backing to carry out the work."

"I'm terribly sorry for your loss, Professor," I said, "and I sincerely hope the work you're doing will pay off—"

"It has," he said. "We're pretty much good to go."

"That's wonderful," I said, "but I still don't understand what it has to do with me."

"You don't?"

"Truly."

He studied me with a peculiar expression, a strange compound of pity and disbelief. "It's because you helped to kill my son, Mr. Rogers," he said. "And I want to understand why."

"What?" I said. "*What*? How dare you. How could you even suggest that I'd harm a child? I want you out of here. *Immediately.*"

"I completed my nanotech work," said Jones as if I hadn't spoken. He didn't move, didn't even bestir himself to get up. Well, quite frankly, he was a tall man, well-built, and the chances of my being able to move him without his consent were laughable. "I hoped that, having done so, I'd feel some sense of closure or peace. But I didn't. You do foolish things when you've too much on your mind and not enough to distract you from it, so I called Katharine. We had a long, painful conversation. But she said something that stayed with me."

I waited; the sooner he'd said his piece, the sooner he'd get out of my museum and leave me and Stephen in peace.

"She said I was unfeeling," he said. "That I reduced everything to the clinical and the mechanical. Treating people like machines, pieces of clockwork—something goes wrong, you take a gear out and replace it. 'Did you ever stop to consider,' she asked me, 'that the reason our son died might have been that he was in pain? Suffering terribly? And we didn't see it. You didn't see it, for all your skill. You didn't see what was wrong. Did you ever stop and ask why?'

"I *had* been all too eager to dismiss the idea that there'd been something wrong in Charlie's life, something I hadn't known about. That perhaps he could have been saved not by some miraculous stroke of nanosurgery but simply by his father coming to him and asking 'Charlie, is everything all right? Is something wrong?' and then . . . just . . . listening."

There was a long pause; Jones's fingertips traced patterns on the table top. I could see the faint white mark on his wedding finger where the ring had been.

"We'd meant to get rid of Charlie's laptop after but couldn't: too many memories of him, and besides, you can never wholly erase whatever's been on the hard drive. Delete it if you want, but the evidence remains. And so I had someone take a look there."

Jones was silent for another moment or two. He gazed at the *Innsmouth Tableaux*, though I suspected sadly that he wasn't devoting his time to an appreciation of my artistic achievements.

"We accessed Charlie's social media profiles," he said. "Twitter, Facebook, that kind of thing. And they were filled, *filled*, with some of the cruellest, most hateful things I've ever seen in my life. Messages that told him he was vile, he was scum, a worthless piece of shit. That his mother would be repulsed if she knew, that we would disown him, drive him out, whip him through the streets of the town"—his voice cracked. "And we wouldn't have. Of course, we wouldn't have. He was our son. But they said that, and they told him to—they told him to kill himself, Mr. Rogers. That he'd be better off dead. He was *twelve years old*, Mr. Rogers. Twelve."

"Mr. Jones . . . Professor," I said. My lips felt dry. "Professor, I'm sorry beyond words for your loss. You're right; it's something I can't imagine because I have no children of my own. It's something no one should have to go through. "

"Most of the people who'd persecuted my son," said Jones, very quietly, steadily and slowly, "were anonymous. They hid behind pseudonyms and aliases and avatars. I don't think even Charlie knew half of them, which makes it worse. It's as if someone just picked him out at random and declared him a target to be destroyed. A funny thing, though: of the nine we could identify, five where dead. They'd committed suicide. Of the others, three were catatonic following full-blown psychotic breakdowns. That only left one; he'd suffered a breakdown but recovered. That, Mr. Rogers, was you."

"No!" I shouted. "No! I absolutely deny that I had anything to do with your son's death, that I could have ever done such a hateful thing!"

From the shadows, out among those exhibits, Stephen laughed: high, hateful, tittering. "Yeah, right," he said, "you bloody could, and you know it, you lying old queen."

"*Fuck off!*" I screamed. "Just fuck off!"

Jones flinched back in his chair. He was very still now, watching me carefully. We looked at each other for almost a minute before he relaxed. A little.

"You *did* have a breakdown," he said. "Four years ago."

"No," I said. "Well, yes. Yes, I had a breakdown, but it was work-related, I told you."

"Mr. Rogers," said Jones, "it wasn't work-related."

"I tell you, it was! Whose life are we talking about here?"

"Do you think I pulled your name out of a hat, Mr. Rogers? I hired private detectives to trace the people who'd harassed my son. Not for revenge, just to understand. They found you. Your doctor, quite rightly, wouldn't break confidentiality, but it was easy enough to talk to your neighbours and the police officers."

"Police officers?"

"Mr. Rogers, you had a full-blown psychotic episode," said Jones. "You smashed the windows in your flat, you cut yourself up with pieces of broken glass—"

My hand went to my chest. Through the thin shirt, I could feel the scars from when I had self-harmed at the time of my breakdown.

He took a square of folded paper from his pocket, unfolded it. "These are their statements. The police and the neighbours all said you were screaming, ranting, raving. You were saying things about 'the hive, the great hive,' and something about 'tentacles in the minds of men, linking us all to the face of God.' Or perhaps 'the god.' Does none of this ring a bell?"

I shook my head, standing, stumbling back. I had to get away. I had to get away from him, away from this man who was saying these terrible things that couldn't be true, they couldn't be. I didn't remember them, I *didn't* remember, I didn't, couldn't—

No.

No.

My legs felt weak; they gave way and I fell to my knees.

"Mr. Rogers—" Jones started to rise.

"Leave him." And there was Stephen: dear Stephen, darling Stephen, kneeling by me. "Do you remember now?" he said. His face was inches from mine: that thin, beautiful face.

"No," I said. "I *don't* remember. I *don't* remember."

"Who are you talking to?" said Jones.

I stared at him and then back to Stephen. "What does he mean? What does he—"

I looked at Jones again, and he was staring with incomprehension. "I don't understand," I said to Stephen. "I don't understand. I don't . . ."

"Shh."

"I can't—I can't—"

"I can," said Stephen, and he stroked my face. "Do you want me to?"

"Please. Please, my darling. Please."

"All right, then," said Stephen, and leaning forward, he kissed me.

And I remembered.

I remembered logging into the computer that night and thinking how odd the patterns flickering across the screen were. They were hypnotic. And then, the hive. The rage. Find a target. Destroy it. Here is the target. Kill him. Kill him. Make him kill himself. Night after night, until he broke. And—

And not just me. Others. So many others. *We are many. The many and the One. We are the One. We are the hive. We are the avatar. We are Cthulhu. Dead but dreaming.*

"Mr. Rogers? Mr. Rogers?"

Someone was leaning over me. Stephen? No.

"Mr. Rogers. Stephen. That's your name, isn't it? Stephen, are you all right?"

"I . . ." I looked up at him. And now, of course, *now*, I wasn't afraid of him any more. "Yes," I said. "I'm fine." I caught his arm and helped myself to my feet. He was staring at me in perplexity, which I could hardly blame him for.

"I haven't entirely been honest with you, Professor Jones," I said. "Because for the last four years, I haven't been entirely honest with myself. You see, when people have asked me about the things I depict, I've always told them that of course they aren't meant to be real. They're all a metaphor for other things. While in fact, they're anything but. I've created and tended this place out of denial. To tell myself, 'It's all just a story; none of it's real.' But my darling Stephen knew better. He always knew better. He was the part of me that always knew."

I released his arm. He stepped back, apparently weighing the prospect of making a dash for it. I side-stepped to ensure I would be in his path.

"You see," I went on, "once upon a time, a very long time ago—*vigintillions* of years ago, to use HPL's own phrase—there were the Great Old Ones, Professor. Creatures you and I can barely conceive of: in terms of their size, their scale, their *nature*. They ruled earth and heaven for billions of years. They were as gods, but . . . all things must end. Something changed. So they went dormant—*dead, but dreaming*—in suitable hiding places. The depths of the Marianas Trench, the gulfs of outer space, the deserts, the mountains: on earth and beyond it, they were and are everywhere, just waiting."

"Waiting for what, Stephen?" said Jones.

He was trying to humour me, but no matter. "They were waiting for *us*, Professor," I told him. "The Great Old Ones could only come back if one of their own kind opened the way for them: at the right time, in the right place. You see the paradox, Professor, yes? They solved it with typical ingenuity: having identified those creatures that would survive the coming change, they modified them to *evolve* along the lines the Old Ones desired. So they would develop intelligence and, with that intelligence, certain ideas and desires and *intentions* would arise—ideas, desires and intentions that would ultimately serve the Old Ones' purpose.

"Of course, even the greatest human mind could only hold an infinitesimal fraction of an Old One's consciousness. But millions, *billions* of human minds, networked—*that* would be a different matter."

"Networked?" he said. "You mean—"

"A gestalt," I nodded, "a hive-mind. And that hive-mind would be the mind of the Old Ones' avatar." I gestured down the aisle. "Great Cthulhu," I said, "the Opener of the Way, the Waker of the Dead, the Old Ones' harbinger and herald."

Jones dashed past me up one of the paths to the entrance. I followed.

He backed away from me: he wanted to flee, but he'd come for answers, and he didn't want to leave without them.

"Why would you kill my son, then?" he cried. "What had he done to you?"

"Oh," I said, "*he'd* done nothing. But his death pushed you in the direction you needed to go, Professor—your work in nanotechnology. That work was vital, you see, to precipitate the final phase."

"Final phase of what?"

"We're all part of the gestalt, Professor. Of the hive-mind. Potentially, if not in actuality. At the moment, anyone with access to a computer, to the internet, to social media can be linked into it at a moment's notice. That was the whole point of the technology, the *true* reason we invented it in the first place. One hypnotic flicker of a screen and millions of minds become one, become *His* mind, Professor Jones.

"But He needed more. Needed to *be* more than a bodiless mind, possessing the crude, weak bodies of humans. He needed to regain His own physical form once again. So as you built in *your* commands and specifications, Professor, you were also building in *others*—forgetting them as soon as you'd done so, of course. Specifications that fulfil not your design but His."

"You're fucking mad," he said.

I laughed. "That's why you've come here, Professor. Because it was time for me to remember. Because I should know. And so should you."

"I'm leaving, Mr. Rogers." The light of the exit was almost in sight.

"Shh!" I held up a hand. "Listen; can't you hear?" And in the stillness that followed, I knew he could. A noise like a vast swarm of wasps, growing closer and closer, louder and louder. "Your little babies are loose, Professor Jones. Their true programming is running now, and they're doing very well. They are fruitful, they multiply, and they replenish the earth with something it hasn't seen in millions of years. With every human brain that lies in their ever-widening path, they're linking another cell into the hive. Until all human minds are linked together to form His." I turned to indicate the great tentacled figure on the throne. "And as their minds are joined, so too will their bodies be broken down and transformed into the matter that will form His new body, when He returns to open the way."

Jones ran for the stairs, but from the streets above, the screams began. Hundreds of them; thousands. Soon to be the screams of millions, of billions. The screaming of a world.

"Listen to them, Professor," I said. "They're afraid. But I'm not. I die happy, Professor, because I die not. I rise, I ascend, I am transformed. I rise in glory!"

And now, Jones began to scream, reeling back from the entrance as the buzzing grew louder. He fell to his knees; his skin and the flesh beneath ran like molten wax.

I raised his arms aloft and threw back my head in laughter, watching as the bones of my fingers rose from the liquefying flesh like R'lyeh's towers from the deep, and hailed the coming of the gods.

{}

Described as "among the most important writers of contemporary British horror" by Ramsey Campbell, **Simon Bestwick** *is the author of the novels* Tide Of Souls, The Faceless, *the serial novel* Black Mountain, *and, most recently,* Hell's Ditch. *Further novels are forthcoming. He's also written many short stories, collected in* A Hazy Shade of Winter, Pictures of the Dark, Let's Drink to the Dead, *and* The Condemned. *Having spent most of his life in Manchester, he now lives on the Wirral with a long-suffering girlfriend. This is taking some getting used to, but he's starting to enjoy it. When not writing, he goes for walks, watches movies, listens to music, and does all he can to avoid having to get a proper job again. All contributions toward this worthy cause will be gratefully received.*

The Judas Goat

Robert Brockway

I don't have a very good imagination.

It was a woman who first told me that. I don't remember her name. She was an online match-up, and like most online match-ups, it didn't go anywhere.

"You're not much for imagination," she said after three boring drinks. "It's lucky you're a scientist."

I'm not a scientist. I'm a research assistant at NASA. My job is more like engineering mixed with cartography. People tune out by the time I get that far. Then, they call me a scientist.

It's a pretty exciting time for us, actually. Eight months ago, we launched the James Webb Space Telescope. It hasn't yet built up the cultural presence of the Hubble. Most people haven't heard of it, but it puts the HST to shame. We find new objects every day. That's been most of my job lately: finding and cataloguing new stars, molecular clouds, even whole galaxies.

If I'm feeling romantic, I tell people I'm helping to explore the edges of the universe.

If I'm not feeling romantic, I tell people I look at blurry photographs all day.

I'm sorry, I meant that as a joke, but it probably comes off like I'm another boring office drone who hates their mundane job. Just the opposite: I love what I do. Even on the off days, I can at least enjoy the methodology. And I love my life outside of work, too. Not that it's anything special. I date. I go out drinking with friends. I have a little girl, Kit, who's the best part of every day. At night, I tell her stories about princesses. I may not be terribly creative, but she likes the stories that I make up best. Well, I don't actually make them up *completely*: I mostly take my favorite movies, censor the violence, simplify the plot, and replace every character with a princess, an evil queen, or a magic frog. Last night, I told her the story of a wandering princess. She came to a land that had just lost its king. His two daughters were feuding over who would inherit the throne, and the peasants were suffering for it. Our clever heroine played both feuding princesses against one other until they destroyed each other, leaving her rich and the townspeople free.

That was the princess version of *A Fistful of Dollars*.

I'm going to tell you a brand new princess story now.

One day, a princess was walking across a wide, open field when there was a noise from the heavens such as she had never heard. It was the gods themselves. They came down from the sky, and they gave the princess a test. The princess was strong and clever and beautiful, but she was still just a girl, and a girl does not work on the same level as gods. The princess did not understand the test and could not tell you what it was.

She could only tell you that she failed.

The gods put the princess to sleep and gave her their mark. When she awoke, she returned to her kingdom, and all was well for a time. She fought with her brothers, for she was quicker than all of them. She danced with her father even though he was big and clumsy. She laughed with her friends, and she fell asleep in her big, soft bed.

That night, the princess dreamt of strange noises from the sky. She heard the crack of sharp thunder. But she slept deeply and did not awake until well into the next day. When she did, she found that she was alone. Her castle was empty, her family was gone. There was no trace of them. The princess searched and mourned, but nobody can search and mourn forever. One day, the princess traveled far away to the kingdom of her aunt, a woman she had never met before. Her aunt was kind, and with time, the princess made friends there.

She fell asleep one night and was troubled again by the noises in her dreams. When she awoke, her aunt's kingdom, too, was empty. Its people had vanished without a trace.

The princess vowed to be alone forever this time, but some vows are very difficult, even though they seem simple when you make them. Eventually, the princess got lonely, hiding in her aunt's empty castle. When a wandering merchant and his family took shelter there one night, the princess broke her vow. They smiled so easily. They laughed and joked and sang and danced, and when they left, she went with them. She lived in their village. Though she was not a princess there, she was happy nonetheless.

She fell asleep.

She dreamed of thunder.

And they disappeared.

The princess carried the mark of the gods, and the gods followed her wherever she went, taking away the people around her. But they never touched the princess.

I never told that story to Kit. It's too tragic. Especially considering that the tale is entirely true, save for two lies. I will tell you what those lies are at the end. You'll have to listen to my story first.

●

"Hey, Victor?" Jan was leaning across my monitor, one of her headphones still in her ear. "I can't seem to verify GL 386-HP. You think we had something there?"

"Maybe," I said. "Let me check."

I ran a search for GL 386-HP, and a result popped up.

Declination: 63° 17' 04.1"

Redshift: 9.62

I opened up the latest exposures sent down. I checked the coordinates. Nothing there. A little spot of unassuming black space.

"Huh," I said. "Guess I was seeing things."

Jan gave me a friendly smile and tucked her other headphone back in. She turned to her monitor.

I tried to forget about GL 386-HP, but it buzzed around in the back of my head all afternoon. Before I shut down my computer, I pulled up the image history from the James Webb. The telescope takes several sets of long exposure images over a period of months, and by compiling them, we can get a massive, fairly comprehensive picture of that part of deep space. Sure enough, two sets ago, GL 386-HP was a little white dot.

A false reading, then. It happens. Distortion. Reflection.

I went home. I drank a pretty fine porter. I watched a TV-edited version of *Kill Bill* while Kit did her homework. Then, I went upstairs, and I told her a story about a princess who had been attacked on her wedding day by a team of other princesses that she thought were her friends, and her epic quest for revenge upon the magical frog who had ordered the hit.

❂

"Hey, Victor?" Jan leaned across my monitor, headphones in. They were blaring something squealing and punky. "I can't verify HD 161859."

I ran a search for HD 161859, scanned to its coordinates in the latest exposures from the James Webb, and frowned at my monitor.

Another little spot of unassuming black. It was right next to where GL 386-HP had been.

"Come look at this," I said, and I gestured for Jan to walk around my desk.

She didn't respond. She frowned a little, but I didn't move my hand. After a few seconds, she reluctantly pulled out her headphones and trudged over to see what I wanted.

"Here's GL 386-HP—that last false positive—two sets ago," my finger settled under the little splotch. "Here it is in the latest set."

A little spot of unassuming black.

"Let's check HD 161859." I could tell Jan was already bored. "Yeah, same thing. There it is on the last set. But on this one? Nothing."

"Weird," she said, though I got the sense she was only confirming that she understood that I thought it was weird more than she was agreeing with my assessment.

"It *is* weird," I said. "One blip is distortion. This is two blips across a span of what? Three weeks?"

"Yeah, keep an eye on it," Jan said, already slipping her headphones in and heading back around the desk.

❂

The weekend.

I took Kit to the mall and bought her an *Adventure Time* backpack. We had dinner at a Japanese place where they flung meat in the air with their knives and made corny jokes. I hung out with a few friends and pretended to be into a basketball game when I was really just into getting a little drunk. I lost at darts, badly.

Monday.

Even when I'm hungover, I'm usually the first in the office. I find that I can shut off hangovers better with something to focus on rather than just sitting around in my underwear, wishing I didn't exist. But I wasn't the first one: Jan was already at her station, staring intently at her monitor. She didn't even have her headphones in.

"Morning, Jan," I said, but she didn't respond.

I lost the morning squinting at spots of light and marking their locations. I stood to head out for lunch and found that Jan hadn't moved.

She was still staring when I got back.

"You okay?" I put a hand on her shoulder.

She didn't respond.

I shook her lightly.

"Hmm?" She said, blinking up at me through bloodshot eyes. "Oh yeah. Sorry, must have been zoning out."

"You've been sitting here for hours," I said. "You look like you just got maced. You getting sick?"

"Y-yeah. Yeah, maybe," she said. "I think I'll head home early."

She was still at her desk when I left at six.

The next day, Jan was still there. Her eyes were bleeding. Her breath came shallow. You could hear the wheeze across the room. I called Alex in, and we tried to coax her away from her monitor. She scratched his cheek open and smashed me in the head with her keyboard. The paramedics were both big guys; they had to call for backup.

Alex asked me a lot of questions. I asked him just as many. Neither of us came away with answers. When I walked by Jan's workstation, I saw what she'd been staring at so intently: a blob of black, empty space located toward the bottom right hand corner of James Webb's latest exposures. GL 386-HP.

I sat down at my computer. I pulled up the images and went back through the last few exposures. GL 386-HP, HD 161859, and now Z6 GND-5865 and a handful of other objects—all gone.

I called Alex. I pointed it out to him. He grunted, acknowledged that it was strange, and joked that it wasn't the strangest thing to happen today. He went back to his office and resumed the endless stream of phone calls about the incident with Jan.

I was all set to leave for the day when Alex tapped me on the shoulder.

"Vic, show me the missing objects again."

He looked distracted. I brought up the exposures. I showed him the empty space.

"What, uh . . . what color would you say that is?" he asked.

"What do you mean?"

"That spot," he pointed to where GL 386-HP had been. "What color is that?"

"There's nothing there."

"No, I know, but what color is it?"

"Black, I guess?"

"No, it's . . . I mean it is, kind of, but it's also . . ."

Alex clenched his fist. "It's like, it's almost . . . but not. It's like a darker . . ." He shook his head and walked away.

Wednesday. Alex didn't say hello to me this morning. He said, "Did you give any thought to it? Can you figure out what color that was?"

I didn't have an answer.

He came by my desk three more times, asking me to pull up the James Webb exposures. He stared at the empty spaces.

Thursday. Alex did not show up for work.

Friday. Saturday. Sunday.

Alex's wife called Monday and said he wouldn't be in. He would be taking some personal time.

I never saw him again.

There were rumors about his disappearance. That's a universal truth: no matter the work, from copywriting to industrial espionage, the gossip is always the same. I heard they had to drag Alex out of his garage. He was surrounded by paints. He had painted every surface. No images—just random smears of color. I heard he gouged out his own eyes on the way to the hospital. I heard they had to keep him in a completely sealed, dark room, or he'd never stop screaming. I heard he was having an illicit affair with the director, and his wife caught them both in gimp masks. I heard the Men in Black came because he'd accidentally contacted aliens. I heard a lot of stupid, unsubstantiated stuff, and I didn't give any of it much thought.

Alex's replacement was a tall woman with enormous lips and frizzy blonde hair. Her name was Elise. She spoke with a slight lisp and seemed very sorry to take the job, like it was disrespectful to the memory of Alex. We didn't hold it against her because, in all honesty, we didn't care. Alex was an all right guy, but he checked out at six on the dot. He didn't bring his personal life to work and didn't ask about ours. He was his job to us, and we were our jobs to him. Elise was different. Right away, she wanted to know how we were dealing with the changes. What we did for fun around here. What music we liked. If there were any good restaurants she should know about, being new to town.

She asked about Alex. I told her. I showed her GL 386-HP.

The empty space was bigger now. Only black where there used to be swirling nebulae and glowing stars.

Within a week, Elise fell mute. It started slow at first. She stammered. She hemmed and hawed in between thoughts, like she couldn't find the right words. Then she started speaking more simply, in mono-syllables. Those became short, staccato bursts of gibberish.

"*Hik no im wo to pat op tra,*" she yelled, pointing frantically. Her eyes went wild.

Eventually, she stopped speaking altogether. She didn't seem to be able to understand, either. She could hear and would jump at noises, but it was like she no longer knew how to use language.

I didn't leap to any conclusions. I didn't assume an empty little corner of a random photograph had something to do with a wave of mental breakdowns occurring in my office. That was too outlandish. But I entertained other theories. We could have some sort of chemical leak. Something in the water, maybe. This job always brought in the eccentrics; maybe it only takes a little something unexplainable to set off a dormant breakdown.

○

I never deigned to believe that the black spot had anything to do with Jan or Alex or Elise.

But I stopped telling people about GL 386-HP.

Just to test the theory, I told myself.

I stopped talking about it, but I didn't stop watching. With each new set of exposures, the emptiness spread. People started noticing. They brought in a technician to work on the system, but he found nothing. He did reboots and uninstalls, cleared something, restarted something else, and left.

The James Webb refreshed, and the emptiness expanded. We emailed people about the telescope. Had them check the cameras. Normal. All across the board.

This is a small industry. You hear the stories.

Like the technician who forgot how to use tools. Some weird targeted retrograde amnesia. He couldn't work the simplest device, just sat there staring at his dumb, useless hands. The woman from optics who suddenly stopped breathing. They got to her in time. They resuscitated her. She's now on a respirator, but the doctors couldn't find anything wrong with her. It was like she just forgot how to breathe.

I left NASA. Not because of GL 386-HP. Don't be silly; it was just burnout.

○

I've been working at the university for three years, and they've been good. I'm helping them figure out a better filing system for scientific images. It's not as sexy as the James Webb, but I like the methodology.

Kit studied and played and grew. I told her a story about a princess who travels back in time to get her parents to fall in love, so she can be born. I told her a story about two princesses who enrolled in Pegasus flight school where they got the code names Goose and Maverick. I told her a story about a princess from the magical kingdom of Nakatomi and how she battled the evil frog wizard, Hans.

Kit wanted a telescope for her birthday. She remembered when I used to talk about the stars.

I gave her my old one. It had been stowed away in the garage for years. I looked through it first. Not because of GL 386-HP. Of course not. Just to make sure it worked.

It didn't.

I looked for familiar objects out in space but found only little spots of unassuming black.

I broke the lenses with a hammer and threw it in the garbage. Kit cried, but I told her I'd buy her anything else she wanted. Anything in the world.

She asked for a Pegasus. Like Maverick, she said.

I laughed; she didn't. We compromised on a weekend-long vacation to a horse ranch out in the desert.

●

Kit had fun today. She rode until she was burnt and exhausted. She looked up into the eyes of the horses, their heads half the size of her entire body, and she wasn't afraid. She's sleeping now in our room while I stand on the porch and watch the sky.

We're so far from the cities. There's no light pollution out here. You should be able to see the arm of the Milky Way. You should be able to see an explosion of stars. You should be able to see *something*. It's not overcast, but the sky is nearly empty.

I can see clouds. Beyond them, the moon. There's Venus and a handful of satellites. At the far edge of the horizon, a spattering of faint stars. But that's it. The vast bulk of the sky above me is just a void of pure and unbroken black.

Like I said, I don't have much of an imagination. But a terrible idea came to me when I put Kit to bed, and I've been watching the sky ever since. I've been standing on this porch for three hours now. I'm watching those little stars on the horizon. One in particular. I call it Harold because I have to call it something, and Harold is a funny name for a star. I can't take my eyes off Harold. It's important.

I don't know what time it is. After midnight, probably.

I thought I just lost it. But no. I've checked and re-checked.

Harold is gone.

The blackness is not a blob or a blotch or a glitch in the system. It's not a spill, pouring over the distant stars. The darkness is blocking the stars out as it comes closer.

I try to picture it. The size of the thing. Something that dwarfs stars, solar systems, whole galaxies—and it's aware of us? Of me? I can't resolve the idea in my head. I think my lack of imagination is the only thing keeping me sane right now.

Now, I'm going to keep my promise. Remember the first story I told you—the marked princess and her quest to find a home?

I told you it was true, except for two lies. Here they are.

The gods were not gods; they were just men.

The princess was not a princess.

She was a goat.

It's a simple herding trick. Feral goats are an invasive species, but how do you find them all? The answer is, you don't need to. You only need to find one, and she'll lead you to the rest. They call it the Judas Goat. Ranchers drive or fly around their property in helicopters until they spot a lone goat. They tranquilize it and fit it with a transmitter. They release the goat, and she returns to her herd. The ranchers follow the transmitter and slaughter the herd but leave the Judas Goat intact. She, following her instincts, finds another herd. The pattern repeats.

The Judas Goat is the ultimate traitor to her own species, but she has no agency in the betrayal. She may not understand what she's doing, but she's killing everybody she loves, regardless. She is being used by things beyond her understanding for purposes that she would surely find malevolent.

The Judas Goat is an old trick. Older than anybody knew. Older than our entire species. Maybe older than the universe. And I have brought its inventor here.

I am sorry.

Robert Brockway *is a Senior Editor and columnist for Cracked.com. He is the author of* The Unnoticeables *from Tor Books (released July 7th, 2015), the cyberpunk novel* Rx: A Tale of Electronegativity, *and the comedic, non-fiction essay collection* Everything is Going to Kill Everybody: The Terrifyingly Real Ways the World Wants You Dead. *He lives in Portland, Oregon with his wife Meagan and their two dogs, Detectives Martin Riggs and Roger Murtaugh. He has been known, on occasion, to have a beard.*

Madness on the
Black Planet

Darrell Schweitzer

In the end, as the two of them descended to the surface of the Black Planet, Astronaut Adam Robinson had only his rage. It boiled up inside him inchoate and incoherent, beneath the level of verbalization or even thought, as he understood at some primordial level, at the base of his brain stem perhaps, that he, and all of humanity for that matter from the beginning of time, had been royally shafted, made ridiculous before a cosmos incapable of responding with even laughter.

It might have been something close to precognition.

The only words he managed utter were, "Oh fuck."

Ten minutes after the lander had separated from the orbiter, something like a shadow had passed over them, touched them, penetrated them in a way human senses couldn't follow, filling his mind with strange visions.

The first objective result of this was that all communications were cut off. The instrument panels in front of him all blinked out, then came back on again, but now nothing responded to his touch or command.

Secondly, his colleague in the seat beside him, Pasternak, had chosen this rather inconvenient moment to go mad. So much for the tight-lipped brilliance that had gotten crews out of sticky situations as far back as Apollo XIII. It wasn't happening this time.

The Black Planet was swallowing them. He saw it outside his window, swelling to blot out the stars. It was not what anyone expected, no frozen landscape of ice and craters like most Kuiper Belt objects, but *pure blackness*, like a negation of the universe where the planet was supposed to be: a planet which truly had no name except for one or two fabulous ones found in ancient and decidedly unscientific texts written by persons of infinite unreliability.

Robinson thought of it as the mouth of Hell, which was equally unscientific.

Indeed, scientific considerations included the fact that, in all probability, their third team-mate, Zhou, left behind in the orbiter, was history by this point.

Pasternak maintained a thin veneer of sanity as he repeated over and over again into his microphone, "Lander to Orbiter, we do not read you. Come in please." But he went on and on at it, like a broken record, until at last Robinson nudged him on the shoulder and said, "Hey, I don't think that's going to do any good."

That was when Robinson could tell that the other man just wasn't there anymore, by the vacant look in his eyes, by the drool that was running down his chin inside his space helmet.

Now the broken record switched to, "Houston, we have a problem. Houston, we have a problem. Houston, we have a problem." That merely confirmed the diagnosis and added to the absurdity, not merely because Houston was so far away that any sort of radio message—in the unlikely event they were still transmitting—would take months to get there, which made any sort of conversation impractical. Besides which, Houston might still be the capital of one of the larger surviving chunks of the former United States, but they hadn't come from Houston, or from any official space agency, not that there *were* any official space agencies anymore, now that cities were burning, oceans washed over continents, and the mad auroras rolled. No, this had been strictly a *private* mission, the brainchild of the last of the surviving grandsons of the infamous Delaroche brothers, oligarchs who could buy or break governments, and who survived and flourished in what newspaper reporters used to call their Fortress of Solitude: in fact an immense compound and artificial island located in the Florida Archipelago near the ruins of Miami, invulnerable to nuclear strikes or large meteorite impacts, so the story went, not to mention mere political revolutions and natural disasters. It had been tried and tested sorely of late, and it was still there, gleaming.

Of course there was a spaceport and if Compton Delaroche, last of the line, desired it to it be used, it was used.

Robinson, Pasternak, and Zhou had only met the old man once, when they were jointly interviewed for this mission. Even then, they'd sat opposite him at the end of an enormously long mahogany table in a darkened room, where they could not see his face clearly. Robinson thought it had rippled, like a flag in a breeze, and his every instinct made him want to rush to the other end of the table and break the bastard's scrawny neck, or else just get the hell out of there, regardless of what was offered, regardless of the state of the world he was fleeing back to. Better to perish among the millions than sell your soul to the Devil, no, something worse than the Devil, something out of the visions that were filling his head now, something he raged against and wanted to destroy for the sheer obscenity of what it was doing to his mind and his world and his universe.

But he had done none of these things, because Compton Delaroche willed that three astronaut candidates be recruited and trained and sent off. There was something in his voice, or in what his mind broadcasted, or in how reality rippled and shifted and changed in his presence so that there was only *one* will and *one* voice and all other living things were but detached limbs animated by his ever-reaching mind.

Now the force that held the lander like a toy in hand set the vessel down gently on the surface of the Black Planet. There was hardly a bump, just the subtle sensation that they were no longer moving.

Robinson turned to Pasternak, who was still babbling into the microphone, checked the seals on his suit and the gauge on his oxygen tank, and then gently led him out of the lander.

"Hey, buddy, you'd better come with me."

"Houston, we have a problem."

"Yeah, I think we do."

He took his crewmate by the arm and directed him down the ladder to the surface.

Now they could both look up and behold the features of the Black Planet. There were stars in the sky, but if it were visible, Robinson could not even make out the Sun, much less the Earth or even Jupiter. All too distant. Specks lost in a star field that looked like gleaming smoke. But they did not search the sky for more than a few seconds anyway, because now the Black Planet did indeed seem to have mountains of gleaming ice, higher than known in the Solar System, an impassible barrier toward which the two men instinctively walked. The rational part of Robinson's mind told him that those mountains must be hundreds of miles away, and, given the lack of atmosphere and the enormous size of the Black Planet (twice the size of Earth, but somehow less dense, so his steps felt impossibly light), very likely hundreds of miles high as well. There was nothing to do but die, as their oxygen ran out in the middle of the featureless plain.

But that was what the rational side of his mind told him, and he was not entirely sure he was in control of himself now. He saw things in memory that his eyes did not see—winged, white, many-limbed creatures rising into space, cities of featureless stone, gardens of frigid fungus in starlight—and sometimes he felt that he was someone else, a disembodied intelligence watching Astronaut Robinson making his way uselessly across the plain, dragging Astronaut Pasternak by the arm.

The rational part of him knew that as soon as the shadow or whatever it had been had taken control of the lander, something had entered his mind, and Pasternak's mind. Pasternak had not stood up under the strain. But he, Robinson, could still think for himself. He was still aware. He felt that rage for freedom that comes to an animal in a trap. It was enough to keep him going.

Much of what followed thereafter didn't make any rational sense. Possibly they covered impossible distances walking, without their bodies growing over-tired or their oxygen running out, or the distances themselves were illusions, or somehow space and distance were not the same here as they were on Earth. It seemed like no more than an hour before they actually reached the foot of those mountains, and he reached out and touched the hard, smooth surface, and all the mountains, as far as he could see, rippled like shapes made of rain, and vanished, to be replaced for a time by the apparition of an almost endless cityscape of black, featureless pyramids and structures that tilted at strange angles the eye could not follow, and of shapes like walking hills moving in and out and between and through these structures to a rhythm he could not follow but which seemed to indicate a kind of dance, increasing in frequency into a kind of frenzy.

Then this too was gone, and he and his companion made their way over trackless miles of wasteland, knee deep in snow so darkly gray it was almost black, toward an ever-distant tower with a burning light in the window, like a beacon, like an eye, irresistible.

By now Pasternak was screaming words Robinson could not make out, words in no human language at all, but sounds that almost meant something in his dreams, in his visions, in whatever pollution was filling his head.

"Houston, I think we have a problem," Robinson said. "No kidding. We really do."

He did not know exactly how he and his companion finally made it to their destination. Perhaps they were lifted up by winged, multi-limbed monstrosities and delivered there. Perhaps the tower was made of bones, but alive, writhing, and many-limbed, and it lifted them up through the lighted window as if shoveling two morsels into its mouth. Pasternak screamed all the way, but then grew silent as they—or at least he, Robinson—suddenly *knew where they were*: inside that meeting room in the Delaroche Complex/Fortress off the remains of Florida.

Something sat at the far end of the mahogany table, clad in a misshapen business suit, wearing a silken mask that rippled like a flag in a gentle wind.

"You can open your helmets. The air in here is perfectly good."

Reluctantly, Robinson unsealed his helmet. No, the air was not perfectly good, but he could breathe it. There was a sharp, acrid smell, like burning, and also a faint but indescribable foulness.

Pasternak fumbled with the catches on his helmet. Robinson helped him.

"Here, refresh yourselves," said the other.

Two plastic water bottles came rolling down the length of the table.

"No, thank you," said Robinson.

Pasternak seemingly couldn't figure out what to do with his.

By this point, like tumblers inside his mind falling at last into place, Robinson found the solution and perfect focus to his own rage. He understood. He recognized that voice, which he had heard at their initial briefing, and in his head and his dreams so many times since. It was the voice of Compton Delaroche, or whatever Compton Delaroche had become or whatever being had impersonated Compton Delaroche all along.

"Fuck you, bastard!"

The yellow mask rippled. The other said, "You have not disappointed me until now. I had hoped that the climax of all of human history would finish on a better line than that."

The lock within his mind sprang open. He was momentarily free. Now he did what his instincts had screamed for him to do at their first meeting. For all the clumsiness of his spacesuit he lunged along the length of that table and caught hold of the thing in the yellow mask. He felt its brittle neck bones crumbling into nothingness in his hands. It felt so, so good. He pounded with his fists as the rest of the body disintegrated and a cloud of thick, choking dust filled the air. He staggered back. He tried to close his space helmet again, but he was too late, because now, after a transition he could not remember or perhaps could not perceive, it was he who was sitting at one end of the table in that darkened room and addressing Astronaut Pasternak, who stood at the other.

The thing, the *otherness,* was inside of him now, awake in his own body, as if he were mad, fractured into a multiple personality, and the prevailing opinion was that the others, the countless monstrous *others,* were real and Adam Robinson was the delusion. His mind was filled with hideous memories that were not his own, of a time on Earth when he—that which had never been Adam Robinson—had appeared in Egypt and beasts licked his hands.

He—Adam—could follow the remaining conversation within the room only as if eavesdropping.

The thing spoke out of his own mouth, first with the voice of Compton Delaroche, then, as it became accustomed, with the voice of Astronaut Robertson.

It was Pasternak who mentioned Kadath in the Cold Waste, the Gardens of Ynath, and "more distant Shaggai." It was he who realized that all through the universe, vast forces were awakening, and, by means Robinson could not begin to comprehend, listening intently to this conversation as it somehow rippled through the very fabric of being.

It was the voice of Adam Robertson that explained that the entire purpose of human existence, the very reason such an evolutionary train of development had ever been allowed to begin, was so that mankind would, at the very end, destroy the Earth, or at least render it sufficiently chaotic that it more suited the desires of the *others* rather than humanity. He, through many guises and many millennia, had shaped events toward the intended outcome. He—that which was *not* Adam—was merely a watchman. Now that humans had, of their own resources, reached the Black Planet, an alarm went off, for if human beings had gained such powers and capacity, they likely had or would very soon carry the plan to its ultimate conclusion.

The stars were right. The time was right. It was not like tumblers in a lock. Wrong metaphor. More like the completion of a circuit.

That which wore Adam Robinson's body turned in its chair and raised a hand. A curtain drew back, revealing an immense circular glass window that that looked out, not on the surface of the Black Planet, but into the depths of space. The star field, like smoke in a wind, rippled. Gaps were appearing in it. Gates were opening.

It was Pasternak, who was mad, who now ran down the length of the length of the table, not to assault anyone, but to leap headlong through that window. The glass shattered. The air roared out of the room, taking with it stray bits of paper, the water bottles, and even a portrait of the original Delaroche Brothers off the wall.

Robinson tried to speak, but his lungs ruptured. A cloud of half-frozen blood spewed out of his mouth. Somehow, he was still conscious. That which possessed his body now didn't need lungs. He couldn't think clearly. His mind was not his own. Other thoughts, other memories, other visions overwhelmed him. He wondered if it meant anything that the first and last human beings in existence were named Adam. Probably not. He tried to form something with the lips, what had been his lips but were now only borrowed as the dominant entity within the body was momentarily startled by the breaking glass. He tried, maybe he succeeded in forming the words *fuck you* one last time, one last shout of nihilistic defiance addressed to the whole universe. Maybe no one heard it, but, he was certain, that was the best epitaph mankind was going to get.

{{

Darrell Schweitzer *has been publishing short fiction since the early 1970s. This present story is, by his count, #334. In the past ten years or so, his work has taken a decidedly Lovecraftian turn, which is fully displayed in his most recent collection,* Awaiting Strange Gods *(Fedogan & Bremer, 2015). His other collections include* The Emperor of the Ancient Word, Transients, The Great World and the Small, Nightscapes, Necromancies and Netherworlds *(with Jason Van Hollander),* Refugees from an Imaginary Country, *and* Tom O'bedlam's Night Out. *His 2008 novella,* Living with the Dead, *was a Shirley Jackson Award finalist. He has been four times nominated for the World Fantasy Award and won it once, in 1991, as co-editor of* Weird Tales, *a position he held for nineteen years. He has edited the anthologies* Cthulhu's Reign *(2010) and* That Is Not Dead *(2015). He is the author of three novels,* The Mask of the Sorcerer, The Shattered Goddess, *and* The White Isle, *plus books on H.P. Lovecraft and Lord Dunsany, and the classic* The Innsmouth Tabernacle Choir Hymnal, *which is used when he leads the choir at Cthulhu prayer breakfasts.*

Drift from the Windrows

Mike Allen

Eden, I'm not a writer. Not like you are. You touch a keyboard, and I swear, five thousand words drop out in thirty seconds. Not for me. I type fast, yes, but I will never have so much to say. Not all at once like that.

Truth is, I'm not much of a talker, either. You know that, right? This, what's happening right now with the words coming from me so easy, that's got to be the state I'm in. My nerves. The chemicals in the air. All those sounds in the other room.

Maybe it's easier that I'm just talking to my laptop. I'm glad I can't see my reflection in the screen. I don't think I could record this if I could see my own face. Even though it's for you.

I need you to understand what all that pain means, what it's for. I hope my words are clear—it's hard to tell, I can barely hear my own voice.

My boss can probably hear me out here. I don't think she cares.

Oh gods, I wish I had known how much you hated SanMorta before we started sleeping together. But when I told you where I worked, you didn't say anything. Why?

Wait, I remember. You told me why you didn't say anything. Because you wanted me that bad. Because you didn't want to scare me off. But you know, I don't think you could have. Your purple hair didn't scare me. Your tattoos, the gauges stretching your earlobes, your nipple rings, none of that scared me. Fuck, even the thought of what my dad was going to say didn't scare me. The bastard had a hard enough time accepting me as a scientist. He wanted me married off to a doctor back home. Seven steps of wedding vows around a fire, jewelry through my nose, the whole traditional shebang.

What he said to me when I confessed I loved a woman—I never told you, did I? You asked me, and I told you not to make me speak of it. You were so respectful of my wishes. Is that why you never talked to me about my job? You knew I'd tell you not to write what you planned to write, never ever to do it, and you didn't want to give me a chance to object? Is that it?

You confuse me so much. But I love that about you. Even now I hope that doesn't change. I hope you come out of this with some of that wildness left inside.

Brady here at work told me. He showed me your blog. The entry about what SanMorta does to farmers.

I know all about that, you know. I don't like it either. I don't even care that they can hear me say it right now. I know why people think it's unfair: those farmers don't have much money, and SanMorta has billions. What harm could this company possibly suffer if someone saves a few seeds? But that's not the point you made, is it? In that blog entry.

Brady told me he found what you wrote because that super-popular activist site linked to it. Spread it everywhere. His eyes were so wide, watching me as I read your blog entry on his screen. Because he thought he was looking at a dead woman. That you and I both were as good as dead.

You're not the first to claim my employer deliberately tampers with crops and uses aggressive legal tactics to sweep it under the rug. But what you blogged, about why they do it . . .

You had to know they would come straight to me. That I would have to answer for your words. In all my soul, I can only find the will to forgive you because you couldn't possibly have imagined the consequences.

If I'm to survive—if *we* are to survive—I can never, ever, let them lose their faith in me.

Know I came home to you that day with a heavy heart. Please, know that. Please.

◉

Sorry, I lost my breath. I think I might have fainted.

It smells like asphalt in here. No, so much worse, like there's a tar pit from prehistoric days in my boss's office and it exhaled all its ghosts into this waiting room.

There's a sweet smell inside the tar, like honeysuckle, like you, and it gets stronger every time I hear your voice through that door, but if I try to inhale you, the tar will kill me. One hundred percent tar, just like the old cigarette ads never said. I'll barf my lungs out, and they'll grow legs and crawl away . . .

I'm sorry, Eden. I don't even remember what I just said. I'm fighting to keep these words sane.

But I remember when I got home and confronted you with that printout. And you just said, "Yeah, I tried to get you fired," like it was nothing. It would have taken me a thousand hours of screwing up my courage to admit something like that, but you just blurted it out! My dad beat me for blurting things out. Your dad did too, didn't he? You told me that, and that wasn't even the worst he did. So how did we grow up to be so different?

Concentrate, Amisha. Keep your focus.

Eden, this is so hard. To fight the drugs we're breathing. To finally speak my secret aloud.

It's like I see you in front of me now, me saying, "What were you thinking? I almost lost my job!"

And your blue eyes went steely, and you said, "That would be a good thing. I think they've brainwashed you, Amisha."

And as I sat there in shock, you snuggled against me on the love seat, like you wanted a kiss. And you started talking about the lateral gene transmission, like I didn't know.

I was too stunned by what you had done to say anything else. I just let you go on.

And much of what you said, I've heard before. That, with genetically modified food, the body doesn't recognize when it's ingested something unnatural. That the body gets fooled into replicating unwanted genes. I couldn't help but laugh when your eyes went all wide and serious, and you told me, "They've proven that the mutant cells start clustering in our reproductive organs first. So children are born with that modified DNA already a part of them."

I know I shouldn't have laughed. It wasn't for the reasons you thought. I was laughing because you couldn't possibly have known how close you'd come to describing what's really going on without actually understanding one fucking bit of it.

And then you yelled at me about how SanMorta gets away with it because they have plants—human plants!—in every level and branch of government, and I know I shouldn't have kept laughing.

But then you grabbed me and shook me!

How could you do that?! You know all about what my dad did to me when I was eight. I trusted you with that! Did you do it deliberately? To hurt me the way my dad would hurt me, so I'd heel like a good little dog?

You're the first person I've known who I ever felt I could be intimate with. And I've even told you . . . that you make me feel safe . . .

Sorry, Eden. It doesn't matter now.

But I keep forgetting what's important because of the atmosphere in here. It's so thick with the Mother's musk, it's like my brain isn't even attached to my body anymore.

Is this thing still recording? It is, bless the stars.

I had to show you that you had it all wrong. It's a miracle I was even allowed to come home to you.

And I admit, it broke my heart in a completely irrational way that you agreed so readily to a tour of our lab. I knew then and there that you had to be plotting something that you'd try to hide from me.

But at the same time, you made me so happy. Because I knew then you had a chance. *We* had a chance.

Oh! Oh no! W-wait, Mother. I'm not finished, don't—Eden, I love y—

●

She let me go.

Looks like my laptop is still working. She didn't touch it.

I don't think she cares about our lives. I mean, our day-to-day lives. And that's why I have hope. I hope what she took from me will help you . . .

I hope they'll make the things the Mother is doing to you proceed easier.

This stench, it's so thick. It makes my head light. I don't know if I'm talking to you or dreaming it all.

Funny that I remember this now: I did worry that you'd be disappointed at how mundane this place is. You know, our labs, they don't look much different than what you find in the biology department at Ferris University—sorry, I shouldn't laugh, especially now. I just remembered your shout of "FU" every time I said that name. Fact is, our labs look junkier. Hah. And you know, the "palace of all evil," as you call it, is just a big greenhouse on the roof. Where we keep all the varieties of plants we're studying. To see what gene combinations show promise.

It's really important, what we do. The heirloom seeds you yammer on about—the world is undergoing drastic changes. I have inklings of what's going to happen, and I still struggle to imagine it. The weather turning haywire won't account for even a fraction of how this planet will transform. What humans will endure. But we'll still need to grow food. We have to adapt our crops.

I don't hear those sounds any more. Maybe it's over. Or maybe my senses have stopped working.

But my laptop is here on the desk. I can touch its warm screen. The little line that the recording program displays keeps pulsing as I speak.

Did I say something about how the Mother doesn't care? None of them care. About our daily lives. My co-workers might care, but they're not the ones that matter. These . . . creatures only care about the big picture and where we fit in it.

But Eden, you were all about the big picture, too. Of course, you planned to put everything you found on your blog. I knew you had a camera hidden in that purse; you never carry a purse. Did someone from the activist website give that to you?

Fact is, I could read your thoughts like a picture book. If I lost my job because of your exposé, if you wrecked my career, I'd be free of this place, and you could deprogram me. Lovingly. And I'd see that you did it all for love and love you even more.

What I kept thinking about, though, when I led to you to my boss's office, was how you grabbed me by the neck and shook me. Like my father did because I wouldn't do what he wanted. So many years, I would sit on his lap, and he would sing to me so beautifully in Hindi, and I would wish I knew the words. I had no warning what was waiting inside him.

Or you. But I *do* forgive you.

Some part of me, though, must hate the thought of happiness for us. Because there was a perverse part of my mind that desperately wanted you to catch on. The way all my co-workers treated you better than any real science journalist would ever be treated, all smiles and happy to show you *everything*, even though you're nothing more than an angry woman with your own little angry blog. The way they just smiled and kept chatting about how we use traditional cross-pollinating when you couldn't hide your boredom anymore. The way my boss greeted you like an old friend after the things you wrote.

She looked her dapper best, I tell you that. I can't believe how pretty she can be sometimes. It's all about her mood, I think. How she wants you to feel.

I could tell you were responding to that aspect of her power, too, Eden. But how could you help yourself? No one can, really. Sometimes, I think my boss is just another human, taken deeper into the Mother's mystery than all the rest of us. Sometimes, I think she's a piece of the Mother, an independent aspect.

What I think is irrelevant.

No one can resist her charms. When she selects someone to interview here, you can bet they'll show up on time. But it's how they respond to *her* boss that's important. Whether they understand and comply, like I did. Or try to fight back. Or start shrieking.

My boss's boss. The Mother. She was waiting for you in the room beyond the office. They told me I wasn't allowed to say anything about her. That I had to let her introduce herself.

My boss was weaving her spell of words. You didn't notice when the Mother started attaching her limbs to you. I did. I couldn't say anything.

Eden, I'm so sorry.

I was hoping you wouldn't scream.

I grew up reading comic books about the many-armed Hindu gods. Sometimes when the Mother takes me, I close my eyes and imagine it's Parvati embracing me. Preparing me for the times ahead. The Mother lets me think this, I think, even sometimes makes it real for me. She wants me to be willing. I don't know what she does for the others. We don't dare talk about that. I wouldn't even speak it aloud now if anyone else was here.

I guess you could say, the same thing you tried to do to me—set up an ambush to force me off the team—I had to do to you. Otherwise, our lives were forfeit.

When I went to the Mother to answer for what you'd done and she took me in her arms, I showed her how useful you could be, filled my mind with visions of all the things you could do for her once she taught you the right way to think. How your voice on our side would make our cause easier. Thank the gods, I saw that she agreed, that you would be spared.

She showed me what she had in mind for you.

I didn't see any other choice.

The Mother isn't like you—or like dad. She's been honest with all of us here about the harm that lies inside her.

Eden, you were absolutely right about some things. You wrote that the reason SanMorta denies that its GMOs cause genetic drift in humans isn't blind stupidity or bureaucratic incompetence. You said they're doing it deliberately and that they want it to spread.

This is true.

You almost even grasped the reason why. You wrote that it was for population control, that the group you're in touch with believes the intruder genes will make everyone more docile, more vulnerable to disease, more dependent on government.

They'll cause changes all right. I can't think about it because it makes me feel so sick I want to vomit myself inside out.

The Mother is just one of multitudes. She and the ancient things she calls kindred are . . . are kind in their own way. When they make themselves known, they don't want bloodshed. They want to claim this world peacefully.

The things they can do with their minds. The ways their forms can change. We can't hurt them. Their bodies—most of what they are doesn't even exist in this dimension. There is nothing we can do to stop them.

Those of us who are useful, those of us who understand and show that we are with them, we have a chance at lives, at futures. A slim chance but a *chance*.

Those who resist, who don't understand, who are not useful. They will just be crops.

There are some, like your father—like my father—who deserve that and worse. But I want you. I want to spend the rest of my life with you. I want you to be with me when this future comes. It's the only hope I have that it will be bearable.

The smells are fading. Those sounds you were making, they've stopped.

The Mother promised me you would still be you when she was done. That you would still look like you. Even, to some degree, still think like you.

Oh, I hope she's kept her promise.

If there's something left in you that questions what I've done, I'll play this because I won't be able to say these things to your face.

But I hope I don't need it. I hope I can just delete it and never worry about us again.

I love you.

{}

On weekdays, **Mike Allen** writes the arts column for the daily newspaper in Roanoke, Va. Most of the rest of his time he devotes to writing, editing, and publishing. He's the editor of Mythic Delirium magazine and the Clockwork Phoenix anthologies, and the author of the novel The Black Fire Concerto, as well as the short story collections Unseaming and The Spider Tapestries. He has been a Nebula Award and Shirley Jackson Award finalist, and he has won three Rhysling Awards for poetry.

You can follow Mike's exploits as a writer at descentintolight.com, as an editor at mythicdelirium.com, and all at once on Twitter at @mythicdelirium. You can also register for his newsletter, Memos from the Abattoir, at tinyurl.com/abattoir-memos.

Chunked

Matt Maxwell

They refused to tell me the name of the ship, only to wait for it.

The deckhand who led me on board the tiny skiff was tall and wrapped in a leather poncho. He stood stooped and black, like a bat wrapping its wings against the cold and wet.

The flensing ship loomed in the water, its reflection cast large in the greasy moonlight. The rain had stopped, and the water's surface lurched slowly, twitching like an animal's lips during dream time. Yellow light spilled from the superstructure, catching steam and smoke from countless pipes and exhaust ducts. The ship made its own weather. Its height was obscured by clouds, leaving only glimpses of what might be above the mist. My eyes swept to the name on the hull, written in white block letters taller than a man. I slid my glasses down to read.

Something touched my shoulder, and I jerked.

The deckhand laughed. "You're just a barrel of laughs." He flinched and lifted his arms, wiggling his fingers, "Ooooooo! I'm a scary monster!"

I sucked back a breath and willed my heart to stop rattling around in my chest. My heart has always been bad. Nothing fearful, but I was acutely aware of sudden turns. They took a physical toll on me.

"You okay?" His amusement cooled down to something harder. "Gotta be made of stronger stuff than that if you wanna step on board. The stuff we catch—"

"I'm well aware of that," I snapped. "And I'll be fine." The pulse rushing through my neck put a small lie to that.

Drizzle ran down the black of his hood as he nodded like he knew I was lying. "Okay, buddy. I mean, no shame in turning back. Hell, most folk wouldn't have even waited on the dock. I mean, they're happy to pop open a cup and eat it cold, but—"

"Knowing where it comes from is another thing."

"Sure enough," he said as he docked the craft at the retractable landing.

I looked up at the metal angles and watched the water sheeting off of the hull like it had just been thrust up from the ocean floor, shedding the Pacific as it settled.

○

The captain was a big man, weight pressing at the seams of the uniform shirt beneath the orange overcoat. It was stained with something, a color that hovered uneasily between moldy green and dirty brown.

"Welcome aboard Meester Lew-ellyn," he said with an accent so heavy that it had its own pull. His lips twitched with the words he held back.

"Thanks," I said as I wiped my glasses dry and replaced them. "Not like Russia out there, right?" I pointed to the rain-slicked windows, yellow drops hanging and glittering in the corners.

His frown could have curdled blood to scabs. "Ukrainian. Not Russian." He spat something from between his big teeth. It hissed into the corner and skittered away into the dark. His lips were stained green from lulu.

"I'm very sorry." The phrase flopped out of my mouth like a beached fish.

"It is okay, Lew-ellyn." His fist thudded against the shirt, right above his heart. "Ukraine only here now." He then swiped at his lip with the back of his hand, not noticing the smear that it left. Brittle chips of something like insect shell hung in the spit.

"I wanted to . . . to thank you for letting me on board on such short notice."

He turned away with a shrug of his shoulders that was obscured by the stained orange fabric. "Your paperwork cleared. And—"

"And?" I stifled a cough, guts kicking. He knew.

The captain's eyes narrowed in mirth. "Never seen EA man actually do the job. Was curious to see what kind of man would wander onto flenser." His hand swept around the bridge. As he turned back, his eyes were lit with a sharpness.

"I've been to the accelerator gateway in Blackrock, Nevada. And to the aeries and tanneries of Bangkok." I lay it out to him like an offering.

"Got my leathers from there. Ain't nothing cuts through these babies." The lingering deckhand slapped his leg, and the sound was sharp.

"So you are a collector? Preserver? I hear about people like that. Who want to see them all."

I shook off the question. "Hard to get a census on ships," I said after a moment. "And I wanted to see the final frontier. I mean, you're after the big one, right?"

"You hear correct." The captain pointed at the helmsman and snapped his fingers. "We finish out that reef, every last one of those bastards. Even the big one down around the horn. They called it *Day*-something. Took a week to process. Quality product, too. Then, we come up here."

Lit from below by the cool glow of his console, the helmsman's downturned lips and protruding mouth made him look like a drowning man. "Locked in, Captain. Take us a day at half power."

"A day?" I asked. "I thought it would be longer." The idea of it having been so close all this time ate at me suddenly.

"Is that fear?" The Captain laughed. "And you have been to Blackrock? Surely, that was more frightening with the colors and the . . ."

"Geometries?"

"Yes. Ge-om-et-ries." He repeated the word, playing with each of the syllables like it was a piece of fatty tuna on his tongue. "The ab-stractions." His finger thrust out from his fist, and he rotated it around his ear and whistled.

"It was safer than you'd think. There was a *distance* between us and the essential at the gateway." I coughed and shifted on my feet. "Tomorrow?"

"Hah!" He fished out a translucent plastic bag from inside his jacket. The instrument lights shone through it, showing turquoise-colored gelatin. Suspended in that were strings of something like fungus and chitin.

Pure lulu.

He took three fingers and shaped a wad before stuffing it into his cheek.

Of course, I knew what lulu did. I also knew it wasn't for me. It made the walls reverberate and let you see around corners and in-between the edges of things. It was critical for flensers, letting them look at the things with the distance necessary to do the job and not go insane. Or only go insane in a useful way.

The captain offered the pouch to the helmsman, who took a generous helping and stuffed it in his cheek. His fingers came out wet, and he stared ahead, uncaring.

A hand reached past me as the deckhand leaned for a pinch as well. The bag stopped in front of me, and the captain shook it. Contents jiggling, they caught the console lights like neon in a splashed puddle.

I held up my hand, palm out. "That stuff gets in the way of my reports."

"Might make 'em sharper," said the deckhand. His words were flabby around the lulu in his cheek.

The captain clapped his hand on my shoulder, and it felt like a dead thing there. "Quiet time. Almost done processing. Caught one in Gulf of California. So many legs." His eyes were black and dead as the lulu took hold.

"A big one, I hope?"

"Only big ones left. Little ones easy to snap up. Use trawl field. Big ones we need to fight. Old school. You see tomorrow."

●

The cabin was no bigger than a rich man's hearse. I slept but not well.

I took a drink from the supply of water that I'd brought on board and tore open the foil on an Icthyo bar. I hadn't sourced it personally, but the dealer was reputable. Who knew what kind of food they'd be serving here? Probably cut straight from whatever they'd caught. That was a little too close to the start of the supply chain for me.

The protein bar was too salty by half, even with the dry crackers. My fingers lingered over the pear in the bag, but I'd save that for a real emergency. Or for trade—as if anyone on this ship would have anything I thought worth giving up fresh fruit for.

A knock rang through the small room, and I pulled my glasses on. "Yes, what is it?" My voice sounded unsure and tentative, even to me.

"Hey, there. Captain thought you might want to know that the timetable's moved up. We're expecting contact in a . . . now."

"Now?"

"Big one, too. Point eight seven hull lengths." He made a sucking sound and said, "Ya ain't scared, are ya?"

"If you aren't, then I'm not."

"Gawd, but you are a terrible liar. Get yourself dressed and on deck if you want to catch the show."

"Is that safe? I mean, to look at it directly?" I gulped. "How about the glasses?"

"Lenses, you mean?" The sneer cut through the door. "You won't find a pair on the ship. Those things mess with your head."

"Good enough for the crews at Blackrock."

"Gutless cowards, all of you. Yeah, put your lenses on if it'll make you feel better."

The sun was out now, but the sea still had a slow roil like molten lead. Churning formed chaotic whorls on the surface, like melting words. It didn't feel like we were anywhere now. Water and sky looked the same in either direction. The wind smelled like fish, like meat left out at low tide.

Something ahead of us surged off the port bow. It broke through the water but wasn't visible through the spray.

The smell swarmed me. I pulled out a mask, holding it to my mouth and sucking in on the bleach and alcohol.

On the level below, black-clad workers shifted and made the line ready. Spools shone silver as they peeled the yellow sheathing off, leaving it aside like jellied snakeskins.

I'd never understood how the process worked, and the metaphysics involved went over just about everyone's heads. What I did understand was that the essentials needed to be grounded in order to be flensed. They existed in some kind of half-life until their state could be fixed, and then, they could be worked. Before that, they were real enough to split the ship's hull in half, just not to be processed and consumed.

"You all know the drill," the voice boomed out of the loudspeaker. "That's cash money out there slithering around in the surf."

Something like an arm broke the surface and made a clawing forward stroke into the sea. Distortion hovered around it, like it was a video only half-loaded, while giant chunks were interpolated or only guessed at. The low sun gave enough light to show a sheath of greenish slime like liquid emerald.

But I knew it wasn't a sheath. It looked like that all the way through:

underwater green, always wet. Sunlight scattered, and my brain imagined it a giant squid half-chewed and spit out by a whale bigger than any on record.

Thousands of meters of grounding cable gleamed, shining like a mirror hammered out into wire thicker around than a man's arm.

Water around the thing boiled. It didn't belong here, violating any reality it touched.

"Good to see you out here, even if it is with crutch." The captain's voice boomed behind me, but I didn't jump this time.

"Crutch?"

He pointed to the lenses and made a face to indicate the mask. "You know why you need those, yes?"

"The smell is revolting."

He laughed. "Your attachment to aesthetic is touching but is wrong." He folded the bag as he stuffed his fingers deep into his cheek.

"Without the glasses, I'd go crazy. Unless I started crazy, that is."

"Ha! None of us is crazy here."

Crazy for lulu maybe.

"So why do I need these things?"

"Sentiment, my friend." He put an arm around me and leaned in close, so I could smell the lulu on his breath, like jellyfish-flavored mints. "You think this is something more than it is." The crinkles on his face deepened as he smiled.

"And what is it?"

"Goop to process. Jobs for a thousand flensers. Heart of thriving industry. Frozen dinners waiting to happen."

He squeezed me like a gorilla squeezing an orange, flush with pride.

"Nothing to be afraid of at all?"

"It only smell bad."

The thing off the port lurched forward like an island cut free and rolling on a storm surge, part liquid, part solid, hideously between states. It raised an arm that looked more like a melting skyscraper sheathed in green glass. The sunlight passed through it murkily, and beneath the skin, veins swam.

I tried to see it like the captain did. Countless individual servings of Benthi-Chow in those bright green and yellow tubs on store shelves. Something boiled up at the back of my throat, and I retched over the rail. My mask hung by one ear in the breeze.

"See, I tell you. You no need stupid mask." The captain's laugh barked out like a seal's. "Look at it like product." He turned to face the target.

The thing seethed in the water, reaching for the ship, neither urgent nor afraid.

"Smile, you son of blubber." The captain's whisper was hoarse and ragged now. He was all up in the lulu. Maybe the words were for whatever he saw in his head and not the thing bearing down on us.

Through the mist was a green hellscape, gelatinous and shifting. There were two black spaces in the center of it, almost like eyes. The urge to rip off my lenses bit at me, but I kept my hands on the rail.

"Fire!" the captain yelled. "Fire to bring supper home!"

No other sound existed after that. Just a horrible woosh that ramped up for the space of a heartbeat and then cut out. Several tons of decompressing propellant hissed around the barrel of the spear gun.

The grounding line shot out in silence, only my brain imagining a *kerrang* of metal against metal. Cable shone hard as it unspooled behind.

I looked up to see the line go tight for a second before going slack as momentum caught up to the spear. It jutted out, embedded some distance below the eyes. Lulu addicts or not, the crew knew their business.

The thing stopped, lowering its arm into the water slowly and curiously, distracted by sensation.

"Throw current!" the captain yelled. "Ground that meat!" The words were muffled as if through a hundred feet of cotton batting.

I felt a galvanic snap. My hair stood up, and my jaw clenched as a somatic shock rolled through my whole body. Were I not holding onto the railing, I'd have dropped to the deck or thrown myself over the side in spasm.

The thing shook once, ripped from a state of shifting to that of leaden certainty, of reality so solid that it could now be cut by knives and carved into bite-sized chunks. It could be reckoned entirely. And now known, the creature stopped moving, only so much gelid meat awaiting the butchers.

○

Seagulls wheeled above it but did not land. Instead, they dodged in and out of the bright white arc lights that played over the massive carcass alongside the ship. Their screams were insane, chattering.

"Is it always like this?" I asked one of the black-slickered men.

He looked up. His features were once strong but now molded into something paler and duller. His lips were stained green. "No. This is different. Gulls usually won't eat this until it's been processed."

Which was smarter than the handful of workers I'd seen down on the muscle shoals floating alongside, kneeling and grabbing up handfuls of slime, licking their fingers clean. They did it mechanically, without joy or shame.

Unrefined lulu.

The carcass was being maneuvered by a series of skimmers, each with grounding hooks attached. They worked with the currents and wind, reading each and calculating the best vectoring paths. Their blades whirred with an eerie pulsing rhythm. The gulls pecked at the machines, seeing these things as nothing more than larger, blacker birds taking pieces of their kill.

Ever so slowly, the drones pushed the titan corpse into the receiving bay at the back of the ship.

I tried to watch dispassionately, as the captain had urged me to earlier with his drunken manner and breath that betrayed appetites that I couldn't dare contemplate. The body floated as teams of men in yellow hoods flashed electric chainsaw blades that bit through the meat. Great strips were flensed away from the mass. They couldn't even wait for it to be lashed down to the work docks, had to get it fresh.

"Beautiful sight, ain't it?" The deckhand settled next to me on the rail, loose and flush with what must have been very fresh lulu.

"I suppose." The green of the thing was bilious now, more yellow than emerald. Maybe it was already starting to rot, locked in our world.

"Enthusiasm, Lew-ellyn," he said in a dire imitation of the captain's accent.

"Sorry. Just that, when essentials are harvested over at Blackrock, it's more like watching a light show or fireworks. This is different."

"Captain's right. You're a preservationist." He whistled, and the light rimmed his face. He looked like a crescent-moon man with the face on the wrong side. "But a man's gotta eat."

"I don't care for seafood." Not that I could think about eating. Even the pear waiting back in my bag in the cabin was rotten in my mind, mealy and slimy.

"Maybe you just need a taste of the right stuff instead. You'll stop fretting." His smile had no reassurance.

Swarms of men were flensing the fiction off the bone and slipping it into giant polyethylene sleeves or siphon tubes that ate giant chunks of flesh as fast as they could be fed. Above, the seagulls continued their chattering—an odd sing-song quality behind it now with a rhythm that was clear to me.

"No," I lied. "I just need to file my report and get back on dry land."

"What report? For EA?" His smile turned wicked now. "Oh yeah, we all figured it out."

I went back to gripping the rail, pressing my flesh to the cold metal to have something to hold onto. Otherwise, my brain would scatter off into a thousand directions. I checked my breath and held it down.

"Figured what?" My lie, for once, convinced even me.

Lips pulled tight against teeth, just a line of green between them. "You. You'd rather have that thing be not real, you know? Half-real. Strong enough to hurt you but invincible. We'd rather have it so we can take ourselves a bite. Solid. Known." He pointed, and even with the weight of the gloves, his finger seemed impossibly skinny.

I let him think he was right. I listened to the sounds of the seagulls and let them make more sense to me than him.

"Nothing to say, Mister EA-report-taker? Gonna let your tears stain the pages?"

The sigh escaped me without thought. A little heavy.

"So, there's the dream, man. Squid meat in vacuum-packed bags. Chunked. Dig it." He waited for a response that I wasn't going to give. Then he shrugged and swept away.

○

Back on the cot, I felt hollow, staring at the metal ceiling, scratched and marked with graffiti from a hundred others. The sound of the seagulls continued somewhere in the back of my mind.

The cabin lurched as if we'd hit something or suddenly picked up speed. I rolled out of the cot and took to the floor before another something shook the whole ship. A red LED dome started flashing along to a chirp that dug into my skull. I slid my jacket on, and I was out the door before it pulsed again.

Clamor bubbled around me and below. Feet and hands hitting the deck and slamming bulkhead doors with empty clangs. Everyone was moving.

The deck shook and jarred, and over the chaos, I heard the screaming of seagulls. They were laughing as the ship yawed. I was thrown to the wall-become-floor before it snapped back sickeningly. Something roared like all the ocean being dumped out in mile-high waves and crashing down.

It must have been the ocean.

Tears welled up. I thought it from the sharp pain in my elbow, which felt broken, having taken most of my weight. It was useless now. But it wasn't that.

Crewmen screamed and cried in reply, gasps of shock welling up in a torrent of realized fear. I could have jarred and preserved it, so thick was it around me.

The ship settled back, but something was wrong. We pitched backward as if a mighty weight at the tail end of the ship was pulling us down. I felt the engines go full in response, a shudder rippling through my feet and legs as I stood uneasily.

The captain started babbling something over the loudspeaker between those incessant chirps. It must have been Russian or Ukrainian, whatever was the language of his heart. As he spoke, the seagulls hushed and the roar subsided, replaced by another sound.

Creaking. A groan ten miles long snaked past me, and I felt the engines go dead with a loud *chunk*. The angle of descent steepened. Outside the door, things went splashing overboard and screaming at one another or the sea or the sky.

Something moved far below me, under the skewed decks. There was a sensation of power, like the engines starting up, but it wasn't that. There was no regularity, but there was unleashed strength. It hammered in every direction at once. The ship shook again, but this time, it was from within. Violent force pulsed as bulkheads below me shattered and tore.

The life vest already felt wet beneath my fingers, but I took it anyway. Tears flooded down my face, hot and stinging, even where they welled behind my glasses. The night wind whipped my face as I slipped out the door and onto the deck. There were no bodies on the deck, just a glistening of fresh emerald slime. That was enough.

The water below was black and choppy with the thrashing of hundreds of limbs and another, larger set of waves driving away from the ship. The whole works heaved as the grounding line drew taut. Something had dived under the surface, and it was still leashed to the ship, bringing it down.

I stood canted at a sickening angle on the deck, high up. There was a moment of dreamy weightlessness and rushing before the concrete slap of impact on the water.

●

The dull fire of my arm roused me. I held onto the life jacket more than I wore it. Above me was night. The gulls still laughed, but now, it was a chaotic sound. There was no rhythm to it.

My head lolled toward the sky, black and huge. I turned, groaning. Rimmed by the remnants of its own strange weather, the bow of the ship jutted out of the calming sea, like a misplaced monolith, suggesting so much of what was happening beneath the surface. The sea lurched, and the hull shook like a toy in a palsied hand.

It slid beneath the surface without me knowing its full name, only the letters -*vidence* written in man-high writing, never to be read again.

§

Matt Maxwell *was born between the assassination of JFK and the first Apollo landing. He started reading horror stories around the time he was ten and never stopped, though they often don't scare him. He's written short fiction for Blizzard Entertainment as well as the series of self-published* Strangeways *graphic novels. In addition, he's written three collections of short stories, two collections of pop culture commentary, a Norse apocalyptic road trip novel (*Ragnarok Summer*), and an as-yet-unpublished near-future science-fiction novel called* Black Trace. *You can read more about him at highway-62.com or on Twitter @highway_62.*

Testimony XVI

Lynda E. Rucker

Classified by: Hastur Project Team
Document by unknown female
Retrieved from Pacific Northwest Exclusion Zone
Top Secret

Something big is happening.

That was what everyone was saying. No, that's not right. "Something big" is a hip club opening, a blockbuster 3D, a new line in holo-tablets. Something *momentous* was happening. But bigger than momentous, even. Bigger than anything that had ever happened before. Bigger than Jesus, as the Beatles once said. Well, as big as Jesus at any rate. Certainly, something on the order of the second coming of Christ—and possibly that very thing. Yes, as big as all that.

A few were in the know even in the early days, of course. But they weren't talking.

Jess talked, of course, but that was at the end and not surprising. I'd always thought he was a crackpot. My best friend Gwen's sometime-boyfriend, ostensibly a philosopher, had clawed his way into a tenured position at the University of Oregon in Eugene before he became famous as a kind of New Age prophet. I think he wasn't such a big deal in academia as he was in pop culture. Maybe he was an embarrassment to his colleagues, but I wouldn't know. I'm a waitress, and I play drums in my time off. Or I did. Anyway, a segment of the media and public thought Jess was a brilliant iconoclast, and he went on talk shows and wrote best-selling books that said things like reality was all just a consensual illusion, and soon, we'd all learn how to do interdimensional travel. All thanks to the assistance of beings from some parallel world (or maybe aliens, I can never remember which) that will push us to the next evolutionary stage of enlightenment.

Jess spent weekdays down in Eugene and came up to Portland to see Gwen most weekends. As Jess saw it, it was the easiest way to keep Gwen and the undergraduates he was fucking as far apart as possible. The joke was on him, really. Gwen knew and honestly, truly could not possibly have cared less. She had her own things going on the side, and really, who could stand having Jess around for longer than a weekend anyway? I asked her once what she saw in him and she just smiled and said, "He's got an enormous cock and he knows how to use it."

Men, in Gwen's world, were good for sex, and for buying you things, and little else. I don't know what made her like that. I said she was my best friend, and she was, but as much as she would happily regale me with stories of Jess's prowess in the bedroom (and the kitchen, and the living room, and on the balcony), she almost never told me anything personal. I don't even know where she was from originally. I guess it doesn't matter anymore. Only it does. It matters that *she* was—that all of us *were*—once. Even though we soon will be no more.

So I don't even know who I am writing this for—for no one, I suppose. But surely there is some power left in human emotion and human intelligence. Before humanity fell, how many brave stands were made throughout our history that no one ever knew about? I don't think that makes those stands any less courageous, any less meaningful. And so this, too, will be lost along with all of the human race. In whatever time we have left, I believe that it still matters that I wrote it down.

○

So they found something off the coast of Oregon, not far from Newport. Who is *they*, you ask me. (You who are not reading this. You who will soon cease to exist along with the rest of us.) Well, you know. The government, the scientists, the powers that be—someone found something, at any rate, and that someone was quickly hushed up. The government and the scientists or the government scientists moved in, and the rumors got started right away: they'd found an alien spacecraft, the ruins of an ancient civilization, a plane loaded with unexploded kamikaze bombs from World War II. It was the North Koreans, it was ISIS, it was Boko Haram, it was some new terrorist warlord totalitarian anti-American organization we'd never even heard of yet, but they were coming for us, oh yes, they were. All of them.

We weren't *just* paranoid. They (the other *they*, not the scientists but the terrorists, the great sweeping mass of fanatical believers that were not-us, and we never once considered our own solid belief in the Western world as the basis of reality equally fanatical) have grown clever over the past decade about the fear you can induce in striking small, soft targets, like a San Diego shopping mall, an Atlanta cinema, a park in Minneapolis. Eventually, you grew numb to the attacks. A dirty bomb in Austin? Large no-go areas quarantined in central Boston? Same old, same old. I was in my late teens when the SWAT teams and the troops started appearing on the streets of Portland, when the checkpoints went up and the curfews began. Old enough to know better, to know it had *been* better once upon a time, but you know, you got used to it. You can get used to anything. Almost.

But before that, for the rest of us, I guess it started with the earthquakes. Growing up in Portland means growing up with stories of how the Big One is coming, probably sometime between later on this afternoon and the next few decades—the 9.5 game-changer that will put anything that's ever rocked California to shame. Even the most conservative of seismologists and disaster planners talk about bridges and railways and buildings and runways ripped from the earth, about death tolls in the thousands.

We always have a few little quakes per year, but just before they found it, there were four or five, and stronger than usual. We tried to laugh them off, but you couldn't help think—is this it, the Cascadia Fault slipping and sliding at last? Are we all going to be living in our own real-life disaster 3D? Geologists were oddly silent on the subject, which only fuelled further and more frantic speculation.

The earthquakes had me on edge, but in those first few days, I didn't pay very much attention to the story about *something* found off the coast. Part of me thought I was above it all. Because I'm an arrogant fuck, every bit as much as Jess, I guess—I'm a girl drummer, I'm good at it, people come to see my band because of me—so what did I care about some new boogeyman? Yet another something that heralded the collapse of civilization as we knew it? We all had a cultivated nihilism about us, wore meaningless cloaks of ironic laughter: who cares, we're all going to die.

We could afford to because we knew we weren't, not really. Not all of us, at any rate.

Now, everything is different.

I can't believe how much I care.

○

Gwen and I met Jess at the McMenamins on Burnside, across from Powell's Books—God, it was only last night. I didn't want to go, but she'd begged me. "Jess was weirder than usual on the phone," she said.

Weirder how? I mean, this is a guy who'd been working with a chemist friend to develop a synthetic version of ayahuasca that he thought would help hasten this spiritual awakening he was so sure was going to happen. He said if the CIA succeeded in getting crack on the streets, he would figure out how to distribute this somehow. Then people would see the truth, and they would rise up.

So if Gwen said he sounded weird, I couldn't imagine what was coming.

He was already there when we arrived, sitting off in a booth as far away from any other customers as possible. Jess was normally a vain guy, but last night, he looked terrible. He clearly hadn't slept in a while. "I've been down in Newport all week," he said. "They called me in. As a specialist. Consulting. You can't tell anybody."

We must have both looked at him blankly. It took a few moments for us to make the connection between Jess and Newport to the story that had been in the news for the last week or so, and then I imagine we still looked blank. What on earth could Jess have to do with any of that?

"A specialist? What kind of specialist?" Gwen said.

His voice shook. "A specialist in making contact with parallel worlds," he said.

"What are you talking about?" Gwen peered at him. "Jess, are you on drugs? Did you take that aya-whatever stuff again?"

He laughed humorlessly. "Drugs!" he said. "Where we're going, we don't need drugs!"

Gwen looked at me across the table. It was a look that said, *what the fuck*?

And, *how do we get out of this*? Then Jess turned to her and took her hand, and his eyes were glistening with tears as he said, "Gwen, will you marry me?"

○

Do I need to tell you that the evening went downhill from there? (You, who are you, gentle reader who will never be?)

Jess said everyone was wrong about what they'd found there off the coast. It was something crazy all right, though. Something they thought at first had crawled up from some part of the ocean that was too deep to measure or explore. *Here be monsters.* They assembled a team of scientists to study it, this leviathan. They wondered if it was dying, coming into the shallows and trying to beach itself. There was a lot of excitement—how had a species of such a massive size gone undiscovered? And was this the basis of all the old legends about sea monsters?

They kept it quiet because they didn't know what it was yet, and because they wanted to fly under the radar of the animal rights activists. Because they also didn't know what they might need to do to the creature in order to study it. They had cordoned off an area of the coast of several miles, so no one could come near their research facility.

Then the dreams started.

They were scientists, so at first, they thought nothing of it.

But they were the same dreams. Or rather, the same nightmares. We asked Jess what they were about, but he just shook his head.

They thought maybe it was some kind of bioweapon, a monster made of organic and mechanical material, and that whatever poison it carried was affecting their minds.

"That's probably it," Gwen said. "That's really scary. How far is its range? Can it reach all the way to Portland? Will we be affected?"

Jess shook his head. "That's not it," he said. "They tested samples of it. It wasn't—it isn't a carbon-based life form."

Gwen frowned. "So, it was all mechanical?"

I got there before she did, or maybe she didn't want to get there. "Gwen," I said. "That's why they brought Jess in. It wasn't anything anybody made. It was from somewhere else. Right, Jess? Everything alive is carbon-based. Maybe it came from another planet, right?"

He nodded. He couldn't speak any more. All of his books were coming true, and he was falling apart in front of us. I thought he was going to cry, and I hoped not because I didn't know what *I* would do in that case.

Instead, we got out of there. We cut over to Morrison and walked down toward the waterfront. I always imagined that if someone told me "the end of the world is nigh," it would be more dramatic, but there wasn't really much of anything to say. Some small part of me hoped that Jess was just freaking out or making it all up, but I knew he wasn't.

We got as far as Pioneer Square, and I grabbed Gwen's hand and said, "Hey, remember when they used to have big crowds in here?" Then I remembered that she didn't, because, of course, we hadn't known one another as teenagers. But for some reason I felt like I had to start telling her and Jess about what it had been like here before everything changed: how there would be festivals or they'd show the World Cup final or a movie on the big screen and thousands of people would throng into the square. Back before it was forbidden for crowds of that size to gather.

They let me rattle on like that for a while, and then Gwen said, "What's going to happen, Jess? Are you going back down there? Are there more of those things coming?"

Jess said, "I'm supposed to go back tonight. I told them I needed to come back for some important papers, that I couldn't do anything further without some of my notes, but I really came back for you, Gwen. I'm serious. Please come back with me. I don't know if I'll be able to come again. I don't know if I'll ever see you again."

Who could have guessed that I would hear the most romantic speech of my life from someone like Jess? But Gwen just looked at him sadly and shook her head.

"No," she said, "and anyway, I don't believe you. I don't believe any of it. Nothing's going to change."

●

That night, Gwen stayed at my place. It was something we did sometimes when one of us was upset or drunk or had missed curfew. I never had a sister but I always imagined if I had it might be like this. We'd lie side by side in my big bed and talk about stuff in the dark—the kinds of things you don't bring up when the light is on.

We lay there that night and talked about what Jess had told us and whether or not we could believe any of it. We got back up and opened a bottle of wine and looked up stuff online: legitimate and whacked-out news stories, forums buzzing with rumors, social media heaving with hearsay. Gwen had her little holo-tablet with her, and we tried to watch the footage some guy had supposedly shot of the outside of the research facility, but it really didn't work that well. It kept stuttering and falling back into just a flat image, and really, it was just a building anyway, so we gave up on that. They—more *they*, nothing sinister this time, just the companies that manufacture holo-tablets—had said the next generation would be out next spring and would work a lot better, but I thought that if Jess was right, this was the last holo-tablet the world would ever know. I felt suddenly sad that it had been kind of a shit product and that we'd never been able to really get off the planet properly or even make decent holo-tablets before we got wiped out.

Gwen took her regular tablet out of her bag and said, "Look, there's so much bullshit out there. We could do this all night and just keep reading crazy theories. I'm going to talk to some people who will know what's going on." She tapped away on her tablet for a while and I wasn't really paying attention, just messing around playing some music and opening another bottle of wine. Then Gwen said, "Okay. Look."

She showed me a video of something, but I didn't know what I was looking at. Not at first, anyway. Then the camera pulled back a little bit. It was murky, a bit like looking at someone's ultrasound of their child. The birth of the death of the world.

We were looking at a thing in a tank. A sea monster. There's no other word for it. It was enormous, and it had so many eyes. You'd go mad with as many eyes as that.

"Where did you find this?" I said.

Gwen shrugged. "You have to go to the dark web to get any of the good stuff," she said. I wondered, not for the first time, what it was Gwen actually did for a living and whether I ever wanted to find out. "The guy who passed this on to me says it's legit."

"Turn it off," I said, my eyes closed, but I felt like just the viewing of the thing brought something unwholesome into the room with us.

○

When I was a child, even though we lived in Portland and not at the coast, I used to have nightmares about the tsunamis they said would accompany the Big One. I imagined the waves towering over me and blotting out the sun. I would try to run, but my legs wouldn't work. Then the water would take me, and the worst part was that I wouldn't drown right away; first I would be cast down to the deepest depths where things lived that ought not to, that we ought to never know about.

That night, the dreams came to Gwen and me. They were like my tsunami nightmares, only a thousand times worse. It felt as though our unconscious minds were being colonized. There was the wave again, and the attempt to run away, and the dragging down into the depths. Only this time, down there deep were cities built on grids that made no sense and architecture that defied reason. We were both shaken awake at the same moment because the quake that was happening around us was real, but in those first startled seconds, we each saw in the other's eyes that we had dreamed the same unspeakable dream.

Then there was just the sickening swaying, the sound of car alarms going off, and people shouting and things falling over and breaking in other parts of my apartment. When it ended, we just sat there and looked at each other for a few more moments.

I wanted to say something to Gwen. When I opened my mouth, a word I didn't know came out, a word from the dream. What I said to her was, "R'lyeh."

I couldn't imagine why I'd said something like that. It upset me so much I just got out of bed and left the room. I went to check the damage: some broken dishes, a bookcase turned over. I actually started to clean it all up before I realized it didn't really matter any longer.

I went back to Gwen. "Get dressed," I said. "Let's go for a drive."

○

Outside, people were spilling out into the streets in bathrobes and pajamas talking about the quake, and there were helicopters overhead. I wondered if we'd get out of the city at all.

But most of the checkpoints weren't even staffed, and the ones that were waved us on with no more than a perfunctory ID check. Gwen said, "Are we going to Newport?"

"I guess," I said, "as close as we can get anyway. I thought we'd see what we could about what's up."

I took the longer scenic route, the one that would take us along the coast from Lincoln City rather than the quicker way down I-5. Although getting out of Portland was surprisingly easy, once we hit US 101 it was clear that lots of other people had the same idea. We were sitting in near gridlock, still a good twenty miles or more from Newport, when Gwen announced, "I'm walking."

"What?"

"Walking," she said to me wearily. "Not all the way to Newport. Not yet anyway. But it's not that far from here to Cape Foulweather, maybe an hour or so."

I started to protest that I couldn't just leave my car there, but of course that was silly. Another thing that no longer mattered.

It actually took us more than an hour to walk to the ocean, but it was a cool, pleasant day. In fact, the sky was so blue you couldn't really believe anything bad could be happening. The same was true when we reached the state park area and made our way down to the deserted beach. One long stretch of blue, ocean meeting horizon, and so tranquil that the clenching in my chest began to loosen. Maybe it had all been a mistake. That had happened to me before: I'd work myself up about something and then getting out for a hike or a drive at the coast, out into nature, would help it all fall back into perspective.

And then the shaking began again.

We looked out across the ocean. As far as the eye could see, shapes were rising from the waters, the sea running off their foul flesh. All the while, the earth trembled and shook. What you knew then was that the reign of man was over, or more to the point, that it had never really begun. That we had been little more than a dream these beings had as they slept and now would banish on waking just as we once banished our nightmares in the light of day. But it was daylight, and the nightmare wouldn't stop.

Gwen is not with me any longer. I am writing this on backs of paper menus in a diner that I walked to back up on the highway. My pen is almost out of ink, so I won't be able to add much. The owner has a generator and has opened the place and is giving out free coffee to people and cooking stuff for them too if they want it, but mostly, nobody has much of an appetite any longer. Near me, two little kids are playing, maybe five or six years old. One of them is wearing a Superman cape. We could use an interplanetary superhero right now all right. In fact, if there's anything out there that can save us, that would be it.

I'm not holding out hope.

Gwen has continued on, on foot. Said she wanted to get to Newport and find Jess. I tried to argue with her. I said she wouldn't get far, that they wouldn't let her in if she did, but she figures it's all gone to pieces so much by this point that no one is in control any longer.

I'd have told you that I would never let Gwen walk away from me like that, that I loved her too much to ever let such a thing happen, but the end of the world does funny things to your priorities. Just like finding Jess, who never mattered, suddenly became so important to her. I knew then we had come to the end of our story together and there was no point in me either joining her or trying to persuade her to come with me.

And you know, maybe she found him. Maybe she did. Maybe they had an ecstatic world-ending fuck. I like to think that's how it happened anyway. It's almost—*almost*—a happily ever after, you know? It's a secret I don't like to share, that I like happy endings, sappy reunions, journeys that end in lovers meeting. We are drawing to our own end here and I still don't know who I am writing this for, writing this to. I have no lover waiting for me, gentle reader, but I was here, and she was here, and we were once

(Testimony XVI ends here)

§

Lynda E. Rucker *is an American writer born and raised in the South and currently living in Europe. She has sold more than two dozen short stories to magazines and anthologies, including* The Mammoth Book of Best New Horror, The Year's Best Dark Fantasy and Horror, The Best Horror of the Year, Black Static, F&SF, Shadows and Tall Trees, Supernatural Tales, Postscripts, *and* Nightmare Magazine. *She is a regular columnist for* Black Static, *and her first collection,* The Moon Will Look Strange, *was released in 2013 from Karōshi Books.*

The World Ends in Neon Yellow

LA Knight

How do you tell the world that it's ending?

My name is Cassie Carter. The people around here call me Ghost because that's what I am. Just one of the wraiths who wander New York, hiding behind our pretty or pallid masks. Beneath mine, I'm faceless. Just another lost pixie of a girl, all sharp bones and mocha skin and boy-cut hair, sleeping in the trees of Central Park to stay safe at night. Probably painting visions in electric color and her own heart's blood across marquees and billboards and ad screens by day.

Faceless wraith girl, but the denizens of the city know me well.

Ice crusts the sidewalks winding through the park tonight. October is a vicious old hag the closer it gets to Halloween, shaking her fist at the local street kids. The snap and burn of her bitter wind slaps my cheeks and pinches my ears. It hasn't snowed yet, but it will. Halloween's tomorrow, and October's letting out all her rage because no way will she agree to just age gracefully and get out of November's way.

I'm on my way back from an advertising job, uneasy on my feet. I don't usually work at night—kids get swept off the street too fast, too frequently, and no one cares but the ones left behind—but I need the cash for an upgrade. So now, I have to be a shadow, a ghost. I touch my tongue to the chip behind my right eyetooth to kill my temporary skinlights and the flashers in the soles of my shoes. No reason to go prancing along like a walking ad for android sneakers.

I stop at the edge of the park to scan the sky. Most people can't see past the toxic haze of exhaust mingling with the billows of steam coming off the skyscrapers, but I can. There's tingling behind my eyes, a wash of warmth that's nice with October cold smacking me in the face; the nanowires behind my retinas let me zoom in on the sky, filtering sludge and smog. Behind it, I find Orion with the three stars on his belt, just like my dad taught me. I find the Pleiades, those seven sisters.

I find that burning-cold beacon trapped between them, screaming bright amidst the star-haze of Taurus. Aldebaran, the Follower. Harbinger of things my dad always prayed would never come in my lifetime. I'm starting to wonder if they'll ever come, or if I've wasted my life preparing for something that will never happen.

The wind slaps harder, bitter cold, and slices right through my jacket. Should've brought a coat. Should've kept my gloves instead of giving them to the boy by the 59th Street entrance. Philip, I think his name is. I hunch my shoulders like that can somehow keep my ears from falling off from frostbite and trudge along the path, kicking aside scraps of trash. Central Park doesn't close until 1:00 a.m., so I've got a little more than an hour before they sweep the paths. As long as I keep my skinlights dimmed and remember to cut the power to my tent, I should be okay.

Detritus litters my way; people think they can just dump their crap right on my doorstep. I can't complain because, legally, I'm not supposed to be here.

A scrap of yellow paper, practically dayglo bright even in the dimness, catches my eye. I snatch it from the air before it can hit my cheek. Three quick blinks to adjust my ocular wiring, and I can read the blocky print splashed across the page. Pins prick the tips of my fingers; my hand convulses around the thick paper, my nails slicing tiny tears.

> *The Rialto Invites You to This One-Time Showing*
> *The King in Yellow*
> *Midnight, October 31st*

The paper crumples easily, and I hurl it against an elm. It falls to the frosted grass and uncurls slowly, a poisonous neon flower mocking me with every paper petal. I hurry past, never looking back as I head for my tree.

I guess my wondering is over.

Sleeping in a beech tree is easy if you've got the gear. People would probably be shocked about the Ghost living in the park when I've got so many good jobs—hacking rich people's tech to blast protest art across their LCD boards pays big bucks—but it grounds me, gives me a toehold in the physical world. The bark offers good traction for my sneakers. Clambering up the tall trunk puts a sweet burn in my calves and gives my fingers something to dig into, almost like punching code into an actual keyboard.

And just like keyboards, everything will soon be obsolete, but not for the reasons most people think.

I string up the tent I keep in my backpack—insulated micronylon flaps on nylon cables, hammock and tent and sleeping bag all rolled into one, braced by cords tied and retied to the beech's limbs. The floor gives when I walk—like jello. Cold to the touch, it warms up quickly from my body heat. No October hag can gnaw my bones in here.

How do I tell the world it's ending? That nothing we do can stop it? Not in the time we have. Probably not at all.

Tomorrow is October 31st. Halloween. The book my dad gave me when I left for New York calls it Samhain. The slip-space between dimensions wavers on nights like that. Splits like an egg sac. Sometimes it spits out things. Nasty things. But I've never been afraid of that until now.

My fingertips trace over the small bumps on my arm from the temporary skinlights. They mask the scars, lines of silver and cerise. Tiger stripes suffused with dormant poison. Scars left by nightgaunt lashes and gug kisses. I'm not afraid of them . . . but I'm afraid of this. Nightgaunts and gugs can be killed. Shot, electrocuted, run over with a car.

Not him.

"If it comes in your lifetime, Cassie, understand this: you can't stop the spread. Maybe you can slow it down, but once it starts, it can't be stopped."

My dad's voice, echoes of memory. I was ten years old then. I'd already written my first codes. Already hacked the school billboards twice to protest unrighteous cancellations—flashing red words screaming: "We want book fairs back!" Before the age of ocular implants and LED skinlights and Xplore chips that let your mind wander cyberspace. Before I'd ever seen the yellow-painted gouges carved into the stone my dad carries close to his heart like a dirty secret.

I tie myself in—not to the tent but to the bit of branch I allow to come inside with me—just in case the tent's cords break in the night. Tomorrow, none of this will matter, but I'd rather die on my feet than plummeting to my messy death out of a beech tree. I tug my blankets over me and close my eyes.

No time for sleep. Not yet. Not now. The dark behind my eyes is just to help me see; eyelids are the best screens in the world.

"*Maybe you can slow it down, but once it spreads, you can't stop it.*" My dad's warning. Truth, like a stone, settling cold in my stomach.

The spread will come. My dad knows it, and so do I. I have to warn him that it all starts tomorrow. He can hole up in the hills around Arkham; no one will bother him there, in our old house that everyone hisses is haunted. Even if they think the old two-story is easy pickings, the mods I put in will keep them back.

Getting to Arkham before the spread hits will be costly, and I have to make it quick. But this is what the Carters have prepared for, and I'm the best at sending out the quick warning; have been ever since I learned to tweet and tumble and pin and blog and hack my way through the web.

Old folks joke about my generation live-tweeting the Apocalypse. I'm counting on the fact that, hells yeah, we will, or this will never work. If it doesn't, pretty much everyone in the world dies in the next forty-eight hours.

Even if it does work, a lot of people are going to be dead really soon, anyway.

I have to tell the world it's going to end. Even worse, I have to make people believe me.

The best thing I ever did was talk my dad into giving me the Xplore implant for my eighteenth birthday. It's what makes all this possible now. All I have to do is let my eyes relax in their sockets, the tightness at the corners ease up, until my eyes just rest in the dark inside my head.

My tongue touches the pressure sensor on my last molar on the left, near the top of my mouth. Neon green and yellow lines cut across my vision, slicing and skewing through each other. Mapping out the path to the internet. I follow the weaving pathway of light in my skull to the coding site I'd bookmarked back in fifth grade. Still my favorite place to work.

I focus on the streams of ones and zeroes floating around the edges of my vision, waiting to be written into sequence so they can do something. The bits and pieces of the world, information ground down to light and electric impulses, all inside my brain. The pearl of the soul of the world, my dad always called it. I can hold everything in my mind when I hit this place up. Touch anything. Search engines beg me to shoot them a question while social media begs me to pin some Disney pics or repost some Tumblr gold. But there's no time for fun. I have to lay the foundations of the alert.

Binary digits sift through my metaphorical fingers as I weave threads of code, twisting and braiding bytes and stringing them together.

With a stray thought, music begins pulsing from the tiny chips in my cochlear implants—earbuds the size of pinheads. Perfect for pretending to pay attention in school. And now, perfect for working, the volume at just the right decibels to keep me sharp as a laser scalpel.

Have to plant the right images into the code. Have to shovel scads of information into nanoseconds, keep it short. Give people a chance to panic and then calm down and figure out how to run. And it won't just be anyone with the green to afford augmentation. When I'm done, this whole city will be one giant neon warning sign.

Scouring DeviantArt and Wikias for pics to embed takes a while. My Xplore implant processes and places everything—the search words "war," "mass murder," "violent orgy," and "global holocaust" are pretty effective for illustrations of what's going to start tomorrow night at midnight. My implant is an Xplore Golden Plus; I get great Wi-Fi reception, even out here in the middle of Central Park surrounded by trees, and my firewalls keep other people with BCI from hacking my feed.

Tired. Everything shifts into place like a charmed game of Psi-Tetris. I leave my signature in the code, the phantom of myself. They call me Ghost for a reason—I can slip in anywhere, and my programs come back to haunt.

Now, just have to release the warning. The trigger word—have to think of a good one. One that ricochets off the radar of every Illuminati and cultist and scholar dedicated to preventing what's been set in motion.

His name. The one who will be reborn in this world on Samhain at midnight. Born at least once before: the avatar of the Golden Death.

My dad taught me about the Deaths. Some are plagues and sicknesses brought from beyond the stars, felling humans like trees and reaping the dead. It hasn't happened in my lifetime, not here. Not since nanotech figured out how to slow cellular decay. Not since antibiotics were augmented with cyber-antibodies; still experimental and ridiculously expensive, but working even now through the right channels to trickle down to all the regular people in the next three or four years. Not the Black Death or the Blue or the White, bubonic plague and cholera and tuberculosis.

My dad warned me of the Golden Death: the King in Yellow and his consort Thale, the Queen in Red. The spread will start tomorrow, and there is no stopping it. Only delay. Delay and delay, and maybe one day, someone will find a way to stop the spread of his power. But it won't be me. I'm no occultist. I'm just the Ghost in the machine.

I key in the last bit of code. The trigger word is the name of the monster, the one who is not to be named, the demon king.

The king who destroyed my mom's world.

"*A king emperors have served,*" my dad always says, and I hate the awe mingling every time with the dread in his voice. "*A king named only at the last.*"

Well, we're almost at the last. Dawn's coming as I prep to pull out of cyberspace, as I cement the trigger word into the code. So I'll name him, the thing I've trained to fight my entire life.

Hastur.

I'm back in the physical world, back in my little nest in my beech tree. I have to call my dad and warn him that the Apocalypse is about to kick our door down.

o

Somehow, I get some sleep as dawn rolls around. When I wake up, it's afternoon, and there's drool on my face. I actually feel rested. And who says bed hair isn't sexy?

Picking through my curls takes minutes because I don't have time to be gentle. It's time to pack up and get moving. I need to be out of the city before I trigger the warning, or I'm probably dead. All hell's going to break loose, and I don't want to be swept up in it.

Unhooking my tent and blankets from the tree and rolling them up tight with the soft swishing of nylon, I stuff everything in my backpack and scuttle down the tree before someone can come along the path and get me stranded up there. Camping in Central Park without a permit *is* against the law.

The moment I hit ground, the hair at my nape prickles. Uneasy in my android sneakers that light up when I key them on with a click of my heels—cheerful green and gold to drive away the nerves. I move along the path and out to the 59th Street entrance.

No birds chirp. No squirrels chase each other through the branches. Distantly, the city noises lie through their chrome and fiberglass teeth that everything's fine. I know better. I'm a Carter, and we come from a long line of nosy people too curious to avoid getting slapped around or eaten by cosmic crawlies. Now that I'm more awake, I can think about being eaten by the things that are going to crawl out of the abyss tonight without breaking out into a sweat.

But I still slip my butterfly knives from my back pockets to the front because something isn't right. The air tastes stale, even here among the trees. The light settles dully in the sky; it's the color of cat vomit. Dry lightning cracks white as bones across the sky, and the trees I've slept in for ten months shudder in their earth.

Maybe, he doesn't have to wait for the play to begin. Maybe, the spell that will suck in the audience isn't what triggers the splitting of worlds. My dad taught me—that was what my mom always told him—but if he's wrong . . .

I have to get out of the city. Now.

Racing for the entrance, the cement jarring my legs with every thud of rubber sole on pavement, I blink hard twice to bring up a miniaturized projection of my bank account. Good—I have enough money for a taxi. No way am I going into the subway. Too close to the sewers. My dad once showed me pictures of what a group of people descended from this guy named Pickman had let out of the New York sewers. Who knows if they're still there or not?

Phantom pain heats the stripes on my arm from the gug kisses. "Kisses" is such a nice, cozy term. It doesn't describe what it's like to have a seven-inch, leathery slit filled with teeth latch onto your skin and punch through flesh to find muscle and bone; what it's like to feel their acid pumping into your body to turn you into soup so they can suck you up like a spider.

No sewers. No subways. Nothing underground ever. I'm taking a cab.

Dashing through the open gates, I give a little skip-jump and yelp, "Taxi!" The need to move, the drive to run—it burns in my blood like liquid lightning. My hands are shaking so hard, I almost drop my backpack.

A fat yellow cab slides up to the curb. That bilious sky stares down at me; I can feel it, like imps clambering along my back to dig their claws into my spine. I jump in the cab and tell the driver—a young man with a mane of locs and sun-kissed skin—to get me to Pelham Manor, a village in Westchester. It's far enough away that I can keep an eye on the growing eldritch storm brewing over New York without getting sucked up in the frenzy of sex and homicide that's going to sweep through the streets like blood.

Assuming nothing tries to eat me.

I close my eyes and slow my heart and my breathing enough to transfer half the money wirelessly to the taxi's cyber account. The meter dings, registering the payment. The cab lumbers away from the curb.

Have to get out of the city. Pelham has a railroad station. I can take a train from there to Essex County. It's a short walk to Arkham from the Essex County Station. I can be home in a few hours. Hopefully, I will live that long. I don't know what's going to come crawling out of the widening split in the world.

○

I pay the driver the rest of his money when we reach the station in Pelham.

"You gonna be okay, Miss?" he asks, frowning.

I nod. It's almost five in the evening. I have to trigger the warning now. People will have eight hours—seven hours to midnight and the hour during the first act of that cursed play—to get out of the city. I don't have to worry about people seeing it. Everyone will see it.

Hastur, I think. I think it hard, hard enough the syllables beat like a heart in my mouth, under my tongue, demanding to be said out loud instead of growled silently in my skull. I feel the code activate, electricity jumping from my coding site to satellites to servers all over New York.

The driver smiles. "Okay, then. You take care out there."

My smile makes my face feel like it's going to crack in half, but I make sure to give him one. He seems nice enough. No reason to be rude.

As I buy a train ticket from a gnarled old ticket master, I activate my Xplore Viewer and zoom in on the aerial view of New York City.

My warning is everywhere: neon letters screaming in slashes of toxic yellow dripping down the sides of skyscrapers and billboards like alien blood; pictures of the horrific things that are going to spread across the city once midnight hits. My code even hacked the feed for the Times Square Jumbotron.

I know a lot of people won't listen. But I also know a lot of people *will*. The people of New York have learned to trust the Ghost because the Ghost exposes the lies and the hidden dangers. I was the one who warned about faulty flu viruses last year; about the crumbling footbridge kids needed to stop biking across and that the city needed to cordon off and repair; about the corrupt school superintendent sexually coercing her students and the district that tried to hide it. Maybe the older folks won't listen, but my generation, they know the Ghost, and they'll know to get out.

This is the only thing I can do.

I watch the chaos spread through the city from my viewer. People scramble for their cars. They flood the subways. I warned against that in my message, but for some, desperation leads to recklessness. It isn't even midnight when blood first splashes crimson on the steps leading to the tunnels. Fights break out on the streets. Windows shatter under blows from cinderblocks and bags of bricks.

Blood seeps between my fingers. Only when the warm wetness drips over my skin do I realize I'm digging my nails into my palms.

I have to believe I did the right thing. I have to believe people are getting out before the real violence starts.

My mom is the only person I know who ever saw what happens when the play *The King in Yellow* is performed and Hastur's avatar steps into the world—and only because of what my great-grandmother recorded of the aftermath before her death.

My mom was the last to see the ruins of Carcosa, a world circling the distant star Aldebaran. The star I watch every night. I always wondered, was it really like my mom described when she used to sing me to sleep?

Along the shore the cloud waves break,
The twin suns sink behind the lake,
The shadows lengthen in Carcosa . . .

Earth will be like Carcosa soon. Delay all I can, nothing will change that. Hastur cannot be stopped. But he can be fought, and I'll fight him: a specter against a monster.

I promise myself this when I get off the train at the Essex Station. I laser etch it into my brain with every step through the strangely peaceful countryside surrounding Arkham.

It's the peace that warns me. Arkham is never peaceful. Too many nightmares call the decrepit town home. Too many secrets fester in the shadows of the gambrel roofs.

Something isn't right. I keep my knife in my fist.

The golden-skinned taxi driver is waiting for me at the gates to my dad's old house. I don't see his cab. Just him, warm brown eyes and gold-kissed skin and dreadlocks dark as midnight. And I realize this has been too easy.

"Welcome home, Casilda Carter."

Casilda. My mother's name—and her mother, and her mother's mother, and on and on. He knows who I am and how I can hinder him.

I know who he is, too.

Clutching my knife, I bare my teeth in a smile.

"You honor me with your oh-so-lofty presence, King Hastur."

The King in Yellow laughs.

He doesn't laugh long.

{}

Counting this story, **LA Knight's** *short work has been published five times (the others are a post-apocalyptic western short, a poem published in a magazine and reprinted in a "Best of" anthology, and a Persian sword-and-sandal short inspired by* One Thousand and One Nights*) and has placed in several HarperCollins online contests. She has written one novel for adults and four fantasies for teens. Nearly all the science and body-modifications mentioned in this story are either currently available or will be (though perhaps not cheaply) in the next two to three years.*

Nimrod's Tongue

Cody Goodfellow

Six minutes after liftoff from the Deimos complex, I climbed out of my coma-pod and murdered my two surviving crewmates. One of them was faking the coma, and it got ugly, but she would've done the same to me. She screamed gibberish in my face as I strangled her while Eater of Shadows watched and jeered at us in synthesized Atlantean dialect. She didn't even recognize her own name . . .

Wasn't it Goethe who said that any time a person speaks and someone else understands is a little miracle? I grew up watching so much shit on TV where the aliens spoke our language. The first time I met aliens, I was terrified beyond belief to discover they had their own language, their own thoughts, their own utterly inscrutable way of perceiving the world, themselves, you. The impulse to crush them as something offensive never quite goes away.

I had to do it. Even though we were able to cooperate enough to launch the ship, we couldn't abide the stink of each other, couldn't stand the nauseous nonsense of each other's speech, couldn't stomach the insect-tickle of each other's incomprehensible thoughts, like ants running 'round the surface of your brain.

I'm keeping an oral diary because I'm afraid that I'll pause in writing this down and look at the preceding paragraphs and recognize not a word, not a letter. I won't listen to it when I'm done. Don't expect anyone to hear it or understand, but it has to be said.

If you can understand this at all, then maybe I've gone insane, and that would give me relief. But maybe it's because you and I are the only ones still sane out of the whole fucked human race.

I was the closest to a rogue archaeologist the Deaver-Wei Expedition could find on Mars out of two hundred thousand colonists. The only funding for archaeological digs on Earth was for rabid collectors who no longer bothered to hide in the black market. We were done, relegated to the dead science annex with the geographers.

I came to Mars as a surveyor and got certified in oxygen-farm engineering when the surveying ran out. I was doing construction in Mariner City's crater arcologies and considering selling a kidney and whatever else to go back home when Dag Strothers summoned me up to Phobos.

Dag had assembled a team to study Mars from its larger moon to find the Martian sister of the Babel Tower. We had to identify potential candidate stones and put our technological ears to them until we heard Liu Wei's voice coming from one of them.

Strothers ran the operation the same way he ran Liu Wei's shipping. A real live war hero, he had turned communication satellites into tactical nukes and dropped them on Cheneyville and half the security compounds on Mars, ending the corporate occupation in four hours. Javier Kroll was our systems expert. Ari Leitner was our medic and xenobiologist. Dr. Khadijatul Kubra was our astrophysicist, charged with the unenviable task of proving Liu Wei's delusion and replicating it in a lab. Bedjina Pierre was an anthropologist, neurolinguist, and the reason I stayed.

Liu Wei made a penny every time someone on Mars breathed and was one of the first to prospect in the asteroid belt.

Wei could afford to indulge in his fetishes for Western cultural junk. He had not so much joined as purchased an American UFO cult and was using his fortune to prove its crazy ideas as scientific fact.

Horton Deaver rode a Section 8 out of the Navy after a nervous breakdown on the submarine USS Barracuda and retired to the Mojave Desert where he almost immediately started hearing voices again. The sounds of the deep ocean had driven him mad; now, he believed he could hear the voices of ancient men, voyagers in outer space, and it gave him peace.

Under a great rock, he built his church. A single 300-ton boulder of vaguely iridescent labradorite, Deaver claimed in his increasingly bizarre pamphlets that an unusual configuration of silicon crystals in the rock made it a "cosmic whisper dish" that focused thoughts and speech for instant transmission across time and space. He claimed they were not manmade, but neither were they natural.

He believed that all the terrestrial planets and Jovian moons had identical stones and that the inhabitants of each had a rapport with the others—that the asteroid belt was an inhabited planet once and that it had been destroyed in a war around the time of the Cambrian extinction on Earth.

Deaver tunneled out a dwelling underneath his rock, his Babel Tower. He listened with all manner of equipment to the music of the spheres and transmitted his own thoughts and entreaties. Slowly, the mad hermit attracted a following of like-minded kooks, and by the '60s, Babel Tower became the focus of an annual UFO festival and Aquarian freakout.

Thousands claimed to have heard the voices, and glitchy, questionable recordings cropped up everywhere, claiming to be the sounds of the Grays or the Lizard People or Quetzalcoatl. When Deaver died in '82, his wife carried on his work as the high priestess of an absurd UFO cult, the Babelians, who dropped acid until they lost all language and engaged in glossolalian gibbering to try to rediscover the mother tongue of the universe.

Their last adventure spawned the infamous Deaver Ping recording. The Babelian faithful had taken to continuously playing Deaver's lectures under the rock and scanning the heavens for an echo. But rather than publish or even reproduce their works, the group devolved in your traditional fringe murder-suicide pact in 1993. It didn't even make national news.

Nobody ever humored the Babelians by testing their claims until Wei bought the remaining federal land in the Mojave Desert and so acquired the Babel Tower. The stone still somehow demonstrated incredible conduction properties unrelated to ordinary granite. The celebrated crystal lattice eluded even microscopic detection. Whether Lu Wei was a true-blue fanatic or just saw a kernel of truth in the weird phenomenon that might become a viable subspace communication system, he went all in.

●

While Strothers and I freebased every Martian geological satellite survey in the records, we bombarded the whole planet with radar and ground-penetrating sonar, looking for a twin to Babel Tower. We even combed it with lasers, hoping to trigger telltale fluorescence. But our job was easy compared to Kroll's.

As Liu Wei read continuously for six-hour stretches under Babel Tower on Earth, Kroll and Kubra scanned from upper atmosphere for an instantaneous ping using six of his own satellites and buying up time on everyone else's.

He paid us to do this for three months. It was the kind of pointless, infuriating job I would've worked to get myself fired from if I didn't desperately need it and if I wasn't in love. Bedjina and I courted and were married.

Security was tight. We were searched and scanned for implants before we went up to Deimos. I remember staring at her when she got sick right after launch off the Elysium Ladder. She whispered a prayer in a smoky French accent and used a sick-sack. Jaw clenched to show she knew I was watching, she dug in the bag to take out a tiny medallion and a leather pouch. I asked, as respectfully as I could, if it was dirt from Mars. It was dirt from Earth, she told me, and to the look in my eye, she added her beliefs were nothing to mock when we were going to try to find the ocean in a seashell.

The dirt came from a hill above Port Au Prince. She was Haitian, from one of the floating city-states on the Caribbean scraped together out of the sea's plastic waste. Her aptitude scores had made her a desirable target, and she was drafted upstairs to the orbital arcologies.

At the end of three months, we had our good news/bad news: we eventually came across a vein of analogous crystal content in a chunk of silica-heavy granite, but it was crushed to gravel a mere ten or twenty million years ago, which was weird because it was out on a slab of feldspar and basalt that hadn't known seismic pressure since long before earth had oceans or a stable atmosphere.

The other good-bad news was that we got our instantaneous ping, but it wasn't from Mars. One of our survey satellites picked it up for about fourteen seconds when it was recalibrating after a breakdown. Liu Wei's voice was coming back to us a good eight minutes ahead of the light-wave from earth, but the signal was coming from further out.

Europa, Ganymede, and Titan were occupied and Pluto even had an automated staging area for interstellar missions yet to come. But unless Wei was laying down an elaborately simple hoax, something out there was bouncing back the signal.

Wei's mining interests combed the asteroid belt for a couple weeks before they found the source. It was deep in the belt, more than halfway to Jupiter.

Passed over by generations of surveyor drones until suddenly it began speaking with our master's voice.

In bed, Bedjina wondered if the stones proved anything besides that we should leave them alone. The Martians destroyed theirs millions of years ago. Maybe they destroyed Vulcan, too. The Vulcanic stone was the only artifact from what must have been a planet comparable with Mars, if not a twin, before it was demolished. Was it so much harder to believe that these stones could destroy worlds as well as connect them?

Even we were kept out of the loop, but rumors came back through the shipyard that the asteroid was occupied when they found it. If there were freefall Deaviants living on it, Wei's prospectors took care of them and spiked the enormous rock with suicide boosters, so it came screaming into Martian orbit in less than three weeks.

Maybe if it had come a little earlier, Bedjina and I might have still been together, and things might be different. Both moody, badly out of sync, we picked on each other. She said I only chased her because she was the most different, the most difficult, and I would never understand her. I told her I hoped I never did because what was love without mystery? Not the right thing to say, and maybe nothing was.

The plan was to examine the asteroid on Deimos, and if it proved to be everything Liu Wei foolishly dreamed it was, he wanted us to set it down on Mars at a corresponding longitude and latitude to Babel Tower on Earth and on a ley line. When Dr. Kubra and I explained that Mars lost its magnetic field a couple hundred million years ago and so had no ley lines, Wei told us the stone would reactivate it if properly placed, and we were directed to a cargo container that contained dowsing rods.

But we believed we had much more than Wei's subspace talking-rock. The asteroid was similar in composition and nearly identical in crystalline structure to Babel Tower. It was unmistakably a piece of a terrestrial planet that once orbited between Mars and Jupiter, proving any number of tinfoil-hat loonies and amateur astronomers correct. We also had proof that Vulcan—we christened it with a bulb of Dag's moonshine—was inhabited.

We were already a cult, worshipping Liu Wei's delusions. Without any significant debate, Strothers and a team of wildcat miners set the thing down on Deimos and domed it.

The stone was similar to Babel Tower in general outline, but a crust of hundreds of spiny crystal growths had accreted up and down its surface. Pits and divots from microasteroid impacts, Pierre insisted, were badly eroded markings not unlike cuneiform. The debate was cut short before it truly got started. It was a moot point.

As soon as the pressure was thick enough to carry a sound wave, the stone began to sing.

Sensors observed nothing beyond some minimal gas exchange and oxidization, but it keened like a tuning fork, rumbled like a stomach. It was Kroll who realized first what the sounds were. Voices. Recorded voices, like ghosts escaping a haunted house ahead of the wrecking ball.

Have you ever been in love? When the sex is no longer conquest but not quite comfort, when the smell of each other has disappeared but still works its magic on the mind, have you ever known that wordless rapport, that feeling of pushing against some barrier, some evolutionary leap that only love could make? I felt it then, looking to Bedjina as she looked at me, smiling shyly as if I'd caught her kissing the medal glued to the inside of her helmet. *The ocean in the shell,* I thought, and she nodded.

That the crystalline matrix of the stone had stored and was continuously emitting the voices was debatable. What was not was the multitude of burrowed holes in the base of the stone, totally unlike any natural weathering. Packed with much lighter volcanic pumice shot through with obsidian shards and scarlet hematite nodules—it had to be metamorphic rock created in an atmosphere. And there were other objects, cylindrical bubbles with the right angles and contours of manufactured artifacts. Cautiously, wary of interrupting the eerie chorus, we drilled into the newer rock and almost immediately hit a harder metal, which shredded the carbon-steel drill bit.

Inside the handmade crevice in the stone, so like the badger's burrow of Horton Deaver's home, we found a gray cylinder that was not just crafted but machined. I extracted one myself and set the spidery diggers to complete the excavation.

Most likely, I thought, it was some kind of fluke, a shucked oxygen bottle or dud demo charge from one of the rogue miners' colonies, somehow sealed up in a lava tube in an asteroid over two hundred million years old. Stranger things happened every day, sure. Because some strange alien artifact would not have had sockets in it clearly designed for cable connections little different from any uni-coax jacks in our homes. It was simple to scan them and fabricate. One socket was mechanical in nature and frozen solid; the other two begged to be connected to electricity and a computer.

By now, the sound of the stone had become orchestral. It shivered with eons of echoes, with all the sounds of a teeming jungle rife with life, not the sterile silence of the void. We were ecstatic, as the ant must be when it beholds the magnifying glass.

I tried to express my joy, but no words would come. A pure animal roar came from my lips, and the others joined in, howling like apes as the loudest voice of all spoke our names.

The noise was so loud now, it was like a light. I reached out into the white icy migraine glow; I reached out for Bedjina Pierre, for anyone, for a hand—

I was screaming for help, we all were, but none of us heard the others' words. Alerts flashed across the faceplate of my helmet, but they were blocky hieroglyphs. Kroll held his hands up, choking on something. His face red, he made these sounds . . .

I've heard that you hear completely foreign languages as strings of maybe four or five phonemes, screening any recognizable pattern from the jumble of alien sounds. The Romans coined "barbarus" to depict the guttural barking sound of Germanic tribes. Kroll was Swiss, Vietnamese, and at least two or three other things. The language coming out of his mouth was not German so much as a German in the full grip of glossolalia, speaking in some primal yet utterly private language, like he was striving to remake a whole language from the syllables of his own name.

Strothers and Pierre both screamed back at him. I reached for Bedjina, calling her name, but every time I said it, she looked more alarmed. I tried to reassure her. She cried, shaking her head, and kicked at me when I came too close.

Kroll kicked off from the stone, headed for the exit. Strothers shouted at him in his own new language. He might have concluded that what had happened to us must be contained. Maybe he believed we were possessed, that he alone was still sane, still himself. Maybe he just thought the wiry, retiring systems analyst was going for a weapon. He lunged at Kroll, who grabbed for a welding torch. Strothers drove a pickaxe into Kroll's chest. With a dying hand on the torch wand, Kroll licked out a blue needle of flame that cut through his own helmet and sheared off the right side of his face.

Bedjina was still backing away from me, eyes wide but unseeing, struggling to speak words. Her speech was a beautiful waterfall of French wreckage, but somehow, it made me crazy to hear it. I tried to say "I love you" in the French she'd taught me, but my attempt sent her fleeing.

I went after her. Strothers came after me. I managed to lock him in the dome with the stone, but he immediately went for the medical chest, and I knew he'd burn his way out with the torch. Bedjina swam up the corridor and locked herself in the common area.

Dr. Kubra came out of her hutch, saw me, and ran toward me with her arms wide, gobbling nonsense. Maybe she thought I'd help her, maybe she thought I was a threat. I could make no sense of her speech, could see only gray empty panic in her eyes. The only thing I could make sense of was the bloody trenching tool in her hand.

I ducked and threw her over my shoulder into the bulkhead and was into my hutch before she recovered. I heard her bash the door with the tool a few times, shrieking and panting.

We had suffered a collective nervous breakdown, some kind of hysterical aphasia. Damage to specific areas of the brain could render one incapable of distinguishing one face from another, and Broca's area and several other loci were associated with language dissociation. We'd just taken a big hit of something, but nothing said it would last.

"Do not fear," said the intercom in an utterly flat, monotonous, halting voice, like a robot that had a stroke. "You will defeat the others and father numerous descendants with their females. They shall make a language of your name."

I looked at the intercom. I wanted to kiss it. I knew I was speaking English—I could hear the words—but the brains of the others had been stirred up with a stick. And yet, the flashing alerts meant nothing beyond their context. I could not make any sense of printed words, so it followed that whatever I was thinking and speaking, it wasn't English.

But whatever my language was, the intercom spoke it.

"You can beat them all, but you must set yourself free."

"How's that?" I asked. Not, *who are you?* The roaring in my brain would not let me ask for anything but relief.

"You must . . . punch a hole . . . trepan yourself. You cannot trust the others to do it for you."

I made sure the voice meant I should punch a hole in my skull.

"That is the only way to be free of it. Your rival is already making your dead friends into a computer."

"How can you understand what I'm saying? Are you talking to them, too? Who the fuck are you, anyway?"

"We are not talking," said the intercom. "I have no body."

○

Eater of Shadows was as true a friend as ever I knew.

That was his name; he told me so. He was an astronomer and magus in Atlantis, and he was right. I only had to punch a hole in my head to be free of the pain. Blood jetted out of the wound, like a swarm of red hornets, splashing off the wall and hanging in microgravity. I floated in an asteroid field of my blood—so ecstatic with relief that I almost passed out before cauterizing the hole.

He told me about the ones from beyond Pluto—the mission computer lexicon shit a brick trying to translate before calling them "barnacle geese"—and how they had colonized Earth, as so many other worlds, and experimented upon humans to expand their intellects, but also to make them useful slaves. Vanished civilizations at Sacsayhuaman and Tiahuanaco in the Andes, in the South Pacific, in Central Asia, and in sub-Saharan Africa built pyramids and yielded up mountains of heads and hearts before weird, indifferent gods. The gods who descended performed surgeries on and sometimes mated with them. All of the enslaved and hybrid peoples either rebelled or were abandoned by the ones from outside—the voice went to Spanish, called them *amigos*—and collapsed utterly into chaos and cannibalism, like domestic pets left to the wolves.

Some shamans and kings left their bodies entirely to fly with their masters into the infinite dark, to behold wonders and learn secrets such as no ordinary human minds could possibly comprehend. This was how Eater of Shadows came to be interred inside the asteroid.

He was a messenger left behind to instruct us when we reached the outer planets. We did not have to be exterminated as a nuisance. We could adapt to the true nature of all creation, open our minds to the unacceptable truth that the universe was alive and consciousness was its preferred diet. We could learn the old ways and sing the old songs and become one with the cosmos, or we could be utterly destroyed.

That was why the stone had fried our speech centers, Eater of Shadows explained, though he clearly knew little more about the motivations of the "amigos" than I did. Such defense measures often stopped upstart subject races from leaving their home worlds, and there were stones such as this one everywhere they had visited in eons of interstellar rape and pillage. Maybe it was a way to keep us down, and maybe it was a way to spur leaps in evolution. Create a catastrophic bottleneck by turning everyone against each other. Whatever emerged was bound to be smarter, tougher, more useful—

The barnacle geese were coming back, and they were closer than we knew. Eater of Shadows showed me the view of the stone chamber, where a spider-drone with one of those ancient cylinders hot-wired to its thorax was plowing the floor. Its scythe-like forelegs gouged the soil of Deimos while its whirring palps sowed the red-black seeds we thought were hematite nodules into the furrows. Not seeds, I was told, but spores.

Other drones patrolled the complex and the shipyard, where most of the 215 workers, staff, and researchers had massacred each other within minutes of our meddling with the stone on the other side of our tiny moon.

Kroll sat in the medical bay, gone from the eyebrows up. A bunch of cables snaked out the holes in his skull to another cylinder. He looked intently at something out of view while joylessly masturbating.

The rest of the cameras were destroyed or showed only blackness and cold.

Strothers was the strongest. Kubra was the smartest. But Bedjina was cleverer, more aggressive than anyone else on the team. I wondered—I still do—if we had still been together, if she still felt about me as I did about her, if we might not be closer than ever. A culture, a species of two. Maybe we could still overcome the alien meddling, and we didn't need to speak. By now, the smell of the others made me sick to my stomach. I didn't realize how angry I was until I packed a bag with medical supplies and water. The bulbs burst in my fists, and I wrenched the door off the cooler. My helmet wouldn't pressurize; Kubra had cracked the visor.

I must have destroyed the whole room in a red fury. I was still swinging at nothing when the hatch popped open.

Strothers sprang into the room and flew into the arc of my helmet. I cracked his jaw and sent him corkscrewing into the bubble wall overlooking the convex lunar horizon. I kicked him, clawed at him and painted the walls with his blood. I backed away, horrified at myself, but he kept dying. I seethed with such rage that I couldn't stop until I'd crushed him like the water bulbs.

He was blind. His eyes were gone, sockets packed with red, soggy gauze held on with surgical tape. He had a choke-chain on. He'd tried to trepan his skull and failed, or someone had done it for him.

I could feel her behind me.

The choke chain jerked taut, and Strothers rose up to trip me. I turned, resisting the urge to lash out with my fists or my mind, wanting only to look into her eyes, to make her look into mine, and see what no language barrier could hide.

She stopped. She didn't let me touch her. The migraine came back harder than ever when I came closer. She'd drilled herself smoothly and sealed the hole with meat-glue several shades lighter than her complexion, which was the color of a sunset through volcanic ash.

We could communicate mind to mind, but she wouldn't let me in. I saw the grim outlines of fortress walls, electric chairs, bear traps, and barbed wire when I pried behind her eyes. She was repulsed by me, but we would have to work together. Bedjina Pierre, Khadijatul Kubra, and I were the only survivors. Kubra had killed Leitner in what looked like self-defense, but then she harvested his and Kroll's skulls and plugged them into some kind of daisy chain with the terminal at the end. She wouldn't, or couldn't, explain what she'd been doing.

Eater of Shadows told me we had to leave before the barnacle geese came back. He was insane even for a disembodied brain in a jar, but he wanted us to survive.

The stone chamber and the airlock were controlled by the others—Kukulkan, a deranged high priest of Tikal; Commander Fiolkov, a Cosmonaut thought to have burned up on re-entry in the '60s; and another who refused to identify herself but emitted bloodcurdling paeans to the Outer Gods until I snipped her speech cable.

The brain cylinders sabotaged the communications network. Without Kroll, without manuals we could read, we could only hack security cams to monitor the rest of the moon, which was again uninhabited, and the surface of Mars.

They were already building pyramids.

Many, if not most of the interlocked Venn-style geodesic domes that made up the bubble-bath skyline of Mariner City were popped and trailing debris on the ghost of a frigid wind. Gangs of eyeless slaves fumbled in quarries and loaded rust-red stones into ore carts under the glare of similarly eyeless but trepanned elites.

Headless, frozen bodies were strewn everywhere and failed to decay, awaiting the collapse of the hydroponic farms and storage. They ran amok inside, naked or clad in each other's skins, conducting endless human sacrifices and building the heads into an aggregate mind big enough to incarnate their god.

When we turned to the stone, the only voice was that of Liu Wei. He must have drilled his own head and begun collecting others long before we found the stone in the asteroid field, and he'd mastered it, coming through so clearly that we could almost see him in burning purple phosgenes on our retinas, staring fixedly ahead in his pleasure dome, wired into a network of hundreds of severed heads. Impossible to tell if he was still reading from his book or giving orders because his speech sounded like stuttering variations on his own name, over and over and over . . .

It was my idea to crash the mission computer and kill everything but life support. The paralyzed spider-drones floated by and fit easily into the airlock. They were ejected at well above Deimos's puny escape velocity. We even got Dr. Kubra to help us attach solid-fuel boosters to the stone.

The spores had already begun to sprout at the foot of the Vulcan Tower. The floor of the chamber was a garden of disintegrating fruiting bodies: soft, pulpy, colorless puffballs falling away to reveal chitinous pupae that twitched disturbingly when you merely looked at them, as if feeding on attention itself.

The pods incinerated all of them.

The jury-rigged guidance system synchronizing the rockets followed through, delivering the 350-ton asteroid on Mariner City in the dead of night when the fires of their sacrifices were visible from Deimos. The Martian capital was exterminated. Vulcan was avenged.

We set out for Earth the next day in Liu Wei's private yacht. Almost immediately when I began to inhale the gas, I felt her hand in my head, and I climbed out of my pod to kill her and Dr. Kubra. I could read none of their thoughts, but I could hurt them as they could hurt me. If we were the last of our species, so much the better. What centuries of inbreeding would make out of the hideous ménage, I could not bear to imagine.

I should follow them out the airlock, but I can't. Not until I get back to Earth. I'm holding Bedjina's pouch of Haitian earth, and I think I'm going to eat it. Not a word, not an image, not a sound from Earth since the moment we dropped the stone on the abomination that was Mariner, a city of two hundred thousand souls.

I'm waiting. I'm only staying alive long enough to go back and see what we did, to see if there's no one left to speak—or if they no longer need to.

{}

Cody Goodfellow *has written five novels and three collections: his latest are* Repo Shark *(Broken River Books) and* Strategies Against Nature *(King Shot Press). He wrote, co-produced, and scored the short, Lovecraftian hygiene film* Stay At Home Dad, *which can be viewed on YouTube. He is also a director of the HP Lovecraft Film Festival–San Pedro and cofounder of Perilous Press, an occasional micropublisher of modern cosmic horror. A collection of his Cthulhu Mythos fiction,* Rapture of the Deep, *is forthcoming from Hippocampus Press.*

The Great Dying of the Holocene

Desirina Boskovich

I find the first capsule as I'm walking along the beach.

At first, it looks like a creature. Some kind of squid-like thing: mutated beyond recognition or perhaps an unknown species.

I squat for a moment beside it, noting the bulbous, misshapen body, the dark, slick arms twitching against the stiff salt breeze.

I decide to take it home.

A shirtless jogger eyes me as I scoop up my specimen. "I'm a marine biologist," I say by way of explanation. He nods skeptically and pounds on past.

I head back across the hilly sand littered with crumpled beer cans and the husks of dead sea creatures. Back in my residence—a glorified dorm, actually, with blank walls and impressively sturdy furniture—I put the specimen on ice and stash it in the freezer.

For the tenth time today, I check my voicemail, hoping stupidly and desperately for a message from Scott, my supervisor at the Underwater Research Lab (Applied Research Division, Triton Enterprises, LLC). I've been on dry land for a month now—about three weeks too long.

Even though it's what I've been hoping to hear, I'm surprised when my former boss's recorded voice crackles on the other end of the line. The sound waves ripple in and out as if to remind me that he's calling from underwater. "Mia," he says. "Was hoping to catch you. Listen, I got your request to be transferred back.

I'd love to have you here, but it's just not in the funding right now. Take care of yourself."

After that, I pour a couple shots of whiskey and settle down to work on my latest paper. It's stupid, drinking while writing, but lately, it's the only way I can bear to think.

I pour myself more drinks. At some point, I stumble over to the bed and pass out, fully dressed, the lights bright above. Once again, I fall into nightmares.

I wake at two in the morning covered in a cold sweat that smells of booze. I swig water to cleanse the foul taste in my mouth, but my brain still feels trapped in the dream.

I grab my specimen and my keycard pass and head down to the lab on campus to take a look.

○

Approximately three hundred miles off the coast—farther and deeper than any aquatic research facility before—the Underwater Research Lab exists, officially, to study the creatures and habitats of the marine environment and the ocean floor. To map the die-outs, record the extinction rates, and chart the mutations, all happening faster than we can scare up the manpower to observe them. It's the great dying of the Holocene epoch, the sixth mass extinction in geological history.

My department. What else is there in this era for a scientist like me to study?

Unofficially, the Underwater Research Lab exists in service of far murkier interests. The staggering sums of funding did not come from federal governments dedicated to environmental preservation. Instead, most of the money to build and run this breathtaking facility came from private industry, businessmen with their own aims and means and mysterious questions.

Still, they needed someone to keep filing the reports about the die-out of *Thecosomata*, maintaining the PR-friendly illusion that the facility exists for scientific inquiry rather than capitalist ambition.

(*Thecosomata* is a pelagic sea snail—a tiny, gorgeous mollusk that floats on ocean currents like a bird on the breeze. Their calcium carbonate shells are thin and delicate, nearly transparent. Increased levels of ocean acidification are devouring them alive, eating through their fragile armor like paper.)

I tried not to know about the research going on in other wings of the facility. Breakthrough techniques in desalination that would allow the treatment plants perched on every coastline to increase their consumption of ocean water with terrifying efficiency. Human body modifications intended to create a new post-human class of divers who could spend indefinite periods undersea, harvesting riches from the teetering ecosystem beneath.

I tried not to know until I couldn't anymore. The politics shifted. Other things . . . happened. They sent me back to shore, "to take a break."

I spend long hours walking the beach because it's the closest I can get to the world beneath, the one that feels like my only real home.

o

At 3 a.m., the lab is deserted. The cleaning crew buffs the floors in a room down the hall. The low drone reminds me of the pervasive sound of machinery that hummed incessantly in the Underwater Research Lab, keeping us alive. That white noise comforts me and helps me work.

My specimen, though . . . it's an odd customer. Sleek and slimy and bedraggled, possessing too many slender appendages and knobby protrusions. The more I look at it, the more I can't tell what it could possibly be.

As I cut into it, the carcass emits a strange odor: not a fish market smell, nor the saltwater tang of fresh oysters, nor the dankness of something rotting beneath the docks. Instead, it almost smells like something burning.

A black viscous substance seeps like oil from its appendages.

(In 1989, the year I was born, the *Exxon Valdez* spilled eleven million gallons of oil into Prince William Sound. The spill poisoned 1,300 miles of coastline, killed one hundred thousand seabirds, devastated populations of otters and orcas and seals, and destroyed untold millions of tiny lives beneath the surface of the sea.)

I look and look, but I can only find one eye.

Somewhere in the building, the cleaning crew is playing Latin pop music. The melodic notes reach me in sweet fragments, fading static in and out.

I make another incision, and the dark liquid rushes in a wave, blood spurting from a vein, and a minuscule drop aerosolizes and lands like a speck of dust in my eye.

For a moment, I can *see* it, hanging and vacillating, dark and pearlescent, a throbbing orb. Instinctively, I blink.

Stupid and dangerous: undersea creatures can harbor harmful toxins, especially now that we've poisoned their world, and the gasping dregs of their species have all gone strange. I shouldn't be working alone in the lab. I should be wearing more protective gear. I shouldn't be working while drunk.

I take a step back, wondering if I should abandon this for now.

That's when my understanding of the creature begins to change.

It seems not so much like a creature but, perhaps, an *artifact*—a manmade object, like everything else floating in the oceans these days. And then, it seems not so much like an artifact but a thumbprint or a chemtrail—a trace left behind by something else.

The music stops and starts again. It's coming closer. It's falling into static. It's gone.

And then, it seems not so much like a thumbprint but maybe an *extrusion*, like the jagged iceberg tip of something poking out from its world into ours. The majority of it hidden, contained beneath the surface, folded into an adjacent but alien dimension.

I'm dizzy and stumbling. I've got to lie down for a bit on the fresh-buffed floor. I retch but manage not to puke.

Here I am, resting: just like they told me to do when they sent me away from undersea.

The viscous substance drips slowly and persistently from the table to the floor.

●

Half of the creatures that came to me for study in the Underwater Research Lab were the equivalent of aquatic road kill. They'd ended up tangled and mangled in the intake pipes of the desalination plants, suction-trapped against the membranes, too large to pass through.

The intake pipes don't discriminate; they swallow plankton, fish eggs and larvae, miniscule mollusks. They devour microscopic creatures by the billions.

Sometimes, I wonder how it must feel for those creatures. They can't *actually* feel, not the way we can, and they can't think, but . . . still, the idea of going along, minding your own business, when suddenly your entire sphere of existence is upended and destroyed.

Our desires are as foreign to plankton as theirs are to us.

The desalination process produces fresh water, fit for drinking, bathing, agriculture, and watering golf courses. It also leaves a byproduct: a salty, brackish, polluted solution, colloquially termed sludge. This contains chlorines, bisulfites, acids, hydrogen peroxide, heavy metals, coagulants, and more, all of which sallies forth into the sea.

The desalination plants on land still use reverse osmosis, running ocean water through thin-film composite membranes; it takes a lot of energy to force all those swimming pools worth of water through these filters.

At the Underwater Research Lab, hands-on experiments tested nanoporous graphene membranes no more than an atom thick: two-dimensional.

If they could get it right, the whole world could change. With just a little effort, we could drain the seas.

When Ian first arrived at the lab, he was on my side. We were fighting the same fight: stealthily gathering our own research on the ecological implications of the desalination process, the tipping points for ecosystems, the die-outs triggered.

We were together, on that and everything, and it was perfect.

But then, he went on one of their diving expeditions. He didn't have the body modifications, yet, so he was weighed down with equipment, lumbering and slow—and he came back different. He'd seen something out there. He didn't know if it was horrible or beautiful, but he wanted to see it again.

After that, everything changed.

○

Some time passes before I pull myself off the lab floor and head toward home. I leave my specimen where it is, though I know it will quickly grow putrid and rot. For some reason, I don't particularly care anymore.

The sun is rising as I trek across campus. The campus seems changed: the buildings squat and skewed, brutally oppressive yet somehow banal. I think unbidden of insect colonies and mazes for rats.

I'm struck with the urge to destroy everything I see, to burn it all down.

I should sleep.

Back in my residence, I close my curtains against the rising sun and hope for sleep without dreaming, but the dreams come back as they always do—I caught them from Ian, sleeping entwined in his narrow bunk night after night.

I dream the jagged silhouette of a forgotten city, rising like an ogre from the deep.

We marvel at our own power, changing the planet in less time than the lifespan of a tortoise. But the stars have been changing, too.

o

There were times when Ian tried to tell me what he'd seen.

Somehow, he'd gotten separated from the others. He was ambiguous on the details. He'd struck out on his own for a moment, over-confident and over-eager; he'd lingered to inspect a specimen; and when he'd looked up, he was alone in the murky waters as far as he could see. The narrative varied in the telling. Finally, he admitted that he had no idea how it happened: in one moment he'd been in a place he recognized, not far from the rest of the crew, and in another moment, it was like he was on a foreign planet in an alien sea.

And there, looming suddenly ahead, a ruin surrounded by swirling waters—there was the city, half-submerged.

He tried to explain its demented angles, its tortured geometry, its sick illusions.

I tried to tell him that, enchanted by the overwhelming strangeness of the deep, he'd stumbled his way into a waking dream.

He remained obsessed.

I began to worry that he might be going insane. Living underwater does that to some people . . . sends them off the deep end.

For someone like me, who'd never found my land legs, it was the opposite. The Underwater Research Lab was filled with strange, secretive types, weird loners with weird obsessions, and I'd reached a place where I finally belonged.

But now, Ian wanted a different kind of belonging. He wanted to join the divers. He wanted to become like them: modified, altered, post-human.

"I have to find that city," he said. "I have to see it again."

I begged him to take a leave on land. Instead, he sought out the director of the aquatic bodymod program—highly illegal but an open secret—and volunteered.

They were ecstatic to have him. They'd been confined to operating on lifers from the prisons: the kind of people who'd sign away all their rights forever in exchange for a shot at freedom, the kind of people they could control. A marine biologist like Ian was a major coup.

Once they were done, he could never go onshore again. Sure, there were rumors about the program, but that didn't mean human beings with flippers and gills were allowed to stroll around on land.

The surgeries were physically traumatic and intensely painful. He'd come back from the lab after yet another invasive procedure—bone-breaking, bone-grafting—pale and weak and woozy from the drugs and still shaking with the pain.

Sometimes, in my nightmares, I hear him screaming. I wake with a start to comfort him, but the screaming is only in my head. It's all a dream.

○

Mid-afternoon, I wake feeling sick. My throat is dry, and my vision is blurry, but none of that is particularly out of the ordinary. I pick up my phone, dial Scott's number. As I listen to it ring and ring, I plan out what I could say. It goes to voicemail. I hang up.

I microwave a frozen burrito and eat it standing over the sink. Then I head back to the lab.

It's empty: unusual for this time of day. The specimen lies crumpled on the table, dry and deflated, nothing more than an empty sack of skin. Greasy trails like the path of a snail streak the table. The dark puddle gleams and glistens on the floor beneath, larger than I remembered.

I poke and prod the wrinkled specimen, take a few samples for testing, then dump it in the trash.

I should clean up the dark puddle too (leaving pools of organic waste on the lab floor is highly against protocol), but I feel uneasy about this. It doesn't make sense, but the more I look at it, the more I feel a kinship to it, as if we're the same, as if it's colonized me with that one tiny drop.

Perhaps, I'm part of it, too, and it's part of me, as all things in the universe are connected and united, if only around the edges and the tips.

(There are creatures that seem to be alive but aren't and creatures that are alive but don't seem it, unless you know how to look. Like coral: an animal, a colony, a living structure. In the Indian Ocean, living banks of corals that have thrived for a thousand years are rapidly going extinct, unable to cope with the heat currents we've dumped into their seas.)

Speculatively, I watch the dark puddle as it watches me, and I think, "You deserve this. You can stay."

In gracious thanks, it allows me to dab one small drop upon the tip of my tongue.

○

Ian begged me to join him. "I still love you," he told me, "and I don't want to be alone." He had changed beyond recognition, both inside and out; he'd changed into something else, and he wanted to change me too.

"You love the ocean," he said. "Imagine this. No more boundaries. No more walls. That whole life on land, you know it's an illusion, right? This is real, down here. The cosmos unaltered, the planet as it truly is."

"Well, kind of," I commented dryly. "But we managed to change it a good bit, too."

"There are deep places," he argued. "Deep places where everything that lives is completely unaware of our existence. Deep places where we never existed at all."

These conversations reminded me of my childhood when all I did was read about the sea. Everyone thought me strange, busting out at inappropriate moments with my tender treasure trove of ocean facts. Even then, I knew where I belonged.

Because the beautiful thing about the ocean, no matter how much you think you know, no matter how much you learn, it's vast and deep and alien, and there's always something more to learn. There's always room to hide.

But I resisted Ian's pleas. I couldn't imagine a life like that, a life like his. I couldn't imagine never again walking along the beach, feeling the sun on my face or the wind in my hair.

Or perhaps, it was just that mundane human fear of giving away too much of myself.

○

I head out to the beach for my evening walk. I can't tell if everything has changed or if I'm the one who's changing, but the world seems altered in ways I can't define.

I keep my eyes out for another specimen. I'm not sure if mine was an odd mutation or the beginning of something new: a migration pattern fatally shifted by the false signals of climate change, or maybe an unfamiliar virus, like that wasting disease that wiped out the starfish and sea urchins in the twenty-teens. Another sample could help me decide.

I find two of the things, and then a third.

Up ahead of me on the beach, a group of young people is dancing around a bonfire and a roiling column of smoke that climbs and shifts toward the sky. Students from the college? It's hard for me to tell these days. The boys are shirtless and the girls nearly so, all of them barefoot and wild-haired, their music discordant and jangling and their dance fierce.

Roasting on a spit over the campfire are two more specimens.

I stand at the edge of the circle. They hardly notice me at first, they are so caught up in their feral laughter and the frenzy of their dance.

The smoke they breathe is heady and intoxicating and filled with strange tidings.

"What are you doing?" I ask.

A boy pauses to laugh. "Making calamari," he says.

The greasy blood of the creature, or the thumbprint, or the extrusion, or whatever it is, drips sizzling into the fire, and the smoke drifts along the beach.

Passing a knife back and forth between them, the dancing children begin to shriek.

●

Soon after I rejected his pleas to join him, Ian moved to the divers' quarters.

Most of the divers were ex-cons: brash, bold, bawdy guys who thrilled at physical danger and lived for risk-taking. A couple women, too. But none of them, not even the women, liked women very much, and they didn't like me. Maybe it was because their creative obscenities always made me wince.

Officially, Ian was there to direct their resource surveys of the ocean floor, cataloging what bounty still remained and where. Their database grew and grew; it had become one of the most valuable assets that Triton Enterprises owned.

Unofficially, Ian continued his obsession with the underwater city, which he'd glimpsed only once—yet he remained convinced that it was there.

I only visited him twice in the divers' quarters where his mutant friends flapped and leered. And in keeping with the unspoken rules, he never visited me at all. It bothered people, that kind of thing.

Then he disappeared.

There had always been disappearances. The ocean was deep and dangerous, filled with skilled predators, sharks and worse. This was not our world, and losses were to be expected.

(The shark is prehistoric and has honed its killing to an art, but in the end, it was no match for us. Hammerhead sharks, which first appeared around twenty million years ago, have declined 89 percent since 1986. At least forty million sharks are killed each year for their fins.)

They were upset to lose Ian, a particularly valuable asset. They'd spent so much money modifying him, but after a week, they gave up the search.

I couldn't bear it.

I guess I went a little crazy for a while, too, driven mad not by the oppression of the ocean but by the finality of my loss. I stormed and screamed and demanded they keep searching. I made threats, falling back on the only power I knew, telling them that I had proof of all the illegal things happening down here and that I'd talk to the media, expose them to the world.

I even demanded they modify me the way they'd modified Ian and turn me into a diver, so I could go and look for him myself.

They diagnosed me with several varieties of psychiatric instability and sent me to the surface.

They could have disappeared me in a mysterious accident like Ian's, so I guess I should be grateful. Mostly to Scott, my supervisor, who probably put his own job and reputation on the line to save me. I know he took a big risk.

If I'm honest, I know I'm never going back to the Underwater Research Lab.

And if I'm honest with myself, I know that Ian didn't have an accident; I'm sure he slipped away to search for the buried city.

Did he waken something, knocking on the door of a place long forgotten?

Or was it wakened already, roused by the screaming cries of a trillion murdered things floating in the sea?

○

People are drifting down to the beach in hiccups and waves, drawn by the music, or the dancing, or the smoke, or the vague odor of roasting meat.

The sun sets terribly and beautifully, a flaring red ball of dancing fire.

I'm swept along with everyone else. Little vials of the black goo are passed around. The dancing grows fiercer, and the fighting gets bloodier. Then, we're moving away from the beach, past the cul-de-sacs and the condos and the storefronts, into the city.

I'm part of it all, breathing deeply, seeing clearly. I'm an ant in a colony that's gotten out of hand, running frenzied with sugar-sick joy, sucking up sticky crumbs with glorious madness before it all gets stamped out for good.

We're smashing through glass, raising our voices in incomprehensible chants, setting the world alight and dancing in the flames.

●

Morning comes. The sun rises wan and confused over the used-up, burnt-out world. We wander back to the beach, wondering if there's anything left to eat.

I stand for a moment and marvel at the coast, dark like an oil slick with drifts of stranded capsules for as far as the eye can see. Across the water shimmers the outline of a monstrous city—which rises roaring from the waves and claws its way back into being.

Desirina Boskovich's *short fiction has been published in* Clarkesworld, Lightspeed, Nightmare, Kaleidotrope, PodCastle, Drabblecast, *and anthologies such as* The Way of the Wizard, Aliens: Recent Encounters, *and* The Apocalypse Triptych. *Her nonfiction pieces on music, literature, and culture have appeared in* Lightspeed, Weird Fiction Review, The Huffington Post, Wonderbook, *and* The Steampunk Bible. *She is also the editor of* It Came From the North: An Anthology of Finnish Speculative Fiction *(Cheeky Frawg, 2013), and together with Jeff VanderMeer, co-author of* The Steampunk User's Manual *(Abrams Image, 2014). Find her online at www.desirinaboskovich.com.*

BROKEN EYE BOOKS

CPSIA information can be obtained
at www.ICGtesting.com
Printed in the USA
BVHW081623220620
581986BV00004B/430

9 781940 372174